THE SHADOWS OF DUST

ALEC HUTSON

ISBN: 978-1-734257427 (print)
978-1-734257441 (ebook)

Please visit Alec's website at
www.authoralechutson.com

In memory of Gerald Warfield
a wonderful mentor and friend

1

KERIN SET his elbows on the worn wood of the ancient balustrade and leaned out over the emptiness. Below him, Drifter's massive flipper churned the rippling dark, etched starkly against the Stream through which they were surging. Silver motes sparked into existence and then vanished with each great stroke, evidence of the tremendous energy the starbeast was expending as he strained against the Stream's contrary flow.

Everything all right? Kerin thought.

Of course.

Through the link they shared he could sense the starbeast's annoyance. Drifter never liked being doubted.

It just seems like you're laboring a bit more than usual.

Something like a snort reverberated in Kerin's mind. *Laboring? The thought that a hatchling of the Great Turtle would ever struggle in the Streams is so ridiculous I want to shake with laughter. But I won't, considering where you've so foolishly and precariously perched yourself. Your grandfather's heart would have burst if he had seen you dangling out over such a turbulent Stream.*

So you admit the Stream is a bit choppy?

Quiet, manling.

Kerin tried his best to hide his amusement. He didn't want to upset Drifter further, as the starbeast was already brooding because they'd left Jegriddsl before the turtle could bathe in the planet's famed sulfite sea. Sharing a psychic bond made that hard, though, so instead Kerin emptied his mind as he stared out into the Stream. Gradually, Drifter's grumbling receded as Kerin lost himself to the beauty of the abyss. At first the Stream was a blackness deeper than the void between the systems, but then slowly vague shapes began to emerge, organic undulations that reminded him of eels slipping through lightless depths. Overlaying this was a sense of something bulging outward against a glistening black membrane, straining to be born . . .

"Kerin!"

He turned from the seething dark just as Nala came into view clambering across one of the wooden walkways bolted onto the side of Drifter's mottled shell. The planks swayed beneath her, but she moved with her usual confident grace, not even bothering to hold onto the guide ropes. Just like the starbeast, she appeared agitated: her ears were erect, and her tail lashed the air behind her.

"Ho, Nala," he called out, pushing himself away from the edge as she padded up to him. "Come to enjoy the view?"

The kyrathi mage spared a disinterested glance at the rushing Stream. "You know I don't see the same things you do."

That was true. It was only through the bond he shared with Drifter that he could experience the terrible beauty of the Streams. Even the feline eyes of the kyrathi couldn't pierce the black through which they were moving.

"Then why leave the Nest? It'll be a fair while before we surface."

Nala gestured at the ramshackle structure clinging to the front section of Drifter's shell.

"I wanted to talk to you about our two passengers."

Ah. He'd been expecting this conversation. Kerin felt Drifter's attention, which had been lurking at the edge of his mind, suddenly sharpen.

"What about them?"

Nala licked her paw and smoothed down her whiskers, something she did unconsciously when she was troubled. "I don't trust them."

"Even the girl?"

"*Especially* the girl."

"Come now, she's a child."

"Exactly. What child would agree to join us out here? You, me, a gobber, and this broken-down starbeast"—Kerin felt a surge of indignation from where Drifter's consciousness touched his own —"chasing fairy tales into the dusty corners of the universe."

"You said yourself that the gobber's chart looks real."

Nala growled in exasperation. "And it does! But what are the chances that an unplundered treehold is floating around out here? We'll almost certainly get to the end of this Stream and find the hold cracked open with all the treasure scooped out."

Kerin shrugged. "Then that will be that. The gobber is still paying passage for himself and the girl, no matter what we find."

"But why is she with him?" the kyrathi persisted, laying her paw upon his arm. He winced as her claws pricked his skin through the weave of his steelsilk shirt, but she didn't seem to notice his discomfort. "You saw the robes she's wearing. The girl is one of those fanatics who worships the Searing Light, and we're far off the trodden paths out here. If things go sour – which they very well might, you know that – she won't last an eyeblink."

Kerin scowled and pulled his arm away, inspecting his shirt for any tears. This was one of his last few decent outfits. "Not our business."

The golden irises of Nala's amber eyes flared wider. Kerin was sure she was going to offer up some harsh rejoinder, but instead she leaned in closer to him, her voice carefully level. "I know your grandfather's code is very important to you and Drifter," she said, "but you have to face the reality that we're not in the guild anymore. We're not bound by their rules." She flicked her ears in the direction of the Nest. "And that also means no one is watching our backs. If the gobber double-crosses us, there won't be a guild response, and if he realizes *that* then he just might try something. You know how gobbers are."

Kerin did, of course. They were infamous throughout this branch of the stellar tributary as being one of the more cunning and greedy of the Younger Races.

He sighed. "All right. I'll come up with you and together we'll get some answers about what's going on."

He could feel Drifter's disappointment as he said this, but he ignored the starbeast. Nala was right: his grandfather was dead, and the guild had cast them out. They weren't beholden to the code anymore. They were alone and adrift in an uncaring universe, and he needed to make smart decisions.

Nala watched him for a moment longer, as if searching his face for something. "I know this isn't how you thought things would play out," she murmured, "but we'll get through it." Before he could push through his surprise at her words, she whirled away and began to scamper back along the walkway. He watched her go, his thoughts churning. Nala was his oldest friend, but she'd never spoken to him like that before. It almost sounded like she was trying to cheer him up.

Things must be much worse than he thought.

～

Protect your passengers, protect their privacy, and protect the integrity of the Starfarers Guild. Those were the three sacrosanct rules that had governed his grandfather's life and the lives of all the eldest members of his family for nearly three centuries, ever since his ancestor had first bonded with a wandering starbeast fresh-hatched from one of the Great Turtle's clutches.

His grandfather never would have considered interrogating paying passengers, unless they threatened the reputation of the guild in some way, and thus came into conflict with the third rule. Their

business was their own. But he and Nala and Drifter were independent streamsurfers now. They couldn't count on the guild's protection
anymore . . . so they needed to be very, very careful.

Kerin followed Nala into the Nest, the largest of the half-dozen
structures attached to Drifter's shell. The gobber and the girl were in
the saloon sitting on opposite ends of a ratty velvet couch. The girl
had her head down, her long pale hair obscuring her face, while the
gobber was hunched over a table that was usually reserved for games
of blood knuckles or t'skelcha, intent on a run of cards he had laid
out. The girl glanced up as Nala and Kerin entered, then seemed to
recede deeper into her dirty white robes. The gobber, on the other
hand, paid them no mind, continuing to mutter to himself as he
snapped more cards down onto the scarred table.

Kerin cleared his throat noisily, and with a frown the gobber
paused in his game and sat back.

"Yes? The man wants what?"

The gobber's Trade was so heavily accented as to be almost unintelligible. He sounded like a drunkard trying to speak a second
language while gargling water.

Kerin folded his arms across his chest, forcing himself to meet the
beady black eyes of the gnarled creature. "We want to know a few
things."

The gobber picked at one of the many bright red lesions pock-
marking his jowls. "Privacy protection, guild rule. Right of the
passenger invoked."

"I'm not a member of the guild anymore."

If this surprised the gobber, his face didn't show it. A tingling
unease spread through Kerin. If the gobber knew he wasn't with the
guild, then he also knew there wouldn't have been an expedition plan
filed anywhere, and that no one would come looking for them if they
disappeared . . .

"I heard, I heard," said the gobber, waving his hand dismissively.
"But sometimes old habits die hard. Thought you might still be
clinging to the old ways."

"We're not," Nala said, her tail dancing. "And we want to know what's going to be waiting for us at the end of this Stream."

The gobber smiled, showing rows of serrated teeth. "Told you the truth. An alvaren treehold."

"But why bring her?" Nala continued, nodding toward the motionless girl.

The gobber was quiet for a moment, his misshapen head cocked to one side, as if considering how much he should reveal. Then he shrugged and leaned forward.

"She's the key."

Nala blinked in obvious confusion. "The key?"

"Aye, catter. The way to get inside where all the goodies are stashed."

"How is that possible?" Kerin asked. "She looks like she'd have trouble figuring out a doorknob."

The girl's head jerked up slightly. *Well, she isn't simple, at least.* Though, in truth, she didn't look very complicated, either. Her unremarkable face was slack, her lips slightly parted. Gray eyes that seemed just a little too far apart watched him dully. He'd have put her age at fifteen or sixteen if pressed, though she could have been a few years younger or older.

The gobber chortled. "The man might be right. But the girl doesn't have to turn the doorknob – she *is* the doorknob. The key and the doorknob!"

Kerin and Nala shared a glance. The gobber saw this and settled back on the couch, a sly grin creeping across his ugly little face.

"The treehold is bloodsealed for alvarens only."

"But the girl's clearly not one of them," Kerin said slowly, as if speaking to an idiot. The excitement he'd felt about the ruins that the gobber claimed awaited them at the end of the Stream began to ebb. If the treehold were bloodsealed, then this expedition would be fruitless. Everyone knew there were no alvarens left in the universe.

They had been the most recent of the Elder Races to transcend, merging their minds with whatever existed beyond the fringes of this reality. They had called it "going to the shoals beyond the stars." A flowery term for what amounted to mass suicide. His grandfather had talked of how his own great-grandpa had met an alvaren once as a young man, in the years before their departure. He'd described the creature as tall and willowy, with huge golden eyes that never blinked, and a cascade of shimmering silver hair. Beautiful and melancholy, like a dying star.

He sighed. This mousy little girl did not resemble a member of that Elder Race in the slightest. Either the gobber was mistaken, or this was all a ruse to lead them into a trap. His trepidation about what awaited them at the end of the Stream strengthened slightly, but Kerin still wasn't too worried: Drifter was a surprisingly ferocious fighter, and it was highly unlikely that any ambushers could contend with a kyrathi battlemage.

The gobber coughed wetly, then swallowed whatever he had dislodged from his throat. "Yes, yes. The girl's not an alvaren. But she's not *not* an alvaren also. A trace of their blood is in her veins from long ago. The faintest of echoes, but the strain is true. The tree-hold will open for her, I have been assured."

"Assured by whom?"

The gobber clicked his mouth shut at Kerin's question and shook his lumpy head.

Nala growled in frustration and turned her attention to the girl. "Why are you traveling with this creature?" Nala asked, but the girl did not raise her eyes to look at the kyrathi, instead continuing to stare at a spot on the floor.

"Don't bother, doesn't speak," the gobber said. "The girl's slave stock, from the catacombs of the Searing Light. She's only been a pain conduit for rich folk."

"A pain conduit?" Kerin didn't like the sound of that.

"The man knows that faith, this one is certain. An infamous madness, as they believe in purity through pain. But the rich believers don't want to suffer, so they make a big donation, and their punishment is inflicted upon one of the temple's slaves. They get their souls cleansed without any of the trouble, the church gets richer, and only a worthless, nameless girl feels anything. Or maybe she doesn't. Hard to read, this one. Incredible to think that all that blood she spilled in the catacombs could have been so valuable to them, if they had only known." The gobber croaked another laugh. "But they didn't! So this one bought the girl for a pittance, and she's gonna bring me more wealth than the Searing Light's ever seen."

Kerin crouched beside the girl, peering into her blank eyes. What the gobber had just described was monstrous, but the universe was full of monstrous cruelties. Was there anything left inside the girl? Or had she been reduced to a hollow shell, her mind effaced by being filled and emptied countless times with purchased agony? There was a low rumble coming from beside him – Nala, demonstrating her disgust at what the gobber had just described. The kyrathi knew well what it was like to be a tool for the powerful and callous.

The gobber moved with surprising speed, reaching across the table to slap the girl's cheek hard with his open palm. Kerin caught her before she went sprawling, steadying the former pain conduit with a hand on her bony shoulder. To his shock, she didn't utter the slightest sound, nor even glance in the direction of the chuckling gobber. She only continued to stare placidly at the floor as a red smear bloomed on her cheek. Nala's growl strengthened, and Kerin wondered if the gobber knew how close he was to being flensed open by kyrathi claws.

"See? As this one said, there is nothing left in the girl."

Kerin felt his disgust rising. To the gobber, she was clearly little more than an object. Should he allow the gobber to use her when it was painfully obvious that she would be discarded once her purpose was fulfilled? Perhaps he should return to Jegriddsl and toss the gobber back into the hazy glimmer den where he'd first approached them. And then what? Adopt the girl? Add another mouth to feed when they were already skirting the edge of starvation? Kerin pushed away that foolishness.

And what if she truly was the key to an alvaren treehold, as impossible as that seemed? The Elder Races had crafted artifacts and sorcery that were far beyond the capabilities of any of the galaxy's current denizens. Interstellar empires had gone to war over the right to plunder an unspoiled treehold, and the great guilds had beggared themselves to buy their mysterious devices at auction. Even the smallest of useless knick-knacks pulled from an alvaren ruin would go a long way towards clearing the debts his grandfather had left him with. Sharing the location of the treehold might even get him back in good standing with the Starfarers Guild.

"We still want to know–"

Kerin. Drifter's deep voice interrupted him, rumbling like distant thunder in his mind.

Yes?

The Stream's mouth is approaching. I hadn't realized we'd gotten so close. We'll be entering the system momentarily.

"What is it?" Nala asked when she saw his expression, concern twisting her features. "What is Drifter saying?"

"We're almost there," Kerin said, rising and turning away from the girl. As he moved towards the saloon's door, he tried to extinguish the compassion that had been growing inside him for the child. What had happened to her was terrible, but he wasn't responsible for saving her or making things right. Given the emptiness in her eyes, she probably wouldn't even appreciate being saved. Nala might balk, but they needed money more than the kyrathi suspected. It wasn't just their dwindling rations – he had it on good authority that the patience of his grandfather's creditors was nearly exhausted. And when that finally happened, the hounds would be let off their leashes.

Kerin passed down a short corridor and stepped out onto the raised deck that extended off the front edge of the starbeast's shell. Drifter's massive green and brown head swelled in front of him like a hummock breaching the water after the tide had receded. The giant turtle cocked his head slightly, and Kerin could see himself faintly reflected in a gleaming black eye as large as a Devali pachyderm.

A point flared in the darkness, then quickly began to swell, until a shimmering curtain stretched in front of them. It bent and rippled like an aurora.

They plunged through it, and with a jarring suddenness slipped back into their accustomed dimension.

Countless stars were spread across the arching expanse, a vast scattering of jewels. Kerin sucked in a lungful of the crisp air, so refreshing after the staleness that permeated the Streams. He'd heard rumors that there were some forsaken pockets of the universe where the air had been pumped out of the systems, and this was one reason why most streamsurfers stuck to the well-trodden paths: the thought of emerging from a Stream into a freezing, airless void was the stuff of nightmares. But perhaps such places didn't really exist, and that was just a tale old handlers told to scare the newly-bonded.

The system was empty of any large planets, as far as he could see, and the giant star at its center was a sullen red veined with black.

"There!" Nala cried as she came up beside him, pointing at a dark shape picked out against the faded glow of the ancient sun. Her eyes were much sharper than his.

Kerin slipped his spyglass from his belt and focused on the hanging object. It was a chunk of rock several leagues wide and dominated by a vast white tree that was growing out of the stone. It was hard to see detail at this distance, but Kerin thought he saw ruins clustered around the base of the tree's trunk, nestled among the squirming roots.

Let's get a closer look, he thought.

Kerin felt Drifter's affirmation, and he had to grip the closest railing to keep from falling as the starbeast lurched forward, its speed quickening. Nala seemed unaffected by the sudden motion, shifting her weight perfectly to compensate for the pitching deck.

"Black star!" cursed the gobber as he arrived beside them and was sent tumbling against the wooden railing, which creaked alarmingly. "Your beast is graceless, handler," he spat, and then snarled in a language Kerin didn't understand.

"Fair warning, if he hears you say that about his swimming, he'll try to send you spinning off the deck the next chance he gets."

The gobber muttered something else under his breath and clutched even tighter at the railing.

Kerin smirked as he turned away to peer through his spyglass again. This was the first time he had seen an alvaren treehold, and he examined the legendary object as they swam closer. The tumbled slabs of stone were indeed the remnants of great buildings – it looked to Kerin like they had not collapsed under the weight of their age, or been felled by wandering void debris, but rather that the mighty tree was in the process of slowly devouring the hold. Great roots had grown over and through the ruins, gripping the stone with such force that in places the walls had buckled and burst under the immense strain. The tree itself was a pale, ghostly white, and no leaves adorned its skeletal branches. To be honest, it looked as dead as the rest of the treehold, though Kerin wasn't sure if that was indeed true. With a pang of remorse he wished his grandfather could have been here to witness this. Kerin knew such fallen grandeur would have stirred his soul.

Lost in his thoughts, Kerin didn't sense the concern swelling in his starbeast.

Kerin, something is coming.

What?

I'm not sure. We're not alone.

"Look!" Nala cried, and a moment later Kerin also saw what she had already seen, a flicker of movement from behind the floating treehold. "Is that . . . is that a starbeast?"

"It is," Kerin whispered hoarsely, unable to believe his eyes.

The thing was a leviathan, easily the biggest starbeast he had ever encountered. A great tapered head emerged first, far larger than the entirety of Drifter, connected to a long sinuous neck. Then a massive body like a small moon slipped around the edge of the treehold's asteroid, great wings outspread.

It was a gigantic dragon, three or four times the size of any he had seen before in his travels. He had never heard of them growing this large. Kerin's fear deepened when he realized that there was no harness around the starbeast's neck, no chains extending behind the dragon to link it with a trailing ship or structure. A wild starbeast?

How had such a creature remained free for all the epochs it would have taken for it to grow to this size?

Drifter! Kerin struggled to keep their mental connection from fragmenting in his rising panic. *Can you escape?*

His starbeast's reply was heavy with awe. *Kerin . . . I'm sorry. This beast is a true ancient. I've come too close . . . It will devour me before I make it halfway back to the Stream's mouth. I've felt age like this only once before . . . in that moment I first emerged from my egg I tasted the residue of the Great Turtle . . . and it was the same . . . so very, very old. Worlds have birthed and died in this creature's life span.* Drifter paused for a long moment, and when he continued there was a new edge to his words, a flavor Kerin had never sensed before. Hopelessness. His starbeast had considered their chances and resigned himself to his fate. *It seems we have swum our last Stream together, my old friend. But there's something else, something strange . . .*

"Bones," Nala murmured. "By tooth and claw, it's just bones."

Kerin's breath caught in his throat. She was right: the great starbeast was only a skeleton. Yet it moved like a living creature made of flesh and blood, flowing towards them. Its vast wings beat up and down, but no membrane stretched taut between the skeletal fingers. How could it fly? What dark sorcery was animating this monster?

The dragon arrested its approach only a few dozen lengths from Drifter, hovering as it slowly flapped its empty wings. Yet that motion couldn't be what was keeping it aloft, as no great gusts of wind buffeted Kerin and his starbeast.

It was huge. It filled their view of the system, occluding the red giant at its core, though snatches of the star could be seen through the gaps between the dragon's ribs.

APPROACH.

The word exploded in Kerin's mind, and he reeled from the force of the command.

Drifter . . .

We have no choice, Kerin.

I know.

If he intends to destroy us, he will. But I think he wants something from us. Hollow hopelessness still tinged Drifter's thoughts, but the feeling was diminished. Curiosity had risen to the forefront of the starbeast's mind.

Tentatively, Drifter pushed himself forward, towards the waiting ancient.

Nala grabbed Kerin, and this time her claws did bite into his arm. "What are you doing?" she hissed. He turned to her. Nala's eyes were wide, her ears flat against her head. The strange girl was beside the kyrathi, clinging to her fur and staring at the dragon with an expression he couldn't fathom. It must be fear, as all sentient creatures would feel fear in this moment. Yet the gobber wasn't afraid, Kerin realized. He was grinning as he watched their reactions.

Kerin lunged towards the gobber and grabbed a handful of his embroidered kaftan, nearly pulling the smaller creature from his feet. "What do you know about this?" he snarled, shaking the gobber.

"Calm, man. It will not devour us today. Or it will, I should correct, but it will not be our deaths."

"What do you mean?"

"Look," the gobber said, pointing with a scabrous finger at the dragon's great skull, which was lowering to meet Drifter's slow approach. Its mighty jaws opened wide, and a great blast of fetid air washed over them as they stared down the starbeast's abyssal gullet. Kerin's eyes watered and he wanted to retch from the smell.

ENTER.

Kerin?

Do it.

Kerin found that he was holding his breath as Drifter passed into the starbeast. It was like a fledgling turtle swimming into the gaping mouth of a hoary old crocodile. Yellowing teeth the length of cloud spires rose around them.

"By the First Mover," he said softly, numbed by the sheer enormity of the creature.

Drifter angled his way down the great hole in the back of the starbeast's mouth, which would have led to its throat if any flesh had remained. Instead, they swam beneath the dragon's spine, each bony link about as large as the great turtle they stood upon. Shoulder blades reared like mountains above them, while ahead massive ribs curved down from the spine to join with a vast white plain: the sternum of the starbeast.

Something was there, a speck of black on the great sheet of bone. Following Kerin's hunch, Drifter moved in that direction. Slowly the dark point swelled, until they were close enough that Kerin could see what it was they were approaching.

The thing was a great throne a hundred span high, carved of some gleaming black substance. The skeleton of a giant humanoid sat straight-backed in the chair, dressed in faded finery, its long dark robes decorated with blood-red starbursts and comets like writhing serpents.

"Streamsurfers," said the gobber, his tone smug, "prepare yourselves to meet Xerivas the Black."

The great skeleton turned its skull to regard Drifter as the starbeast's flippers touched bone.

"Oh, nebulas, no," whispered Nala.

Staring at the glimmer of cold light recessed in the creature's eye sockets, Kerin knew with absolute certainty what this thing was, and fear coiled in his chest. A lich was before them, as impossible as that seemed, an immensely powerful sorcerer who had somehow avoided the inevitability of entropy by rendering its core essence immortal. There were only a handful who had ever accomplished this feat, and each was legend: Juth-neth-kava, Scourger of Worlds; Nul the Forsaken; The One Who Walks Alone. Empires trembled at their names and paid obeisance when they passed through their systems, sacrificing thousands if they demanded a blood tribute to replenish the ranks of their undead hordes.

But who was Xerivas the Black? Why had Kerin never heard of him? And what could a lich possibly want with *them*?

"Best we don't keep him waiting," the gobber said, stumping over to where a rope ladder was coiled on the deck. Grunting with the effort, he tossed the ladder over the side, and then without glancing back to see if they were following he started to climb down.

Kerin and Nala shared a long look before turning together to face the huge skeleton. It was clearly watching them as well.

"I suppose . . ." Kerin began.

". . . We have to follow," Nala finished, then smoothed her whiskers with a trembling paw. She turned to the ashen-faced girl. "Come, child. I think we've been summoned."

2

THEY STOOD on the white plain, staring up at the seated skeleton towering above them. The ground beneath their feet was not as smooth as it had appeared from afar: its age was evident up close, so cracked and pitted that it more resembled coral than bone. At the base of the throne was a jumble of more human-sized skeletons, some clothed in the shreds of rags, others not. The gobber shuffled forward and went to his knees, raising his arms in supplication before the lich.

"I have returned, lord, bringing the child and the streamsurfers you desired!"

A jolt went through Kerin at this – the lich desired *them*, as well as the girl? His surprise faded quickly, to be replaced by a wash of cold dread. Whatever this ancient sorcerer wanted must be terrible . . . he had never heard of a mortal surviving an audience with a lich. He eyed the remains heaped around the throne uneasily.

With a grating crackle the skeleton looked down, a cloud of dust exploding from its neck as one of its vertebrae popped loose. It regarded them in silence, the suffocating power of its presence nearly forcing Kerin to join the gobber on its knees. The shards of light sunk deep within the lich's eye sockets glimmered with a merciless, inhuman intelligence. Kerin felt like he was being peeled apart beneath that terrible scrutiny, and he struggled not to look away. His jaw ached from being clenched so hard, his nails biting into his palms.

He wasn't sure how long he stood there on that empty white plain, trapped like an insect pinned to a collector's board, but suddenly he was brought back to himself as something soft thumped against his leg. This broke the spell, and he tore his eyes from the lich and found that it was Nala's tail that had touched him. The digits of one of her paws flickered, almost too fast to see. Guild cant, but modified to account for her being a kyrathi. Even if the lich somehow was familiar with the Starfarers Guild's hand signals, there was no way it could understand what she was saying. This was a language unique to Nala and him.

Does it know what you are?

Kerin swallowed, unsure how to answer. Could the lich sense that he was Anathema? No sorcerer had ever been able to before, but he'd also never stood in the presence of such a powerful being. Xerivas was attuned to the higher mysteries, very different from mages such as Nala, who could only crudely manipulate the energies coursing through the universe. He gave a tiny shrug to convey his uncertainty.

"Lord, has this unworthy one pleased you?" the gobber whined, an edge of desperation to his voice.

Kerin was just starting to consider grabbing Nala and sprinting back towards where Drifter waited, then seeing how far the starbeast could get before the dragon tore them to shreds, when a hollow rattling issued from the lich. The great skeleton slumped in the throne, its neck lolling, as if the life force animating it had suddenly vanished.

A moment later one of the skeletons sprawled at the chair's base twitched, then rose to its feet as smoothly as if a puppeteer had pulled it up on invisible strings. This skeleton – which might have once been human – was clad in a tattered dark robe, and in its bony grip it clutched a long black staff. Topping the staff was a tusked silver skull, a faceted red jewel recessed in this dead beast's forehead. The harsh light that had burned in the giant skeleton's eyes had been transferred to this new avatar, and Kerin knew with absolute certainty that the being called Xerivas had descended to meet them.

He fought the instinct to step back as the lich shuffled forward. The gobber ground his brow into the bone they stood upon, not daring to look up, his breathing fast and panicked. The creature was mumbling some mantra, the same phrases in his grating language repeated over and over again.

"I am Xerivas the Black." The lich's jaw remained closed, even as his sibilant whisper shivered the air like the tolling of a distant bell.

"I'm Kerin thon Talisien, bonded to the starbeast Drifter," he struggled to say, his mouth dry. "This is my companion, Nala."

"A mage, a channeler with some facility for manipulating aether." The lich turned his attention to the kyrathi.

Nala managed to meet Xerivas's cold, lambent gaze, but Kerin could see the tension thrumming in her. The fur was raised on her slightly arched back, and her claws were unsheathed. "I am a battlemage," she said. "Once lashed to a ghenabakan dreadnought."

"Congratulations on your freedom," the lich intoned hollowly. "Few minds can survive the breaking of such shackles."

The kyrathi's whiskers twitched, but she did not reply. After a long moment, the lich glided past her and came to loom over the girl. Xerivas extended his arm and brushed a bony finger against the former pain conduit's face. She was frozen, seemingly trapped in the prison of the lich's attention.

"And this one. You did well, D'zerjin. This is indeed the child I needed."

The girl's expression remained empty, but a tear trickled down her cheek.

"And us?" he asked, surprising himself with his own audacity. "The gobber said you needed us as well."

"Silence, man!" the lich's servant screeched. "How dare you have the arrogance to question our lord!"

The heel of the black staff thumped against bone as Xerivas approached Kerin once more. When the lich's scrutiny returned to him, a sharp pressure began to build behind his eyes. He blinked, as if this could dispel the pain, but the feeling only intensified as the ancient sorcerer halted a few span from him. The avatar of Xerivas was so close he could have reached out and grabbed a handful of the lich's threadbare robes. Kerin was tall and broad for a human, but the skeleton overtopped him by more than a head.

"I do, mortal. I charged my servant with obtaining two things on Jegriddsl: the first was this girl, for the ghost of alvaren blood haunts her veins. Long have I sought one such as her. And the second were stream-surfers with the reputation of returning successfully from dangerous places laden with the wealth of the dead."

"Tomb robbers," Kerin murmured, realization dawning. "Your creature sought us out because of what we did on the Mandati barrow moon." So it had not been random chance that the gobber had approached Nala in the glimmer den.

"I know not what you have done, mortal. But D'zerjin must believe you are capable of accomplishing what I require."

"And what is that?" Kerin whispered, dreading the undead sorcerer's answer.

With the creak of long-disused joints the lich swept out his arm that held the black staff, pointing the tusked silver skull at the floating treehold.

"I greatly desire something that is inside this treehold. For these are no ordinary ruins, streamsurfer. This is the Crucible, where the alvarens forged their greatest artifacts. When it was time to leave this reality they locked arcane wonders away inside. Many years have I spent scouring the galaxy for this treasure room, which they had hidden well, only to then find I cannot enter. The sorcery of an Elder Race threads this stone, ancient wards and defenses fashioned to keep out ones such as myself."

"But not us?" Nala asked, and at her interruption the lich turned smoothly to face her.

"Not you," the lich answered, his voice crackling like ancient

parchment. *"You mortals are too weak to ever wield the artifacts within, and thus you should be able to slip beneath the barriers. We shall work in concert to recover what I desire: you will lay down a path to the innermost sanctum, one that I may follow, and then I will come and claim the prizes within."*

Kerin knew with blinding certainty that whatever the alvarens had left here should never come into the possession of a lich. Entire worlds might be put in danger. "Why would we do this thing for you?"

When Xerivas finally replied, emotion laced his dry voice for the first time – something that might have been a hint of amusement. *"Because if you do not, I will eat your souls."*

Kerin had been to a hundred different worlds in dozens of systems, and never had he seen a once-living organism as large as this tree. The lich's skeletal starbeast could have nearly disappeared among its vast, tangled roots. It was like a mountain made purely vertical, soaring up and up and up, until finally spreading out into a great canopy that even without any foliage obscured most of the stars above the treehold.

Dizzied by the vastness, Kerin tore his gaze away and instead watched the creature that had deposited them at the base of the tree as it slowly flapped its way back to the waiting dragon. Their transport had appeared to be an amalgamation of monstrosities welded together to make some new horror, kept aloft by a pair of wings that might have been scavenged from the corpse of a huge bird. Kerin had counted three heads and a dozen limbs, all sprouting from a body that reminded him of the great ungulates that roamed the carnivorous grasslands of Thrys.

Kerin wasn't sure where this creature had come from, but he suspected that an undead legion lurked somewhere in this system. Every story about liches he'd ever heard spoke of the vast reanimated armies that accompanied their masters as the dead sorcerers traversed the universe seeking power and knowledge, leaving blighted worlds in their wake

"What do you think we'll find in there?" Nala asked softly, coming to stand beside him. From her tone she was imagining all sorts of dreadful possibilities.

Kerin joined her in staring at the great door set among the tumbled slabs of stone – despite the general devastation of the ruins, this seemed the only entrance into the treehold.

He shook his head. "I don't know, Nal. This place housed the artificers of an Elder Race – all I know is that there will be treasure beyond our wildest dreams."

The kyrathi grunted in agreement, folding her slim arms across her chest. Kerin's gaze drifted to the gobber, who was leading the pain conduit towards the door. The tattered black figure of the lich waited for them beside the entrance like the spirit of Entropy guarding the gate to Oblivion. The girl stumbled in the scree littering the treehold's surface, and the gobber grabbed her by her arm and roughly pulled her along.

"We're going to die," Nala said matter-of-factly.

Kerin frowned. "*I* don't plan on doing that."

The kyrathi chuckled grimly, shaking her head. "Ever the optimist, just like your grandfather."

He opened his mouth to tell her that was unfair when suddenly the lich's desiccated voice sounded nearby. It was as though he was standing next to them instead of a hundred paces away.

"Join us."

Nala and Kerin shared a look, and he could see in her eyes the fear she was trying to push down.

"Last chance if you want me to douse the lich in aether," Nala said, flashing a weak smile. "Since we battlemages are only really good for one thing." She didn't have to finish that thought, as he knew what she was referring to: rampant destruction. But as spectacular a mess as the kyrathi could make when she unleashed her power, liches were as close to gods as existed in the universe. Other than the beings that claimed to actually *be* gods, of course.

"I doubt that would do anything except make him annoyed," Kerin replied with a sigh.

"And you would be correct," came the harsh whisper again. Nala flashed Kerin a guilty look, as if embarrassed to have been caught gossiping by the person they were talking about. *"Come, nothing grates on me more than having to wait for mortals. I'm the one with all the time in the universe."*

That almost sounded like a jest. Surprise flavored Drifter's thoughts as they intruded on his own, as if anything other than a dread pronouncement from Xerivas would be unthinkable.

He was alive once. Perhaps he still faintly remembers what humor was.

He could sense Drifter's incredulity through their bond. *Well, don't try any of your terrible jokes on him. I like you better with the skin on.*

So do I. Probably best not to keep him waiting, then.

Speaking of waiting, do you expect me to stay here gazing up at this thing's ribs while you are traipsing around in there? It's very creepy. An image of what Drifter was seeing materialized in Kerin's thoughts. The plain of pitted bone stretched before him, broken only by the giant skeleton slumped in its throne. It seemed to still be watching the turtle, despite the light having vanished from its eye sockets.

Kerin summoned up some sympathy, knowing his starbeast would sense it.

I'm sorry. But I think if the lich gets distracted with what's occurring over here then the dragon's attention might wander as well. If that happens, I want you to try and slip away . . . and to be ready if I call for you.

Do you actually have a plan?

No, but you never know what the future might bring.

That also sounds like something your grandfather could have said.

Just be ready.

He felt a surge of agreement from his starbeast, and then was pulled back to his present surroundings as Nala's tail thumped him again. "We need to move," the kyrathi said sternly. "I don't want to test the lich's patience."

Kerin followed her as she picked her way over the chunks of stone and bits of fallen masonry towards where the others waited beside the treehold's door. When they arrived at the great slab of stone, the lich struck the ground hard with the end of his staff and the gobber shoved the pain conduit roughly in the back. The girl stumbled forward, nearly smashing her head against the entrance. After she caught herself, she stood swaying and staring emptily at the feature-less stone that was less than a hand-span from her face.

The lich watched this without moving, but Kerin thought he could sense annoyance radiating from the dead sorcerer.

Cursing, the gobber stomped over beside the girl and grabbed her limp arm, then slapped her open hand against the door, her fingers splayed.

"The moment of truth," Nala whispered. Even the lich seemed excited, craning his skull forward and readjusting his bony grip on the staff. The slight breeze swirling over the asteroid suddenly strengthened, stirring Xerivas's tattered robes.

Nothing else happened.

The gobber looked around, as if searching for a sign that the girl's presence had done something. He pulled her hand from the stone and then smacked it down again, harder than before. Again and again. Everything was silent except for the sound of the girl's palm striking the door. For some reason, Kerin found he had to fight back the laugh that desperately wanted to escape. He was fairly sure the lich would end him if he couldn't control his mirth, so he kept silent. Though then he would know once and for all if being Anathema protected him even from the sorcery of dead archmages.

It never came to that. As the gobber tried to lift the girl's hand for the ninth or tenth time he suddenly found that it was stuck fast. Grunting in surprise, it took him a moment of straining to realize that it wasn't the pain conduit who was keeping it fixed to the stone. When that happened, he let go of her like she was diseased and scrambled backwards, nearly tripping over the hem of his long kaftan.

The girl glanced back at them, her eyes wide. From the way her arm was moving, Kerin could tell she was trying to pull her hand free. She looked terrified.

"Will she be all right?" Nala asked, concern clear in her voice.

The lich did not answer, merely continuing to watch as the girl's struggles intensified.

A stronger gust of wind buffeted the treehold, dislodging stones higher up the ruins and making the pain conduit's long hair writhe. Kerin blinked as swirling grit entered his eyes, and he wasn't the only one affected as the kyrathi yowled in pain. When he could see clearly again a moment later he found that the girl was panicking, desperately thrashing back and forth as invisible fingers tugged at her robes.

She screamed, wordless and raw. *Damn the lich* Kerin thought, starting towards her, but before he could cross half the distance to the girl a terrific crack like thunder split the air and he was knocked backward, flying.

He lay sprawled for a few moments, dazed, his head whirling, until the feeling returned to his limbs, and then with some effort he stood again. Nala and the gobber were also climbing to their feet unsteadily, though the lich looked to have been unaffected by the blast. The girl had collapsed, slumped against the stone, and was cradling to her chest the hand that had been stuck to the door.

The door...

With grinding slowness it was opening, swinging inward.

Kerin moved as quickly as his tingling legs could manage, stumbling over to the girl and kneeling down beside her.

"Are you all right?" he asked, taking her closed fist and gently prying open her fingers, afraid of what he would find. But there was only a single small pinprick of blood in the center of her palm. Something like relief shivered across her face as she saw this as well, then she wrenched her hand away from him with a sob and began rocking back and forth.

"The door opens."

Kerin turned from the girl to find Xerivas looming over them, and fought back the urge to drag the girl away from the lich's unsettling presence. The undead sorcerer was staring into the darkness that had been revealed when the entrance to the ruins had finished swinging wide.

A wash of musty air billowed out, redolent of dust and death. It smelled like the places his grandfather had once brought him, forgotten ruins and the dingy backrooms where black-market dealers trafficked in the detritus of the past.

Darkness churned within the treehold, seemingly impervious to the illumination now spilling in from the outside. Kerin slipped a small lightsphere from his pocket and shook it gently, kindling the crystal at its core, then rolled it into the black. For a brief moment the radiance swelled brighter . . . but then it flickered and vanished, like a candle's flame placed under glass. In that brief moment before the light was extinguished, Kerin thought he saw something long and sinuous moving in the dark.

"Xerivas," he asked nervously, preparing to grab the sobbing pain conduit and retreat from the entrance, "can you sense anything in there? I could have sworn I—"

A tendril erupted from within, slithering across the stone and coiling around the girl's leg. "No!" Kerin cried, scrabbling for the hilt of his belt knife while also holding on to her with his other hand. There was a strange translucence to the tendril, like it was not fully real, but as it touched her flesh it hardened into something solid and glistening. The girl screamed in pain. Kerin hacked with his knife, but the rubbery flesh barely parted. "Nebulas, lich, do something!" he cried, putting all his weight behind his blade as he sawed harder. He cursed himself for not drawing his grandfather's sword first. Then, as quickly as it had attacked, the tentacle uncoiled itself from the girl's leg and retracted back into the dark. Where it had touched her the pain conduit's skin was red and mottled.

"Get up!" Kerin cried, trying to pull the girl to her feet, but when she put weight on her leg it collapsed beneath her. Cursing, he hooked his hands under her arms and began to drag her away from the door. A lance of crackling green aether flashed past them and was swallowed by the blackness. Kerin spared a quick glance behind him as he pulled the pain conduit to safety; Nala was crouched on the shoulder of a tumbled statue, her paws limned by emerald flames. Suddenly a rending shriek emanated from inside the treehold, so loud he was forced to let go of the girl and clap his hands over his ears. When it subsided, he drew his grandfather's sword, the veins of gold threading the dark blade seeming to shine even more brightly than usual.

Then, silence. No one moved – even the wind seemed to be holding its breath. Gobbets of green flame tumbled from Nala's paws to hiss and sputter upon the ground. The gobber's gnarled, teak-brown scalp and tiny black eyes were just visible from behind a chunk of white stone.

Nala gracefully leaped down from where she had been perched. "Did I—"

Without warning a writhing maelstrom of tentacles exploded from the darkness. Kerin screamed as a half-dozen of the grasping arms wrapped around his limbs and began to drag him inside the treehold. He thrashed, but the strength of the thing was overwhelming; where the tendrils touched his skin it burned, but they were not hot – rather, the slimy flesh was beyond freezing. His sword nearly slipped from his numb fingers as one of the tentacles tightened around his wrist.

He heard the panicked cries of his companions, and out of the corner of his eye he saw the pain conduit being pulled towards a darkness that was suddenly riddled with gnashing mouths of many different sizes, all filled with curving fangs. Shapes pulsed in the black, reminding him of things he had half-glimpsed while staring deep into the Streams.

The tendrils shuddered as a chanting suddenly began; each booming pronouncement was made in a language he did not know, imbued with a festering power that made his Anathema blood throb. The grip of the tendrils slackened, then loosened enough to allow him to slip his arms and legs free. In astonishment, he watched as the mouths and tendrils dissolved, becoming greasy black smoke that was then drawn towards where the lich stood intoning his incantation with his staff upraised. The red gem in the forehead of the silver skull pulsed like a beating heart as the foul mist flowed into it and vanished.

"By the Great Turtle," Kerin managed hoarsely as the last shred of the smoke disappeared. Xerivas stopped his chanting and slowly lowered his staff. It must have been Kerin's imagination, but it now looked like a smile curved the skull's tusked mouth. The gem had changed as well, its once flawless red veined with darkness.

"What was *that*?" Nala asked, picking herself up off the ground.

Xerivas swung his staff in front of himself so he could more closely examine the jewel. *"An eldritch horror from beyond the stars,"* the lich rasped, tapping a bony finger against one of its black-threaded facets.

"Oh, is that all?" Nala growled sarcastically, examining her elbow where a patch of fur had been scraped away.

"Yes. We are lucky this one had dwindled so much due to starvation." Satisfied with whatever he saw in the gem, the lich turned his attention to the gaping entrance of the treehold. Shadows still choked the interior, but they seemed far less foreboding. They weren't moving, at least. *"I have never heard of such an entity being summoned by the alvarens. I can only assume it was drawn here by what lies within, and could not escape once it had entered."*

"So whatever we are looking for must appeal to such creatures?" Kerin asked.

"That was not a creature, as you conceive of such things. It did not slip from a womb or evolve from a lesser being. It is . . . a pathos of the uncaring cosmos manifested, given form by interacting with your subconscious."

"Right, well, whatever," Kerin muttered, grimacing as he limped over to check on the girl. She seemed to be recovering quickly, the red burns lacing her flesh already fading. He investigated himself and saw the same, though his pain was receding at a slightly slower pace.

"How do you feel?" he asked the girl, not expecting any sort of response. To his surprise, though, her gaze did flicker to meet his own for a moment, and before he looked away he thought he saw some measure of awareness. Relief, maybe? Gratitude for how he had tried to help her? Kerin gripped her arm gently as she struggled to her feet;

the leg that had been seized by the horror trembled slightly, but this time it took her weight.

"*Something else comes,*" the lich intoned, and Kerin's blood went cold. His hand flew to the hilt of his sword, though in truth he had little faith that anything inhabiting these ruins could be harmed by a weapon he wielded, even his grandfather's sword.

From the depths of the treehold drifted a cloud of swirling silver motes. When they reached the door's threshold the glowing specks stopped and slowly began to coalesce, a gradually brightening radiance seeping from them until they merged, and an image took shape.

"*No!*" the lich shouted, and Kerin tore his gaze from whatever was materializing to see Nala lowering her arm uncertainly, the green aether she had summoned around her paw dwindling. "*This is not a threat.*"

Its nature was revealed moments later as it finished resolving into a hovering spectral humanoid – an alvaren, Kerin suspected, as the wraith strongly resembled how his grandfather had described that vanished people. It was tall and inhumanely thin, dressed in flowing robes that rippled in an unfelt wind. Its eyes were large and lacking pupils, its mouth a thin slash, and like his grandfather had said the most striking feature of the alvaren was the luminous silver hair that tumbled past its slim waist. It regarded them silently, its hands thrust into the long sleeves of its robes.

"Is this a ghost?" Kerin called out to Xerivas, trying to keep his voice steady. "If so, this is sort of your specialty, right?"

"*Not a ghost,*" Xerivas replied softly. There was an odd flavor to the lich's words. He almost sounded . . . wistful? "*An echo.*"

For an echo, it seemed remarkably aware of its surroundings. The transparent alvaren turned slightly so that it was facing them all, then slipped its hands from its robes and steepled its long fingers. Its mouth moved, and for a moment there was no sound. Then the words came, slightly delayed, a tumbling of musical utterances.

It wasn't Trade, or any of the other half-dozen languages of which Kerin had a cursory understanding. The tone was far from threatening, though, so he slipped his hand from the hilt of his sword and glanced at Xerivas, who seemed absorbed by whatever it was the alvaren spirit was saying. He was just about to ask for a translation when something shifted in his brain, like the pieces of a wooden puzzle box slotting into place to reveal what was hidden within, and the lilting words of the alvaren suddenly made sense.

"—and I beg you, strangers, to abandon this place. Much tragedy has been brought about by those who thought themselves worthy of bearing the artifacts of my people. Even we who crafted them did not always wield them wisely, much to our shame." The apparition spread its arms wide. "The Crucible is cursed, and this curse will follow you forever if you venture within." With that pronouncement, the alvaren bowed its head and dissolved, the glimmering silver motes winking out of existence.

"Cursed?" Nala said into the silence that followed.

"*A desperate attempt to deter those poised to plunder the treehold,*" the lich muttered. "*Curses are nothing more than superstition.*" Xerivas waved a skeletal hand at the open door and a sourceless light swelled within the treehold, illuminating an ancient stone corridor. Black lichen encrusted the walls and dripped from the ceiling, and the only decoration Kerin could see were strange abstract statues flanking the way that reminded him of waves cresting. These were carved of some opalescent material that gleamed nacreous, like the inside of a sea-creature's shell.

"*Find your way to the heart of the ruin,*" Xerivas commanded. "*I will follow after I have unpicked the webs the alvarens have left behind. Disarm any mundane traps and destroy what guardians they have left to protect the forge, the chamber at the heart of the Crucible. But if you value your lives, do not try and take up any artifacts you may find.*"

"Why do you need us again?" Kerin asked, peering down the length of the passage to where it terminated in a stone archway inscribed with runes.

"*Your passage will cause a disturbance, and the eddies in your wake will help me to see what sorceries the alvarens left for ones such as I.*"

Kerin didn't understand what the lich was talking about. "Such things won't harm us?"

"*I do not believe so.*"

And you wouldn't care in the least if they did, Kerin thought bitterly. Well, there was little he could do now, unless he feared what might be lurking within the treehold more than the lich eating his soul. With a sigh he turned to Nala, squaring his shoulders.

"Let's go."

3

KERIN HAD DELVED into dozens of ancient ruins in the two decades since his grandfather had swooped into his life and liberated him from the sodden wreck of his mother. The old man had been fascinated by what vanished peoples had left behind, but he'd adhered to a strict personal code that kept their investigations purely scholarly. He'd taken rubbings of ancient carvings, transcribed pictographs etched into walls, drawn careful illustrations of the artifacts they'd discovered, but never had he plundered the wealth of the dead that had so often been there for the taking. Kerin had always found that ridiculous, a harmless eccentricity, until he'd opened his grandfather's books after his death and discovered just how deeply in debt they were. Then he'd been outraged.

This alvaren treehold seemed surprisingly banal, given it was the creation of an Elder Race. They could have been pacing down the corridors of one of the obsidian-sheathed ziggurats on Mun or the barrow of a Mandati exarch, as just like in those ruins it was all merely crumbling stone and chambers choked with rubble. Kerin had always imagined that the structures of the more ancient and advanced species would somehow be immune to time's ravages, or at the very least bursting with strange objects, but that was very clearly not the case. Except for the odd, flowing sculptures, it certainly looked like the treehold had long ago been looted of anything valuable. At first he'd thought these were simply for decoration, but then he'd realized that the soft light filling the ruins was actually subtly emanating from the abstract statues.

Kerin kicked at a chunk of stone littering the corridor, sending it skittering ahead. "It's strange your boss was so nervous about coming inside," he told the gobber, who had been muttering to himself ever since they'd entered the ruins.

The gnarled little creature glared at him, as if annoyed by Kerin's interruption. "Not my boss, man. My lord. My *god*. And if you think there's nothing here except what you see, Xerivas has greatly overestimated you."

"He's right," Nala said, pausing to inspect one of the sculptures, which unlike the others was glowing a pale blue. "I have only a sliver of the senses of a full-fledged sorcerer, but even I can feel the power flowing through these ruins. It's like a tide, surging in and out." She pointed a claw at the pain conduit, who was stumbling along as if in a daze. "And she can feel it too, I'll wager."

"Either that or she's still suffering from that horror that grabbed her."

Nala shook her head. "I don't think so. It seized me as well, and now there's nothing more than a faint ache. You? There were more of those tendrils touching you then anyone else, but you seem to be fine."

"That's true," Kerin admitted. The pain the creature had inflicted had faded surprisingly quickly . . . almost as if it had never been real to begin with. Could it have been some kind of illusion? And if so, had it been crafted by the alvarens . . . or Xerivas? Why would the lich do such a thing if the attack had been, in truth, a clever deception?

He turned these thoughts over as the passages they followed sloped downward. There were other corridors branching off, but this way was larger and the only one lined by more of the radiant sculptures. Kerin didn't fancy braving the shadow-choked alternatives, he had to admit, especially given what they'd already encountered lurking in the darkness of the ruins.

He was just starting to worry that they wouldn't recognize the forge room that Xerivas wanted them to find when they descended a short flight of stairs and arrived at what could only be what they were looking for.

Two large sculptures flanked an entrance to a darkened room, the tongues of their frozen opalescent flames bending together to form a shining archway. Although the area beyond was lightless, Kerin could tell that it was much larger than any chamber they'd yet encountered in the ruins. Kerin's skin tingled as he passed through the door, as if for a moment he'd been assailed by countless invisible insects. Nala must have felt it as well, for she gave a little yelp.

As they entered the soaring space, a light kindled within a great crystal sunk into the ceiling. Kerin sucked in his breath at what was illuminated.

The great chamber was shaped like a dome, with the walls veined by the tree above; it looked, to Kerin, like the stone had been laid around the twisting roots, as there was no buckling or bursting as would have happened if the roots had crept down slowly over the ages. They'd even extended into the floor, which was a thick sheet of dark glass or crystal, the tips of the roots interweaving and forming a lattice beneath the surface. Through the smoky glass and the gaps between the roots Kerin could faintly see the blackness of the void and even a few glimmering stars. They must be at the very bottom of the treehold.

Seven blocks seemingly carved from the same iridescent material as the sculptures were the only furniture in the room. Six were arrayed in a circle, with the seventh in the middle of this ring. Upon each of these plinths a different object rested: the closest to where they'd entered the chamber displayed a gleaming red mask, another held a crystal rod, another a golden spider with green jewels for eyes. The air was heavy and swollen with power, like just before a violent thunderstorm. Sorcery, so strong it was making his eyes water and his Anathema blood race in his veins.

Kerin walked slowly into the room, his boots ringing on the crystal floor. His mouth was dry at the thought of the wealth one of these artifacts could bring, as anything the alvarens had thought so highly of that it would be enshrined in this chamber must be of incalculable value.

One object in particular drew his attention. It was a nondescript gray cube, but it rested on the center block, as if in a place of honor. Slowly he approached the artifact. He reached out his hand. Somewhere behind him he heard the gobber yelling, but it was like the sound was coming from very far away.

The air above this central plinth shimmered. He blinked, startled, and hesitated as the alvaren specter materialized – he thought it was the same one, but he couldn't be sure. It stared down at him with desperate, pleading eyes, and then spoke.

"Stranger, this place is not for—"

"*Do not touch that!*"

The alvaren wraith gasped as the lich's voice echoed in the chamber. It raised its fluttering fingers as if to ward away something Kerin could not see, and then dissolved into a faintly glowing mist.

Xerivas stood just beyond the room, on the other side of the glowing archway. "*On your life, mortal, step away from the artifact!*"

"What does it do?" Kerin called back, edging closer to the cube. The gobber barked some insult at him in its grating language, apparently appalled by his audacity.

"*That does not concern you!*"

Kerin's heart was thundering, but he drew himself up and met the lich's smoldering gaze. It didn't seem like the ancient sorcerer was capable of stepping into the forge; the wards Kerin had felt passing beneath the archway must be keeping Xerivas outside. His gaze flicked from the cube to the lich and back again. This thing was a powerful creation of an Elder Race. If he delivered it into the clutches of a lich he could be sealing the fate of billions. Entire star systems might be consumed.

"I just want some assurance—"

A coruscating bolt of black energy struck him in the chest,

sending him tumbling backwards. He gasped, trying to breathe, his cheek pressed against the cold crystal of the floor. The stars faintly glittering far below whirled and danced. Somewhere, someone was screaming. Nala? The girl?

He rolled onto his back, his hand going to the charred hole in his steelsilk shirt. Gently he explored what was beneath, expecting to find bubbling flesh or a gaping, bloody cavity, but his skin was smooth and unbroken. His Anathema blood had protected him, thank the First Mover.

He sat up, his head spinning. The lich's arm was still raised, crawling with the same dark energy that had just knocked Kerin over. As their gazes met, Xerivas's bony jaw fell open in an almost comical expression of surprise.

A moment later, the lich was consumed by a wave of crackling green aether. Heated air washed over Kerin, followed by the smell of ozone. Nala had lifted the floodgates inside herself, and from her extended paws was issuing a torrent of aether, enough to blow a hole in the side of a fortress. She'd never unleashed this amount before in an enclosed area, to Kerin's knowledge, and he felt a stab of fear that she would accidentally cook the girl if she was standing in the way of the sorcery.

Then as quickly as it had erupted the flow of aether stopped. Nala swooned and she looked like she might collapse. Kerin's fear gave way to hope, as surely she must have destroyed the physical form of the lich. Beyond the archway an emerald inferno raged, almost too bright to look upon.

From the blaze stepped Xerivas. His robes had been burned away, and green flames crawled along his bones. He gestured in the direction of Nala and sent the kyrathi flying backwards. Somehow her feline instincts took over, as she managed to twist herself so that she landed on her paws on the far side of the chamber.

Kerin climbed unsteadily to his feet, bracing himself with his hand on top of the plinth. His fingers brushed the cool metal surface of the gray cube, and he picked it up.

"*Let it go, mortal,*" thundered Xerivas. The aether flames had dwindled to only a few flickering patches, except for the tusked silver skull topping his staff, which continued to blaze like a torch.

A terrific crack sounded from above, and both Kerin and the lich looked up. The roots threading the ceiling and walls were starting to move, tearing free of the stone. A chunk of rock that would have caved in his skull shattered on the floor not a dozen paces from where he stood. Fissures were spreading as the chamber began to collapse.

The lich hissed in frustration and raised his burning staff. The light crystal set in the ceiling flickered and dimmed, and through his Anathema blood Kerin could sense a massive wave of sorcery swelling in the lich. He stumbled as the floor buckled, a thrashing root emerging from where it had previously been trapped below. Shreds of darkness were swirling around Xerivas, pulsing with malignant power. The lich pointed the silver skull straight at Kerin just as the building wave began to crest.

Blinding light.

Kerin cried out, his vision obliterated by the searing brilliance. He fell to his knees, his Anathema blood throbbing like nothing he'd ever felt before.

Silence.

Was he dead?

Slowly other colors seeped into his sight. The whiteness receded, leaving only pale islands behind. He blinked, trying to focus on the lich.

Xerivas was gone. The floor where he'd been standing was blackened, and the wall and part of the archway behind him had been obliterated. His staff lay on the ground, still clutched by a bony hand that had been sheared off at the wrist. What had just happened?

Another quake shook the chamber, and a larger piece of the ceiling tumbled down. Kerin looked around wildly. The gobber was cowering in a corner, staring in shock at the pain conduit.

Kerin gaped as well. The girl was holding an alvaren artifact, the one that looked like a crystal rod, pointing it at where the lich had been standing moments ago.

The gobber shrieked and held up his arms as she turned it

towards him. "Mercy!" the creature gibbered just before a beam of raw energy erupted from the rod and lanced across the room to consume him utterly.

"Nebulas," Kerin whispered.

Somehow the girl seemed to hear this, and she swiveled so that the rod was now aimed at him. Her face was empty, completely devoid of emotion.

Numb terror washed over him. "Wait, no!" Kerin cried, steeling himself to meet the death he saw in her blank eyes.

The treehold convulsed. Kerin somehow managed to keep his balance, but the girl was thrown from her feet. She landed heavily on a pile of freshly-fallen rubble and did not get up.

The roots were writhing, shattering the stone above them and rising from the floor below, sending jagged chunks of crystal thrusting upwards. This chamber – maybe the entire treehold – was being crushed by the great tree. Was there any chance of escaping before everything collapsed? Clinging to the faint hope that the tree would subside again if they fled this chamber, Kerin stumbled towards where the pain conduit lay sprawled. She looked so still and peaceful that for a moment he thought she was dead, but when he knelt down beside her he realized that her chest was still rising and falling.

"I don't think we're wanted in here," he muttered, scooping her into his arms and standing with a pained grunt. She was heavier than she looked, and he was very sore from absorbing the lich's sorcery.

Another quake, the strongest yet. Above them, one of the largest roots ripped free, sending the great crystal embedded in the ceiling crashing down. He turned and tried to shield the girl's body with his own as it shattered into countless flying shards.

"*Ah!*" he cried as pain blossomed in his back, and a moment later he felt warmth begin to flow. He could still move, though, so the steel-silk must have blunted the worst of it.

The chamber had been plunged into semi-darkness, with the only light coming from the shimmering remnants of the crystal and the pearly luminescence of the tree's roots.

"Nala!" he cried out.

"Here!" she called back from the blackness that shrouded the far side of the forge. Green aether flared around her paws, and his heart leapt to see that she could still move.

"We need to leave! Follow me to—"

Before he could finish, another quake shook the treehold and with a rending shriek a huge fissure shuddered open. Nala's green-limned hands waved frantically as she tried to catch herself, but to Kerin's horror she tumbled into the widening crack and vanished.

"No!" he screamed, numb with shock. Not Nala! For a moment he could only stand there, swaying, as the treehold continued to break up around him.

It was the girl who brought him back to himself. She squirmed in his arms, moaning as she fought for consciousness. Kerin had a strong desire to drop the pain conduit and run as fast as he could from this place, but something stopped him. Maybe it was resignation – there was no way he was escaping this. He raised his eyes to what was left of the ceiling. He wanted to see his death coming.

Kerin.

He felt a stab of sorrow as the starbeast slipped into his mind for the last time. *Drifter.*

You're alive.

Not for very much longer. Kerin struggled to form the next thought, as if he was refusing to admit what had just happened. *Nala is dead.*

She's not, but you will be if you don't get out of there right now.

What?

Go to where you last saw her. Quickly.

Kerin staggered across the chamber to the rent in the floor carrying the limp pain conduit. When he got to the edge, he looked down and gasped.

Drifter's shell filled the emptiness below the treehold. Nala was perched on the tallest structure grafted to the starbeast, the gently rounded glass roof of his grandfather's solarium. He wasn't sure how she could possibly be keeping her balance, but her arms were outstretched towards where he was gaping down at her.

"Leave the girl and let's go!" Nala cried.

Kerin glanced at the face of the unconscious pain conduit. He remembered her empty expression as she had pointed the crystal rod at him . . . the rod. It was still in her hand, even though her fingers had gone slack. He tried to rip it from her grip, but it wouldn't come free. Something was wrong. The rod seemed to be *melting* into her hand, its crystalline substance flowing across her skin.

"Leave her!" Nala screamed again. "I can't take both of you!"

Ignoring her words, Kerin sank to his knees and adjusted his grip on the girl. Holding on to her arms firmly, he leaned forward, lowering her so that Nala could reach her legs.

"Damn you for a fool, Kerin!" the kyrathi snarled as she wrapped her paws around the girl and in one smooth motion slung her limp body over her shoulder. "Wait for me!" she cried, and then leaped down from where she'd been standing. She laid the girl on the deck – none too gently – and looked up just as another great shudder passed through the treehold.

Kerin glanced over his shoulder to see the walls caving in and the last bits of stone around the roots in the ceiling collapsing. If he waited any longer he knew he would be crushed.

He jumped.

For a moment, time slowed to a crawl as Drifter swelled larger below him, and then the glass roof of the solarium exploded. The last thing he saw was his grandfather's desk rushing up to meet him.

4

KERIN AWOKE.

The first thought he had, as he swam back to consciousness, was that he was not dead. And the second was that he wished he was. Every bone and joint in his body ached, and his back felt like it had been scourged by a cat o' nine tails.

He lay on his bed in his cabin under a scratchy wool blanket. He knew he hadn't laid himself down by his own volition, because this had been his mother's blanket from when she was a child, and it always stayed in the chest at the foot of the bed. Nala, then. It must have been, as the bandages wrapping him had been applied in the distinctive spiral technique of the ghenabakan navy. Also, they were the only two residing on Drifter these days.

No. That wasn't true anymore. The girl should still be alive. He closed his eyes as the memory of what had happened in the treehold hit him like an avalanche. Kerin swallowed, trying to sort through the madness. Everything had happened so fast. The lich had attacked him, not knowing about his Anathema blood. In response, Nala had unleashed her aether, but the lich had shrugged that off. Then the girl had channeled through one of the alvaren artifacts an absolutely mind-boggling amount of raw stellar energy. One of these events – he wasn't sure which – had woken up the treehold, and then it had promptly decided to kill all of them.

How had they survived? He glanced out his cabin's small window and saw flowing black. They were in a Stream. Relief washed over him, and he sagged back into his bed. Somehow they had managed to evade the undead starbeast and slip out of the system.

Drifter?

Ah, you're awake. Wonderful.

What happened?

You executed a perfect dive through the roof of your grandfather's favorite room. Made quite a mess.

Kerin did the mental equivalent of an eye-roll. The starbeast was so infuriating sometimes. *No. I mean how did we get away?*

I moved my little flippers as fast I could. The dragon seemed sluggish and confused after the treehold turned murderous, and we made the Stream mouth before he even thought about starting to follow.

More good news. If they had enough of a head start, then Drifter might be able to lose any pursuers in the myriad branchings of the stellar tributary.

And where are we going?

Actually, I was waiting for you to wake up and tell me. As of now, we're swimming in the opposite direction of where we just were.

Probably a good idea.

The door to his cabin swung open and Nala stepped inside.

"You should knock," Kerin said. "I could have been naked."

"I already saw you naked," the kyrathi responded with a snort, settling herself in his reading chair. "Or do you think Drifter changed you into your sleeping robe?" She gave a little chuckle at the face he was making. "Oh, don't be such a prude. Without fur, you always look naked to me. Just an ugly shaved ape."

"Hmm," Kerin sniffed, pulling the blanket up higher to hide his bare chest. "I had no idea I was so disgusting to you."

"I'm used to it," the kyrathi said with a wave of her paw. "Though

I'd prefer to never have to dig dozens of glass shards out of your body again, so please don't go jumping through any more windows."

"I'll try my best," Kerin murmured, pulling back the sleeve of his robe to inspect his arms. His skin was a lattice of angry red lines, but he seemed to be healing well. Another benefit of being Anathema, to go along with his resistance to base sorcery, was that his bones knit back together in weeks instead of months, and cuts went from open and weeping to faint scars in almost no time at all.

"How long have I been sleeping?"

"We left the treehold's system a little less than a solar standard day ago."

"And the girl?"

The kyrathi's eyes narrowed to slits. "Still out. I'm burning vel sticks in her cabin to keep her under for a while yet. I don't want her waking."

Kerin struggled to sit up, concerned by something in Nala's tone. "Why not?"

The kyrathi uncurled from her seated position and stood. "You should come see for yourself. Can you walk?"

Kerin threw back the blankets covering him, then took a deep breath and slipped from the bed. He hurt all over, but the pain was manageable. Wincing, he hobbled after the kyrathi as she left the cabin.

Nala had put the pain conduit back in the passenger quarters that she'd been sharing with the gobber during their week-long voyage out from Jegriddsl. A fog of blue-tinged, sweet-smelling smoke assailed him as he crept inside, tickling his nose, and he had to fight back the urge to sneeze. The vel sticks were smoldering inside an incense burner he thought he recognized from his grandfather's collection. Such objects had been strictly off-limits while his grandfather had been alive, but Kerin was well past caring at this point. Most of it was junk, anyway, as he'd found out when he'd tried to hawk a few pieces.

The girl looked peaceful, her breathing deep and regular. There was no hint in her face that she was suffering at all from anything that had happened back in the treehold, either physically or in her dreams. A lantern had been placed on the bedstand, and its guttering crystal was making shadows dance in the darkened room.

"What are we looking for?" he whispered as Nala silently padded over to beside the bed. The kyrathi turned back to him and laid a claw against her mouth, then drew back the edge of the quilt covering the girl's right arm. Kerin sucked in his breath at what was revealed.

Something sheathed the pain conduit's arm from the tips of her fingers to her elbow. In the gloom, it could almost be mistaken for the kind of formal glove worn by ladies of a certain social standing, but Kerin knew immediately that this wasn't a normal piece of clothing. He crouched down closer, hesitant to touch the strange covering but achingly curious to see if his suspicions were correct. Whatever it was, it didn't look soft. There were no folds or wrinkles like what gathered in cloth or leather; rather, it appeared hard, like a fitted gauntlet. Kerin remembered the alvaren rod the girl had used to obliterate the lich's avatar beginning to melt as he tried to tear it away from her hand, a crystalline ooze clinging to her skin, crawling up her wrist . . .

He swallowed and stood, glancing at Nala. She was staring at him meaningfully. He raised his hand and started to sign using guild cant, but she shook her head and gestured for him to follow her outside.

After Nala had shut the door behind them softly, she whirled on him, her tail lashing. "What do we do?" she hissed.

Kerin shrugged. "I don't know."

The kyrathi gestured furiously at the closed door with a claw. "You brought her on board. Surely you had some reason why."

"I wasn't going to just let her die," he said defensively, crossing his arms.

"Who is she to us?" Nala continued in a heated whisper. "A damaged, possibly deranged girl who has known nothing except a life of being filled and emptied countless times with purchased pain. Who can conceive of what grudges she holds against the universe?

And now she has an Elder Race weapon grafted onto her. If she wakes up and triggers it – by accident or not – she could vaporize a large chunk of Drifter and send us all tumbling out of the Stream and into the void."

Kerin held up his hands to try and stop the kyrathi's tirade. "All right, all right. I hear you. But how was I to know the artifact would bond with her? And what do you want me to do about it now? Sneak back inside and smother her with a pillow while she sleeps?"

"Not a bad idea. Want me to do it?"

Kerin couldn't tell if she was joking or not. He thought she was. He hoped she was. "No," he told her sternly.

The air vibrated as Nala began a low, dangerous growl, and the hair on the back of his neck started to prickle. Usually when he heard that sound it meant that someone was about to be clawed, so it was time to put some space between him and the kyrathi.

"I'm going up to look at the charts," he said. "Don't kill her while I'm gone. If she wakes, try to be nice. Or come find me, but make sure she's not panicking."

Nala glared at him a moment longer, then turned and stalked off, her tail lashing. Kerin watched her go until she'd vanished down the stairs leading to the lower deck, feeling uneasy.

She's scared.

Nal doesn't get scared, he informed Drifter, a bit more forcefully than he'd intended.

She doesn't feel fear when she's got an enemy across from her and aether crackling in her paws. But there's nothing for her to fight right now, yet our lives are in danger. She's helpless, and that terrifies her.

You think I should toss the girl over the side? he thought bitterly.

I do not, the starbeast answered calmly.

Kerin sighed as he made his way to the spiraling stairs that led up to his grandfather's solarium. *I know this.* His boots rang on the metal steps as he started to climb. *Did you see through me what happened to the lich?* he thought, trying to change the subject. *Do you think it's gone?*

Yes, I saw. And no, it's not.

He expected the second answer, but still his heart fell a little at Drifter's quick response. *Didn't look like there was very much left of him.*

I've been swimming through the stars for centuries, Kerin, and I've heard many stories about sorcerers like this Xerivas. Their physical forms may be destroyed, but their consciousness merely retreats to another host. The only way to end a lich's existence is to find its core essence – its soul, if you will – and destroy the phylactery that houses it.

Great, Kerin thought as he reached the top of the stairs and put his hand on the ebony knob of the door to his grandfather's sanctum. *Well, maybe this lich will cut his losses and let us go.*

The starbeast's silence concerning this possibility was deafening. With another sigh, Kerin turned the handle and entered the solarium.

Or what was left of it.

Much of the copper frame that made up the curving ceiling had been mangled when he had come crashing through, and only a few panes of glass were still intact. The rest were scattered about, a thousand glittering shards that crunched beneath his boots as he came to stand in the center of the room. His grandfather's desk where the old man had sat and watched the Streams rushing past bore the imprint of where Kerin's shoulder had caved in the wood. He vaguely remembered twisting in the air just before impacting the desk, and, all things considered, he had been lucky not to have broken his neck in the fall. Even his Anathema blood wouldn't have brought him back from that.

The ancient brass telescope that had been his grandfather's second most prized possession must have taken a glancing blow, as the legs of its tripod had snapped off and sent the device crashing to the floor. Kerin bent over to pick it up and noticed the lens was cracked, and a little swell of sadness hit him. Damn. Another memento of his grandfather lost. He turned to find a place on the damaged desk for the optical tube, and his foot bumped something lost amongst the slivers of glass. His heart went cold when he saw it was the gray cube from the treehold.

How did it get here? He swallowed, eyeing the object like it was a venomous snake. He must have kept it in his hand when Nala and Xerivas and the girl had started tossing arcane energies around. Or maybe he'd slipped it into his pocket in the chaos and forgotten about it? Hesitating slightly, he crouched down and scooped the artifact from the floor. Like he remembered, it felt as if it had been forged from a single piece of cool, smooth metal. His Anathema blood did not stir, as it had in the past in the presence of powerful sorcery. If the lich had not desired the cube, and it had not been placed in such a place of honor inside the Crucible, he would have thought it was a paperweight, or something equally as useless.

Carefully, he placed the remnants of the telescope and the cube on an intact section of the splintered desk. A thought struck him, and he glanced up again at the blackness of the Stream surging past. Should he just toss the cube out into the dark? Let it tumble out of the Stream and into the void beyond? It would fall for eternity, forever out of the reach of monsters like Xerivas. He hefted the cube again, considering doing just that, but found himself hesitating. Perhaps it was the ghost of his grandfather in the room willing him not to do such a thing to a priceless remnant of a lost people. Or, more pragmatically, maybe they would need the cube as a bargaining chip if the lich managed to find them. He set the cube down once more, hard enough that it made a solid metallic clunk, and willed himself not to think any more about dropping it into the Stream.

He had more important things he should be concerned with right now, like figuring out where they should go. Kerin went over to the cabinets built into the wall and rifled through the mess of loose papers inside until he found the star charts for this section of the stellar tributary. They were coated with a layer of dust, and it didn't seem like anyone had referenced them for a generation or so, but that mattered little, as it was very rare for the Streams to ever shift. While he was there he grabbed a dusky stoppered bottle of something that looked so alcoholic as to be potentially poisonous. He desperately needed a drink right now.

Kerin laid the yellowed parchment down, searching through the maze of Streams and systems for a familiar name to orient himself.

There, on the edge of the map, Jegriddsl had been written in a neat, archaic script that Kerin recognized as belonging to another of his ancestors, the one who had drafted most of these charts. Even back then, the planet had been an important hub, as a half-dozen Stream mouths converged in its system. Kerin found the Stream the gobber had paid them to take, and he followed numerous branchings until it emptied into the unnamed and uninhabited system where they'd encountered Xerivas and his monstrous starbeast. It was the only mouth in the treehold's system, so it must be where they'd fled back to after what had happened in the Crucible.

Kerin righted the chair that had been knocked over during his fall and sat. He put his finger on the Stream and started to trace their route. These charts were such confusing tangles that it was very easy to lose one's place.

Drifter, he thought as his finger approached the first branching, *did you take this smaller rivulet or stay in the main Stream?*

I did not like the feel of that small Stream, so I remained in the larger. I took the following branch, then continued past the next two converging mouths and chose the third, headed towards the Umbral Cluster.

"Mmm," Kerin murmured, finding the Stream through which they were currently swimming. *The Umbral Cluster. That was smart. It's a warren out there, easy to get lost.*

Which is usually bad, Drifter replied, and Kerin could sense the pride in the starbeast from being praised.

But of course right now we want to get lost.

My thoughts exactly.

Kerin drummed his fingers on the dry parchment. The Umbral Cluster was on the fringe of the Known, and only in recent years had a few of the major star-spanning empires begun to contest the worlds within. He'd heard that the Qan Hegemony had won a bloody war against a powerful pirate queen to lay claim to a handful of systems. He dredged his memories for their names: H'shen, a world of blue sand deserts and tarry oceans; Bel Atoch, uninhabitable except for its polar regions, where league-long ice worms were hunted for their vision-inducing organs; and Reaver's Rest, the only planet in the cluster with a significant population, known throughout the stellar tributary as a haven for miscreants and villains. Kerin opened one of the desk's drawers and took out a crystal tumbler. With some effort, he uncorked the mysterious bottle, grimacing at the smell that escaped, then splashed a little of the foul liquid in the glass. He leaned back in the chair, swirling his drink and mulling the possibility of stopping at the Rest. It was a dangerous place, but perhaps after the fall of the pirate queen the qan had made things a bit more civilized.

Kerin knocked back a healthy swallow of his drink. If it was poison, he didn't want to end up half-dead.

Searing warmth slid down his throat, stripping away layers as it went. He stifled a cough as the liquid pooled in his stomach and started to curdle. "Drega's dugs, that's good," he wheezed. A few more glasses of this stuff and he would forget all about the troubled girl with the Elder Race weapon melded to her arm who was sleeping below in his passenger berth.

His eyes wandered over the map. There were dozens of systems in the Umbral Cluster, but only nine with names. The others were uninhabited, with maybe, at most, a gas giant or two and a few barren chunks of rock tumbling around their star. Good places to hide, but they only had provisions for a few more days stored on Drifter. No, they needed to go somewhere out of the way, but still large and developed enough that they could resupply themselves and not stick out as strangers.

Kerin took another bracing gulp of his drink. Hideous stuff, but absolutely what he needed in this moment. His finger drifted aimlessly, tracing the Streams crisscrossing the cluster, right up to where the Known merged with the Unknown. Some of the Streams plunged through that invisible demarcation, though the cartographer hadn't bothered to guess where they went. Instead, they trailed into blank parchment, empty except for a few fanciful drawings of monsters and horrors. Many explorers had ventured into the Unknown, but few had returned. The ones that did spoke of Streams that were wild and dangerous, with surging currents that could exhaust even the strongest of starbeasts. Every fresh handler heard from grizzled streamsurfers of the things that had been sighted or experienced beyond the Known: ghost starbeasts endlessly swimming, voices that called out from the black in strange tongues, and creatures that dwarfed even the largest starbeasts briefly breaching the boundaries of the Streams, infringing from the void beyond, and then vanishing again.

No, even if the lich chased them to the edge of the universe he'd rather turn and fight than flee into the Unknown. Hopefully, though, he wouldn't have to make that choice.

His finger had come to rest right on the edge where the Umbral Cluster gave way to mystery. There was a system there, its old name scratched out and a new one written in a different hand than the rest of the map.

Dust.

He'd been there, long ago. It was one of the first places his grandfather had brought him after the old man had come blazing like a comet into his life. He remembered it as a sleepy settlement squatting in hollowed stone spires that had been carved out by an earlier, vanished people. They'd stayed with a woman who had had some sort of relationship with his grandfather – there had been many such women, across a frankly astonishing number of worlds – and the only other thing of note he could recall was that his nightmares had been so vivid. He'd dreamed of dark little children, watching him crouched from the shadows . . . he shivered, despite the warmth flowing through him from the drink. He hadn't thought about Dust in years.

But it was perfect, for more than one reason.

He found Nala on the upper deck that jutted off the saloon. The kyrathi was leaning against the balustrade staring at the Stream through which they were plunging, seemingly lost in thought, a steaming mug cradled in her paws. She glanced over as Kerin joined her, then quickly looked away again. He said nothing, sipping from the cup he'd brought down from his grandfather's solarium. The numbness brought on by the mysterious spirit had overwhelmed the stinging in his back, for which he was grateful.

Silence hung between them for a while. Pushing through the pleasant fog now hovering over his thoughts, Kerin tried to discern from Nala's posture whether she was still angry with him or not, but the kyrathi's mood was as enigmatic as any cat's – she might have already forgiven him, or she might be preparing to swipe him with her claws.

Very well, he'd be the one to break the tension, as he needed to find out where he stood with his crew mate. Kerin took a fortifying gulp of his drink and then turned to her.

"Nala—"

"She's still asleep," the kyrathi said, cutting him off. "But I don't think she'll suffer any permanent injuries. She should be fine by the time we get where we're going."

Kerin's mouth closed with a click, surprised by her tacit admission that she'd been wrong to wish harm on the girl by letting him know she expected her to reach their destination. He swallowed what he'd been about to say with another mouthful of the bracing drink. That was good, not that he actually thought in his heart of hearts that she would ever have hurt the girl.

The kyrathi stirred the contents of her mug with a claw, swirling the bits of meat that floated in the silty liquid. "Where are we going, Kerin?"

And now came the other potentially difficult conversation. "Drifter is taking us to the Umbral Cluster. I'm thinking Dust."

Nala's eyes narrowed. "Dust . . . I've never been. Heard the name, though, a while back when we were on Heth. Another streamsurfer talking about his last swim . . . said he'd come from the cluster, and that Dust was a Mandate world now."

That pierced the comforting haze he had been floating through. *Nebulas, can we ever escape the void-cursed Mandate?*

"Truly? That's a long way from the imperial core."

Nala shrugged, rolling her shoulders in a way a human could not. "They're ambitious, been gobbling systems these last few years. And with the qan pushing in from the other side, maybe they thought they needed a claim to the cluster before it all fell to the reptiles."

Kerin sighed. Much of their recent misfortune was connected to the Mandate – though, if he was perfectly honest with himself, the imperials had shown surprising leniency when he and Nala had been caught trespassing in an exarch's barrow. After the Mandati soldiers had first appeared he'd imagined a short walk off a gallows' pier was in his future, but the magistrate in charge had let them off with a fine and a warning. Word had still gotten back to the guild, however, and old rivals of his family had used this debacle to oust them. And *that's* why they had become the sort of streamsurfers who took on risky contracts from random gobbers.

"Well?" Nala said, and from the twinge of annoyance Kerin heard, he realized he had missed something she'd said while his thoughts had been wandering.

He took a guess at what that must have been. "I still think we should go there. We weren't banned from Mandati systems, and Dust is a good place to lay low for a while. Better than the Rest, especially if that planet now bows to the qan matriarch."

Nala grunted in agreement to this. The kyrathi and the qan were ancient enemies, stemming back millennia to when they had both been enslaved by the same Elder Race. But while the qan had managed to establish their own interstellar empire in the epoch since their old masters had vanished, the kyrathi had never overcome their solitary natures, and instead had been subjugated to various other peoples ever since. Most recently the militant ghenabakans, in whose breeding pits Nala had been raised.

For a moment, the kyrathi looked mollified by what he'd said, but then her eyes narrowed suspiciously. "There's something else, another reason you want to go to Dust."

Careful, careful, Kerin thought, trying to look as innocent as possible. "No, nothing, I promise," he said, holding up his hands as if to show he wasn't hiding anything. Instead he managed to spill his drink down the front of his shirt. "Oh, bloody stars," he muttered, staring in chagrin at the spreading stain.

Nala turned away in disgust. "Go clean yourself up and lie down, you're drunk. I promise not to kick the girl over the side if she wakes up."

5

KERIN'S FINGER traced the golden cracks threading the glistening black substance of his grandfather's sword. The imperfections resembled lightning strikes, how they started thicker down near the plain storm-gray metal handle, then gradually grew more attenuated as they made their meandering way towards the slightly curved tip of the blade. No blood-groove ran along its tapering length, and the glassy smooth material it had been fashioned from resembled obsidian, but while that volcanic rock shattered easily, his grandfather's sword had proven capable of cutting through nearly anything.

He had asked a dozen different experts if they had ever seen such a weapon before, and all had shaken their heads. Most had then tried to buy the sword from him, sometimes for extravagant amounts, but Kerin had never been tempted, even when he could barely afford Drifter's feed. It was the one item of true value – other than the star-beast, of course – that his grandfather had left him. To sell the sword would be to finally turn away from his family's legacy.

Kerin upended the bottle over his cup and waited for the last few silty drops to trickle down. Had he really finished it all? When had that happened? He remembered coming into the saloon and sliding onto the threadbare couch where the gobber had been sitting not so long ago, lost in recollections of his brief time on Dust. This – and the bottle he carried – had led him further down the paths of memory, to simpler times when he'd been much younger and had revered his grandfather, the famous streamsurfer. Which had, in turn, resulted in him unsheathing the old man's sword, laying it upon the scarred table, and becoming lost in the glimmering flaws incised into the blade.

Mercy, his grandfather had called the sword. A stupid name for a weapon, Kerin had come to realize, in the years after the luster of his grandfather's legend had faded in his mind. Truly, naming any object like it was a person was silly, and yet every time he looked at the sword all he saw was *Mercy*.

"They better hope I don't show them *Mercy*," Kerin slurred, mimicking his grandfather's gravelly drawl. Oh, he'd thought that was *so* funny. He must have said that a hundred times to Kerin, referring to intractable bureaucrats, guild rivals, and the stablemasters who invariably attempted to gouge them when bargaining for Drifter's stall.

Kerin lifted his glass and was surprised to find it empty. He frowned, reaching for the bottle, only to discover that its contents had also mysteriously vanished. He briefly considered pushing himself from where he slouched to go rummage through the saloon's cabinets in the hope that something had magically appeared since the last time he'd gone looking for a drink but couldn't make it to his feet before subsiding with a resigned grunt. Maybe he'd lie down here instead until Drifter stopped swimming in circles. Just for a little while . . .

KERIN.

Someone was stomping back and forth along the inside of his skull. No, not someone - an entire regiment of ghenabakan heavy infantry was on parade, drums beating and horns blaring.

He cracked open gummy eyes and sat up, groaning. Nala must

have passed through the saloon, as the only lightsphere that hadn't been extinguished was the one hanging over the table. Grimacing, he lowered his eyes from the pulsing radiance, studying the imperfections in the wood in front of him.

What had dragged him back to consciousness? He'd need at least another six sandglasses spent asleep before he could wake up without boots trampling his brain into mush . . .

KERIN.

His own name exploded in his thoughts, bellowed by his starbeast. He rocked back on the couch, smacking his head against the wall.

"Ow," Kerin moaned feebly.

YOU MUST WAKE UP.

"I'm awake," he said aloud, then realized what he'd just done and sent the same message hurtling across the bond he shared with his starbeast. *I'm awake.*

Thank the whorled shell. What in the abyss are you thinking, drinking yourself into oblivion when we're at this moment fleeing from a lich and his dragon through dangerous Streams? Despite the haze blanketing Kerin's thoughts he could still sense Drifter's frustration. *Every generation of your family has gotten progressively more foolish. I shudder to think what being bonded to your spawn will be like.*

All right, Kerin thought, kneading his temple. *I'm sorry. Why did you wake me?*

I've been trying to rouse you for a quarter of a glass. At this point, only a few options are still available.

Kerin's thoughts sharpened. *What do you mean?*

There's something up ahead of us in the Stream. It feels like another starbeast, but it's just . . . sitting there.

If it's not moving at all, then it must be dead. Starbeasts did not often perish in the Streams, but when that happened their corpses could last for centuries, until they finally tumbled into the void or were hauled out by another streamsurfer hoping to sell some rare body part to an alchemist or chirurgeon. Organic matter did not seem to decay in here, one of the many ways in which the Streams differed from the rest of the universe.

It's not, Drifter replied. *I can sense its thoughts, but they are very alien. Not shaped by any handler I'm familiar with, an unknown sentience.*

That unnerved Kerin. Young starbeasts were imprinted by the first handler they bonded with, their personality often a reflection of this original formative relationship. Drifter, in some ways, was like a bridge to Kerin's own distant ancestor. But while the many star-faring races molded their starbeasts differently, over time the great creatures had learned to understand and communicate with each other in their own pidgin dialect. If Drifter claimed he did not understand the starbeast they were approaching, that meant whatever had tamed it had come from outside the region of the stellar tributary they were familiar with. A disquieting thought.

Kerin heaved himself to his feet, just managing to catch himself with a steadying hand on the table before he fell back again. Nebulas, he needed all his faculties right now. He staggered over to the bar, which was barren except for a few empty bottles, and grabbed a dented metal jug. There was a water barrel beside the bar, and he pried off the lid and plunged the jug within. Steeling himself, he poured the cold water over his head, and sobriety hit him in a crystalline wave that left him gasping.

"*Gah,*" he spluttered, rubbing his face hard. That would have to do. He returned to the table and grabbed his grandfather's sword, then headed for the exit that led out onto the upper deck.

Like inside, only a few lightspheres were still glowing. Drifter's great head was twisted half-around so that the turtle could glimpse him out of the corner of his eye.

Sopping wet and brandishing Mercy. At least I know you're taking this seriously.

Kerin ignored Drifter's tone. The ancestor who had shaped the turtle's personality must have been an annoying bastard. *How much longer until we reach the other starbeast?*

It could be moments. We're close.

Kerin strode across the deck to where a large brass bell hung. His hand went to the cord, but then he hesitated – Nala slept lightly and would certainly be awoken, but what about the girl? How potent were the vel sticks that were keeping her asleep?

He really didn't have a choice. If there was danger up ahead he would need the battlemage at his side. Gritting his teeth, Kerin rang the bell loudly.

Within moments, Nala appeared on the balcony off her cabin. Her quarters were in another, smaller structure attached to Drifter's shell, slightly below the deck he stood upon. She didn't waste any time, swinging onto the walkway that spiraled up to the Nest and then taking off at a run. She rarely unleashed her full speed and agility, but it was on display here as she leaped from plank to plank and dashed across swaying ropes, finally soaring over the emptiness to arrive beside him.

Her ears were pinned back, and claws unsheathed as she approached. "Is it the lich?" she asked, staring past the Nest at the blackness churning behind Drifter.

"No," Kerin said, indicating in front of them with a jerk of his chin. "We're coming up on a starbeast. Not moving, Drifter says, but not dead either."

Nala's eyes narrowed. "Injured . . . or an ambush?"

"What would lie in wait in a Stream?"

"There are stories . . ."

"Stories that are found at the bottom of tankards."

There ARE stories, Kerin, don't dismiss the possibility, Drifter admonished him. *I've spoken with starbeasts that claim to have escaped such attacks, and starbeasts do not tell tales.* He paused. *Well, most of them do not. We don't drunkenly boast to each other, at least.*

"Speaking of the bottom of tankards," Nala murmured, looking Kerin up and down.

"I'm fine," he growled, and she gave a little snort at this.

Kerin, up ahead and starboard.

His attention sharpened on the roiling blackness of the Stream. At first he could see nothing, just the vague shapes that always seemed to lurk at the edge of perception out here, but then he noticed one that did not fade away with the rest.

"I see it," he said to Nala. "On the right, a half a league or so in the distance."

"I see nothing," she replied, craning her head forward as if that would somehow give her his starbeast-shared ability to pierce the Stream's darkness. "What is it?"

"It looks . . . like an insect. A big insect."

A beetle, Drifter clarified.

What race bonds with such starbeasts?

None that I'm familiar with.

Kerin's anxiety deepened. If Drifter had never encountered such a creature, it did suggest strongly that it came from another, very distant branch of the stellar tributary. Or the Unknown, though he'd never heard of sentient races and starbeasts dwelling among those corrupted Streams.

Whatever it was, he didn't want to stop and find out.

It's still not moving?

Yes. And I can't see any structures or creatures on its carapace.

Then continue past it. Speed up, if you can. If it starts to stir to life, I want to have enough of a lead that it has no chance of catching us.

It won't, Drifter told him confidently. A trace of arrogance, but Kerin knew it was warranted. Size was usually correlated with speed among starbeasts, and he could tell that the insect was much smaller than Drifter.

"I can see it," Nala hissed, her claws digging into the wood of the balustrade.

"We're not stopping," he told her.

"Good. We've had enough excitement recently."

Kerin could feel the effort Drifter was expending. His flippers were scooping great chunks of the invisible substance they were swimming through, each mottled limb fairly wreathed in glimmering silver sparks. The turtle's vast head was straining forward, displaying the long, wrinkled neck he usually kept hidden.

The beetle flickered past, almost too fast to make out any details.

Kerin thought he'd seen movement on the glistening black body, but it might have been his imagination. He turned away as it quickly receded and began to merge again with the blackness of the Stream.

"Well, that was anticlima—"

AH!

Kerin was thrown forward as Drifter's speed suddenly decreased, sending him smashing him against the balustrade. He heard the snap of wood as part of it gave way, but enough of the ancient posts held that he was kept from tumbling off the deck and onto the turtle's shell. The pain he'd been trying to ignore in his back flared again, spots dancing in his vision as he came dangerously close to throwing up everything he'd drunk earlier.

He realized in a numb panic that Nala had been tossed over, and she was even now sliding down the starbeast's shell. She yowled, scrabbling desperately for purchase. Below her, beyond the curve of the shell, yawned the endless abyss.

"Nala!" he cried, and then had to look away as she tumbled closer to the edge. Nebulas, no! This was the death that streamsurfers dreaded most, falling off their starbeast and into the Stream, then passing into the void to plummet endlessly through the dark until finally claimed by hunger or thirst...

Choking back a sob, he forced himself to look again. He gasped in relief to see Nala had managed to arrest her slide by sinking her claws into some imperfection in Drifter's shell. She couldn't start to climb up, though, as Drifter was convulsing. All she could do was try not to lose her tenuous grip. Kerin also had to cling to the balustrade's remaining posts to stop himself from plunging over the side, and his heart leapt as the wood creaked alarmingly.

Drifter, stop it! Nala will fall!

Get it off!

The starbeast was thrashing his head back and forth, trying to be free of something. Which was exactly what he was doing, Kerin realized, as he suddenly noticed the glistening strands clinging to the great turtle – and it wasn't only his head. Silky filaments were stretched taut across the entirety of Drifter, laying against his shell and tangling his flippers. It was as though he had swum directly into a vast net.

Calm, Drifter he commanded soothingly, trying his best to keep his own fear from bleeding across the bond they shared. The star-beast clacked his great beak in frustration, but Kerin felt the turtle's panic start to subside. As it lessened, so did his struggles. Kerin glanced again over the side and saw that Nala had steadied herself and resumed her climb back up the shell. As he watched, she arrived at one of the wrist-thick strands, and without hesitation she raised her paw, which was now sheathed with crackling aether. When the green flame touched the strange material it blackened and quickly shriveled, eventually flaking away in a cloud of ashes. Her aether crawled farther along the thread, burning it up as it spread, until finally the sorcery dissipated.

"What is it?" he called down, and Nala glanced up at him.

"I'm not certain, but it sure feels like a web."

Coldness pooled in Kerin's stomach. A web. The Weaver in Darkness? No, these strands looked nothing like the creation of the Weaver or its spawn, nor had that entity ever been known to unspool its silk in the Streams. *Drifter, how long until you can swim normally again?*

Not until you remove a lot more of this stuff.

Grimacing, Kerin hefted *Mercy* and looked around. Another strand had fallen upon the deck, and he hacked down. His sword sliced through easily, but it didn't disintegrate like when touched by Nala's sorcery.

I can cut it, but it still remains. Aether actually burns it up, so we'll need Nala to free you, I think.

We don't have time for that, Kerin.

What do you mean? he asked his starbeast, though he had a sinking feeling he knew what Drifter was about to say.

The starbeast behind us has started moving. It's coming right for us.

By the time Nala joined him again on the deck the ambushing star-beast was visible and rapidly growing larger. Its small, blunt head was dwarfed by a fat thorax, seemingly too large for the spindly legs carrying it closer. It certainly wasn't the fastest starbeast he had ever encountered . . . but it didn't have to be to catch its prey, if it could set traps like the one they had blundered into. Luckily, Kerin couldn't see any mandibles or claws or other sharp extremities that could injure Drifter while he was helpless, but now that the beetle had nearly come alongside them, he could see that its back was swarming with smaller insects. There were dozens of them crowding the edge of the beetle's shell, chittering and waving their scythe-like arms. It was difficult to gauge their exact size from this distance, but to Kerin it looked like they might be at least as tall as a man, with the bent legs, thin bodies, and bulging eyes of mantises. Jagged red markings covered their black and green carapaces like war paint.

"Have you encountered such things before?" Kerin asked.

"No," replied Nala. "They look like savages. I don't see any structures or weapons at all."

He wanted to ask Drifter, but the bond between them had been frayed close to breaking by the starbeast's panic at being tangled by the threads. No need to remind him that hostile raiders were almost upon them.

"They certainly don't seem friendly," he murmured, his grip tightening on *Mercy's* hilt.

"No, they don't," Nala replied, aether flaring around her paws, which caused Kerin's Anathema blood to stir in response. "I think we can assume ill-intentions."

With a grunt, she hurled a crackling green glob in the direction of the insect starbeast. It carved a glittering arc through the Stream, trailing wisps of energy like a comet, and came down well wide of the beetle. The mantis-men swarming its back raised their scythe-like arms in what looked like celebration of her miss.

"First one was a warning shot," she muttered, "and the idiots don't seem to realize that."

"No more warning shots," Kerin told her as the beetle's speed quickened.

Another green fireball tumbled towards the approaching star-beast, but this time it impacted on the creature's shell. Burning chunks of aether exploded in all directions, but none of the mantis-men were caught in the blast, and when the sorcery dissipated the beetle's carapace looked charred but unbroken.

"Again," Kerin said, his unease rising as the beetle continued ever closer. Was it going to try and ram Drifter's side? His starbeast was quite a bit larger, and a blow from his flipper would send the beetle spinning away. Not to mention that if Drifter managed to free himself and brought his head about, his beak would crunch through the insect's legs like they were reeds.

"No holding back," Nala assured him, and then summoned a much larger sphere of roiling energy and sent it spinning right towards the greatest concentration of the mantis-men. Some of them flinched backwards, but one with white markings instead of red stepped forward and raised curved arms that looked to have been dipped in black paint. The air directly in the path of Nala's aether shimmered and crystalized into a translucent circle of gray ice. When the sorceries collided, a crack like thunder shivered the air. Kerin's Anathema blood pounded in his veins, and although the disc fractured into countless fragments, the aether blast also evaporated into nothing.

"Tooth and claw, another mage," Nala growled.

Kerin sighed. This would make things much more difficult.

The mantis-man sorcerer waved its serrated limbs and a dark-crystal lance began to coalesce from drifting ice-motes, hovering beside him.

"A Path I've never seen before," the kyrathi battlemage muttered. "And it, unfortunately, seems strong in both attack and defense."

Kerin frowned. Nala's sorcery certainly leaned in one direction, as was the case with most other mages. That would put her at a disadvantage here.

The mantis-man shaman brought one of his black-painted arms

down sharply and the gleaming lance shot like a ballista bolt across the rapidly shrinking distance between the starbeasts, aimed straight at Nala. She raised her aether-limned paw and sent a stream of fire hurtling to meet it, but she was a heartbeat late and the sorceries smashed together only a few dozen paces from where they stood on the deck. The lance shattered, chunks of the crystal skittering around Kerin's feet, a blast of frozen air washing over him. Nala kicked at one of these fragments even as it started to dissolve.

"He's powerful," she said, her voice sounding slightly strained. "I'm not sure if I can help you with the others."

"Maybe they won't try and board now that they know you're a mage," Kerin said hopefully, but as soon as he said this one of the mantis-men crouched down and leaped off the side of its starbeast.

"Oh, dear," he sighed as the creature soared across the gap between Drifter and the beetle and landed safely on the lower deck. The mantis-man whirled back to face his kin and raised high his scythe-arms, clashing them together as if encouraging the others to make the same jump.

"Kerin . . ." Nala began warningly, but he was already moving. If enough of those creatures crossed over, then they'd have to surrender. His only hope was to throw the boarders back before they established a foothold on Drifter. Hefting his sword, he dashed down the narrow path to the lower deck. It took him only moments, but while he was running he saw a few more of the mantis-men make the leap. To his satisfaction, he saw one of them fall short, plummeting out of sight. The four mantis-men already on Drifter lowered the arms they'd been waving around to inspire their brethren, and those still on the beetle who had been preparing to jump hesitated, their antenna shivering in what Kerin assumed was consternation. Something flashed above him, followed by a sound like crashing waves. The shaman of these creatures must indeed be powerful if he could contest with Nala – the kyrathi had more facility with aether than any other mage Kerin had ever met.

Kerin reached the lower deck and charged towards the mantis-men. They whirled as one, almost as if they shared the knowledge of his approach, raising their arms to meet him while chittering through their mandibles. Those scythe-arms looked as hard as bone, wickedly serrated on their undersides and tapering to barbed points. Long scratches covered the limbs, as if these arms had successfully parried metal in other battles.

That might have given him pause, if he was carrying a normal sword.

He lashed out with *Mercy*. The closest mantis-man brought his arm up to deflect the blow, but the dark blade sheared through the chitin like it was flesh, barely slowing. As the limb tumbled to the deck the creature reeled back, green ichor pulsing from the stump. Kerin lunged at another of the mantis-men, but it hopped away with surprising quickness, out of the reach of his sword. Their faceted eyes flicked to each other and then to their wounded companion, who was now keening with pain as it huddled on the deck, cradling its severed arm.

"Had enough already?" Kerin snarled, feinting forward, which made them draw back even farther. "Rather pathetic bunch of pirates, aren't you?"

In reply, they leaped at him at him with perfect synchronicity, the barbed ends of their scythe-arms hurtling at his head.

"Nebulas!" Kerin cried, scrambling backwards. They were too fast, though, and he had to throw himself to the deck and roll away to avoid getting impaled. He found his feet quickly, but they were even faster, and he barely managed to block another slash. The mantis-man who'd nearly disemboweled him drew back, hissing, a deep fissure where *Mercy* had cut into his chitin. The other two approached more warily, fanning out to come at him from different angles. Kerin kept his sword up, shifting quickly from one to another to try and keep them from rushing at him. Things were already looking bleak, but the prospect of him surviving eroded further when he saw that the mantis-men had resumed their boarding of his starbeast. The wooden planks shivered under his boots as a half dozen more of the creatures thumped down on the deck.

"I accept your surrender," Kerin said, and he hadn't expected the creatures to understand but the two circling him emitted a clatter of hisses and chirps that sounded like it might be laughter. Above him, the crash and boom of sorcery had gone ominously silent. Kerin sighed, adjusting his grip on the hilt of his sword, which had become sticky with ichor. So here was how it would end – hacked apart by insects in a nameless Stream. His grandfather would have—

A star went nova.

Kerin was flung backwards, his vision consumed by radiant white light. He'd dropped his sword, and then scrabbled for it blindly on his hands and knees. His face burned, like a phosphorous fire had just erupted in front of him. He would be surprised if he still had his eyebrows, but he had no time to check as right now his overriding concern was finding *Mercy* before he was dismembered by the mantis-men.

Slowly his sight returned. Kerin lunged for a dark lump on the deck near him, yelling triumphantly, but this quickly changed into a pained yowl as his hand closed upon the serrated chitin of the arm he'd lopped off earlier. Throwing the limb aside, he scrambled to his feet, preparing for his flesh to be torn away by clacking mandibles.

But instead the mantis-men were turned away from him, watching as their starbeast convulsed. The back half of the great beetle had vanished, right about where its thorax merged with its distended abdomen, and thick yellow fluid was tumbling from its ruptured body in a vile, viscous torrent. The insect's front legs were swimming fiercely, straining to keep itself aloft, but Kerin knew this was an exercise in futility. The starbeast would sink until it passed beyond the boundaries of the Stream and entered the void beyond. Or that was the widespread belief, anyway. No one really knew what happened because nothing ever slipped from a Stream and returned.

What had just occurred?

The beetle drifted out of sight, Kerin's last glimpse of the creature its antennae waving frantically. For a moment the mantis-men still on Drifter stared after their starbeast, and then they surged as if of one mind to the edge of the deck. Kerin thought they were simply going to watch their compatriots dwindle into oblivion, but as they neared the balustrade each gathered themselves and leaped. Not one of them hesitated or glanced back at where he stood, watching in open-mouthed astonishment.

"Huh," he grunted as the last of the pirates disappeared over the side.

Blinking away the islands floating in his vision, he found where his sword had fallen and scooped it up.

"Nal!" he cried as he pounded his way back up the walkway, not even bothering to sheathe his blade. "Nal, did you see what—" His words caught in his throat as he reached the upper deck.

The kyrathi crouched beside the former pain conduit, who was sitting splay-legged on the wooden planks with her head down and shoulders slumped, staring at the glittering arm in her lap. Kerin slowed, uncertain of what had happened. Nala glanced over at him before returning her attention to the child in her filthy white robes. In that brief moment, Kerin saw the terror in the kyrathi's face. He approached cautiously, unsure whether he should sheathe his sword or not. This might be their last chance to avoid the same fate as the starbeast that was even now tumbling into oblivion.

She must be the cause of the sorcery that had consumed the star-beast. The amount of raw energy that had just been unleashed was many magnitudes greater than what Nala or any other mage could harness. Even a full contingent of battlemages yoked to a shriving crystal aboard a ghenabakan dreadnought couldn't summon such an aether blast. He shivered.

This girl might be the single deadliest weapon in the entire stellar tributary.

And right now she was crying silently, snot and tears running down her face.

Kerin. Drifter's strained voice slipped into his head. *I want to swim again.*

He shook himself, returning *Mercy* to its sheath. The greatest fear of any starbeast was being incapacitated in a Stream, and Kerin could sense Drifter's barely suppressed panic.

"Nal," he said softly, and the kyrathi's frightened eyes found him again. "We have to get moving. I saw you burn away one of these threads. Can you free Drifter?"

"I think so," Nala replied, rising, but she looked hesitant to leave the side of the crying pain conduit, her gaze flicking between the girl and one of the thick strands that lay across the starbeast's shell. "What if she . . ."

"I'll take care of her," Kerin promised, sinking down so that he was at the same level as the pain conduit's slumped head.

The kyrathi padded away, the fur on her back bristling and her tail twitching in agitation. Kerin watched her go until she vaulted over the side of the balustrade and disappeared.

He licked his lips. Despite the assurance he'd just given the kyrathi, he had no idea what he should do. Should he touch the girl? What if she responded instinctively, so lost in her own head that she lashed out without thinking? And then tore a hole in Drifter like she just had done to that other starbeast?

Perhaps he should leave her alone. Let her sit here and cry and when she was recovered somewhat then try and reach her . . .

Her head lifted slightly, her dull gray eyes focusing on him. She looked miserable. And different. The face he remembered from the journey out from Jegriddsl hadn't been plump in the slightest, but it also hadn't been nearly this sunken. It looked like her skin had tightened over her bones, the flesh beneath disappearing.

"Hungry."

Kerin started. Her lips had barely moved, and the rasping whisper was almost inaudible, but she had definitely spoken.

He swallowed nervously. "Can you stand?"

She shook her head slightly.

Kerin tried to keep his attention on her face and not the Elder weapon resting in her lap. "May I . . . may I help you inside? Get you some food?"

A barely perceptible nod.

Slowly Kerin knelt beside the pain conduit and gathered her into his arms. He could feel her stiffness, the tension thrumming in her small body. She was terrified, but was she afraid of the crystal swallowing her arm, or him?

"Don't be frightened," he said, trying to comfort her. He wondered if she could feel his own heart flailing wildly in his chest. The girl did not reply.

He carried her back inside the saloon and over to the couch, then gently put her down. She sank into the collapsed cushions, staring at her limp, glittering arm like it was a serpent coiled in her lap.

"I'll find you something to eat," he said, slipping behind the bar. There were a few small sacks of dried rations stored back there, including hardtack that could be used to mortar together a stone wall, and a handful of sad white tubers covered in layers of green fuzz. In the galley he could prepare some hot food, maybe cook some rice and a few of their precious few remaining eggs, but he'd have to leave the pain conduit alone here unless he dragged her halfway across the shell. And from the way she seemed to be melting into the couch, he didn't think disturbing her at this moment would be a good idea.

Tubers it was, then. Kerin grabbed a knife and began cutting away a disturbing amount of green growth. A strange sense of unreality settled over him as he made a small pile of glistening slices. Not a quarter of a glass ago he had been fighting for his life against insect pirates, and now here he was preparing a snack for a half-comatose girl in his saloon. Suddenly he remembered Nala's secret cache, something she thought he knew nothing about. He turned and began rummaging behind the empty glass bottles that in his grandfather's days had contained an impressive variety of exotic spirits, eventually pulling out a tiny, nondescript wooden box. He laid it on the bar, flipped it open, and was instantly overcome by the smell of spices and burnt sugar. Inside were a few translucent squares flecked with red, Nala's greatest vice. She might burn him to a crisp for sharing her Felisian sugar candies, but after glancing again at the sickly-looking tuber slices, he made a captain's decision that desperate times called for desperate measures.

Leaving the tuber behind, he brought the box of sweets to the pain conduit and placed it on the table in front of her. For a moment she continued staring blankly ahead, as if her thoughts were very far away, and then her eyes fluttered as the smell reached her. She raised her hand to take a sweet, but then a shiver of revulsion went through her as she realized which arm she'd reached out with.

"Here," Kerin said, plucking one of the candies from the box, trying to draw her attention away from her gleaming limb.

With some effort, the girl dragged her gaze to what Kerin was offering and took the sweet with her trembling, still-very-fleshy hand. She sniffed the sugar square curiously, and then tentatively bit down on a corner; almost instantly her eyes widened, and she quickly stuffed the rest of it in her mouth.

Kerin winced at the sound of crunching as she enthusiastically chewed the candy, but the girl didn't appear bothered at all by its hardness, and after swallowing she reached for another.

She seemed to forget about her arm, the tension seeping from her body as she focused completely on consuming the sweets as fast as possible.

Kerin watched the dwindling supply with some apprehension, knowing Nala was not going to be pleased, but he also couldn't help but share the pleasure the former pain conduit was obviously experiencing. This was the first time he had seen her with her guard down.

"Do you have a name?" he asked softly, and he could actually see her withdraw a little, the frantic movement of her jaw slowing as she trained her gaze on the table.

"I'm Kerin," he said. "Though you probably know that already. I'm sorry I didn't introduce myself earlier. I didn't know you spoke Trade."

Her gray eyes flickered to him and then back to the table. For a long moment she was absolutely still.

Kerin thought she had fully receded again into herself when suddenly she spoke.

"South Sept, Nine Ghelthing."

"That's . . . your name?"

A tiny nod. "The last time a Sister of the Thorns woke me she called me that." The former pain conduit blinked, as if surprised that she had said that much. Maybe it was the most she'd ever spoken. Her voice sounded ragged from disuse.

South Sept, Nine Ghelthing. A strange name. A sept was a part of a temple, wasn't it? And a ghelthing was the currency of Jegriddsl. Nine wasn't very much, maybe enough to buy dinner in a halfway decent tavern.

"The last time? You mean, other days you had different names?"

The girl stared at the square of spiced sugar in her hand. "Yes. Some days I was West Sept. Other days Crimson Nave. Always, I was Nine Ghelthing. It was the amount the Prioress decreed when I was given to the Searing Light."

Kerin felt a pang of sympathy as he finally understood. Supplicants had paid the price of a lamb shank and a flagon of ale to have this girl tortured for their sins. He found his mouth was dry.

"Well," Kerin said, forcing himself to smile. "That name is too long for me to remember. Can I call you Sep?"

A long hesitation, and then another small nod.

"Very good, Sep—"

"Take this off," she pleaded, raising her crystal arm. "Please." Her face trembled, as if she was on the verge of breaking down.

Kerin licked his lips, unsure what to say. "I, um, I don't know if—"

"Please," she said again forcefully.

He shook his head. "I wish I could, Sep."

She let loose a hitching sob, tears trickling down her face. To his alarm, Kerin thought he saw a shimmer of light pass up the girl's arm.

"All right," he said, raising his hands with his palms out, as if asking for calm. "All right."

The light flared brighter. She was shaking now, the sweet in her hand seemingly forgotten, but he knew she was listening to what he was saying with a desperate intensity.

"We're going somewhere," he said soothingly. "A planet called Dust. There's a man there who can help you. A wise man."

The glimmering radiance in her arm faded slightly. "A wise man," she repeated. "Like the Red Vicar?"

"Yes," Kerin said in relief as whatever had been rising in the girl subsided.

Sep breathed out slowly. "We have to hurry," she said, raising her arm further so that her long sleeves fell away. Kerin just caught himself from gasping when he saw that the crystal had crept past her elbow with glittering fingers, reaching towards her shoulder.

"It's eating me."

~

Kerin was dozing when Drifter's sudden lurch into motion jolted him awake. He sat there for a moment, confused as to why he had fallen asleep on a stool in the darkened saloon, and then the memories of what had happened washed over him in a tumbling rush. Swallowing away the dryness in his mouth, he straightened, wincing at the pain in his neck. Across the table from him the former pain conduit – no, her name was now Sep – was sprawled out on the couch, snoring softly.

He quested out with his thoughts. *You're free.*

Yes, thank the Great Turtle Drifter replied at once, which usually meant he'd been waiting impatiently for Kerin to wake.

Any lasting damage?

Just my pride Drifter responded with a mental sniff. *Though there's a lot of sticky residue covering my shell. I want a bath badly, but I don't remember any large bodies of water on Dust. Maybe the stable hands can give me a good wash.*

I'd advise making friends with them, then Kerin thought, standing and stretching. *We have no extra funds for pampering.*

Then I just might pull rank and make you give me a scrub.

Pull rank? Just who do you think is captain around here?

Another psychic snort. *A fiction that I might have to finally dispense with, unless you do what I ask.*

Kerin didn't dignify this with a reply as he stood and went over to the water barrel. The ache in his head that had vanished during the excitement earlier had returned with a vengeance, and his throat felt like he had been gargling sand.

So there are other reasons you chose Dust.

Kerin hesitated, his battered tin jug poised over the brackish water. *What do you mean?*

We're going to see a wise man who can help her. I believe that's what you told the girl.

Kerin sighed and plunged the jug into the barrel. *You were eavesdropping again. You know I don't like that.*

I was trying to focus on anything other than the fact that I was caught in a giant net. If I had panicked and started thrashing, Nala might be tumbling through the void right now.

Fair enough Kerin thought, sipping the stale water. This did nothing to diminish his headache, and his gaze wandered to the empty bottle on the table. Or was it truly empty? Maybe there were a few drops down at the bottom . . .

Wise is not the word I would use to describe the one you're thinking of, Kerin. Knowledgeable, perhaps.

Pretty much the same.

The fact that you think that concerns me. A wise man would do his best to mitigate the threat of the weapon, even if that meant destroying it. He will not do that.

A shiver of movement drew Kerin's attention. He glanced towards the door and saw Nala motioning him to join her on the deck. Setting down the jug as quietly as possible, so as not to wake the sleeping girl, he joined the kyrathi outside. Drifter's massive flippers were straining hard as the starbeast gathered speed, silver sparks erupting as they churned the Stream's unnatural darkness.

Freeing Drifter looked to have been an arduous ordeal. Nala's fur was sticking up in places, matted by whatever substance had comprised the threads that had ensnared Drifter, and she was clearly exhausted, her shoulders slumping and her amber eyes half-closed. But she roused herself as he arrived beside her, reaching out with a claw to hook the sleeve of his shirt.

"The girl is sleeping?"

Kerin nodded. "Whatever she did took a lot out of her."

Nala's gaze flicked to the saloon and then back to him. "I saw what she did," she murmured urgently, her claw pricking his wrist. "She killed a starbeast, Kerin! With a single blow! The power she unleashed . . . it was like standing beside a star."

Kerin opened his mouth to disagree with this obvious hyperbole, but the kyrathi shushed him with a growl.

"I'm not exaggerating. As part of our training in the navy, before we were lashed to a dreadnought, the adepts of my cohort were tied to ropes and lowered towards the ghenabakan sun. It was to strengthen us, to see how long we could suffer the heat before we pulled on the ropes and demanded to be brought back up. I lasted the longest of my cohort, and while I dangled there far above that maelstrom I cast my senses down into the depths of the star. I felt the unquenchable fire at its core, the roiling power that seemed to be birthed from nothing." Her whiskers twitched. "And that was what I felt on the deck, Kerin. Whatever sorcery that occurs in the deepness of a star is also happening in that girl's arm."

"Sep," Kerin said softly. "Her name is Sep."

"She told you her name?"

"I gave her a name."

The kyrathi let go of him, throwing up her arms. "You gave her a name? Kerin, you must not let yourself get attached. She cannot stay with us. We can't protect her."

Kerin snorted softly. "It seems like she can protect herself."

Nala showed her frustration by licking her paw and smoothing her whiskers in a single sharp motion. "She's still just a frightened girl. And are you sure Dust is the place to bring her? A Mandati world? What would the imperium do with such a weapon? Can you imagine the havoc the Golden Emperor could wreak in the stellar tributary if he dispatched his legions with *that* power at their disposal?"

Kerin's jaw tightened. "So we're back to talking about throwing her overboard?" he whispered, glancing in the direction of the darkened saloon.

Nala visibly slumped. "No, no. We owe the girl—Sep, did you say? —we owe her our lives. I just think we need to tread very, very carefully. We're only streamsurfers, Kerin. I'm a reasonably proficient battlemage, you're Anathema with an antique sword, and Drifter is not quite the slowest starbeast in the tributary"—a low grumble came from where Drifter's mind brushed his own—"but we're swimming in waters that are much too deep for us. A lich? Xerivas was just a taste of the powers that will be drawn to the girl. Sorcerers and gods and Transcendents beyond our understanding will converge if they find out what she is capable of doing."

"Then we need to hide her."

"Well, she needs to learn how to control herself. Killing a starbeast out here in the Streams where there are no witnesses is one thing, but what if something happens down on Dust and she lashes out blindly? Such a story would spread like wildfire throughout the Known."

Nala ran a shaking paw over her crusted fur. She looked to Kerin like she was on the verge of collapsing.

"Go sleep," he urged her. "I promise, we'll be careful when we get to Dust. My grandfather had friends there, and something like a safehouse. We'll hide for a while, long enough to be sure Xerivas isn't still hunting for us. That will give us enough time to figure out what we should do." Kerin flashed Nala his most confident smile. "Don't worry, I have a plan."

The kyrathi's eyes narrowed. "That's what I'm afraid of."

6

REALITY SHIMMERED and twisted as Drifter exited the Stream.

A bracingly cold wind washed over Kerin where he stood upon the deck, and despite the burning in his lungs he breathed deep, reveling in how fresh the air tasted after so long spent in the Streams. It was like being trapped underground for weeks, and then emerging from a cave to find oneself perched high on a mountain, a great vista spread below.

This view was grander than what could be found on any peak, though. Around them, a shroud pricked with countless glittering points wrapped around the system, stars beyond number. An endless profusion of worlds and peoples unfurling into infinity. All he knew, all his family had ever explored was but one small branch of the larger stellar tributary, which itself was only a fragment of the Known. What mysteries and wonders could be found out there? Was there another streamsurfer on the other side of the universe gazing out at the distant light where they had just arrived?

It was enough to make one feel insignificant.

At the center of this system smoldered a faded orange sun. It looked tired, worn out. Kerin had always found the life cycles of stars interesting. In their youth they blazed with white hot impudence, and then over the grinding of the eons they gradually subsided to yellow, and then orange . . . but finally, right before their deaths, they flared again bright red, some even swelling larger, like an old man fighting to rise from his sick bed as he raged against the approaching dark. The star in the unnamed system where they'd found the tree-hold had been in its death throes, although the life-span of stars was so long that even dying took millions of years.

Nala was right. This system belongs to the Mandate now.

Kerin tore his gaze from Dust's sun, looking around for what Drifter had noticed. *How can you . . . oh.*

Off the starbeast's port side, a long, sleek shape slid through the emptiness. It was not merely a shadow picked out against the stars, as motes of blue bioluminescent light glimmered where its flesh was not sheathed in dark metal armor or encrusted with wooden structures. Kerin could see the shape of a great ballista clinging to its mantle, though he took some comfort knowing Drifter's shell was so thick that it could not be pierced by even the largest bolt. A lucky shot to the eye, however, would certainly mean his death. On the other end of the great creature a nest of tentacles squirmed, with two of these limbs much larger and longer than the rest.

A war kraken, the sharp tip of the Golden Emperor's lance. The Mandate had absorbed other star-spanning races as it expanded and had incorporated many other species of starbeast into its menagerie, but the creature now known as the war kraken had been the first. And it was what made the imperium such a formidable military power. Fast and agile, with grasping arms and a razor-sharp beak, the kraken had seemingly been designed as a near-perfect predator.

Kerin let out a sigh of relief when he realized that the starbeast was not following. A sentry, then, merely set to watch what emerged from the Stream. The Mandate's hold on Dust must be tenuous if it felt that the entrance to this system needed to be permanently guarded.

He could sense Drifter's distaste as the creature dwindled behind them. Many generations ago, his starbeast had run afoul of a kraken, and still had scars from where the hooked barbs at the end of its tentacles had latched on to his shell. That particular kraken, if it still existed, now sported several fewer arms. Or so Drifter claimed. His starbeast had a habit of embellishing past adventures. Since his family did the same, he wondered idly which had first imprinted this trait on the other. Maybe his grandfather was not truly to blame for his tendency to exaggerate, as his personality had been shaped by the starbeast he had been bonded to as a child.

A rustle of cloth came from behind him, and Kerin turned to find Sep hovering in the open doorway to the saloon. The girl had become withdrawn again since the ambush by the insects, haunting the starbeast like a skittish ghost, sometimes only scurrying from her quarters to claim the food and water he left outside her door. Kerin had decided that if he wanted to try and build on the fragile foundation of trust he'd established, then he'd need to get his hands on more sweets, or perhaps some chocolate.

Yet here she was, emerging from the shadows to witness their arrival. Kerin offered a friendly smile, but the former pain conduit shrank away, melting back into the darkness of the saloon. He sighed and returned his gaze to the rapidly swelling sun. A vast gas giant loomed starboard, layered by shifting bands of emerald and azure and encompassed by a hazy golden ring. Kerin pulled out his spyglass and scanned the orbit of the great planet, quickly picking out a few drifting shadows that he thought must be moons. He made a mental note to find out later if there were any trading towns worth visiting out there; sometimes on the frontiers of a system supplies could be purchased at a significant discount, especially if any of those moons were suitable for growing crops or raising animals.

"She'll need some new clothes."

A jolt of surprise nearly made Kerin drop his spyglass. He fumbled it away and found that Nala had silently padded up beside him and was now leaning against the balustrade, the strong wind rippling her fur.

"I'll take her to a shop as soon as we settle with the stables."

The kyrathi shook her head. "Dangerous. The robes she's wearing are grubby and tattered, yet still recognizably from the temple of the

Searing Light. The gobber said he paid them for her, but the more I think about it, the more likely it seems that he bribed someone, or simply stole her away. And if that's the case, a stir might be made if she's spotted."

"And a stir would likely not end well for anyone," he agreed.

"You see my point."

"Then what do you propose? We can try and hide her in the stables, but any halfway competent stablemaster will realize she's there. Or one of the other starbeasts might tattle."

Nala clicked her claws on the balustrade as she considered this, her amber eyes thinned to slits. "Draw out your bargaining with the stablemaster. Be the obstinate skinflint I know you are, and while you're doing this, I'll rush out and buy something for her to wear."

"I can do that."

"Just don't get him so annoyed we have to leave. I'm very much ready to enjoy the trappings of civilization for a while."

"So long as those trappings aren't too expensive. The gobber paid half upfront, but berth and feed for Drifter will take a large chunk of that."

Nala's claws tightened on the wood. "We really need to make some money, Kerin."

Kerin indicated the green and blue gas planet with a small jerk of his head. "I saw some moons over there. Maybe the Mandate has already turned one of them into barrows ripe for looting."

The kyrathi's response to his jest was a low growl.

With some effort, Kerin managed to keep himself from smiling. He probably shouldn't remind her of the disaster that had brought them to their current impoverished state, or at least refer to it so flippantly. If Nala finally decided she was sick of him, she would have no trouble finding a spot among the crew of any starbeast in the tributary.

"There," he said suddenly, pointing at a small red coin that had appeared in the distance. "That's Dust. We'll be there in less than three turnings of a sandglass. Best go get ready."

The kyrathi murmured agreement, but she stopped him with a

claw on his sleeve as he turned away. "Oh, Kerin, did you see what happened to my sugar sweets? They seem to have disappeared."

"Hmm," he grunted, stroking his chin in mock-thoughtfulness. "Must have been the gobber. You know how they are, the thieving bastards."

~

Shreds of indigo mist clung to Drifter as the starbeast descended through the clouds. Below them was a rocky, rust-colored expanse etched with meandering lines where once water had flowed. The landscape was not completely dry, though. In a few places oases of gray-green water welled up, fringed by a riotous assortment of blossoming plants. These were some of the only blotches of color marring the monotony, save for the striations of umber and ocher layering the canyon walls that their shadow flowed over as they swam across the golden sky.

"I can see where the planet's name came from," Nala said, leaning out over the balustrade to watch the landscape unravel below. "Looks dry as dust down there."

It seems my memory was correct. No chance for a swim here. Drifter's thoughts were heavy with resignation. It almost seemed like the great turtle's head was hanging a bit lower than usual.

Let's not give up hope yet.

Maybe I can come back here and splash around in those puddles.

That's the spirit! Kerin thought brightly, but he sensed Drifter's glumness as the starbeast receded from his mind.

"What are those?" Nala asked, pointing to where a collection of crooked, rocky spires were emerging from the red earth. At varying heights, threads were strung between these formations, which looked to have been pricked with many tiny holes. Kerin drew out his spyglass and was surprised to find that the threads were actually rope bridges, across which tiny humanoid shapes were moving, and the holes in the spires were windows and entrances.

"A settlement," he said, focusing on a line of waddling gray pack animals with spiraling horns. Kerin saw a child perched on a knob of rock near where the men were lashing bales to the backs of these beasts point and jump up and down excitedly, shielding her face from the sun as she watched them pass overhead. Then the town was gone, dwindling behind them, and Kerin turned his spyglass to the low, rumpled mountains rippling the horizon.

"I was very young when I last came here," Kerin told the kyrathi, "but my memories are starting to return. Most of the people on Dust live in those rock spires. They weren't the ones to hollow them out, though. The structures are ancient and were once the homes of the first dwellers of this planet."

"Any of those first dwellers still around?"

Kerin shook his head. "No, I don't think so. They vanished long ago. My grandfather told me they must have been primitives and couldn't survive when the rivers and seas dried up. They didn't even leave behind any writing or pictures, so far as I remember."

"Surely there must be bones. Artifacts, or at least whatever tools they used to carve out those spires."

Kerin shrugged. "Maybe. I don't recall my grandfather mentioning about that. Then again, everything from that time in my life is hazy, to be honest, and I was far more interested in swords and starbeasts than the crumbled remnants of a dead civilization."

"So, not much has changed, is what you're saying," Nala said, squinting at the rapidly swelling mountain range.

"People don't change," Kerin murmured in reply, "we just get better at hiding ourselves."

"What a delightful rationale for never trying to improve yourself as a person," the kyrathi said sharply, and to this Kerin could only offer up a shrug.

Nala hissed something under her breath and stalked away. As the distance to the mountains dwindled, he heard her banging things together inside the saloon, perhaps searching again for her missing Felisian sweets. He probably should do something nice for her when they got to Dust. The stress of the last few days clearly had her on edge and losing the kyrathi to another streamsurfer would be like a knife to the gut. They'd been through a lot together, he and Nala. And despite all his mistakes and miscalculations she'd stuck by his side . . . hopefully, she hadn't reached the limit of her patience.

Drifter ascended to clear the ragged little range, plunging into the bank of purple clouds shrouding the tallest peaks. For a few moments, the starbeast was swaddled by an indigo murk, and an irrational fear stabbed Kerin that a cliff-face would suddenly loom out of the fog directly in front of them. Then they burst from the cloud and he had to blink as sunlight washed over them again.

On this side of the mountains spread a city. For most other inhabited worlds this would be a backwater town, a fourth-tier city that would only glimpse a starbeast if one passed high overhead on its way to more important places. But Kerin knew this must be Sanctum, Dust's largest city, as the vast expanse of white fabric covering its stables rippled like a pale sea in the wind. Yet again he was impressed with Drifter's flawless memory, as the starbeast had led them unerringly to the settlement despite decades since last visiting this planet.

Beyond the stables crouched the city, an unimpressive collection of rock spires with smaller adobe dwellings clustered around their bases. Some of these mottled structures looked to be a single story, but others were layered like insect hives, speckled with many openings. In a few places, white stone gleamed in the harsh sunlight, and Kerin guessed that these were buildings freshly constructed by the planet's new overlords. The Mandati always sheathed their government buildings in the same flawless marble that was only found on their home world. He certainly didn't envy the starbeasts who had to haul blocks of the stuff through the Streams.

Drifter angled his approach so that he was descending towards a gap in the sea of white cloth. There were many such openings scattered about, cut to allow starbeasts to enter. Only a few were adorned with strips of colored fabric, which meant that a starbeast was occupying the berth below.

Not the most luxurious accommodations Drifter thought as they entered the stables, his bulk settling on a great mound of dried rushes. *But it will do.*

Kerin had to grip the balustrade as Drifter used his flippers to awkwardly edge closer to the huge water cistern that abutted several other berths, all of which were empty. He felt a flood of satisfaction from Drifter as the great turtle lowered his head to the murky water and began to drink.

Kerin could see clearly only two of the other starbeasts in the stables, both far enough away that he couldn't be certain of their breed. One looked humped and vaguely amphibian, and the other might have been draconian, though far smaller than the lich's great skeletal monster. Both seemed to be sleeping in the shafts of sunlight slanting down through the openings above their berths. Most of the rest of the wide expanse was empty, save for the cisterns and rushes that had been laid out. In the far distance he could glimpse indistinct shapes that must be other starbeasts. From the dry crackling that was coming from below Drifter as he shifted, Kerin knew most of these berths had been waiting a long time to be occupied. No one had changed the rushes in many months.

The size of the stables was certainly ambitious, given that Dust was a backwater planet on the edge of the Known. Maybe the Mandate had ordered them expanded.

"Company coming," Nala said from beside him. The kyrathi was peering into the hazy distance, where a smear of brown suggested the stables ended and the city began. Kerin almost drew out his spyglass again, but then he saw what she'd already noticed: a man was approaching astride one of the same horned animals they'd glimpsed earlier. The creature was hairier than he had realized, covered in long fur than nearly trailed to the reddish earth, and despite its stocky build and stumpy legs it was galloping towards them at an impressive pace. The man on its back bounced up and down like he might fly off at any moment; he held no reins, instead clutching handfuls of his steed's long hair, nor did he sit a saddle. His legs were almost enveloped by the hirsute animal, making it seem like he was some strange chimera of beast and man.

"Stablemaster," Kerin said, and Nala grunted in affirmation. Then she turned to him, holding out a paw.

"I'll make a foray into the city and find some clothes for the girl."

Kerin stared at the kyrathi's paw for a long moment, then reluctantly handed over a few Jegriddsl ghelthings.

Nala shook the coins with a frown, making them clink together. "So you want me to just buy a burlap sack to stuff her in?"

Sighing, Kerin added a few more ghelthings. "That's all I can spare, unless Drifter doesn't care about being fed while we're here."

At this, the great turtle raised his dripping head from the cistern and moaned pathetically.

"Don't worry, you great complainer," Nala said loudly, then leaped nimbly over the railing and scampered down the curve of Drifter's shell. She didn't bother with uncoiling any of the rope ladders, instead simply leaping when she reached the shell's edge. It was several dozen span at least to the red earth, but since Nala was a kyrathi her legs didn't shatter when she landed, and moments later she was scurrying across the shadowed plain towards the city.

If she was smart, she'd take that money as an advance on her wages and desert, unencumbering herself of a starbeast that had incurred the enmity of an undead archmage. Kerin wasn't too worried, though. Many reasonable excuses for abandoning Drifter and him had come and gone over the years. Still, maybe this was the grain of sand that would crack the glass.

It was, he admitted, a fairly large grain.

"Who is that?"

The words were barely a whisper. Kerin turned to find that the former pain conduit had emerged onto the deck, her shoulders hunched and her head lowered, as if she expected to be punished for asking that question. Sep had found a blanket somewhere and wrapped it around the arm and hand that had been fused with the Elder weapon, hiding every trace of the crystalline flesh. Her shy gaze flickered to Kerin and then back to the rider.

"It's the stablemaster," Kerin replied. "He'll take care of Drifter while we're in Sanctum."

"Sanctum?"

"The city." Kerin pointed at the distant buildings.

"Why are we going there?" Fear trembled her voice, and she clutched protectively at the blanket swaddling her arm.

"Remember the wise man I told you about? He lives there. He might be able to help you."

She said nothing, but when Kerin approached the side of the deck where he could best converse with the stablemaster he heard the whisper of her slippers as she followed a few paces behind.

He laid hands on the worn railing as the old man reined up below by yanking hard on the hair he was clutching. The beast snorted and shook its shaggy head, but it came to a halt in a cloud of rust-colored dust.

"Ho, streamsurfer," the stablemaster called up, doffing his straw hat and grinning broadly. There were more gaps than teeth in that smile, and the man's pale blue skin was etched with dark age-veins, but he looked spry enough as he fought to control his ornery mount's stomping and shuddering.

"He's blue," Sep murmured.

"Aye, a native Duster," Kerin replied out of the corner of his mouth as he waited for the stablemaster to calm his beast. "They were the first settlers here when the Stream to the Umbral Cluster suddenly opened. Thalani is their people's name, if my memory serves. I've met them on other worlds. They scattered widely after the cataclysm that destroyed their original masters."

The old man had finally gained control of the animal by leaning forward and slapping its broad skull repeatedly. When he looked up again to where they stood on the deck Kerin raised his hand in greeting.

"Ho, stablemaster," he shouted down. "Well met. I am Kerin thon Talisien, bonded to Drifter."

"Talisien?" the stablemaster said, and even from this distance Kerin could see the man's bushy white eyebrows lift. "There's a name. Thought I recognized this turtle. I ne'er forget a guest." His gaze traveled the length of the starbeast until he locked eyes with Drifter, who had again raised his head from the cistern as he turned to stare at the stablemaster.

I remember this one.

A shiver of surprise went through Kerin as a third consciousness infringed upon the bond between him and his starbeast.

An' I remember you too, hatchling of the Great Turtle. Pleased an' honored to see you again.

"Withdraw, stablemaster," Kerin called down through gritted teeth.

"Apologies, Bonded," the old man replied, ducking his head, though in truth he didn't sound very sorry.

Kerin frowned, crossing his arms. Anyone could forge a bond with a single starbeast, but only those with a very special talent could communicate with all of them. Whisperers, they were called, and such an ability was as rare as being born Anathema. The few others like this stablemaster that Kerin had met had all worked for the Starfarers Guild as trainers for novice streamsurfers and their starbeasts. Even back then, Kerin had felt violated when the instructors spoke with Drifter when his consciousness was also touching the great turtle. This was a common reaction among the other handlers he'd known. The bond between a starbeast and his chosen was an intensely personal one.

Kerin sighed, trying his best to set aside his annoyance. He was still holding out hope for a good price on feed and berth. "Accepted, stablemaster. What's your name?"

"Jenks, streamsurfer. Please to meet ye and yer daughter." He flourished the straw hat he held in greeting.

Kerin opened his mouth to correct this misapprehension, then decided to let it slide. Perhaps Sep's presence would engender a little extra sympathy.

"How are things on Dust?"

The old stablemaster shrugged and spat out a wad of red. "This ain't a free world anymore, but ye probably figured that out already. Some folk are happy about that, some aren't."

"And you?"

Jenks squinted up at him with an unreadable expression. "Stables are gettin' a bit more business. Though the Mandate dug out a lake on one o' the moons for their beasts. Squids prefer swimmin' around in water, y'see, an' we never built our own pools. This isn't like those big fancy stables y'all have elsewhere." He looked away, staring at the distant dust-shrouded buildings. "Then again, it ain't all about the silver and gold. I was fleet helmsman when we first came to this world. We was just a bunch o' slaves fleeing what happened to the scalies when the Sword swept through the systems." Jenks spat again, then wiped at the redness staining his mouth. "Turned out freedom was just a dream. Shoulda known it would end sooner or later. Is what it is, I suppose."

Kerin nodded in the direction of the other starbeasts. "So these aren't Mandati?"

"They ain't. The squat fella is crewed by gobbers. Traders, they say they are. The drake is part of the guild. Not sure what brought it out here." He scratched at the distended age-veins creeping up his neck. "Your grandad was a guild man, yeah?"

"He was. We're not."

The stablemaster met his gaze placidly, chewing on whatever was in his mouth. "Maybe I heard something 'bout that. Can't remember."

"Best things stay that way," Kerin said, putting an edge to his words. He would greatly prefer if the Mandate didn't know they had arrived. The barrow-moon incident had been resolved already, but some might be aware of the problems it had stirred up between the empire and the guild. Nebulas, even the stablemaster of this backwater world had somehow heard.

"Gobbers . . ." Sep whispered beside him, staring out at the froglike starbeast crouching in the distance. The distaste in her voice set Kerin's alarm bells clanging, and he leaned closer to her.

"Strangers. Nothing like that one who took you from the temple."

"So we doin' business here?" shouted the stablemaster, shooing away a cloud of insects that had formed around the head of his mount. "Or you gonna steal that gulp of water and meander somewhere else? Fair warning, ain't no other stables on Dust."

Kerin glanced to where Sanctum fringed the tented plain. Nala had already vanished, but he imagined she'd need at least another flipping of a glass to return with clothes for Sep. And once he struck a bargain here, Jenks would insist on making sure no one else was left aboard.

"No other stables, eh? Does that mean you charge something outrageous?"

The stablemaster looked affronted at the thought. "Me? I'm what the high-falutin' folk would call a benign monopoly. Twenty Mandati tribunes a day for berth and feed, or the same in silver from wherever y'all hailed from."

Kerin inwardly sighed. That *was* an excellent price to stable Drifter. Much lower than that, and Jenks here would likely lose money during their stay. Yet he needed to delay. Well, it wasn't likely he and the stablemaster were ever going to be friends, anyway.

"Ten tribunes."

Jenks spluttered in indignation, nearly choking on whatever he was chewing on. "Ten? Ten? There isn't a stable in the tributary that would charge that!"

"Maybe I could go to eleven."

All residual traces of friendliness fled the stablemaster's darkening face. "Nineteen and a half, you grave robber."

Ah, a personal attack. That will make this negotiation much more enjoyable. "Eleven, and I'll let you salvage anything my starbeast leaves behind." Not that this fellow wouldn't already do that, which made this perk something easy enough to give away.

"Nineteen," Jenks called up coldly, then reaching into a pouch at his waist he withdrew what looked like a pinch of leaves and stuffed them into his mouth, chewing furiously in obvious agitation.

Kerin smiled. He was starting to enjoy himself.

Nala returned much earlier than Kerin expected, which he appreciated, as the bargaining had broken down into a grinding war of attrition. She appeared suddenly beside the stablemaster's beast, causing it to *whuff* in alarm and stamp its stumpy legs, but Jenks had become so exasperated he barely spared her a glance as she used one of Drifter's flippers to reach the shell, and then scampered higher to where she could swing herself onto a walkway.

"Maybe it's best if ye jus' pull up stakes and be on yer—"

Kerin interrupted Jenks's growled suggestion by clapping his hands together loudly. "No need, stablemaster. I agree to you terms, seventeen and one quarter tribunes a day, with any washings extra. You are truly a shrewd negotiator."

The old man scowled, and then spit with even more vehemence than what he'd shown previously.

Nala finally arrived on deck, panting, and pressed the pile of folded clothes she'd brought into Sep's surprised arms. "Change," she gasped, struggling to get out the words, then pushed the girl back towards the saloon.

"Agreed," the stablemaster called up sullenly. "Now come on down here an' pay me for two day's lodging. And ye best be sure I'm bitin' whatever silver ye hand over."

Foreign thoughts pushed their way into his head, another unwelcome intrusion. *This one always so difficult, turtle?*

Drifter's chuckle reverberated in Kerin's mind. *You have no idea, stablemaster.*

7

AFTER JENKS HAD DEPARTED in a huff and a cloud of dust, clinging to his great hairy beast as it thundered back across the plains, Kerin went and quickly gathered what he would need during their stay in Sanctum. This was made difficult by the fact that he didn't know how long they would be laying low in the city. He wasn't even sure how much time would have to elapse before he could be certain Xerivas wasn't still hunting them. But since the last of the gobber's money would run out in, optimistically, a fortnight, there was no need to plan for an extended visit. Three changes of clothes, *Mercy*, his lucky blood knuckles set, his copy of *The Startreader's Almanac*, the strange gray cube he'd acquired in the treehold, and a few battered novels he'd been meaning to re-read. Everything except his sword he threw into an ancient rucksack that had once belonged to his grandfather and then slung that over his shoulder.

Back on the deck he found Nala and Sep waiting. Gone were the former pain conduit's filthy and frayed white robes, replaced by a billowy, high necked blue dress that reminded Kerin of something a homesteader on a frontier planet might wear. Which made sense, since that was a perfect description of Dust. Nala had also purchased a pair of long white lady's gloves, and these combined with the dress's frilled sleeves completely hid the alvaren artifact that was slowly consuming her arm.

The kyrathi had made some other efforts to make the girl more presentable: her face had been scrubbed, her eyes shaded fashionably with kohl – the provenance of which was a mystery to Kerin – and her pale hair pulled back and pleated into a braid. The thought of Nala fumbling with the girl's hair almost made his lips twitch into a smile, but he restrained himself when he saw the nervous uncertainty in Sep's lowered gaze. She was clearly feeling self-conscious about this makeover, and any humor he showed very well might be misconstrued.

"Civilization awaits!" Kerin said with a cheeriness that wasn't entirely feigned, going over to the edge of the deck and tossing a rope ladder over the side. He gestured grandly for Nala and Sep to go first. The kyrathi sighed heavily as she brushed past him, then began to descend one-handed, somehow managing to do this gracefully while carrying a pair of travel bags. Sep was next, and as her head disappeared over the edge of Drifter's shell he felt the starbeast stirring in his mind.

Any idea of how long we're going to be here?

No. I'd expect ten days, at least. If an undead horde hasn't invaded this system by then we can poke our heads up and see if the coast is clear.

Annoyance seeped across the bond between them. *Ten days is a long time, Kerin.*

Sleep. Get fat. Work on your art. Swap some stories with the other beasts, or that stablemaster. You two seemed like old friends.

Grumbling something unintelligible, Drifter receded from Kerin's mind as he swung himself over the side. The starbeast would almost certainly get lonely stabling here for so long. Their bond would grow more attenuated as the distance between them grew, until they were no longer able to communicate except for flashes of intense emotion, but that couldn't be helped. Maybe he'd find a way to come visit, if he could somehow make nice with Jenks. Such visitations were usually at the discretion of the stablemaster.

When they all stood on the plain, Nala handed one of the bags she was carrying to Sep. The girl's brow furrowed as she took it, as if she couldn't fully grasp the idea that there were things in the universe that now belonged to her.

"Another dress and a few baubles I've picked up over the years," the kyrathi said as Sep undid the clasps and peered inside. The girl's gray eyes widened as she reached within and withdrew a bracelet of polished red stones.

"Forgot where I got that," Nala said, scratching her neck. "Been cluttering up my quarters for a while."

"It's mine?" the girl whispered, seemingly unable to tear her eyes from the bracelet.

The kyrathi waved her paw, as if dismissing the gift as nothing of importance. "Yes. I don't wear jewelry."

In slow wonder Sep slipped on the bracelet, settling the red stones on the cream-colored fabric of the glove that covered her untainted arm. She turned her wrist this way and that, engrossed by how light slid over the gleaming stones.

"Let's get going," the kyrathi said gruffly, shouldering her bag. As she passed Kerin, she noticed his slight smile and leaned in close. "Means nothing. We're still dropping the girl when we find a good landing spot for her."

"I'm sure there will be plenty such places here on Dust," he replied innocently. Nala scowled and kept on walking.

Traversing the vast stables took the better part of a turned glass. Most of the way was shadowed, the huge swathes of white fabric above them rippling in the wind, but occasionally they passed beneath the gaps where starbeasts could descend into the berths, and they could see violet clouds scudding across a sky of burnished gold. The color seemed to have deepened since they'd entered the stables, suggesting to Kerin that the day was fading.

The structures they had glimpsed from afar turned out to be massive storehouses, piles of feed and vegetables visible through the gaping entrances. There was also a large, penned area where at least a hundred striped, bandy-legged animals milled about snorting and braying. Kerin would have been charged significantly more to stable Drifter if his starbeast was a carnivore. Even the small drake currently in residence here could eat a dozen of these creatures a day.

Beyond these buildings was the edge of the city proper. Mounded beehives constructed of something like adobe hunched beside the narrow street, their lowest and largest tiers given over to small shops and other businesses. Stairs climbed their facades to the higher levels, which diminished in size as they ascended and appeared to be mostly residential. Laundry was strung outside some of these dwellings, and blue-skinned thalani etched with deep age-veins sat on stools smoking pipes and watching the streets below.

Those streets were busier than Kerin had expected. They must have entered a market area, as carts piled high with goods choked the way ahead, surrounded by jostling shoppers. Blue children with unblemished skin ran giggling through the crowds, chasing a waddling orange lizard that somehow kept just far enough ahead of them to remain out of reach. Nearby, a man in a pointed white hat was grilling finger-long insects over charcoal, wooden skewers thrust through their bulging thoraxes. The fact that the smell was making his mouth water was depressing. He'd subsisted for far too long on hardtack and tubers.

He needed some real food.

"Come on," Kerin said, motioning for Nala and Sep to follow him as he joined the stream of thalani filling the street.

Music from performers playing strange bladdered instruments skirled around them as they pushed through the crowds, rising above the hum of countless conversations. Even for him, who had gone many times from the bleak solitude of the Streams back to the tumult of civilization, the transition was jarring. He kept checking over his shoulder to make sure that the girl hadn't stopped and curled into a terrified ball. She certainly looked overwhelmed, her wide eyes darting between the many distractions, but she was still managing to match his pace despite her stream legs having to adjust to the stationary solidity of the planet.

The street eventually spilled into a larger plaza fringed by structures very different from the adobe beehives and rock spires they'd seen on their way into the city. Kerin instantly recognized some of the distinctive architectural designs – this must be Sanctum's religious district. Very often the temples to the various powers of the universe were clustered near a city's stables, as the first thing many travelers wanted to do after feeling the ground beneath their feet again was go give profuse thanks to whatever being they worshipped that they had survived their journey.

Most of the major faiths were represented, though many by little more than icons and altars heaped with flowers or other offerings. In front of some, men and women in priestly vestments claiming to represent the truth among the varied choices perched on wooden stools, exhorting the crowds. Others needed no such marketing. The gray-stone walls of the Sower's temple were veined by creepers speckled with bright flowers, a vibrant garden visible through its humble trellised entrance. Elsewhere, a small shrine encrusted with chunks of quartz glittered. From the laughing face carved into its stupa this one must be dedicated to Mekros, a Transcendent that had become known as something of a trickster god. Hunched by itself in one corner of the square was a jumble of black rocks, almost certainly the place where brave souls could entreat the nameless god of entropy to spare the ones they loved. And in the center of the space was the newest and largest temple, a gleaming building of pure white stone carved with ostentatious flourishes. This was the Mandate's contribution to the universal pantheon, where citizens of the imperium could show their devotion to their immortal Golden Emperor.

The plaza was even busier than the market street had been, and Kerin wondered if the thalani were, by their nature, an extremely devout people, or if they'd arrived during a festival. The sea of blue faces was not uniform, though, as other races and beings speckled the crowd. As they crossed the plaza and passed close to the Golden

Emperor's temple Kerin noticed that the first settlers of Dust were giving the structure a wide berth, and that the ones flowing in and out of its elaborately carved doors were almost entirely Mandati. The imperials resembled the thalani in many ways, but their skin was milk-white, and covered to varying degrees in intricate red tattoos which writhed as though alive.

"Kerin!"

He turned back to Nala, and realized immediately why she sounded so alarmed. Sep was no longer near them, having drifted in the direction of where a small crowd had gathered around a woman dressed in black leather standing on a block of stone. Half of her head was shaved perfectly smooth, but on the other side, long dark hair tumbled nearly to her waist. Black markings that looked like tear tracks trickled down her cheeks, and at her waist was coiled a whip studded with tiny thorns. Behind her loomed a jagged temple of black iron, seemingly constructed with too many sharp edges, as if a great pile of weapons had been melted together and fashioned into a building.

Oh, nebulas, he thought, immediately realizing what this place must be. This was not what they needed right now.

He moved to follow her, but a surge of thalani in yellow robes chanting something unintelligible and clanging cymbals together suddenly blocked his way. Cursing, he shoved through them, and the droning mantra deteriorated into cries of outrage.

"Sep!" he cried, finally reaching where the girl stood at the edge of the crowd watching the woman in black. The former pain conduit's lips were slightly parted, her eyes unblinking. He grabbed her by the arm, but she didn't seem to notice.

"We are all children of the void!" the woman shouted, turning so that her gaze encompassed all those who had gathered. "Sparks in the abyss! We are alone. We are birthed from nothing, and to nothing we shall return!"

Kerin saw to his dismay that Sep's lips were moving as she whispered the words at the same time the woman spoke them.

"Life is shaped by pain. It drives us. Controls us. We are slaves to it! Only when we immerse ourselves fully in agony, learn how to accept it, can we rise above our base nature and become something more. Something pure."

"Enough of this madness," Kerin hissed, starting to drag Sep away from the priestess. The girl struggled to stay, but he was too strong.

"You!"

Kerin glanced to the priestess and saw that she was pointing at them with a long black nail.

"Yes, you child! I sense in you a yearning for purity! To have weakness washed from your body, so that what remains can be filled with cleansing light!"

"I do," Sep murmured, straining against Kerin's grip.

"You don't," he hissed.

She twisted around to face him, her expression pleading. "You don't understand," she said. "The Light can heal me." She raised her arm, as if reminding him what was under the glove. "I can be made pure."

The former pain conduit wrenched herself away from him with surprising strength, but when she turned towards the priestess again she found Nala blocking her way, the kyrathi's amber eyes slitted.

"Child," Nala said, her voice ragged. "This is not what you truly want. I promise you on the souls of my siblings. Please. Come with us. Let me explain why you must not return to that life." She stepped forward and touched the girl's wrist, her paw covering the bracelet she had gifted her.

Kerin's Anathema blood tingled as Nala sent a carefully woven burst of sorcery up Sep's flesh and blood arm. The girl blinked, a tremor passing across her face as her hand twisted around to clutch at the kyrathi's fur. Then she sagged, and Kerin had to lunge forward to catch her. He glanced up at Nala, who was staring at the limp pain conduit with such sadness that his own chest began to ache.

"We have to take her away from here," the kyrathi said. "Away from that woman. Follow me."

~

They carried Sep through the temple district and down one of the larger side-streets, drawing a few curious stares. No one moved to intervene, though, probably assuming the girl had been over-whelmed by the crowds or an upwelling of religious fervor. Still, it didn't speak very highly of the vaunted Mandate governance that a man and a catter could carry a young girl away without being questioned. Kerin actually hadn't noticed anything that resembled a constabulary or city watch, oddly enough.

Sep stirred in their arms just as the street they were traversing emptied into another large plaza. This space was dominated by a great tree growing out of a block of white stone, the few leaves speckling its gray branches flashing silver and gold. Not alive, then. Either the tree was beyond ancient, fossilized and then adorned with bits of gleaming metal, or it was simply an elaborate statue. The sight of it made Kerin think of the Crucible, though that apparently-dead alvaren treehold had eventually turned out to still be very much alive.

This area seemed much older than the previous one. Instead of recently-built religious structures, tapering rock spires like crooked fangs ringed the plaza. These were much taller than the hive-like buildings, some of them soaring hundreds of span upwards, though they were also pocked with holes that Kerin knew to be windows for the dwellings within. The thick bases of these spires had been given over to restaurants and cafes, their tables spilling out so far into the plaza that some actually sheltered beneath the tree's glimmering branches. Delicious smells wafted from where open-air grills had been set up, making Kerin's stomach clench.

The girl's gray eyes fluttered open. For a moment she didn't seem to know where she was, and then she twisted her neck around, as if looking for something.

"Where is the Light?" she whispered, squirming to be put down.

"Behind us," Nala said, helping Sep find her feet. She swayed dangerously, and Kerin had to grab her arm to keep her from falling.

"I must go to it. That was a Sister of the Thorns. She can help me."

"Wait," Nala said gently, putting herself between the girl and the street they'd just left. "Let us find some food first. Aren't you hungry?"

Sep blinked. She sniffed, apparently for the first time noticing the aromas filling the square. Kerin could actually see her awareness of how famished she was growing in her face.

He gently started to pull her towards an empty table, and after hesitating briefly she followed him with stumbling steps.

"Here, sit," he said, helping her into one of the rickety chairs around a table of pitted dark wood. She'd looked listless just moments ago, drained of energy, but the scent of meat cooking somewhere nearby was bringing her fully awake. Sep twisted around in her chair, searching for the source, her eyes now wide.

"I want food," she murmured, and as if summoned a stout thalani matron materialized beside the table, making the girl jump. Her skin was a deeper shade of blue than most of the others Kerin had seen, and she'd applied some cosmetic to try and cover up her age veins.

"Food we have, my lovelies," she said, offering a smile that flashed gold. "Drink and glimmer, as well."

"What's that meat I smell grilling?" Kerin asked, finding his own seat.

"Khedrin," the woman said. "We serve 'em up on kebabs or smothered in onions. Goes good with a nice dark stout."

"Let's get one with onions and two kebabs," Kerin said, fishing in his belt pouch for a handful of ghelthings. The woman raised a skeptical eyebrow when she saw the unfamiliar currency. She picked up one of the silver coins and studied its stamp of a double-headed dragon.

"You lot are from far away. Jegriddsl, is it? I have to check an' see how this changes to tribunes."

Kerin waved his hand in understanding. "Of course. Should be a similar weight."

The woman bit the coin then slipped it and a half-dozen others into the front pocket of her apron. "Well enough. Should be good for a round of drinks as well. What's your poison?"

"The stout," Kerin said quickly. It was all he'd been thinking about since she'd mentioned it paired well with the meat.

"Tea, whatever you have," Nala said, her paws on the table. Kerin knew she was dying to scratch the rough wood, but she was smartly waiting until the serving woman had taken their order. "Throw in a few little chunks of the meat, the bloodier the better."

"And you, lass?" the woman said, turning to Sep. The former pain conduit stared up at the large woman with round eyes, her lips slightly parted like she wanted to say something but couldn't drag forth any words. The thalani frowned, a flicker of unease crossing her face at the girl's strange behavior.

"Do you have any hot chocolate?" Kerin asked, and the woman tore her gaze away and turned to Kerin with an expression that was almost like relief.

"Aye. You're lucky, came in from the Rest just a few days ago. Sweet as the Mother's milk."

"A cup, then, for the girl," he said, and with one last glance at Sep the woman hurried away.

Almost immediately came the shriek of Nala's claws digging into wood. Kerin hoped these fresh gouges would go unnoticed, though this wouldn't be the first time he'd had to compensate someone after the kyrathi sharpened her claws. Another screech put his teeth on edge, but Sep didn't even seem to notice the furniture destruction that was occurring. Her brow was furrowed, and her lips pursed like she was deeply considering something she couldn't understand. Kerin felt a rising apprehension about what that could be.

Suddenly her head jerked up, gray eyes finding him. "Who is the Mother?"

Kerin blinked in surprise. That wasn't what he had been expecting.

"What?"

"The Mother. That fat woman said, 'sweet as the Mother's milk.' Is it her mother? How does she remember the milk was sweet?"

"Um, no, no," Kerin said, shaking his head. "Not her real mother.

The Mother is a goddess. She's popular among the poor and the downtrodden."

"That woman did not look poor. She has meat to sell."

"She's not, I don't think. Her people, the thalani, were enslaved by another race. Something terrible happened decades ago – an insane Transcendent called the Sword cut a bloody swath through the stellar tributary, obliterating entire systems. The Unfettering, it was called, because the slave-races were allowed to escape while their masters were wiped out. This was one of the planets the thalani fled to in the time called the Diaspora. Any worship of the Mother is probably a holdover from when their ancestors toiled in the fields and work-shops under the overseer's lash."

Sep cocked her head to one side, the confusion in her face deepening. "Why do they not worship this Sword? The one who freed them?"

Kerin shifted uncomfortably. "Well, for one thing, the Sword's crusade eventually ended in defeat . . . and his spectacular obliteration by the archmages of the Triumvirate and a few piqued Transcendents."

Understanding grew in the former pain conduit's eyes. "So he was not a god. We were warned of them in the temple, these false gods. Shadows thrown by the Light. Sister Radiant called them . . ." Sep's face scrunched up as she scoured her memories for what she had once been told. "Temptations."

Nala snorted. "There is no one all-powerful god, child. This mess of a universe is proof enough of that. Too much suffering for there to be someone watching from on high who loves us. There are plenty of powerful beings, though most of them care not a whit about the little people bowing and scraping in their temples."

"Suffering is proof of the Light's love. It is through suffering that we gain meaning. Pain washes away our impurities, making us worthy of salvation." From Sep's singsong cadence this sounded like a litany she had heard many times before.

Nala crossed her arms across her furred chest, her eyes narrowing. "And you were given others' pain, yes? You helped make them pure?"

Sep nodded slightly.

"Why could *they* not suffer, if they believed in this madness?"

"I was blessed," Sep said softly. "I was chosen to take their pain. I brought them into the Light."

"But were you tortured on behalf of the poor?" Nala pressed, her voice rising in anger. "The sick? The ones that truly suffered every day of their miserable lives? Or did some rich bastard pay to have you hurt, believing *he* would benefit from *your* pain?"

The girl seemed to be wilting before the increasingly impassioned kyrathi. If she was still wearing her temple robes, Kerin thought she would have pulled down the cowl to hide her face. There was no place to retreat to in her new clothes, so instead she lowered her face and stared blankly at the table.

Sympathy flared in Kerin. The girl had lived her life in the catacombs of the Searing Light, her entire existence ordered and given meaning by its strictures . . . to have that challenged, the reason for her suffering questioned . . . it must be difficult. Terrible, even. There was a small chance Nala could help her escape the prison of her faith, but Kerin knew that it was far more likely that the girl would retreat into her beliefs and lash out at those who dared question them. But what could he say?

Sep shifted uncomfortably, mumbling something under her breath.

"What's that?" Kerin asked gently.

"Nine ghelthings," the girl repeated, still not raising her eyes from the scarred wood.

Nala and Kerin shared a glance. The kyrathi's seemed to have spent her anger, as she slumped back in her chair looking faintly embarrassed.

Kerin knew what Sep meant, and he suspected Nala did as well. It wasn't just the rich whose pain the conduit had taken. She knew the price to have her suffer was something even a day laborer could afford. Barely more than the cost of the meal they were even now waiting to arrive.

Nala opened her mouth, then seemed to reconsider whatever she'd been about to say, the click of her sharp teeth coming together filling the silence that had fallen. Kerin also wasn't sure how far to go here. If Sep saw herself as a martyr, purifying others through suffering, should he even try to disabuse her of this belief? Would it truly be better if she came to realize that the only reason for her lifetime of pain was to fill the coffers of whatever holy man was perched at the apex of the church?

This seemed like a revelation that would be received better if she arrived at herself. Nala appeared to have come to the same conclusion, as she had turned away from the slumping girl and was watching the swirl of pedestrians passing beneath the canopy of the plaza's great tree.

The awkward lull was mercifully broken when the serving woman returned carrying a steaming platter.

"Food!" Kerin said, clapping his hands in anticipation.

"No tea," the thalani matron said apologetically as she slid her burden onto the table. "But I had 'em slip some giblets into boiled water, just like I know you catters like. Now, you folks enjoy, and holler if ye need anything else." With that, the woman turned and swayed away, but Kerin only noticed this peripherally, his attention fully absorbed by what had been delivered.

On a wooden trencher was heaped a pile of crisped onions and chunks of browned, sizzling meat. Beside this was a pair of skewers that could have doubled as stilettos, both threaded with more of this meat, though fattier pieces, as well as an assortment of charred vegetables he couldn't recognize. There were also several small ceramic bowls placed at the edge of the platter filled with dark sauces and fresh-chopped chilis. And of course, their drinks. Kerin hefted his tankard, grinning in anticipation when he found it chilled.

A cold dark beer and a pile of barbecued meat. At this moment, he could think of few things better in life.

His first swallow was like finding a waterskin in the sand after wandering for days in a desert. Amazing how a single drink could make all the anxieties brought about by dealing with bone dragons and insect shamans and starbeast-killing girls melt away.

That last anxiety-conjurer was even now staring at the pile of food in front of her in wide-eyed wonder. She reached out slowly with a trembling hand and plucked a slightly charred piece of khedrin – whatever that was – from among the strands of caramelized onions, then placed it carefully in her mouth.

Kerin couldn't help but vicariously enjoy the stages of pleasure that moved across the girl's face, from surprised delight as she began chewing, to rapturous bliss when she finished and began sucking the juices from her fingers. Whatever theological matters had been troubling her seemed to have been forgotten as she scooped up another handful of meat and onions and shoveled the food into her mouth, her eyes bright.

Nala's paw flashed a few words in guild cant. *Teach girl use spoon yes? Disgusting. Like animal.*

Kerin shrugged in reply. He was waiting for when Sep got around to trying the hot chocolate. She just might faint again.

A shimmering drew his attention from the girl. The thalani milling beneath the great tree had parted to allow through a small group of Mandati. Four were soldiers, their armor forged from white overlapping plates that looked more like ceramic than steel, red metal crests on their helmets marking them as elite k'zar warriors. The last was most definitely who they had been set to guard: a beautiful woman just as tall as the warriors, long-limbed and lithesome. The gossamer shift she wore was faintly transparent, allowing the squirming tattoos covering much of her body to be glimpsed through the fabric. She'd attained at least the seventh rank in the empire, maybe even eighth, which meant she was likely high up in the bureaucracy. The shimmer that had distracted him hadn't come from her clothing, though, as thrusting out from her back was a set of iridescent wings like might be found on a dragonfly, the day's fading light making the individual panes of membrane flash gold.

Usually the sight of a chimericist's handiwork filled Kerin with revulsion, but here the work of the Mandate's mixmages actually enhanced the woman's already ethereal looks. That fey beauty was unfortunately marred by the scowl twisting those perfect lips as the woman strode across the plaza, her k'zars hurrying to keep pace.

"Look," Sep whispered, finally having noticed the Mandati noble-woman. The chunk of meat she'd been holding slipped from her grease-stained fingers as she twisted to follow the woman's progress. "She has wings—"

White light knocked Kerin from his chair.

His face was pressed against stone, his head ringing. Gasping, he pushed himself to his hands and knees, struggling to focus through the hazy veil that had descended across his vision. His thoughts were fractured.

What?

Had happened?

Nala?

Sep?

His Anathema blood was thrumming in his veins. Somewhere nearby had been a massive surge of sorcerous energy. The girl?

No. She was sprawled out on the ground beside him, limp, her eyes closed with her face slightly blackened and smeared with kohl. Nala was beside her, covered in the wreckage of their meal. The only movement from her was the twitching of her tail, but it was enough to send a jolt of relief through Kerin.

He staggered to his feet. There were screams. Wailing. Several limbs from the plaza's great tree had been ripped loose. A few others were still attached, wreathed in jade flames. Beyond the tree a massive chunk had been torn from the base of one of the rock spires. Whatever wave of power that had flowed across the square had exploded from there. Corpses were everywhere, severed arms and legs scattered about. A young thalani girl was stumbling through the dead, her expression dazed and disbelieving.

Of the winged Mandati noblewoman there was no sign, but a blood-streaked, red-crested white helmet was lying a dozen paces away from where he now stood swaying. It took him a moment before he realized that a face was still staring out from within, eyes blinking frantically. The rest of the guard's body was missing.

"Nebulas," he muttered dully just as a crack like thunder sounded from nearby. He jumped, expecting another wave of aether, but this did not happen, nor did his Anathema blood warn him of any unseen sorceries. More grinding and splintering, and then a large rock bounced down the outside of the spire that had suffered the brunt of the explosion, shattering when it struck the ground. More debris followed this first piece, sifting from higher up.

The spire moved.

"Oh, no," Kerin said, bringing his foot down intentionally on Nala's tail. She came awake spluttering and hissing, claws unsheathed, but her rage dissipated as soon as she saw the plaza's devastation.

"The girl did this?" the kyrathi asked as Kerin bent to haul Sep to her feet. The pain conduit's head lolled to one side, her eyes fluttering. She wasn't ready to stand on her own, but a shiver of pained awareness passed across her face.

"No," Kerin grunted, pausing to scoop up their bags from among the wreckage. He slung them over one arm as he began to drag the limp girl towards an alley where two nearby rock spires nearly brushed together. "And we have to get out of here. Now!"

"Why?" Nala asked.

As if in answer to her question, another fracturing boom sounded and Kerin glanced over his shoulder just as a huge chunk of the uppermost reaches of the spire sloughed away. It seemed to take forever before it struck the ground and made the world heave and buckle. Kerin barely managed to keep his feet, continuing to half-carry Sep while also looking at what was happening behind them in the plaza. A wave of gray dust billowed out from where the shard of the rock tower had fallen, rushing across the plaza. The burning tree vanished as it was enveloped, then Kerin had to turn away as dust washed over him. He coughed, blinking away the grit in his eyes. An ashy haze had descended, limiting what he could see to only what was right around him – Sep and Nala and toppled chairs. Both his companions and also the strewn furniture had been transformed into gray wraiths, coated by a film of dust.

Sep pulled away from him, stumbling towards the alley mouth. Muffled explosions were happening behind them, but Kerin didn't know if these were from another building collapsing or more sorcerous eruptions. He followed closely behind the girl, not wanting to wait around and find out.

The light had become muted, filtered through the hanging dust, but still he noticed movement from the shadows within the alley. A small shape huddled there, he was certain, barely larger than a child. It flowed like water in the blackness, and he had the distinct impression that it had turned to regard him. Kerin slowed, stopping at the mouth of the alley, seized by blind terror. It looked exactly like the children that still haunted his dreams, the watchers from the darkness he thought he'd imagined when he was younger and his grandfather had brought him to this planet.

"Come on," Nala hissed, grabbing his arm as she passed him.

He yelped in pain, glancing down at the red lines she'd left on his dust-smeared skin, and when he looked up again the presence in the alley had vanished. He shook his head, trying to clear it. The blast must have jarred something loose in his mind and sent old memories rattling about.

The space was narrow, barely wider than the width of his shoulders, and blessedly empty of demonic children. There was actually more light than he had expected, the tapering spires rising up on both sides like red pillars supporting a roof of beaten gold. Garbage littered the way, potsherds and lengths of broken wood and soft organic matter that squelched unpleasantly under his boots. Ahead of him, Sep fell more than once as she rushed towards the brightly illuminated exit of the alley, but the explosion that had knocked her out cold just moments ago did not seem to be bothering her much now as she scrambled back to her feet and continued on.

Then they were stumbling out onto another street, this one far less busy than the others they had seen in the city. Or perhaps most of the people had fled after the blast in the adjoining plaza. A few still remained, thalani with their necks craned to watch the spreading cloud of dust stain the sky. One very plump woman glanced at them as they tumbled from the alley, then screamed and took off in a comical, jiggling run.

Kerin couldn't really blame her, as they did look frightening. There was so much dust coating Nala's tawny fur that she might have passed as part snow leopard, and Sep could have played the lead in a *kabuchen* ghost opera. Kerin assumed that he was likewise completely covered in white ash.

"Where do we go?" Nala asked, her voice trembling. She sounded shaken.

Sep also appeared to be treading the edge of trauma, her wide eyes staring blankly at nothing.

Kerin licked his lips, to his immediate regret as he had to spit out a mouthful of dust. When he straightened, he scanned the rock spires thrusting up in this area of the city. Hoping, praying, begging whatever power out there might take pity on them. Hadn't they suffered enough? Hadn't they—

"Yes!" he shouted, pointing at a twisted spire rising in the distance. It looked like a crooked finger beckoning them closer, and it matched perfectly with one of his few clear memories of his earlier time on Dust.

At his outburst, Nala and Sep had turned to him, their faces slack with exhaustion and misery.

"Follow me," he said, and set off.

8

Bells began to clang as they hurried through the empty streets. Kerin felt eyes watching from behind shutters and peepholes, but none of the thalani who had retreated inside their adobe dwellings emerged to challenge them. They looked suspicious, he knew, a kyrathi and a couple of pale-skinned strangers covered in dust hurrying from the direction where a spire had partially collapsed, and he wondered what rumors their passage might ignite.

He couldn't worry about that now. They needed to find safety before they attracted the attention of the Mandate. Their innocence would be realized eventually, he was sure, when the true cause of the explosion became apparent – whatever that was – but if their initial interrogation discovered the crystal swallowing Sep then she would vanish into the imperium, never to be seen again. They would find a way to remove the weapon, even if it killed her, or force her to become a tool for the Golden Emperor's ambitions.

"Someone's coming," Nala warned him. "Heavy boots, many of them."

"Soldiers?"

"Almost certainly."

"Then we hide." Taking Sep by her uncorrupted arm, Kerin

pulled her towards a smaller side street cluttered with abandoned carts piled with vegetables and fruits. He guessed their owners must have rushed inside and slammed the doors before the blast's echo had faded, and Kerin was starting to suspect that something similar had happened before.

They hunkered behind a cart mounded with ridged purple fruit, and as soon as they had settled Kerin heard the same clomping that Nala's much better ears had been the first to notice. The sound swelled until a squad of Mandati soldiers briskly jogged past the entrance to the side street, perhaps two dozen in all. These were not the elite they had seen earlier guarding the chimeric noblewoman; their armor was a dull gray instead of bone-white, and their helms lacked the red crest that would mark them as k'zars. Still, a member of the Crimson accompanied them in his flapping red robes, struggling to keep up with the soldiers. His protruding belly wobbled, and his tonsured scalp gleamed with sweat as he struggled for breath, but Kerin knew that this Mandati battlemage could obliterate the rest of that squad with a thought. The Crimson were as much responsible for the victories of the Golden Emperor as his legion of war-krakens.

Nala let out a slow breath as the sound of the squad faded. Her claws were gripping the side of the cart so tightly that the wood had splintered.

"Lucky the mage was distracted. Otherwise he might have sensed me."

Kerin rose, plucking one of the purple fruit from the pile in front of him. "Whatever happened back there, the Mandate is taking it seriously. The Crimson looked like he was risking a heart attack running with those soldiers." He twisted off the rind and bit into the fruit's speckled flesh. Deliciously tart.

As he chewed he noticed Sep staring at him in disapproval. "What?"

"You shouldn't steal," she said sternly, pointing at the half-eaten fruit he held.

Kerin blinked in surprise, unsure how to respond to this. He glanced at Nala, but she only shrugged.

"Fine," he sighed, digging in his belt pouch with sticky fingers and finding a ghelthing. He laid the coin carefully where he'd taken the fruit, then grabbed a few more, throwing one towards the still-frowning girl. She caught it awkwardly. "That should be about what I paid for," he said, tossing the pit of the fruit he'd just finished over his shoulder.

"What do you think is going on?" Nala asked, still staring off in the direction the Crimson had gone. "Is the planet under attack? The Mandate?"

"Not from anything above," Kerin replied, squinting up at the purple clouds threading the sky. "We would have seen something."

"Rebellion, then," Nala said, slipping around the cart to peer down the deserted street.

Kerin shrugged. "Maybe. A small world like this, though, fighting against the Mandate . . . it's hopeless. The Golden Emperor could flood Dust with more soldiers than there are inhabitants on this mudball. Perhaps it was a lone terrorist. Or maybe it was an accident. Someone dropped an ancient family heirloom and it turned out to have been infused with Elder Race sorcery." He joined Nala at the mouth of the little street. The flower of dust and ash that had bloomed over the plaza when the spire collapsed had mostly wilted. Soon, the faint smear that lingered would merge with the darkening sky, and only the incessant ringing of the bells would remain to remind the rest of the city that something terrible had happened.

"Whatever is going on," he continued, "we need to lay low. The Mandate might start sweeping this area, looking for survivors . . . or suspects." He raised his dust-covered arms. "And it's fairly obvious we were there when the spire fell."

Nala nodded, then turned and motioned for Sep to join them. She did, holding the fruit he'd given her so tightly that her fingertips had broken the skin, as if she couldn't decide whether she wanted to throw it away or join him in enjoying something they hadn't truly compensated its seller for yet.

Odd that a church which encouraged the torturing of innocents would have instilled such rigid morals strictures. He had never understood religion.

~

The neighborhood of the twisted spire was much poorer than he remembered. The streetlamps here were few and far between, and nearly all their dangling spheres had been shattered to get at the light crystals within. The road was also far less well maintained, pocked with holes or missing cobbles, and no sweepers had come around in quite some time to clean up the dung and garbage. Kerin wrinkled his nose at the vile smell as he stepped around the corpse of a dog-sized lizard, flies encrusting its bloated white belly.

The rock spires were more thickly clustered here, and far fewer adobe structures lined the way. Kerin guessed that those buildings were newer and where Dust's middle class had moved. It was the poor and desperate that still squatted in the ancient homes of the planet's original inhabitants. Some of them were out and about, untroubled by the distant alarms bells. They hurried past, hunched and furtive, glancing quickly at the strangers who had ventured into their realm before returning to their own business. At least there were no Mandati to be seen.

"You came here with your grandfather?" Nala asked dubiously as a drunk stumbled out of a nearby alley and collapsed against a wall.

"I don't recall it being so . . . derelict," Kerin replied. In his faded memories, this street had more resembled what they'd previously seen in the city, with cheerful crowds frequenting bustling shops and restaurants. Either this area had deteriorated badly, or he'd led them to the wrong spire.

But it was unlikely that there was another that matched his recollections so perfectly. It looked like a giant had reached down and given the top of the ancient structure a twist, rippling the stone and making the peak cant at an odd angle. None of the other spires he'd seen today shared this characteristic.

The entrance was a soaring arch, large enough that Drifter could have poked his head inside. Strips of colored cloth fringed the curving rock above, faded with age, and lurid graffiti decorated the outside walls. A few older thalani men, their dark blue skin webbed by age-veins, sat around a stone table that had been placed in the shadow of the archway. Kerin felt their suspicious attention as he passed inside the spire.

"Tooth and claw," Nala murmured as the great space opened up above them. Most of the spire was hollow, and they could see all the way up its tapering height. A great spiraling staircase was built into the walls, allowing access to the levels that ascended to the apex of the building. Kerin guessed that there were more than a dozen of these tiers, each with doorways leading into individual domiciles. Just enough light was trickling through the countless small holes that pocked the walls to shroud the interior in a perpetual twilight, and large, winged shapes fluttered in the distant gloom. To their right was something that looked like a cage festooned with pulleys and ropes. Most of these extended upwards, but one thick cable stretched taut to where a cowled figure hunched beside a massive windlass and one of the striped animals they'd seen earlier at the stables. The beast stared at them dully, its long tail flicking away insects.

Long ago, Kerin had stood in this exact spot, and nothing seemed to have changed in the intervening years. The ancient thalani and the beast yoked to the contraption matched perfectly with his memories, except that when he'd been a boy they'd loomed much larger.

"This way," he said to Nala and Sep. The thalani lifted his head slightly at the sound of their approach, but his face was still hidden within the hood of his robes. Kerin hoped the old man couldn't see well. If he refused them it would be a long and arduous climb up the spire.

"Ho, grandfather. We've come to visit Bas Jelaska."

A trembling, age-veined hand emerged from a long sleeve. "Ninth level," the thalani rasped as he unfolded spidery fingers, revealing an empty palm. "Red door."

Ninth level. Not as high as he'd feared. Still, it wasn't a climb he wanted to make right now, with Sep and Nala swaying on their feet.

He fumbled in his belt pouch and then deposited a ghelthing in the old man's hand. A drastic overpayment for this service, but Kerin would prefer to be in the old man's good graces if others came around asking questions about strangers that had been seen in the area.

"Inside," commanded the thalani, and Kerin ushered his companions into the metal cage, then swung shut the door. The platform was planks of old wood that creaked alarmingly under his boots, and he had to fight back the urge to exit this device and head for the stairs instead.

"Is this safe?" Nala hissed as the old man crept painfully towards where the animal placidly waited.

"Perfectly," Kerin said with far more confidence than he actually felt.

A switch had appeared in the robed thalani's shaking hand. He raised his arm slowly, and Kerin wondered if the animal would even realize it had been commanded to move when it was finally struck, but when the lash came it descended with surprising speed and viciousness. The animal brayed, surging forward, and Kerin nearly lost his balance as the cage jerked from the ground and began a rapid ascent.

Sep gasped and clutched at his arm to steady herself, goggling over the side at the receding sight of the windlass turning as the animal tried to escape the switch. "Light save us," she murmured softly.

Kerin patted her hand reassuringly, even though his own heart was lurching in rhythm with the cage's swaying.

Despite some creaking and grumbling the rickety contraption arrived in one piece at the spire's ninth tier. Keeping his gaze well away from the now-tiny shapes far below, Kerin crossed onto the small wooden platform extending out from the stone walkway. He then helped Sep disembark, while Nala leaped the gap with her usual grace.

"Will this woman remember you?" Nala asked, strolling closer to a couple of bamboo cages hanging outside the closest door. A frantic explosion of beating wings and terrified chirps erupted as she peered between the bars.

"Hopefully," Kerin replied, starting on the curving passage that hugged the spire's wall. The way was littered with stools and tables and stunted fruit trees growing out of ceramic pots, but the only resident they saw was a thalani child crouched over a small army of wooden soldiers. He was so immersed in his imaginary battle that he didn't hear Kerin approach until the streamsurfer was only a few paces away. When the child finally did glance up, his face went slack with shock, his color fading from indigo to azure, and then in a frantic scramble that sent soldiers scattering he vanished through a cracked-open door.

"And if she doesn't?" Nala pressed.

"Then we find an inn," Kerin replied, his pace quickening as he caught sight of a familiar red door. "Though it would have to be a rather miserable place, given our lack of funds."

Kerin paused before knocking, glancing back at his companions. Both looked utterly bedraggled, singed by the initial explosion and then smeared by the wave of dust that had washed over the plaza after the spire's collapse. He was sure he didn't look any better. Sighing, hoping that he wasn't about to come face to face with a complete stranger, he rapped his knuckles on the ancient wood.

Shifting came from inside, then a muffled thump. Footsteps approached.

"Who's there?"

"Ah, hello. Bas Jelaska? My name is Kerin thon Talisien, we met a long time ago. I was with my grandfather—"

Kerin paused as he heard the sound of a deadbolt sliding back. The door opened slightly, still secured by a chain. A slice of a woman's pale face appeared in the gap, her vivid green eye narrowed suspiciously.

"I remember you. You ate me out of cakes and cried a lot about your mother."

Kerin blinked in surprise. He didn't remember *ever* crying about his mother.

"Well, uh—"

The face visible through the door shifted slightly to take in Sep and Nala. "Where's your grandfather? And did you all just rob a bakery? Why are you covered in flour?"

An amused snort came from the kyrathi.

"Cal is dead. Please, we need your help."

A long silence followed this. Kerin was half-afraid the door would slam shut, but then he heard the chain being unhooked.

"Behave yourself," Bas Jelaska said as the door opened wider.

Kerin immediately saw why, as the small woman standing in the entrance had a massive crossbow leveled at his chest. He took a reflexive step backward, wondering how easily an accident could occur given the strain the weapon must be putting on her thin arms. Yet he couldn't detect a wavering in the quarrel poised to rip through his body, so hopefully she was stronger than she looked.

He raised his hands to show that they were empty. "It's good to see you again," he said, not daring yet to step over the threshold.

Bas Jelaska barked a laugh and lowered the crossbow. "Ha! Now that sounds like something Cal would have said." She gave a little jerk of her head to indicate they should enter. "Well, come on in. Don't get flour on the furniture."

Kerin edged into the domicile as the woman tossed her ancient weapon onto a threadbare divan. He winced, half-expecting to hear the thrum of a quarrel being loosed into the cushions, but apparently the crossbow hadn't been fully wound.

He heard the shuffle of feet as Nala and Sep joined him inside. Bas Jelaska stepped back, eyeing them critically. She was smaller even than the girl, barely up to Kerin's chest, but she didn't look frail in the slightest. Her face was more lined than he remembered, and her golden hair was now mostly gray, but otherwise she didn't seem to have aged much in the last twenty years.

"Is that dust?" Bas Jelaska asked, her head tilted quizzically as she examined them. After Kerin's affirming nod she sighed. "You arrive on Dust covered in dust and decide to come visit just after I've dusted." She pointed at wooden chairs scattered around a small table. "There. Sit there. Should be easy enough to clean."

They meekly went where she was indicating and sat. As he did, his let his gaze move from the old woman and wander around her home. It was a small space, cluttered by old furniture and odd decorations, a large circular window dominating one wall. Through the smoky glass the golden sky was a dull bronze.

Bas Jelaska crossed her arms and studied them with pursed lips. "So Cal is dead. How did it happen?"

"His heart . . . or maybe his brain," Kerin began, wondering why the woman sounded angry. "Something just gave out. I found him in his favorite chair, watching the Stream flowing past. Drifter knew he was slipping away and had withdrawn from their bond." He swallowed, surprised by the emotion the memory was stirring up. "He looked peaceful. Content."

"Drifter? Oh, yes, the starbeast." Bas Jelaska's jaw seemed to unclench, and she sighed. "Well, he was always his own man. It's fitting he died in the Streams, I suppose. It was the only place he truly felt at home."

Kerin nodded slightly, a tightness in his throat. She *had* known his grandfather well.

Bas Jelaska went over to a black cabinet inlaid with mother-of-pearl birds. She rummaged for a moment and then pulled out an ancient bottle and a pair of long-stemmed glasses. She regarded the faded label for a moment, her expression inscrutable.

"This was our drink," she said, depositing the bottle and glasses on the table. "Kelcha. It's made from fermenting the golden rice they grow here on Dust. The first time we met we stayed up all night drinking it and arguing about everything. I only drank it when he came through, but I always made sure there was a bottle here for when he did." With some effort she pulled out the cork. "We might as well finish it now." She poured a measure into the two cups. The liquid roiled and eddied like the sky during a storm. Bas Jelaska lifted her glass and waited for Kerin to join her. She held his gaze for a moment with her brilliant green eyes, then sighed. "Goodbye, Cal," she said simply, then downed the amber drink in a single swallow. Kerin followed. He had been expecting something harsh and biting, like the mysterious alcohol he had discovered in his grandfather's solarium, but the rice-wine was surprisingly smooth.

Bas Jelaska set her glass down with enough force that Kerin thought it might have cracked. Her eyes grew distant, staring at something only she could see. Reliving past memories, he assumed, just like he was.

Kerin remembered being mildly afraid of Bas Jelaska during the time he'd spent in this apartment. She'd been forceful and confident, loudly challenging his grandfather when he'd said something she disagreed with, though he couldn't recall what it was they'd argued about. So different from the withdrawn and sullen mother he'd recently left behind. *She* had barely put up a fight when his grandfather had arrived and told her he'd be taking Kerin with him back to the stars. He couldn't imagine Bas Jelaska ever doing the same. Even as a child he'd recognized the most basic distinction between the two women: his mother could only conceive of herself as a victim, no matter how much her circumstances were her own fault, while Bas Jelaska owned all her choices and, as his grandfather had told him, strode through life without apology. At the time he hadn't understood what that had meant, but he'd still realized that Bas Jelaska was different. Now, thinking back, Kerin wondered if his grandfather had brought him to Dust so soon after liberating him from his life in the slums of Deval so that he could experience living for a short while with a woman the diametric opposite to his mother.

Or maybe he'd just wanted to find comfort for a time in her arms. Ascribing higher motivations to his grandfather's behavior had proven foolish before.

Bas Jelaska blinked, returning to herself. She took in Nala and Sep like she was seeing her guests for the first time. "And you two. Streamsurfers, are you? I'd offer you a drink of this, but I know kyrathi abhor human spirits, and you, young lady, are far too young. Some hot water for you both, at least?"

"That would be nice," Nala said, and Sep nodded ever so slightly.

The former pain conduit seemed intimidated by the older woman's crackling presence, her shoulders hunched and her gray eyes fixed on the table.

Bas Jelaska bustled over to a small fireplace set in one of the walls and used a poker to stir the smoldering embers. A kettle was already suspended on a metal rod, and she briefly lifted the top to check its contents.

"So I imagine you didn't swim through the Streams just to tell me about Cal," she said over her shoulder as she took down a dried sausage that had been hanging from a hook and began slicing it into small pieces.

Kerin shared a quick glance with Nala. "We're actually a bit down on our luck. Hoping to turn it around in the cluster."

Bas Jelaska snorted loudly. "Ha. You and I both know this isn't the kind of place you'd come to do that." She waggled the knife she held at him. "No, you all are hiding from something."

"Laying low."

"Big trouble?"

"Barely worth mentioning."

She squinted at him, then resumed her chopping. "Hmm. You lie like your grandfather."

He smiled back innocently.

"You're going to ask me if you can stay here," she said, bringing the sausage over on a dish and setting it down in front of Sep. "And I'd be a fool to let you."

"I promise you there's nothing—"

He snapped his mouth shut when she sliced the air with the knife. "But there's history between Cal and I. Old and deep history. I owe him for something that happened before you were born. So you can stay, if you behave yourself." She pulled out another chair and sat down heavily, then tossed the knife onto the table with a clatter and reached again for the bottle of rice-wine. "And, truth be told, I haven't had visitors for a long while. I'm interested in the stories you've got to tell, and the news from beyond this miserable little planet." She refilled his glass and then her own. "But you can start with telling me your names."

The story Kerin told had enough roots trailing down to the truth that it tumbled out easily enough. He began by telling Bas Jelaska about the debt they'd been left with after his grandfather's death – probably not hard to believe if she truly knew Cal well – and how a clumsy attempt to clear it had led to a misunderstanding that exiled them from the Starfarers Guild. This, in turn, had forced them to take on a risky contract from a gobber who wanted transport to an out-of-the-way system. But it had all been a ruse, and they'd been ambushed by the gobber's friends. They'd fought their way free and fled to the cluster, and, right now, were hoping to rest and regroup while keeping their ears open for whispers about lucrative contracts.

When he was finished, Kerin sat back feeling satisfied. The best lies, he'd long ago learned, were heavily leavened by the truth.

Bas Jelaska's face was not entirely devoid of skepticism, but she seemed willing to accept most of what he'd laid out.

"And this?" she asked, making a broad gesture that encompassed all three of them. He knew she was referring to their general state of dishevelment. "What happened to you?"

Kerin gave an exaggerated shrug. "No idea. As soon as we got Drifter settled in the stables we went to find some food . . . we were sitting outside a café in a large plaza with the statue of some great tree and suddenly something exploded. Brought down one of the spires and the dust from that washed over us while we were beating a hasty retreat."

Bas Jelaska's eyes widened. "A spire fell? In the Bowery? Nebulas. So that must be the reason the bells have been ringing all afternoon. There's been another attack."

"Who is attacking?" Nala asked, leaning forward in interest with her elbows on the table.

Bas Jelaska shifted, suddenly looking uncomfortable. "They call themselves the Black Dawn. Freedom fighters in their own minds, maybe in a fair number of the regular thalani as well. Terrorists to the Mandate and the rest of the locals." She took a quick gulp of her drink. "Led by one called Mazrem Tou, though that's not his or her real name. It means something to the thalani, harkens back to when they were slaves before the Sword came and broke their shackles. Anyway, they're fighting to be free of the Mandate, make Dust an independent world again."

"By blowing up their homes," Nala said contemptuously.

"At first it was just graffiti, pamphlets, nothing violent. But the exarch of Dust wanted to stamp it out quick. He came down hard, a few people died, and things have escalated in recent months. Somehow the Dawn got a hold of wraith crystals, probably from the black markets on Reaver's Rest. They've ignited several already, damaging the barracks here and killing a few soldiers. This would be the first time one was used in public." She scowled. "Things are about to get dark, I think. You all have picked the wrong time to visit."

Kerin thought back to the sorcery that had been unleashed in the plaza. Wraith crystals certainly made sense, though they were rare and expensive, and he couldn't understand how the revolutionaries of a poor backwater had gotten their hands on them, let alone more than one. They came from the caverns of the world of Wraith, halfway across the stellar tributary. The mages of that planet had learned how to pour tremendous amounts of aether into these indigenous crystals, and the sorcery remained dormant until shattered. Then it was all released at once, causing massive devastation.

"And you?" Bas Jelaska asked, turning to Sep. "You're not a streamsurfer. How did you end up with these ruffians?" The girl did not respond, keeping her eyes lowered, but Kerin had learned enough about her to see the tension in the way she was holding herself.

Bas Jelaska frowned, turning back to Kerin. "What's wrong with her?"

"She's very shy," Kerin explained. "She belonged to the gobber.

Before that, she was a pain conduit in the church of the Searing Light."

Some of the hardness in Bas Jelaska's face melted away. "Poor child," she murmured. "I've heard stories of what goes on in those temples... does she speak?"

"She does," Kerin assured her. "Or, at least, she started to after her former master got reduced to dust."

"She's trembling," Bas Jelaska said, concern in her voice. She stood, then came around to crouch beside Sep. "Child, come with me. I'll draw you a bath and get you cleaned up. I will not hurt you, I promise." Gently she laid her hand on Sep's arm – the one not being turned to crystal, thankfully – and surprisingly the girl did not pull away.

Kerin glanced at Nala and saw that she was also looking at him in alarm. The truth about Sep's condition would be impossible to hide if Bas Jelaska cared for the girl.

"I will help her," Nala said quickly.

"No," replied Bas Jelaska with a firm shake of her head. "I'm no stranger to trauma. Forty years ago I sat just like this poor girl is now, a prisoner of my own mind."

Kerin inwardly sighed. He couldn't see any way to keep the alvaren weapon a secret.

"There's something wrong with her arm," he blurted. "We have to be careful."

Bas Jelaska's brow drew down in confusion. "Wrong?"

Well, no turning back now. He reached out tentatively towards where Sep's gloved hand rested on the table. "Can we show her?" he asked the girl softly. "Maybe she can help."

Sep didn't turn to look at them, but he saw her neck move slightly as she swallowed hard. Then her other hand slid across the table and slowly pulled off the glove with a hiss of cloth.

It was the first time in several days that Kerin had seen what the alvaren weapon was doing to her. The flesh below her elbow had completely vanished, replaced with glittering, faceted crystal. There wasn't a boundary that clearly demarcated the two; a swath of skin above the crystal was turning opaque, already rendered partially translucent, bones and veins and muscles clearly visible. There was also something else, thin, dark filaments stretching from the transformed arm and extending into where she was still only flesh.

To Kerin's surprise, Bas Jelaska did not gasp or cry out when the state of the girl's arm was revealed. Instead, her voice remained steady and calm.

"What is causing this?"

"We don't know," Kerin replied, again skirting the edge of a lie. "It's another reason we're on Dust. Maybe we can find help here."

"The Mandati mixmages?" Bas Jelaska said dubiously. "They usually deal only with organic matter."

"Not them. Someone else."

"Ah," the old woman said, her voice suddenly turning flat. "You're talking about the Antiquarian."

"Yes," Kerin said, feeling Nala's eyes boring into him. He hadn't wanted her to find out that was the reason he'd chosen Dust. Hopefully he could explain before the kyrathi drew her own conclusions about this. "He was a friend of my grandfather."

"An acquaintance," Bas Jelaska said, an edge to her tone as she corrected him. "A business associate. A dangerous man . . . if he is a man." She made a gesture, as if dismissing the topic. "But I don't want to scare this poor child further." She lightly touched the back of Sep's head. "Come, child. Don't be afraid. We'll get you out of these dirty clothes and give you a good wash, and I promise to be mindful of your arm. Now, come on."

The scraping sound as Sep pushed back her chair surprised Kerin. She slowly stood, and Bes Jelaska raised herself from her own crouch and began to gently guide the girl towards a passage leading deeper into the apartment.

When they'd vanished, Nala leaned closer to him, her whiskers trembling. "The Antiquarian?" she hissed angrily. "Who is that? Why didn't you tell me he was the reason we were coming here?"

Kerin sat forward, lowering his voice. "The Antiquarian is why my grandfather used to visit Dust, but don't tell that to Bas Jelaska. He's an expert in the artifacts of Elder Races and ancient sorceries. And he's independent, not part of a university or scholar cabal. Out of the entire universe, I can't think of someone better to examine Sep and the thing consuming her arm."

Nala's eyes narrowed suspiciously. "Then why not tell me this earlier?"

Kerin shrugged. "Like Bas Jelaska said, he doesn't have the best reputation. Maybe even verging on villainous. I guess I was afraid that if you'd heard of the Antiquarian you'd argue against coming here. But my grandfather knew him well. They had a relationship. I promise, Sep will be safe."

Nala studied him carefully, as if weighing how much stock she should put in what he was saying. Finally, she leaned back and crossed her arms over her chest. "Fine. So long as the girl's well-being is foremost."

"It is," he promised, and then abruptly stood and stretched. "Ah. I'm in desperate need of a drink and a little relaxation. It's been a long time out in the Streams. You stay here with Sep; I'm going to find whatever dive streamsurfers hang out in on this planet. Listen to some whispers and get a sense of what's really going on around here."

"Just remember to keep a low profile," Nala said evenly, still giving him that measuring look. "Your family's name is clearly known around these parts."

9

As soon as Kerin exited the spire he felt like a great weight had been lifted from his shoulders. At least for a little while he was leaving behind the mantle of captain, the responsibility of caring for Nala and Drifter . . . and also, he was forced to admit, Sep as well. Despite his best attempts at remaining detached from the girl, he was now thinking of her as one of his crew. Which would make what he'd almost certainly eventually have to do all the more difficult. Kerin had no illusions about the likelihood of finding a way to separate the artifact from the girl without harming her.

Sighing, he pulled up the collar of his steelsilk shirt. In the indigo sky a pair of silver moons had risen, one a tarnished coin and the other a gleaming scimitar. With the coming of night the temperature had dropped, and he regretted leaving his heavier clothes back aboard Drifter. He'd forgotten how much colder it was on this planet when the sun vanished.

None of the streetlamps in the neighborhood contained working crystals, but the twin moons gilded the spires and the cobbles beneath his feet with a patina of silver. More light spilled from soaring entrances or infused the windows speckling the great structures rising around him. This area had seemed nearly abandoned earlier, but now Kerin realized that its inhabitants had merely been hunkering inside while the warning bells were tolling. Those had finally fallen silent while they'd been with Bas Jelaska, though the air still seemed to be trembling with an almost febrile intensity, as if another disaster was only a breath away.

But perhaps that was just his nerves. The last few days had contained a decades' worth of excitement and danger. Usually they plied the Streams ferrying passengers between systems, or transporting small, valuable cargo for those who hoped to avoid the scrutiny given to the larger starbeast trading caravans. Years could pass between encountering pirates or inhospitable locals, and he'd only had to swing *Mercy* in anger a few times, most of those when planetside, after a bout of heavy drinking.

Drinking like he planned to do tonight, honestly. No carousing, though – at least nothing that would result in spilled blood and the attention of the Mandate authorities. He had more than enough problems simmering without having to also ask Nala to bail him out of the local gaol. Nebulas, she wouldn't like that at all. She might just—

The feeling of being watched yanked Kerin from his thoughts. His eager strides slowed, and he took in his surroundings with a fresh wariness. He was being foolish, passing down dark, unfamiliar streets while distracted. A quick way to end up a punctured corpse stashed in one of these alleyways.

He scanned the darkened openings between the spires, wondering where this creeping sense that he was being observed was coming from. There were a few others sharing the street with him, but everyone seemed to be trying their hardest to ignore each other, heads down and pace hurried.

Perhaps he was being paranoid. A useful trait, but annoying at times. His natural inclination to expect the worst had saved him before, but sometimes he wished he could just blithely float through life—

There. A cold shock went through him when he saw a patch of shadows tremble. Up ahead, a gnarl of rock bulged from near the base of one of the spires, creating a pool of darkness from which he was sure someone was watching him. The shiver of movement had immediately stilled, but it hadn't been his imagination. Something was crouched there.

His hand drifted to *Mercy's* hilt. Perhaps it was a dog, or one of those orange lizards he'd seen waddling about. Or a waif, staring enviously at his nice clothes and bulging money pouch.

But he knew in his heart it was none of those things.

Kerin stalked closer to the rock overhang and whatever lurked below. He'd swum ancient and forgotten Streams, stared out into the abyss, refused a lich's demands. A shadow the size of a small child could not frighten him. He pulled a lightsphere from his pocket and kindled the crystal within. Radiance flared and the darkness melted away, revealing only a scarred rock wall and a scrawl of graffiti. Kerin unclenched his jaw, giving his head a small shake. What was wrong with him? Why was he seeing these shadows again? Were they actually memories stirred up by returning to Dust?

His heartbeat slowed. Nebulas, he needed to be sword-sharp right now, and here he was jumping at phantasms from his childhood. Angrily, he shoved the sphere away . . . though he did not extinguish its crystal, which allowed the muted light to seep through the pocket of his shirt. He knew he must look ridiculous, but he didn't care. To the void with them all. If anybody snickered at him for needing a nightlight he'd show them a handspan of *Mercy* and send them scurrying.

Kerin's gaze lingered where he'd thought he'd seen the shadow for a few more moments before he finally turned away. He really needed a drink.

∾

In every port on every planet there was at least one tavern where streamsurfers congregated. Usually such places could be found near the stables, as procuring a stiff drink was often high on a new arrival's list of priorities. Perhaps a quick detour first to visit the shrine of whatever power they believed had shepherded them safely through the Streams, and then soon after that the consumption of copious amount of alcohol would commence to help lubricate their transition back to society.

Streamsurfers almost always preferred their own kind over the company of groundlings. There was something about the long, lonely voyages through the Streams that those who dwelled their entire lives planetside could never understand. You could try to explain it, the sense of what it was like standing on a starbeast as it plied the stellar tributary, the abyss that churned around you seething with glimpses of things beyond comprehension, but invariably such attempts failed. So streamsurfers sought each other out, because only their own kind could understand what they had experienced.

If he hadn't been staying with one of his many paramours scattered throughout the tributary, his grandfather had usually lived at surfer taverns whenever they were stuck on a planet for an extended period. When he'd had to go out to buy supplies or visit with prospective customers Cal had been different, on edge, twitchy like a glimmer junkie. It was only within the confines of the local streamsurfer haunt that this tension sloughed away, and he seemed completely relaxed. Kerin had spent countless evenings sitting with his grandfather in these taverns, swapping stories of the Streams or casting blood knuckles with guild friends, or simply enjoying a drink and a companionable silence with others who knew what it was like to slip between the stars.

Kerin's guess about where the local streamsurfer haunt would be found was eventually proven correct. He knew it was what he was looking for immediately, as much from intuition as anything else: a freestanding adobe building much smaller than the huge beehive structures where most of the thalani dwelled, bedecked with red paper lanterns. Golden light and the hum of conversation spilled from the open windows, through which he could see a swirl of activity, and beyond the tavern he glimpsed the rippling fabric of the stables glowing white in the moonlight. Those that were bonded often tried to stay as close as possible to their starbeasts.

Several of the letters on the sign hanging above the door had corroded into illegibility, but Kerin believed it spelled out The Fell Whimsy. An odd name for a tavern, but in truth it sounded like something a streamsurfer would call their establishment. The more esoteric or mysterious or bizarre the better.

He pushed inside, nearly colliding with a thalani woman who was carrying a tray laden with bubbling mugs.

"Careful, sweetface," she called out as she swayed around him, somehow not spilling a drop. "Tables are all full up, but there's space at the bar."

He blinked, his eyes watering from the pall of reddish smoke that hung heavy in the cramped room. Gleaming brass and copper contraptions squatted like huge metallic insects on each of the half dozen tables, burbling and hissing as glimmer addicts sucked on snaking tubes. There wasn't an empty chair in the tavern, and around several tables groups had clustered, waiting their turn to partake of the glimmer or get into the various games being played. Mostly this was cards, but the rattle of blood knuckles being cast somewhere made his ears perk up. To his surprise, more than half the patrons were thalani, which suggested that The Fell Whimsy was popular with the locals as well. That did make some sense. On larger worlds, streamsurfers were often seen as dangerous outsiders and trouble-makers, but here on these frontier worlds the native folks appreciated the brave souls that kept them connected to the rest of the stellar tributary.

Kerin pushed through the crowd and bellied up to the bar, a beautiful slab of golden wood that looked to have been carved from the body of a single great tree. Just how such a piece had made its way to this arid and forest-lacking world was probably a tale worth hearing, and Kerin stored away that question as a conversation starter for later. The hulking thalani behind the bar approached, laying his hands upon the wood and leaning forward. Kerin saw that while one of the man's arms was the same dark blue as the rest of him, the other was a deep copper and noticeably more fine-boned. The skin on the same side of the barman's face as the different-colored arm was scarred and pitted, like he'd been burned, or maybe savaged by something vicious.

Kerin always felt uneasy when he gazed upon the handiwork of a Mandati mixmage. The idea of grafting organic matter to a different, still-living body made him squeamish, but in certain instances – like replacing missing limbs – he could countenance the chimericist's sorcery. So long as the new body part was sourced from someone or something that hadn't died for the purpose of offering up a piece of itself. It was when such alterations were made in the name of vanity that he shook his head.

"What's your drink, surfer?" the barkeep rumbled, and Kerin realized with a flash of embarrassment that he'd been staring at the man's arm. He looked away, making a show of perusing the bottles lined up against the wall. He drummed his fingers on the bar top, surprised by how the golden wood seemed to vibrate at his touch. The loss of the dark stout earlier was an aching hole in his heart, but he could still taste the drink Bas Jelaska had shared with him on his tongue. What had she called it?

"I had some sort of rice wine that's bottled right here on Dust. Golden color, very smooth."

The weary impatience in the barkeep's face vanished, replaced by grudging respect. "Kelcha," he said warmly, turning to pluck a bottle with a label Kerin recognized from the assortment behind him. "Best thing to come out of the soil round here. You want it with glimmer or without?"

"I'll take it pure," Kerin said as the barkeep poured a healthy amount into a red-crystal glass.

"Only way to drink it," the thalani said, sliding the drink in front of him. "That would normally be a tribune, but since you just arrived, first one's on the house."

Kerin raised the glass in a salute and then took a sip. This vintage was slightly fruiter, but just as easy to drink. A very dangerous kind of wine.

"So you came in on that turtle today?" the thalani said, wiping at something invisible on the spotless bar top with a rag.

Kerin set down the kelcha with a contented sigh. Already he could feel his tension seeping away. "Aye."

The barkeep grinned. "Jenks was in here earlier grousing about you. Apparently you drive a hard bargain. Also said your family is pretty well known in guild circles."

Damn. Kerin's rising feeling of well-being suddenly and sharply subsided. So much for staying in the shadows. Well, hopefully the Mandati streamsurfers didn't frequent this place.

The thalani must have seen something in his face. "Ain't no one going to be picking quarrels here, friend. Or if they do, I'll set them straight right quick. Those guildsmen in the back have been watching you since you came in, but if they try anything, the next thing they'll feel will be their arses hitting the cobbles outside. Grudges get checked at the door here, the Whimsy's a place for drinking, not fighting."

Kerin twisted around and immediately spotted who the barkeep was speaking about. Through the glimmer haze and the shifting crowd of patrons a young man with bright silver hair was staring at him from a booth set into the far wall, surrounded by his crewmates. Even if Kerin hadn't been able to see the golden starburst sewn into the streamsurfer's tunic he would have known him for a member of the Starfarers Guild, as the boy had the same casual arrogance that Kerin had once wrapped himself in like a second skin. Their gazes met, but the guildsman didn't nod or raise his drink in greeting.

He clearly knew who Kerin was, and he wasn't going to be friendly.

About which Kerin couldn't care less. He flashed a too-broad smile and gave a jaunty wave, and this seemed to annoy the streamsurfer. A flicker of anger passed across his face, causing his lip to curl.

Kerin dismissed the boy by turning back to the bar. He took a deep drink of the rice wine, draining the glass, and savored the warmth as it spread out from his belly. A few more swigs of kelcha and he would be itching to invite the cocky guildrat to meet him in the alley outside the bar. Perhaps he should slow down a little, he grudgingly admitted to himself. Then again, maybe he should provide what the boy clearly had coming to him. Might be best for him in the long run, honestly.

The thalani barkeep was polishing an already gleaming flagon, his scarred features crinkled up in amusement. "His name's Gereld, and he's the one bonded to the pretty little drake in the stables. They're here on official guild business, I hear, but they've been resting their wings for nearly a month now. No one knows what they're waiting for."

Kerin heard the unspoken question. "It's not me," he told the barkeep. "Pure chance we ended up on Dust. And we won't be staying longer than we need to."

The thalani grunted, setting the flagon he'd been polishing down beside a collection of its equally spotless fellows. He opened his mouth as if to say something, but then his eyes widened slightly, and he quickly turned around.

Kerin blinked in surprise at the barkeep's broad back, wondering if the arrogant streamsurfer and his friends were even now pushing through the crowds behind him, intent on avenging the good name of the Starfarers Guild. His hand drifted slowly to *Mercy*'s hilt, his fingertips brushing the cool metal. He just couldn't seem to stay out of trouble these days . . .

"Hello, stranger."

It was a feminine voice, low and deep. Bordering on sultry.

"Buy you a drink?"

A woman appeared beside him, leaning casually against the golden bar. She was young, maybe about his own age, though there was an air of confidence about her that suggested she might be older than she looked. Or maybe she was just very aware of her effect on others. Kerin hadn't seen such a beautiful woman in a long, long time. She was even more striking than the Mandati noblewoman from the plaza: she was slender, her limbs long and graceful, and it seemed like she had been poured into her red-leather outfit. Her tight clothing nearly matched the color of her hair, and her skin was only a shade removed from the alabaster white of the Mandati. He didn't think she was from the empire, though. Her eyes, for one, were like nothing he'd ever seen on a human before, a lustrous gold flecked with little bits of jade.

And he'd been staring into them for a half-dozen heartbeats. Kerin swallowed, tearing his gaze away and returning it to the barkeep, but the thalani had moved down to the other end of the bar to attend to a customer.

He cleared his throat. "What, um, were you thinking? About the drink, I mean."

She shrugged. "Something with a bit more bite than what you just had. Kelcha is an old woman's drink around these parts."

"Are you, uh, from Dust?"

A slight smile curved her lips. "No. But I've been around here long enough to know what's worth drinking." She rapped her knuckles loudly on the bar, drawing the barkeep back to them. "A bottle of Zino's Tears," she said. "And two glasses."

Kerin thought he saw wariness in the thalani's eyes just before he ducked down to rummage for her order, and his unease deepened. Who was this woman? Usually he'd assume she was interested in a transactional relationship, given her rather provocative clothing and how brazenly she had approached him. But in this case he didn't think so. She was too confident, too sure of herself. And of course she'd offered to buy *him* a drink. Maybe she was a streamsurfer, out hunting for a tryst in port that didn't have much in the way of suitable options. Was he still a dashing figure, despite still not having cleaned up from what had happened in the plaza earlier?

Perhaps he was underestimating his rakish charm. Kerin offered what he thought was his most alluring smile as the barkeep set a bottle and pair of chipped tumblers on the wood between them.

"I'm Panil," Kerin told her. It was a name he'd used before when visiting planets that might not remember his family fondly. Bad enough that he'd told the stablemaster who he was, and that the guildrat in the corner had recognized him. He should, from here on, try to limit who knew they were here. Maybe Xerivas had servants all over the tributary, like the very flesh-and-blood gobber they'd encountered on Jegriddsl.

The woman poured a splash of the unsettlingly black liquor into both glasses. Then she raised the one closest to her, waiting for him to do the same. He did, trying to avoid getting lost again in her beautiful eyes, and brought his glass to his lips.

"No, you're not," she said, and tossed back her drink.

He coughed as the liquor scorched its way down his throat, nearly making a mess on the bar top.

The woman watched him splutter with amusement, then stuck the tip of her tongue out between her lips.

The sense of familiarity that accompanied this expression was jarringly strong, but for a moment he couldn't place from where. Then realization struck Kerin so hard he nearly staggered backwards. "Tess?" he rasped, barely able to speak.

She nodded ever so slightly as she reached to refill her tumbler. "So you haven't forgotten about me completely," she said breezily as more of the sluggish black liquid slipped from the bottle.

"Tess, what are you doing here?" he managed, resisting the urge to clutch at her arm. His head was spinning. How long had it been since he'd last seen Tessa? Fifteen years? Sixteen? He remembered her turning back as she had vanished into the jostling crowds on the edge of Heth's stable, sticking out her tongue impishly in the same manner she had just done a moment ago. She'd been painfully thin and gawky back then, all knobby legs and arms, not yet a woman grown. That was no longer the case.

One side of her mouth lifted as she swirled the tarry contents of her glass. "Oh, I'm fine, thanks for asking. And how has life treated you, Kerin?"

He shook his head, trying to order his scattered thoughts. "I'm sorry, Tess. It's just shocking to see you. How have you been?"

She shrugged. "Tears and laughter. Flax and silks."

"Your eyes," he let slip, realizing a moment late that this might be sensitive for her. "I mean, they're different. It's why I didn't recognize you."

"Well, our last memories of each other are from when we were children," she replied. "If it wasn't for the sword at your side I wouldn't have known you were you. Especially since you're all . . ." She indicated him with a flick of her wrist. "Dirty."

"There's an explanation for that," Kerin assured her, suddenly self-conscious about how destitute he must look. Of course, the entirety of his wealth *was* contained in the half-full pouch at his waist, but his current disheveled state was not from lack of money.

"And I have a similar explanation for my eyes," she said, fluttering her lashes at him. "There was an accident, and I could only see again if I visited a chimericist. So I did."

"A mixmage did that?" he asked in wonder, studying the contours of her eye sockets. "The work is flawless."

"It wasn't cheap," said Tessa with a tight smile. "And in some ways I'm still paying off that debt now."

"Talisien."

His family name, spoken with a surprising amount of venom. Kerin knew immediately what he would find when he turned around. The only question was whether the young guildrat had mustered the courage to confront him on his own, or if he'd dragged over the rest of his crew. He sighed, wondering if it was Tessa's attentions that had incited the boy to finally confront him. It must have been maddening when he'd been dismissed and ignored, then watching as Kerin was approached by such a beautiful woman.

Kerin turned slowly, still holding his glass. He casually took a drink, trying to exude calm confidence even as his heart fell a little when he caught sight of the guild insignias stitched on the tunics of the five rather beefy fellows standing behind the boy.

"That's my name. Who might you be?"

"Gereld t'Sahn," the boy shot back, almost triumphantly.

Inwardly Kerin sighed. Of course. The silver color should have been a dead giveaway, since everyone in that huge, inbred clan shared the same hair. "Son of Balloch t'Sahn?"

"Yes," the boy said with a fierce grin.

Kerin sipped his drink. "Your father's a bastard."

Gereld flushed, his fingers twitching. Kerin knew he badly wanted to reach for the filigreed silver hilt at his side, but he was smart enough to know that once he did that there would be no turning back.

"You want nothing to do with this one, my lady," Gereld finally snarled, addressing Tessa. "He's a thief. A grave robber. He was caught red-handed on a barrow moon carting away the treasures of an exarch, and when the Mandate realizes he's here I'm certain they'll clap him in irons or send him scurrying back to the stars clinging to his old turtle." He sneered. "Maybe I'll go tell them myself."

Tessa arched her eyebrows. "You'd turn in a fellow streamsurfer? Once a member of your own guild?"

"He's been cast out. There's no one in the tributary who cares what happens to him."

"I see," Tessa murmured, studying Kerin with what he hoped was mock-pity.

"Yes. The Mandate might even reward me for informing them."

"Oh, I doubt that."

"Do you?" Gereld said, the cold arrogance returning to his voice. Apparently with that contradiction he'd decided Tessa wasn't worth pursuing.

"Yes. Because they already know he's here." Tessa reached up to the red-leather collar that covered most of her throat. Keeping her expression placid, she pulled it down, showing what was beneath.

Kerin gaped. Upon her neck writhed red tattoos, the mark of a citizen of the Mandate. He couldn't be sure what rank she had attained, as that would be indicated by the total amount of markings scrawled on her, and right now her body was almost entirely covered by her tight-fitting garb. She could be anywhere from a second to a seventh – a higher rank was unlikely, as her face was entirely unblemished. Unless she wanted to keep her citizenship in the empire a secret some of the time. But that would only make sense if—

Tessa's brow creased in concentration, and the twisting red tattoo suddenly darkened. For a moment it was a squirming black snake, and then just as quickly it returned to its original color.

Oh.

Oh no.

Gereld's face had turned a shade of yellow that reminded Kerin of cured vellum. His eyes were bulging like he couldn't believe what he had just witnessed.

"You're a ... you're a ..."

Tessa continued to smile through his stammering. "Yes, I am a Shroud of the Inquisitarium. And if you don't want me to take a hard look at what exactly you and your runty flying lizard are doing here on Dust, I suggest you walk away. Now."

The boy shot Kerin a final look of loathing and then turned quickly on his heel and made for the door. His compatriots followed close behind, nearly falling over each other in their haste.

Kerin couldn't take any pleasure in watching the guildrat get humiliated. He felt numb. The Inquisitarium was one of the most feared organizations of the tributary, employed by the exarchs and the Golden Emperor to maintain order within the borders of the Mandate. They were the daggers in the dark: part secret police, part investigators, and part assassins, ruthlessly excising any threat to imperial rule.

Or at least that was the rumor. But the Tessa he'd known would never – *never* – have allowed herself to become such a tool.

She must have seen the disbelief in his face. "It's true," she said, closing her strange new eyes. Something passed across her face that suggested either exhaustion or sadness. "And as to your first question, why am I here . . ." Her eyes snapped open again, and whatever he had glimpsed for that moment was gone. "This planet is a hotbed of sedition. The thalani refuse to accept that they are now part of the Mandate."

Kerin raised his glass and drank deep of the vile black spirit, unable to keep his hand from trembling. Tessa? A Shroud? Of all the shocking events and revelations of the last few days, this was the one farthest beyond the bounds of possibility.

"They were slaves once before," he whispered. "They do not wish to be again."

Tessa's mouth twisted. "They have no choice in the matter. If the Mandate withdrew tomorrow from the cluster, it would only be a matter of time before another of the great powers swooped in to take the empire's place. Would they prefer sloshing through the breeding pits of the ghenabakans? Tending the algae fields of the Qan Hegemony? Sacrificed to rise again as foot soldiers in a lich's legions? The Golden Emperor takes far better care of his subjects than most, even those recalcitrants who refuse to become citizens. He allows them to live their lives, with all the benefits the Mandate brings to its systems. Stability, protection, trade."

"You sound like a true believer."

Tessa shook her head. "I'm not the child I once was, Kerin. And neither are you. I think we probably have both done things that would have horrified our younger selves. But this shedding of innocence happens to everyone . . . or the universe breaks them." She sighed, falling quiet for a moment. "I'm on Dust because the Black Dawn somehow managed to assassinate an exarch."

"Truly?" The surprises continued. Exarchs were drawn from the ranks of the Mandate's most powerful archmages, and the layers of protection wrapping them – both sorcerous and otherwise – should have made them beyond invulnerable to a bunch of ragtag revolutionaries.

"Yes. And not just any exarch. Charvenak had been a favored apprentice of the Golden Emperor himself. Even a Transcendent should not have been able to murder him so effortlessly."

Kerin's curiosity was piqued now. "What happened?"

"He was found dead in his chambers. His wards were intact, and there was no sign of physical trauma."

"Poison?"

"Nothing in his blood. And no common substance could have harmed him anyway. It was like his spirit simply . . . abandoned his body."

"Perhaps a sorcerous rival?"

"No trace of sorcery was found, at least nothing ever encountered by the mages of the empire."

"But you're sure the Black Dawn are responsible?"

She stared into her nearly-empty drink as if an answer could be found in its silty dregs. "He'd been marked for death by the Dawn for things he'd done trying to root them out. And then he died. Until I have further proof, I'm holding them responsible."

"So you're here to find out what happened and bring the guilty to justice."

Tessa set her glass down hard with a clink. "Yes. In fact, I have other things I need to be doing tonight. My coming here to the Whimsy was supposed to be just a brief stop to say hello to an old friend." She must have seen the question forming in his face, because she hurriedly continued. "Information is hoarded by the Inquisitarium. Your arrival was noted today and brought to my attention, and I know you well enough to realize that this place would be where you'd spend your first evening on Dust." She tossed a generous handful of tribunes onto the bar and began pulling on the red-leather gloves she'd removed earlier when she'd started drinking.

"Did you hear my grandfather is dead?" Kerin blurted. He'd been avoiding broaching this topic, but she should know if she didn't already.

Another quick shiver of emotion passed across her face. "Yes," she said simply, stepping away from the bar.

"Can I see you again?" Kerin asked, suddenly afraid that she was once more going to walk out of his life and vanish.

One side of Tessa's mouth lifted. "Come by the magistrate offices tomorrow around the tenth glass. I'm working out of there, as the Inquisitarium has no permanent presence here on Dust yet. Though that might change if we have more days like today."

"You mean the explosion in the plaza?"

She nodded. "They nearly killed the new exarch's daughter. I can't imagine what kind of reprisal would have happened if they'd been successful. I fear it would have been bloody and indiscriminate. We *must* end this insurgency before too many innocents suffer." She withdrew a featureless black disc slightly larger than a coin and held it out for him to take. "Show this to the guards when you arrive, and they'll bring you to me." Her golden eyes lingered on him for a heartbeat longer, then she turned and strode away.

He continued staring at the door for a long time after she'd vanished. Tessa was here on Dust. And she was a citizen of the Mandate. Not just a citizen, but a member of the Inquisitarium. If his grandfather's ghost had watched what had just unfolded his heart would have stopped a second time. Of all the people he had ever known, Tess would have been the absolute last he'd have expected to become an agent of the Golden Emperor.

He raised his glass, but then realized he had no desire to drink any more tonight and set it back down again. He knew he should be happy knowing that Tess was still alive – he'd wondered many times what had happened to her after she'd left their crew – yet there was a sadness starting to gnaw at his insides. More of Zino's Tears might well lead to real tears, and that wasn't a path he wanted to go down right now.

Sighing, he pushed away from the bar.

10

WRAPPED IN HIS THOUGHTS, the streets of Sanctum passed in a vague blur as Kerin made his way back towards Bas Jelaska's spire. Late night snack vendors called out to him from behind makeshift grills as they brushed marinade onto the carapaces of cooking insects, and groups of scantily clad thalani women clucked their tongues in an attempt to lure him over to where they lingered in the puddles of light below hanging spheres.

He ignored them all.

Tessa. There had been a time when he'd been sure that their destiny was to be together. That they'd stand side by side on Drifter's deck as the Streams flowed past, carving a place for themselves in the tributary. He'd imagined them becoming legends in the guild, eclipsing the fame of his grandfather and all of Kerin's other storied ancestors. They would bend the universe to their will, taking what they wanted from life with both hands.

And then that fantasy had been shattered. The memory of that day still sent a pang through his heart. They'd alighted on Heth to stock up on supplies and meet with a merchant who had been looking for a courier to deliver some important documents to a distant system. Tessa had seemed quiet in the days leading up to their arrival, but nothing to suggest what was coming. Then, almost as soon as Drifter's flippers had touched the blue grass of Heth's stables, she'd thrown a ladder over the side and started to descend. He'd been surprised, wondering what was on this world that was so important she couldn't wait for his grandfather to conclude his negotiations with the stablemaster.

Kerin remembered his shock when he'd realized she was carrying a bulging travel bag that must have contained nearly everything she owned. He'd rushed to the edge of the deck, calling down to her as she reached the ground and paused to adjust how the huge bag hung from her shoulders. But she hadn't looked back or responded, setting off towards the crowd of hawkers and merchants clustering on the edge of the stables. He'd started to follow her, but then a hand had fallen on his shoulder.

"Tess is leaving," his grandfather had told him, and the sadness in the old man's voice had shaken Kerin. Up until then, he'd never heard such emotion from his grandfather. Tessa's actions hadn't been a surprise to Calvin. She'd told him, and he'd kept it from Kerin. The bastard.

Ever since that day, Kerin had imagined what might have happened if he'd pulled away from his grandfather and chased Tessa into the crowd. Was it possible he could have convinced her not to leave them?

But he hadn't. He'd watched, numb and broken hearted, as she turned back just before vanishing and stuck out the tip of her tongue. Had she been crying? Somehow, he couldn't remember. Every other detail of that moment was etched diamond-sharp in his memory, except for what emotion she had been showing. Or maybe there hadn't been any tears. Maybe there had only been relief and joy, and the gap in his remembrance was his mind trying to protect him from the truth.

And now they'd been brought together again. Ten thousand systems were spread throughout this branch of the stellar tributary. What was the chance that they would find each other on the same frontier planet on the edge of the Known? It felt like fate. It felt like destiny.

Neither of which Kerin believed in.

A clattering from a nearby alley brought his hand to the hilt of his sword, but it was just one of those damned lizards chasing a rat into the shadows. He relaxed, frowning, and squinted at the silhouettes of the spires picked out against the stars. They were also speckled with glimmering points, but the color was different: the light filling the windows was golden and warm, while the smaller stars beyond the spires gleamed white and sharp. Perhaps Tessa had tired of the cold beauty of the stars and the Streams that bound them together. She'd not been born a streamsurfer and had lived the first eight or so years of her life on the outskirts of a poor city on a backwater world. Tessa had come into his life when she'd tried to pick his grandfather's pocket. Cal had caught her, of course, and she'd thrashed and squirmed like she knew he was going to cut off her hand. Kerin remembered standing there frozen in the bazaar, his jaw hanging open as this whirlwind of snarled red hair tried desperately to free herself from his grandfather's grip. Her terror had been so raw, so real. He'd been about the same age as her and had been travelling with his grandfather for less than a year, and he hadn't known his grandfather well enough to guess what he would do. Back in the slums of Deval, if one of his mother's lovers had caught a thieving urchin there would have been blood spilled. But his grandfather had only waited until she'd exhausted herself, and then as she watched him warily with wild eyes, her body heaving in panic, he'd taken a coin from his pouch and pressed it into her hand. After that he'd let her go, and she'd disappeared between the dusty pavilions like a terrified mouse, clutching the coin to her chest.

At the time, Kerin had been sure he'd never see her again.

But after they'd swum nearly to another system she'd crawled out of a barrel half-stuffed with hardtack, crumbs in her hair. And she'd stayed for seven years, until that day on the blue fields of Heth when she'd abandoned them.

Abandoned him.

He swallowed back a surge of emotion. Something had changed in that moment for all of them. Age had finally seemed to catch up to his grandfather, bowing his shoulders and deepening the lines of his face. He'd been more melancholy afterwards, spending far more time in his solarium watching the Streams. There had been less laughter, and he'd been quicker to anger. It was like the fire inside him had been dampened. Kerin felt that he had never been the same either. His dreams had constricted after Tess had left, becoming far less ambitious. No longer did he imagine becoming one of the legendary streamsurfers. Now it was enough just to keep Drifter swimming between the stars, with enough money in his pouch to sleep in a comfortable bed and enjoy a good meal in port.

The canted apex of Bas Jelaska's spire emerged from the shadowy forest rising in the distance. Would Nala ever abandon him like Tessa had? The mere thought sent a cold shiver through him. He'd be alone, except for Drifter. He imagined wandering through the empty rooms as a Stream surged outside, playing t'skelcha silently by himself in the Nest under the pitying stares of his ancestor's ghosts. The hollow ache in his chest intensified. He couldn't lose Nala. How could he continue if he did?

His legs were burning by the time he reached the ninth tier of the spire. Apparently, the old man and the beast that turned the windlass had already retired to their beds – he should have expected that, given how deep it was into the night. Luckily he hadn't drunk himself into oblivion like he'd planned, because he probably would have passed out somewhere on the endless steps spiraling up the inside of the spire . . . and that was presupposing that he would have even successfully retraced his path through the city to get back here.

He fumbled his way past the doors of the other families living on this level, careful to avoid tripping over the detritus he remembered seeing earlier. Without the daylight trickling through the cracks and holes in the walls the interior of the spire was draped in near-total darkness, although a few large luminescent moths shed just enough radiance that he knew he was going in the right direction. Even still, he had to catch one of the insects and hold it caged and fluttering within his laced fingers to make sure that he'd reached Bas Jelaska's red door with its recognizable flourishes of black metal.

He suspected that those inside were already sleeping, so instead of waking them up by rapping on the door he pushed lightly with his shoulder and was pleasantly surprised to find that Bes Jelaska had left it unlocked. As quietly as possible he slipped inside the darkened home; he was tempted to release the glowing moth he was still holding, but then thought better of it and tossed it back into the hallway before closing the door.

The entrance to the corridor leading deeper into the apartment and presumably to beds was a square of deeper blackness. He decided the idea of stumbling around in the dark where three females were sleeping was a poor one, especially since he knew one of them answered her door holding a crossbow. So he was sleeping out here.

Kerin carefully crept across the room towards the hunched shape of the divan, remembering just before he flopped down to check to make sure that same crossbow was no longer there, nor any of its quarrels. Bas Jelaska must have moved it, as all he felt was frayed fabric, and so he unlaced his boots, unbuckled his sword belt, and laid down with a satisfied sigh.

As soon as his head touched a cushion exhaustion swept over him. It had been a long, overwhelming day. And tomorrow would be even longer. First, he was sure he was going to accept Tessa's invitation to meet in the late morning. The thought filled him with no small amounts of both excitement and trepidation. He was desperate to know what had happened to her in the decade and a half since she'd left Drifter, but also worried that she might have changed beyond recognition. What had he told Nala? People don't change, they only get better at hiding themselves. Was that true? Was the Tessa he had grown up with still there beneath those squirming black markings?

And then after his meeting with Tessa he should go to see the Antiquarian. Who knew how long Sep had before the alvaren artifact completely consumed her? Or would it simply stop at some point? Surely it wouldn't change her entire body to crystal, would it? His imagination conjured up an outlandish scenario where crystallized alvarens were fixed to the fronts of starbeasts like the figureheads on terrestrial sailing boats, ready to smite their enemies with vast amounts of conjured stellar energy.

He shifted, trying to get more comfortable, and as he did so he saw something that sent a spike of fear through him. Looming over the far end of the divan was a formless shape, a blacker shadow cut from the darkness. Immediately he thought of the things he'd glimpsed on the streets of Sanctum, those ancient memories that had somehow been given substance by returning to this world. But maybe this was all in his tired mind. Yes, surely there was nothing really there, he was just being a ridiculous fool—

The shadow moved, coming partway around the end of the divan.

Terror held him fast. Kerin wanted to cry out, to scramble from where he lay, but the only part of him that still seemed capable of moving was his heart. He fought the paralysis, a cold sweat breaking out. This was exactly like what had happened all those years ago; this might have even been the same divan where he'd watched unable to move as a shadow of a child drifted closer . . .

"Are you awake?" A voice asked softly, and Kerin let out a gasp of relief. Sep. Sep was standing in the darkness.

He pushed himself into a sitting position. "Oh. You scared me."

"I'm sorry," she said, settling on the end of the divan.

Kerin rubbed his arms to banish the last lingering chills. "It's fine. Are you all right?"

He heard her fingers running along the fabric. "Yes. Bas Jelaska is kind. She washed me and told me good things."

"That's . . . nice."

"She said I was safe. That no one could hurt me when I was with her. And that you would find a way to fix me."

"I will try my best. I promise you."

Sep was silent for a moment. When she finally spoke again it sounded like she might be struggling not to cry. "I feel different these days. For so long I wanted to talk. The words were inside me, but when I opened my mouth I couldn't make them come out. And now . . . now they spill out so easily, like water."

Kerin was quiet, sensing she had more to say.

"If this wise man makes me like I was before, will I lose my words? Will I fall into myself again and become lost once more?"

Kerin wanted to reach out and touch her, but he was afraid he might accidentally brush against the spreading crystal. "I don't know, Sep. But I don't think what has changed in you will revert to what it was before. And we're here with you. Bas Jelaska and Nala and me. We'll keep you safe."

A shiver of movement came as Sep raised an arm and rubbed it against her face. Kerin heard her sob, and he wished he knew what he should do. Embrace her? Keep saying comforting things? He really was not very good in these moments.

Eventually Sep grew quiet, and he felt her rise from the divan. She started to move away, but then hesitated, and he sensed that she'd turned to face him again.

"You saw it, didn't you?" she said through her sniffles.

"Saw what?"

"After the big light made the rocks fall. We ran to the small street. There was something in the darkness. It saw us, and you saw it back. I did, too. And then it was gone."

He swallowed away the dryness in his throat. "I didn't see anything," he whispered as a wave of prickling numbness washed over him. "There was nothing there. Go back to bed."

The clatter of crockery brought him awake. He sat up on the divan, blinking in the honey-colored light spilling through the large window. Late morning, he thought, and for a brief moment, fear seized him that he had slept past the time he was supposed to call upon Tess, but then he realized that the smoked glass was deepening the color of the sky outside.

"What time is it?" he mumbled, twisting around to where Bas Jelaska was laying out plates heaped with fruit. Sep and Nala were both seated at the table, but they did not seem so interested in this first course. They were both watching the small fireplace, from where Kerin assumed the delicious smell of cooking meat was drifting.

"Morning vespers sounded not too long ago," Bas Jelaska said, using a pair of tongs to flip the sizzling strips. "Ringing out praise for the Golden Emperor."

Kerin subsided back on the divan, relieved. He had time, though he had to eat quickly. Sanctum wasn't a large city, and he thought it wouldn't take him longer than a turning of a glass to find the office of the magistrates. He should try and make himself presentable, though. He was still covered in the filth and sweat from yesterday.

"Come eat," Bas Jelaska said, transferring the crisped meat to a plate as Nala and Sep watched in anticipation.

"Where's your privy?" he asked as he stood and stretched. His head felt pleasantly buoyant – thank the stars that he hadn't indulged as much as he'd intended last night.

"Third door on the left," Bas Jelaska said, gesturing with her tongs at the passage leading deeper into her apartment. Then she slid the plate with the meat onto the table and the girl and the kyrathi fell upon it like starving wolves.

"Save me a little," he begged them as he made his way towards where Bas Jelaska had indicated. There he found a room with a copper pipe that with the turn of a faucet discharged water into a basin, similar to what he had seen on other Mandate worlds. He remembered many years ago helping his grandfather carry buckets of water from the communal well outside the spire, and this was a very welcome improvement. The imperials did take sanitation very seriously.

After scrubbing away several layers of dirt and grime he returned to the main room expecting to find nothing but a glistening puddle of grease where the meat had been. To his surprise there were still a few pieces, though Nala did not seem very happy about this.

"Thank the girl," she said when he raised his eyebrows at her. "She insisted we keep some for you."

He nodded in appreciation at Sep as he slid into a chair and reached for the last of the meat. It tasted deliciously fatty and gamey, and he wondered if this was the khedrin that he hadn't had a chance to try the day before. The loss of that meal and its dark stout accompaniment still stung.

"Are you going to see the Antiquarian today?" Bas Jelaska asked, taking a bite of one of the fruits that had remained untouched in the scramble for the meat. There was an edge to this question that suggested she still thought it was a bad idea.

"In the afternoon," Kerin said. "I think Sep should stay and rest here until then."

Nala peered at him suspiciously. "And what will you be doing?"

He swallowed the last greasy morsel, wishing he had a cup of strong black coffee to wash it down with. "I met an old friend last night at the tavern," he said nonchalantly. "And we're going to catch up."

"Friend?" The disbelief in Nala's voice was slightly hurtful to him, although – he had to admit – not entirely unwarranted.

"Tessa is here on Dust," he said simply, reaching for one of the fruits.

Kyrathi faces were not suited for evoking surprise, but he had been around Nala long enough to know that she was shocked to hear that name. She'd never met Tessa, but the girl had featured prominently in many of his grandfather's stories. Some of which had even been true.

"Truth?" Nala said, and he noticed that her tail had started to twitch. "What are the odds? Why is she here?"

"Pure chance," he said, hating himself even as the lie tumbled out. "She's part of a crew passing through the cluster." If Nala knew Tessa was now a Shroud of the Inquisitarium she would bristle at the thought of him meeting with her, maybe even demand he stay away. And that was something he couldn't do.

The movement of Nala's tail became more pronounced. He suspected that if he was sitting closer to her he would be able to hear a low growl.

"Sep told me something interesting this morning," Bas Jelaska said brightly, obviously trying to break the sudden tension.

"Oh?" Kerin asked, avoiding eye contact with Nala as he took a bite of the wonderfully sour fruit.

"She said she's seen a Shadow."

Kerin coughed, spraying bits of pulp on to the table.

Bas Jelaska's mouth twitched. "And she said she thought you'd seen one as well. In an alley near the Bowery after the Dawn ignited the wraith crystal."

Kerin shook his head. "We were both still reeling from what happened," he explained. Then he paused, realizing what she'd said. "Wait, what's a Shadow?"

"You don't remember?" Bas Jelaska asked, cocking her head to regard him quizzically. "I was woken up by your screams years ago. You had seen one watching you when you first stayed here."

Kerin tried his best to keep his expression free of the coldness filling his chest. "I remember having some bad dreams back then."

"That was what your grandfather told you," Bas Jelaska explained. "Because he didn't want to frighten you. But the Shadows are very real."

Kerin set the half-eaten fruit down, his appetite gone. Was *this* a nightmare? Or was Bas Jelaska playing a joke on him?

"Then what are they?"

The old woman shrugged. "Who knows? There are plenty of theories but little evidence. We know they've been here since the thalani first settled the world, and that they're harmless. Many Dusters go their entire lives without seeing one."

"What about you?" Kerin asked. His breakfast was now sitting like an iron ingot in his stomach.

"Twice," Bas Jelaska said softly. "Once on the street, staring at me from the shade cast by a trader's wagon. I wasn't sure back then if it had been my imagination. The other time was in this very spire, and I have no doubt in what I saw. Twilight had fallen outside, and I had just passed through the entrance down below. It was late summer, I remember, and the air felt swollen. As if the rains were coming, which happens only a few times a year. The light filtering into the spire was a deep purple, but not so dark that I couldn't see the Shadow standing right there, in the center of the spire, bold as day. I swear it was looking right at me. That it *saw* me. And then it was gone."

Kerin stood awkwardly, nearly knocking over his chair. "I have to go," he said, hurrying over to where he'd left *Mercy*. He hoped that none of them could see his hands shaking as he buckled on his sword belt. "Sep, I'll be back after midday. And then we'll go see about your arm."

The office of the magistrates had not been difficult to find. A thalani on the street had waved vaguely to the south-east, and as he moved in that direction he noticed that the ratio of blue skin to white started to change. By the time the first of the gleaming marble buildings appeared there were as many citizens of the Mandate around him as native Dusters.

Most of the imperials he saw flaunted their tattoos, the shifting red designs marking their faces and arms. The more that covered their bodies, the higher the rank they had attained in the empire. And with rank came freedoms. Those in the first rank – the one group entirely bereft of tattoos – only had the freedom to serve. Slaves and those born as indentured servants occupied this lowest rung of Mandate society. The second rank was the freedom to work, the third the freedom to breed. The apex of the pyramid was the tenth rank, the freedom to rule. Only members of the government – exarchs and the most powerful generals and sorcerers – ever achieved this rank. Above and outside this hierarchy existed the Mandate Golden Emperor, his authority absolute and inviolable.

The street leading to the cluster of white-stone buildings had been blocked off, a line of gray-armored soldiers barring the way of non-citizens. Most of the Mandati that were being let through had the tonsured scalps and pale blue robes of bureaucrats. Probably a prudent decision, given that the revolutionaries here had access to Wraith crystals that could topple spires, but it might make his life more difficult.

Kerin approached one of the guards, a large fellow that looked carved of granite, his face a nest of writhing red tattoos. Likely he was only a third or fourth rank citizen, but the lower classes of the empire often tried to exhibit what markings they had achieved prominently. The upper classes, on the other hand, were much more circumspect. Such displays among the aristocracy were considered gauche. Kerin cleared his throat, and the warrior's flat gaze slid to regard him.

"Ho, soldier," he said, touching his forehead with two figures in a Mandati gesture of respect. "I need to get through. I have a meeting in the magistrate's office."

"What's your business?" he asked in obvious boredom.

"It's with a Shroud of the Inquisitarium."

The soldier's eye twitched. Kerin could see disbelief warring with wariness in his face.

"No Shrouds on Dust," he said, but he sounded uncertain, as if he'd heard rumors to the contrary.

Kerin withdrew the small black disc Tessa had given him the night before and held it up.

The effect was instantaneous. With a sharply indrawn breath the soldier stiffened, then looked around frantically. "Commander Hellius," he said loudly, the pitch of his voice higher than it had been a moment ago. A soldier with a golden crest on his helm glanced up from the document he was examining.

"What?" said the officer in annoyance. Then he saw what was in Kerin's hand and visibly paled. After shoving the papers he'd been checking back into the hands of the shocked citizen standing in front of him the commander beckoned for Kerin to come closer.

"Who gave you this?" he hissed, positioning his body so that the token was shielded from the crowd around them. "And bloody stars, hide it. Do you want to cause a panic?"

Kerin hurriedly slipped the disc away again, surprised by the officer's tone. "A Shroud gave it to me last night. Told me to come here today at the tenth bell."

"I know it was a Shroud. Did he or she have a name?"

"She. Tessa."

The officer licked his lips nervously. "I mean her name in the Inquisitarium."

Kerin shrugged. "She didn't tell me that."

"What color was her hair?"

"Red. And she has golden eyes."

The officer took off his crested helm and ran his hand through his greying hair. Then he let out a slow breath. "That's her. Alright, follow me. We'll see if we can find her." He turned back to the soldier Kerin had initially approached, gripping him by the arm. "Verix, you have the command here. Do not tell anyone what you just learned, understood?"

The soldier thumped his chest with a closed fist. "Aye, sir!"

Sighing, the officer donned his helm again and motioned for Kerin to follow him. "I don't know why the Shroud revealed herself to you. But best you keep it to yourself. A lot of folks will get very worried if they find out one of the emperor's knives has come to Dust."

Apparently the rumors about the Shrouds were true, that they were feared even more within the boundaries of the Mandate than outside. How in the abyss could Tessa have become one?

The officer led Kerin up a flight of broad steps and into a forest of white pillars. Clerks and administrators rushed this way and that clutching scrolls and sheaves of parchment to their chests, their footsteps ringing upon the marble floor. A haze of incense like might be found in a temple spiced the air, making Kerin's nose itch.

But where an altar would have been placed in the very center of the building was instead a large desk of gleaming black wood, behind which sat an ancient thalani with deeply etched age veins. He was writing something in a ledger, his sleeve pulled back so that it wouldn't accidentally smear the ink. Red tattoos crawled along his forearm, reaching towards his bony wrist. To his surprise, Kerin realized that this was the first thalani he'd seen that had become a citizen of the Mandate. Unless others had been hiding their markings . . . which would be wise, given the state of affairs on this planet.

They halted in front of the desk, but the clerk didn't set down his stylus until the officer cleared his throat loudly. "This one was summoned by the Shroud," he told the old thalani. "Has a token to prove it."

The clerk gave Kerin a measuring look. One of his purple eyes was covered in a milky film. "Let me see it."

Kerin produced the disc again, and the thalani grunted. "She is waiting for him in the gardens."

The officer nodded sharply and turned away. Kerin fell in behind him as he began to make his way deeper into the building, towards where a slice of the golden sky was visible beyond the marching pillars. There were more soldiers here, standing stiffly at attention with their hands on the long hafts of black-metal halberds. The officer Kerin was following snapped off a clenched fist salute, but the guards continued staring straight ahead without any acknowledgment.

They came to a set of steps leading down into a sunken courtyard garden. Paths set with iridescent stones wended around fanciful statues of Mandati starbeasts and robed men striking heroic poses, with the centerpiece a pool of silvery water. Only a single variety of plant filled the entire garden, a twisting vine spotted with large white blossoms. In the flower beds it had grown together into vast tangles, sending out tendrils that wrapped around every statue and trellis. Kerin had never been to the Mandati home world, but he knew that this flower was ubiquitous there, with entire plains transformed into vast white expanses that lapped against the walls of their cities like living seas.

Tessa stood on the edge of the pool, her hands clasped behind her back as she gazed out at the glass-smooth water. Kerin knew it was her even though she'd traded her red leather for a loose-fitting black tunic and a cloak with the hood drawn up. She was the lone occupant of the garden proper, though a few thalani in the garb of servants were at work pruning the white-blossom tendrils that had spilled from their beds and were attempting to creep up the steps and into the surrounding buildings. Kerin could actually see the vines slowly writhing like blind serpents, unsettlingly similar to the tattoos inked into the flesh of Mandate citizens. The only sounds as he and the soldier walked along the paths were the scuff of their boots on the stones and the slithering of the surrounding tendrils as they knotted together. Kerin couldn't imagine the effort it must take to keep these paths clear.

Tessa turned when she heard them approach. Even though her face was shadowed by her cowl he could see the dark smudges beneath her eyes. It looked like she hadn't slept since he'd seen her at the tavern.

"Good morning, Kerin," she said, then turned to the officer accompanying him. "And you are dismissed, eptian. Return to your command."

"Yes, mistress," the officer said in obvious relief, thumping his chest and turning sharply on his heel.

She watched his hurried retreat for a moment, tucking away a curl of her red hair that had escaped her hood.

"They are all scared of you," Kerin said.

"There are some rather scary stories about Shrouds," she replied, turning to him. "Some true and others not." She reached out towards a nearby copper trellis, and one of the dangling vines uncurled to meet her hand, tightening around her wrist.

"The muxin flower has always been the symbol of the Mandate," she mused, examining her new bracelet as it moved. "Even here on Dust, it wants to expand aggressively. It doesn't realize how inhospitable the conditions truly are for it. Away from this water it would quickly wither and die."

"Sounds like a lesson for the empire."

She pulled her arm back sharply, breaking the vine. For a moment it still clung to her, and then it fell away. "Perhaps." They watched the fragment squirm on the stones for a few moments, until it grew still.

"Tell me about your crewmate. The kyrathi."

Kerin blinked, surprised by the question. "Nala? She's been on Drifter for about eight years now."

"I hear she's a battlemage who served in the ghenabakan navy. That intrigues me. She was lashed to a shriving crystal aboard a dreadnought, I assume? I've never heard of anyone remaining sane after breaking such shackles."

"Now, there's a tale," Kerin said with an affected drawl.

The corner of Tessa's mouth lifted in amusement. That turn of phrase was what his grandfather had always used just before launching into one of his stories. So she hadn't completely forgotten about her time as a streamsurfer.

"Tell me."

For a moment he hesitated, slightly annoyed by the note of command in her voice. Then he set that feeling aside – she was clearly accustomed to authority. He supposed he could forgive her for forgetting that he was not a citizen of the Mandate.

His thoughts returned to the day they'd found Nala. The memories were tinged with a sense of unreality, as if what had happened had been nothing more than a vivid dream. "We were making a swim to one of the far-flung systems out among the Embers. I don't even remember what we were delivering. Golems, maybe, to work in the asteroid mines. Anyway, we exited the Stream and before we even realized what we were seeing Drifter started panicking." Despite so many years having passed he couldn't hold back a little shiver of dread. "The Stream's mouth had emptied into an asteroid swarm where the prospectors had set up their operation. But it was hard to tell that's what it once was, as all those floating rocks had been bound together in a vast web."

"The Weaver in Darkness," Tessa murmured.

"Yes. And it wasn't just those asteroids. The silk filled the entire system, stretching all the way to the star at its center. Not that very much of that sun could be seen, though, as it had been completely cocooned in layers of gray threads. Only a tiny amount of radiance was seeping through, which had plunged the rest of the system into perpetual twilight."

"I'm surprised you didn't turn and flee immediately. What if the Weaver had still been lurking there?"

"Drifter realized fairly quickly that the Weaver was long gone. I still wanted to jump back into the Streams, but you know my grandfather. One of the great legends of the tributary had been there. He couldn't resist having a look around."

Tessa snorted and shook her head. "Of course."

"We didn't get very far. Apparently a ghenabakan dreadnought had had the tremendous ill-fortune of exiting the Stream while the Weaver was still there. We found the withered carcass of the starbeast bound to an asteroid, and despite my very strident objections Cal insisted we have a look inside."

"Like a cat with his curiosity," Tessa muttered.

"He'd apparently always wanted to set foot in a dreadnought." Kerin was sure Tessa understood why. The ghenabakan starbeasts were unique in the stellar tributary, as instead of carrying or pulling structures their streamsurfers actually lived within the great creatures in tunnels and chambers carved from their rocky flesh.

"And there you found the kyrathi."

"We *only* found the kyrathi," Kerin corrected her. "There was no sign of any of the ghenabakans or their slaves. Even the other battlemages who had been yoked to the same shriving crystal were gone. It was just her, still holding on to the crystal, nearly dead from dehydration. The way she was staring at nothing, I thought her mind had been shattered, but when my grandfather touched her she started screaming."

"Did she remember what happened?"

"Nothing. The last memory she had was of a rush of cold air as the dreadnought slipped from the Stream. Then blackness until we brought her back to herself."

"Probably better she can't remember," Tessa admitted. "Did you find anything else in that system?"

"We fled as soon as we got her aboard Drifter. Another stream-surfer was traveling with us back then, and while we'd been exploring the corpse of the dreadnought he'd noticed something strange about the cocooned star. If you stared long enough you could see what looked like hundreds of enormous shadows moving within it. After he pointed that out to us we decided it was time to leave."

Tessa pursed her lips. "Do you know what those were? Because I think I do."

Kerin nodded. "Later we heard the stories about how the Weaver in Darkness lays its eggs within stars, and then after they hatch its spawn eat their way out, leaving only an empty stellar husk behind. I'm not sure if that's truly what those things were, but I'm glad we didn't stick around to find out."

Tessa was silent for a long moment. "You know," she finally said slowly, "my instinct is to assume you're carrying on Cal's tradition by spinning an elaborate tale only slightly flavored by the truth."

"It's actually almost entirely true."

"Almost?"

"There were no baby Weavers. We were just terrified after traipsing through a dead starbeast and decided we'd had more than enough of that system."

Tessa sighed. "Then why not just say that?"

"Because the . . . embellished version was the story Cal told all his guild friends. I heard it so many times it became more real than what actually happened."

"Your whole family is mad, do you know that?"

"Is that why you left?"

"It certainly made the decision easier."

Kerin smiled ruefully. He'd missed Tessa so much.

"Why did you leave?" he asked suddenly. "I have to know."

She turned away, lapsing into silence, the only sound the sibilant hiss of the crawling vines. Finally her lips parted, and she seemed to be gathering herself to say something.

"I—"

"Shroud!"

Kerin whirled around as a woman's angry voice sliced through the tranquility of the garden.

"Oh, bloody stars," he heard Tessa murmur to herself.

The woman from the plaza was rushing down the steps, her iridescent dress swirling and the wings protruding over her shoulders trembling with what looked to Kerin to be agitation. Behind her hurried her three remaining k'zar bodyguards; they all appeared somewhat battered, as one walked with a pronounced limp, another's arm was in a sling, and the last had a livid scar curving down the side of his face. The woman, on the other hand, seemed to have escaped the explosion yesterday without a scratch.

"Don't say anything," Tessa whispered as the woman stormed through the gardens towards them. It was probably his imagination, but it almost looked to Kerin like the flowers shied away from her passage.

"Shroud!" the woman repeated when she reached them, crossing her arms across her chest and glowering at Tessa. "What are you doing here?"

Tessa regarded the irate woman calmly. "Mistress Dierdra," she said, inclining her head slightly. "I am gathering my thoughts. The garden helps me to think."

The woman glanced around in disbelief, as if this was a ridiculous claim. Her gaze briefly alighted on Kerin, but then moved on, dismissing him as irrelevant.

"You should be doing, not thinking. You should be out there" — she jabbed a finger at the spires rising beyond the Mandate buildings — "not in here. I nearly died! I lost one of my k'zars, and you know how hard they are to replace!"

Tessa let the waves of the woman's anger break against her, and

Kerin was impressed she managed to maintain her placid expression. "What would you have me do?" she asked, in what sounded like genuine curiosity.

The woman's insect wings thrummed the air. "Ask questions, kick down doors. Torture someone! I don't know, you're the one trained for this! If all the Shrouds were as useless as you the empire would have long ago collapsed!"

Kerin thought he saw a slight hardening in Tessa's expression. The woman might have noticed this as well, as her anger seemed to have subsided a little when next she spoke.

"We just need to be aggressive. My father agrees with me about this. The more incidents there are without bringing anyone to justice, the more people will think us weak."

"We are getting closer. Their carelessness will rise with their confidence. We must be patient."

"And what if while we're patiently waiting for them to make a mistake they kill my father? *Me*?" Kerin half expected her to stamp her foot in petulant rage, but instead her wings flickered even more forcefully. "Drag someone important out of their home! Someone who is *suspected* of harboring separatist sympathies! Make an example of them publicly. We need to show that we are the rulers of this planet!"

"Your advice will be taken under consideration," Tessa said coolly.

"Under consideration? You *will* do what I command!"

"Remember your rank, Dierdra. You do not have the authority to command me."

The woman sneered, shoving her finger in Tessa's face. "I know how the empire works, Shroud. Unlike you, *I* was born into it. Born to a man who has attained the freedom to rule. The freedom to command you. And don't forget *I* have his ear."

With that she whirled around, her long dress shimmering. With her back stiff and head held high she strode away, her k'zar guards falling in behind her. The wings on her back were beating so frantically that Kerin wouldn't have been surprised at all to see her briefly lift from the ground.

Tessa didn't say anything until the woman had vanished into the building.

"That was actually more pleasant than I was expecting."

"She's the exarch's daughter?"

"Oh, yes."

"I saw her yesterday in the plaza just before the spire fell. She didn't look happy then, either."

Tessa's golden eyes moved to him. He thought he saw mild surprise that this wasn't his first time seeing the exarch's daughter.

"She's never happy," Tessa said with a sharp shake of her head. "Growing up in extreme privilege seems to render some people eternally dissatisfied."

The feeling of something touching his leg made Kerin jump. He glanced down to find that one of the vines had crept onto the paths and had snared his ankle, so he stepped back quickly, ripping himself free.

Tessa brought her boot down on the squirming tendril, grinding it into the stones. "Let's go somewhere else. I hate this place."

She led him into the only building abutting the gardens that did not have soaring pillars or imposingly vast open spaces. It was squat and functional, seemingly not to have been designed for impressing visitors. There were no ornamental flourishes decorating the walls or doorways, no bright frescoes of krakens or shining figures staring down from the ceiling. Tonsured clerks were absent in the narrow corridors, replaced by soldiers in the dark gray armor of the legions. This was the barracks, Kerin assumed. Most of the men they passed did not take heed of them, save for those more heavily tattooed and wearing gold-crested helmets. These officers stiffened when they saw Tessa, thumping their chests even as they averted their eyes. Apparently the knowledge that a Shroud had come to Dust hadn't trickled down to the common soldiers, but their officers had been informed.

A wooden clattering swelled as they approached a wide doorway with a pair of crossed stone swords upon its lintel. The space beyond sprawled for a thousand paces or more, open to the golden sky, the floor nothing but churned earth. Squads of soldiers were training here in groups of six, shuffling their sandaled feet as they practiced moved together. They followed a clearly scripted pattern, raising the bucklers strapped to their arms while those next to them swung their short, broad-bladed swords.

"The Mandate's legions are highly regimented," Tessa said, raising her voice over the bellowing of shouted commands and the clash of practice weapons as they moved between the drilling cohorts. "A single legion is six thousand soldiers, but the entire army is built on the strength of these six-men squads. They train together every day, until they fight seamlessly as a single unit. Ten of these together are under the command of an eptian, the officers with gold crests on their helmets."

The precision with which the small groups of soldiers moved and fought impressed Kerin. He could see that granting autonomy to these squads would be beneficial, especially if they could retain their discipline and cohesion when integrated with a larger force. But what were he and Tessa doing here? Was she making some point about the Mandate's military strength? He didn't need convincing that the empire was among the more formidable powers of the tributary.

They traversed the training grounds until they came to where a grizzled old soldier was overseeing a half-dozen duels. The combatants here seemed to be officers, with crests of various colors adorning their helms and their cuirasses embellished with intricate designs. Tessa went over to a barrel from which many identical sword hilts were emerging and drew forth a wooden practice blade. The older soldier watching the duels started when he caught sight of her, his face darkening, but then recognition replaced outrage and his color drained away. Tessa ignored the man entirely as she tossed the sword to Kerin and pulled out another for herself. She studied it critically and then took a few swings to test the balance.

"Longer than what I prefer but shorter than *Mercy*, so we'll be equally disadvantaged," she said, running a finger along the nicked and dented edge.

"Excuse me?"

She pointed the tip of the wooden sword at his chest. "Let's see if you've been keeping up with your bladework."

"We're going to fight?" he asked, surprised.

Tessa leaned in closer to poke him lightly. "Practice. Just like old times."

"We never used to train together," he said dumbly. "Grandfather didn't allow it."

"Really? I must have misremembered," she said, grinning at his confusion. "Now, prepare yourself."

Unsure what Tessa was playing at, Kerin fumbled with his sword belt and laid *Mercy* down in the dirt. His grandfather had never invited Tessa to the lessons where he had taught Kerin how to fight, and she had likewise shown little interest. But she had apparently learned in the years since she'd left Drifter, as she was carefully laying down two swords that had been hidden beneath her cloak. Both were short and thin bladed, with gleaming golden hilts. On one the pommel was carved into a roaring lion and the other a snarling dragon. She shrugged off her cloak and shook her head, which sent her red curls tumbling down her back.

Kerin sensed the attention of the nearby dueling officers, quick glances out of the corner of their eyes as they parried and thrust. The older soldier must have likewise noticed this, as he let loose a string of invectives and creative threats that resulted in suddenly much fiercer clattering.

Tessa stepped away from where she'd piled her belongings and beckoned for Kerin to join her. He did so with some trepidation, still unsure why she wanted this. His grandfather had been renowned in the Guild for his swordsmanship, and Kerin had surpassed him. He had height and strength on Tessa, as well as experience. Kerin shook his head at the absurdity of it all: a decade and a half apart, and within a day they were crossing swords, albeit ones made of wood.

"Are you ready?" Tessa asked, settling into a guard position.

Kerin raised his sword, mirroring her stance. "Yes."

She lunged forward with startling speed, and Kerin just managed to catch the blade with his own and turn it aside. Her recovery was nearly instantaneous, and he desperately warded away her flickering sword as he gave ground. Nebulas, she was fast! He gritted his teeth and tried to seize back some of the initiative, but he was far too focused on defending to launch a counterattack. The tip of her sword slipped past his guard to thump him in the ribs. He winced, stumbling, and the next blow caught him in the wrist.

"Ah!" he cried, the hilt dropping from his numb fingers.

Tessa took a quick step back and lowered her blade. He stared at her with wide eyes, rubbing his wrist, then bent to retrieve his sword from the dirt. Well, that was humbling. Kerin had always fancied himself an expert swordsman, and nothing in his life up to this point had disabused him of that notion. He'd killed brigands and pirates and sent cocky streamsurfers sprawling bloodied in the alleyways of a dozen ports. But Tessa had made him feel like a child. She'd moved with a flowing grace that had looked almost like a dance.

"Again?" she asked, pulling up her long sleeves. The red tattoos writhed, as if excited by what had just happened.

"I suppose so," Kerin muttered, taking a few practice cuts to test his throbbing wrist.

Tessa crooked a smile, bringing her sword up. The tattoos on her forearms darkened, a momentary flicker, and this was followed by scattered gasps from the soldiers. They were all watching now, even the old captain, their swords dangling at their sides.

"You're showing them what you are," Kerin said, not yet readying himself.

Tessa nodded slightly. "Shrouds are feared and respected. By revealing that I've come to Dust, I am sending a very clear message that this world has the attention of the emperor. The destruction yesterday convinced me to emerge from the shadows." Her gaze traveled between the silent soldiers.

"I wondered why you displayed yourself publicly in the tavern last night."

"That was for the locals, and by extension the Dawn. *This* is to improve the army's morale."

"So you're saying I was right to go easy on you?" Kerin said finally, lifting his sword into a ready position.

"Yes, thank you so—"

Before she finished speaking he attacked, hoping to overwhelm her before she was fully prepared. To his surprise, though, she expected just such a ploy, and her sword leapt smoothly to meet his. Still, the force of his slash sent her back a step, and he pressed forward, putting all his strength behind each blow. He felt a little surge of triumph as he saw faint lines appear at the corners of her refashioned eyes. Tessa might be able to draw upon some well of Shroud training, but he was still much stronger, and she could only hold him off for so long. He grinned savagely, his own swordplay becoming wilder as he sensed her defenses crumbling.

There! He saw the opening and lunged, the blunted tip of his blade thrusting towards her unprotected chest. He'd knocked her sword aside a moment ago, and even with her preternatural quickness there was no way she could intercept the strike.

Then she spun away, and his sword passed where she had been a heartbeat before. He stumbled forward, off balance, and before he could turn to follow Tessa her sword rapped the inside of his knee hard. His leg collapsed, sending him sprawling into the dirt. For a moment he could only lie there, shocked at the speed with which he'd lost again, pain radiating from where she'd struck him.

"Are you all right?"

With a groan he rolled onto his back. Tessa loomed over him, silhouetted by the golden sky. Not far away the officers who had been dueling were staring slack-jawed.

He blinked against the brightness of the day. "My leg hurts. And my pride."

She grunted a laugh and held out her hand for him to take. "Don't feel bad," she said as he let her help him to his feet. "The Inquisitarium employs the finest weapon masters in the Mandate." She paused, then added: "And truth be told, the chimericists have done a little more than just give me new eyes. The sinews and tendons of some very large and very dangerous predators have replaced what I was born with."

Kerin frowned. It sounded like they'd fashioned her into a killer. Was that what she wanted when she'd walked away from Drifter all those years ago?

"Now, if you'll excuse me," she continued, "I haven't finished giving the men something to talk about." She turned to the old soldier who had been overseeing the training officers. "Captain," she said, brushing back a lock of sweaty hair that had fallen across her face. "Who are the three best swordsmen here?"

The soldier blinked watery eyes. He looked as stunned as the rest by the display Tessa had just put on. "This lot, Mistress? Probably him and him and him." The three men he'd pointed out paled noticeably.

"Excellent. I will spar with them now."

The old man swallowed, the bulge in his neck bobbing. "Uh, certainly. Which would you like to duel first?"

Tessa gave a throaty chuckle, her sword slicing a quick pattern in the air. "Oh, you misunderstand me, captain."

11

THE FLOOD of change that had washed over Dust in the years since last he had been here had seemingly left the Old Market untouched. Crowds surged among a labyrinth of dusty tents, hawkers at the open flaps inviting passersby to peruse the goods within, and greasy smoke rose from the grills of street food sellers to smear the sky of beaten gold. Kerin half-expected to see his eight year old self wandering wide-eyed through the open-air bazaar, clutching at his grandfather's hand.

"The Antiquarian is here?"

Kerin understood why Nala sounded so dubious. This did not look like where a specialist in Elder Race artifacts would set up shop. Cheap tin pots and pans festooned the outer wall of one tent, while in front of another a silver-bearded thalani swept out his arms to encompass the piles of dried nuts and figs heaped on a table. The market was an assault on the senses, and he felt dizzied by the swirling chaos.

A plump thalani matron jostled Kerin as she pushed past him, and he winced as her elbow found his bruised ribs.

Nala noticed his flinch of pain, her eyes narrowing. "What exactly did you get up to this morning? You look like you got trampled by a herd of tamana."

"Nothing," he muttered, turning away from the kyrathi to try and find Sep. She was drifting between the stalls and tents, pausing occasionally to examine the wares on display.

Nala snorted. "Fine. Nothing," she said, and moved closer to where Sep was goggling at a collection of spinning tops that appeared to have no intention of ever stopping.

Kerin's fingers probed his side, trying to tell if anything was cracked. His Anathema blood would deal with his injuries quickly even if a rib or two had been broken, but in that worst-case scenario he would be limited at least for a few days.

Not that he should be swinging a sword anyway. A hot flush of shame rose in him at the memory of how easily Tessa had beaten him. His grandfather had been a famously good swordsman, after all, and Kerin was better. But Tessa had toyed with him like he had been a novice. The thumps she had given him ached, but it was the wounds to his pride that would take a lot longer to heal.

The memory of this morning was already tinged by unreality. If his body wasn't throbbing with the legacy of the duel he might have convinced himself it had all been just a strangely vivid dream.

He returned to himself as Nala approached him again. The kyrathi was holding a blue confection of spun sugar piled atop what looked like a pinecone.

"Come back to this planet, streamsurfer," she said, her tongue darting out to lick the treat. "And tell us what we're supposed to be looking for."

Kerin pushed down the emotions Tess had stirred up earlier. He might revisit them later . . . but more likely they'd just lie there festering in some dark corner of his mind. That was the best way to deal with such things, another lesson imprinted on him from his grandfather. Introspection should only be attempted when armed with a strong drink, and abandoned as soon as any uncomfortable truths swam up from the depths.

"As I remember, the Antiquarian's shop wasn't in the crowded part of the market. Let's find our way deeper and then explore. We're looking for a large tent painted with red eyes."

"Hmm," Nala grunted as she surveyed the crowds in front of them. She took another lick of the sugar and then gestured with the delicacy towards a less-trafficked path wending away from the central area of the market. "Let's start over there."

The outskirts of the Old Market were an entirely different experience. No jovial merchants loudly proclaimed the quality of their goods from outside tents, no sweets-sellers or snack-peddlers cluttered the way, no rag-wrapped beggars sprawled in the dust with trembling arms outstretched. There were also no browsers here, with the few cloaked thalani he saw hurrying through the twisting side streets to eventually vanish within tents and pavilions decorated by esoteric symbols. Kerin caught a few glimpses when patrons disturbed the hanging flaps, but he saw little in the shadow-draped interiors. He had his suspicions about what was being sold, though, as from one he caught the unmistakable whiff of glimmer.

They explored the recesses of the market for what seemed like several glass turnings without success, every question he asked about the Antiquarian met with confusion or thin-lipped hostility. He thought he saw a flicker of recognition in the faces of several of the thalani, but none were willing to offer up more than vague gestures that did little to narrow their search. It wasn't until they had passed into the shadows thrown by the spires fringing the edges of the market that Nala suddenly drew in her breath sharply.

A moment later he saw what she had already seen: a sprawling tent pressed up against the rock wall rising behind it, its cream-colored fabric decorated with stylized red eyes of many shapes and sizes.

"Is that it?" she asked, and Kerin nodded. "Doesn't seem like this Antiquarian gets much business."

"I don't think he's interested in casual shoppers," Kerin replied, slowly approaching the large tent. Nala was right, though. This area of the market seemed abandoned, with not a single living soul visible. The nearby tents were dark and shadowed, and none had been set up within a dozen paces of the Antiquarian's shop, almost as if they were shying away from it. Only the eye-adorned tent had a thin trickle of light escaping from between its closed flaps, though there were no sounds coming from within.

Kerin glanced at Nala and Sep and found them both looking at him expectantly. Sighing, he strode forward, pushing into the tent.

And stopped in surprise.

This was not what he'd remembered. Kerin had been expecting the vast space inside to be cluttered with the detritus of the past: broken statues looted from distant ruins, mysterious machines scarred by rust, and chests and tables covered with various sorts of strange objects. He had a distinct memory of wandering among artifact-choked shelves as the dust glimmering in the gloom made his nose itch.

But it was all gone. The tent had been emptied of all these wonders except for a single black desk pushed up against the far wall. Tentatively he edged into the darkened space. It looked like the Antiquarian had closed up shop, but why had his pavilion remained?

"Well, this was a waste of time," Nala said from behind him, then sniffed. "Wait. There's a smell here. Some strange musk..."

"Look," Sep said, and Kerin turned to see that the girl was pointing at the desk.

He squinted, then stepped closer to see better what she'd noticed. As he did this, a light crystal hanging from the ceiling flickered to life, sending the shadows scurrying.

Something was seated behind the desk. It was small, barely tall enough to fold its furred red arms on the polished black in front of it, and even still Kerin suspected it was sitting on a pile of somethings, as the chair looming behind it looked human-sized. The creature wasn't moving, and as Kerin crept closer he wondered if it had been stuffed. But no, he could sense the regard in its glittering black eyes.

This was a creature he had never encountered before in the

stellar tributary. Its face was long and vulpine, and a small pair of spectacles perched on the end of its nose. Over its red fur it wore a green vest done up with golden buttons, a handkerchief poking from its breast pocket. The fox-man – and Kerin was fairly sure it was a male – had kept its claws laced in front of it as Kerin approached, staring at him silently. What in the abyss had this thing been doing here sitting in the dark?

"Is that the Antiquarian?" hissed Nala in a low whisper. Kerin couldn't be sure, but he thought the fox-man's whiskers might have twitched at the kyrathi's question.

"No," Kerin replied softly. "He was a lot more . . . human. Or he looked human, at least. Sort of."

The fox-man watched this muttered exchange without apparent interest. Did this thing speak Trade? Was it one of the Younger Races he was unfamiliar with, or a pet that someone had dressed up in a strangely formal outfit?

"Ah, hello," Kerin said when he finally stood before the desk. He towered over the small creature, and it tilted its head slightly as it continued to regard him with placid equanimity. "We are looking for the Antiquarian."

The moment stretched. Kerin tried to be patient, wondering if he was waiting on a response from a dumb animal. Nala gave a long sigh of exasperation, and Kerin was certain he knew who would break first in this unfathomable stand-off.

He was wrong.

Stiff fabric rustled as the fox-man unfolded its claws and leaned over slightly to pull open a drawer. With some effort, it lifted a large book bound in cracked black leather and laid it on the desk, then followed this by placing beside the tome a silver inkwell and an iridescent writing quill. Small claws found where a strip of red cloth had been placed between the pages, and the creature opened the book to that spot. It was blank, no writing or illustrations, just an empty white expanse.

The fox-man took up the quill again and dipped it into the inkwell, then peered at Kerin through its spectacles.

"Name?"

Its voice was high and reedy, with an accent that sounded archaic. Kerin glanced over at Nala, who shrugged.

"Uh, Kerin thon Talisien."

It might have been his imagination, but he thought he saw the fox-man hesitate ever so slightly. Then it sat forward and began to write, the sound of the quill scratching the paper unnaturally loud. Kerin frowned as he watched it work. Even though what it was writing was upside-down to him, he was still fairly sure it was just gibberish. No written language looked like a child's doodling.

The fox-man finished whatever it was doing with a flourish, set down the quill, and shut the book so forcefully that the crack made Sep gasp in surprise. A moment later the wooden drawer rasped open and the book disappeared, along with the writing implements. When the desk was clear, the creature removed its spectacles, polished them briefly with its handkerchief, and settled them once again on its long snout. Its claws clicked as it laced them together.

"Master will come to you," it said.

The feeling of drifting through a dream was strong. "Do you know when?"

The fox-man did not reply, but its lips curled back slightly to reveal sharp little fangs.

Kerin wasn't sure what that meant. Was it amused? Angry? "Do you mean tomorrow? A fortnight? It's just that what we need to discuss with your master is rather time-sensitive. Perhaps I could—"

"When ready, Master comes. If child is dead, much condolences."

Kerin blinked. How had the creature known about Sep? He looked over at the former pain conduit, who was staring wide eyed at the fox-man.

"I . . . see," Kerin said slowly. "Well, how will he contact us? Do you need to know where we're staying?"

"Master come to you," the fox-man repeated, and this time its words were flavored by what Kerin took to be annoyance. "If nothing else, go. This one very busy."

"Yes, clearly," Nala murmured beside him. The fox-man's whiskers trembled, and it shifted its liquid black eyes to the kyrathi.

"Very well," Kerin said taking Nala by the arm and steering her towards the tent's entrance. He pulled aside the flap so that Sep and the kyrathi could exit, turning back to the strange creature just as the light crystal above them sputtered and died. The last thing he saw before the darkness rushed in again was the fox-man sitting motionless behind the desk, its little paws neatly folded. Then he shook his head and followed his companions outside.

They returned to a busier section of the market, one dedicated to toys and various other small curios. Kerin thought he knew his way out from here, but he wasn't in any great rush to return to Bas Jelaska's spire. Sep seemed enthralled by the goods on display, pausing to examine the cleverly fashioned and luridly painted puppets dangling from one awning, then with a sharp indrawn breath rushing over to where glittering crystals in a panoply of colors had been laid out on a velvet blanket.

Kerin enjoyed watching the girl browse, with her childlike expressions of wonder whenever something new caught her eye. He walked slowly a few paces behind her, wondering idly what their next course of action should be. He'd been hoping that by the time they'd left the Antiquarian's tent the alvaren weapon would no longer be part of Sep, but he supposed that such an outcome had always been wishful thinking.

"So, do we just wait?"

Kerin understood the frustration in Nala's tone, but all he could do was shrug helplessly. "What else can we do?"

The kyrathi's tail thumped his leg, lashing about in irritation. "It's not what you want to hear, but what about the mixmages? The Mandati are the best in the tributary at manipulating flesh."

Kerin sighed, turning away from Sep as she scurried between merchant stalls and facing the kyrathi. "You know we can't do that."

A low rumbling started deep within Nala before she spoke. "Even when that thing on her arm reaches her shoulder? What happens when it starts to consume her vital organs, or her throat? When it's on the verge of *killing* her?"

Kerin felt his own anger start to rise. Nala wasn't being fair. Of course he wanted to save Sep, but how could they do that if it meant this starbeast killing weapon tumbling into the Golden Emperor's arms? "Look, Nala—"

He hesitated as the kyrathi brought her paw up sharply to quiet him. Her amber eyes were thinned to slits as she peered past Kerin.

"What?" he asked, twisting around. All he saw were tents and stalls and a steady stream of shoppers.

"Where's the girl?" Nala hissed.

Nebulas, she was right. Sep had vanished. Could she have disappeared into one of the tents, enticed within by the wares displayed outside? Surely if she'd been kidnapped he'd have noticed . . . or a large swath of the market would at this moment be a smoking ruin.

"Sep?" he called, going over to where he'd last seen her. A pair of young thalani browsing the assortment of crystals glanced at him incuriously.

"Did you see a young foreign girl?" he asked them, but they shrugged and turned away.

Kerin pushed his head through the crystal merchant's tent flap, but inside was only a jumble of boxes and an obscenely fat man bent over a worktable examining a chunk of unpolished green stone with a jeweler's loupe. The fellow looked up in surprise, his eyes magnified by the large lenses strapped to his face, and after muttering an apology Kerin quickly withdrew.

Where had she gone? Could she have just wandered off and gotten lost?

"Hey, *kalaman*."

The voice was coming from around the edge of the tent and pitched low enough that only Kerin could hear. With his hand on the hilt of his sword, he stepped closer so he could see into the narrow space. A thalani man was squatting there, dressed in rags, his hood pulled low so that his features were shadowed. Kerin could tell that the stranger was fairly young, as the arms emerging from the frayed sleeves were not etched deeply with age veins, though they were pocked by the evidence of a struggle with some disease.

Had the beggar been talking to him?

"Yes, you, *kalaman*. Gots something to tell you."

Kerin moved to fill the mouth of the small alley. He spared a glance over his shoulder and caught Nala's eye, then beckoned her over with a jerk of his head.

"Friend with a catter," the man said with a low whistle. "Rare as blue diamonds, that."

"You want to say something to me?" Kerin asked, coming closer to loom over the huddled ragman.

"Aye," the beggar said, then coughed wetly. Kerin took an instinctive step back. Perhaps the plague scars were more recent than he had first thought.

"Your girl, yes? You lost her."

Kerin narrowed his eyes, peering into the labyrinth of fabric walls behind the thalani. "I did," he said, his sword hissing as he slowly drew forth a hand-span of *Mercy's* strange blade.

The beggar raised his arms in mock terror. When his sleeves slipped away more of the ravaging from whatever disease had afflicted him was revealed. "Oh, please, don't hurt me!" the thalani cried, and then rasped a chuckle.

"What happened to her?" Kerin asked, not letting go of the hilt or pushing his sword back into its scabbard.

Nala appeared beside him, her fur brushing his arm in the alley's close confines. "Kerin, who is this creature? He smells sick."

"He claims to know what happened to Sep." Kerin turned back to the beggar. "You saw something? Did you see where she went?"

"The girl found some friends," the thalani said, sketching a random pattern in the dust with a blackened finger.

"Well, we'd like to meet these friends, too," Nala growled, and Kerin felt his Anathema blood stir as jade fire flared around one of the kyrathi's paws.

"Ah, a catter battlemage! Rarer and rarer." The beggar pushed himself to his feet with some effort, nearly toppling into the wall of one of the tents. He pressed his diseased hands together and bobbed his head obsequiously. "But your friend, yes? Come."

Kerin met Nala's eyes briefly as the thalani turned and began to hobble away from them. With a disgusted sigh the kyrathi extinguished the aether she had summoned, then moved to follow the beggar. Kerin fell in beside her, preparing himself for whatever they might find. Here where the tents from several shopping streets came together was a twisting tangle of cloth alleyways, and the perfect spot for an ambush. He couldn't help but imagine blades slashing at them through the tent walls.

Kerin stiffened as they turned onto the main passage running behind the tents. It was not empty. The diseased beggar was hobbling towards where three others were waiting, dragging his scabrous feet in the dust. Relief washed over Kerin when he saw Sep was one of them, absorbed in a shimmering egg-shaped crystal twisting on the end of a silver filament. A thalani in stark white robes, his cowl thrown back to reveal a young, handsome face, was holding the crystal out for her to take. Slowly she did just that, her fingers closing about the braided silver string as she stared into the crystal's depths. When she took it, the man smiled and turned away from her to face Kerin and Nala. The other stranger had been staring at them since they emerged, his expression far less friendly. He looked like a thug, with mismatched armor and scars crisscrossing his bald blue head. They almost seemed ritualistic, and Kerin wondered if he would recognize something about the man's allegiances if he was more familiar with the criminal underbelly of Sanctum.

The beggar staggered a few steps closer to the strangers and then collapsed in the dust with a pained wheezing. The grinning robed thalani and the scowling thug ignored him, keeping their attention fixed on Nala and Kerin.

The kyrathi's tail brushed his leg, and he glanced down to her paw as she quickly signed three words in guild cant.

Boy. Mage. Powerful.

Not great news, but wouldn't this fellow be surprised if he tried to throw his sorcery around. Kerin loved the expression on the face of cocky mages when their aether was swallowed up by his Anathema blood.

"Ho, strangers," the young thalani said, pressing his open palm to his chest. "A pleasure to meet you. M'name's Rel, and my friend here is Kapper." Kerin took note that he didn't introduce the beggar sprawled near his feet. "You all must be with the girl." He jerked his head in her direction, but he kept his gaze locked with Kerin. "Sep, these folks here those you were talkin' about?"

Sep dragged her eyes from the crystal to briefly acknowledge Kerin and Nala with a nod, then returned her attention to its glittering facets. Kerin sniffed, his blood stirring. The air was flavored with subtle puissance, and Kerin thought this sorcery was leaking from the crystal Sep held. A glamor of some kind, he suspected, to hold her mind in thrall.

"What do you want?" Kerin asked flatly, crossing his arms. "Why take her away from the market?"

The young thalani's eyes widened. "Take her away? Nah, *kalaman*. The girl liked the crystals, so I offered to show her a special one. Happened to want to talk t'you, too. But not out there with so many watching. Quiet place for a quiet talk."

"You wanted to talk to me?"

"Aye, Kerin," the mage said. "Ripples been spreading ever since your turtle touched Dust."

He knew his name. That was disconcerting. "What do you mean?"

Rel held up three fingers, each encircled by a ring of thick black metal. "Well, let's recount. First you were there in the Bowery when the spire came down. Folks remember seein' a couple of pale offworlders with a catter sitting under the tree. Sort of thing that sticks in people's minds, you understand." One of the fingers vanished. "Then that night you were approached by a Shroud down at the Whimsy. She seems mighty friendly with you, by all accounts." Another finger disappeared, and the thalani waggled the lone remaining digit. "Now, today, you go lookin' for the old man, that

Antiquarian, after a jaunt over to the offices of the magisters in the morning." The mage stared at his closed fist and slowly shook his head. "Nebulas, *kalaman*, you didn't just bump your head on a hornet's nest. You went through the forest with a stick knockin' em from the branches."

Kerin had grown progressively colder as the mage had listed off what he'd been doing over the last few days. This encounter certainly wasn't random. They'd been watching him. But who were 'they'?

His suspicions were strong enough that he decided to fire an arrow off into the dark. "You're with the Black Dawn?"

Rel's grin widened while the thug's scowl deepened. "Clever!" the young thalani cried, clapping his hands together. "Aye, we come here representin' the Dawn."

"What do you want with us?"

"Well, for one thing we'd like to know what you an' the Shroud got to talkin' about."

Kerin's blood suddenly began to burn a little hotter. Sorcery was thickening the air as the mage wove some spell, likely to discern if Kerin told the truth, or perhaps to compel an honest answer. There were many flavors of magic, and Kerin knew this mage walked a Path about as far from Nala's battle sorcery as one could get. This was something far more subtle, likely rooted in illusion and deception and telepathy. Mind magic.

But of course the sorcery slid off him like water poured on glass, unable to get its hooks into his brain. A shiver of pained surprise went through the mage, his grin vanishing. Beside him the thug stirred, concern deepening the lines on his face.

Kerin pretended like he hadn't noticed anything. "I knew the Shroud before she joined the Mandate. She was a streamsurfer, an old crewmate of mine, and a friend. We were just catching up."

Rel swallowed, blinking away his discomfort. "A friend? Do Shrouds have friends, Kapper?"

"No friends," the scarred thalani rumbled. "Mixmages cut out their hearts an' pour in poison. Gives 'em the souls of serpents. So it's said."

"So it is," the mage murmured, studying Kerin. "But I'm not going to go so far as ta call you a liar, Kerin thon Talisien. I will warn you, though. She sought you out, and that means she has a use for you. And her purpose here is to extinguish the Dawn, grind the Mandate heel down on the folks here with freedom still singin' in their blood. Now, we'll be watchin' you. Take a stand against us, and we'll have to come visit where you're stayin', with that old historian Bas Jelaska over in the crooked spire. But if you stay out of the Dawn's business . . . Well, then we have no problem. You understand, *kalaman?*"

Kerin relaxed slightly. They weren't here to kill them, but to warn them away from what was none of their business. He could respect that, and he actually wished he wasn't Anathema, so it was possible for the mage to see the truth of this in his mind.

"Understand," he said, trying to sound convincing.

"Good, I—"

"Rel!"

The thalani mage turned in surprise to the beggar, who was pointing a mottled finger at Sep. The girl was still staring into the spinning crystal, ignoring what was going on around her, but she was no longer alone.

Kerin cursed, reaching for his sword hilt. Three small Shadows hovered around her, their insubstantial limbs flickering as they stroked her motionless body. She didn't appear to have noticed, though their fingers were rippling her clothes and stirring her hair.

For a moment no one moved. Then Kerin surged forward, *Mercy* ringing as it slid from its sheath. At the sound, Sep turned to him, and for a brief moment she stared into a Shadow's featureless face. Her eyes widened, but before she could scream the apparition dissolved like the morning mist.

Kerin hastily thrust his sword away and knelt beside her. She was taking great gulps of air, and fear stabbed at him that she would panic and accidentally unleash the power of the weapon devouring her arm.

"They're gone, you're safe," he said soothingly, and after a moment her breathing began to slow.

"Rel," the thug Kapper said slowly, "is the ash—"

"Quiet!" came the hissed command, but not from the slack-jawed mage. Rather, the beggar on the ground had spoken, and to Kerin's surprise the large thalani did just that, closing his mouth and rubbing his stubbled chin with fear in his eyes.

Kerin took the crystal that was still dangling limply from Sep's hand and tossed it in the dirt, then began to guide her back the way they'd come. As she clung to him, he could feel her shaking.

None of the Black Dawn men said anything, but he could feel their eyes on his back until he turned the corner and the market's bright bustling was once more in front of them.

12

THE FOLLOWING days were largely spent confined to Bas Jelaska's home. Kerin insisted that Sep stay within the spire, though Nala made several short trips to purchase kyrathi treats and essentials, and he made a brief foray to see how Drifter was holding up in Sanctum's stables. The starbeast was keeping busy with his art, sketching vast mandalas in the loose earth with his flippers, and Kerin suspected that the stablemaster was coming by to swap stories of the Streams with the great turtle. He tried not to let this bother him too much, as Jenks had indeed demonstrated his amiability by allowing Kerin to even visit Drifter. It was perfectly within the rights of stablemasters to close the stables to handlers if they were not arriving or departing. Streamsurfers were a jealous lot, and the thought that someone seeking to be bonded might be ingratiating themselves with *their* starbeast had led to blades being drawn many times before. Most stablemasters avoided the possibility of blood being spilled by restricting access to the stables.

Jenks had proven accommodating, however, and allowed him a short visit. So Kerin had told Drifter of all that happened in their short time on Dust, and the starbeast had been stunned into mental silence to learn that Tessa was here on the planet. He'd tried to pick apart the roiling storm of emotions this news had created in the turtle, but there was honestly too much going on to know what he was truly feeling. Kerin thought he'd caught snatches of sadness and affection and even anger. That last emotion surprised him, but Drifter had still asked Kerin that if he saw Tessa again he should tell her to come visit him.

Otherwise he stayed inside Bas Jelaska's spire, bored and restlessly waiting for what he hoped was the Antiquarian's immanent summons. But as the days slowly shuffled past he began to worry that no invitation was forthcoming. It was surreal knowing that the Inquisitarium, the Black Dawn, and the Antiquarian all were very aware that they were on Dust – and even staying in the home of Bas Jelaska – yet apparently none of them thought they were worthy of more attention. If any of those factions had only known that the bearer of an Elder Race weapon capable of conquering star systems was, at that very moment, gorging herself on spiced chocolate and taking long afternoon naps they would have torn apart the city trying to claim her.

Strange days.

On the fourth morning since their expedition to the Old Market, Kerin awoke to find Bas Jelaska seated in an overstuffed chair in front of the room's circular window. The divan where he'd been spending the nights was almost too comfortable, and he likely would have slept for a few more turnings of a sandglass if a strange acrid smell hadn't dragged him from his dreams. Slowly he sat up, blinking away the stickiness that was trying to keep his eyes from fully opening.

"Morning," Bas Jelaska murmured. She took a long draw on the cheroot she held, then expelled a stream of shimmering blue smoke. Most drifted through the cracked-open window, but some remained, wreathing her head.

"Morning," Kerin replied with a yawn, then glanced around the room. "The others still sleeping?"

Bas Jelaska tapped ash into an urn beside her chair. "I looked in on them and the girl was curled up next to the kyrathi like she was one of her kittens."

Kerin grunted. Nala had taken to sleeping in the same bed as Sep ever since what had happened in the market. He wasn't sure how he felt about that. The kyrathi was clearly growing more and more attached, but Kerin had no illusions about what would likely happen to the girl. She was being devoured – or perhaps transformed – by an artifact that was beyond the comprehension of almost anyone in the stellar tributary. Its makers had left this reality more than a century ago. Coming to the Antiquarian was an act of desperation, and Kerin had been steeling himself to find out that the girl was beyond saving. He didn't want to think about the pain Nala would suffer if she realized they could do nothing.

Bas Jelaska watched him through the glittering pall of smoke. "Strangest thing . . . When I went into their bedroom I found that someone had brought more lightspheres inside, so that it was bright as day while they were sleeping."

Kerin shifted uncomfortably. They hadn't told Bas Jelaska about meeting the emissaries of the Dawn or the Shadows that had shown such interest in Sep. He'd feared that if the old woman knew she'd have forced them to leave, and with his dwindling funds he could only afford a few nights in an inn before they'd be on the streets or forced to take Drifter back to the stars.

"She's seen the Shadows again," Bas Jelaska said matter-of-factly, then drew deeply on her cheroot.

Nebulas, she was shrewd.

Kerin cleared his throat, thoughts racing. Maybe he could convince her Sep was still worrying about what she'd glimpsed before, or perhaps that she was having nightmares, or . . .

His confabulations shriveled under Bas Jelaska's flat gaze.

"The Shadows returned," he said with a resigned sigh. "In the market. Three of them, fluttering like moths around a flame."

"Three?" Bas Jelaska said, sounding surprised. He thought she was going to say more, but then she sank deeper into her chair, a faraway look in her eyes.

"Aye. They were touching her, playing with her hair. Like children might do." He shook his head. "I don't know why."

Bas Jelaska brought her attention back to him again, her expression suggesting she was deeply disappointed in him.

"Truly? It seems obvious, doesn't it? It's her arm."

"Her arm?"

Bas Jelaska blew out a plume of blue smoke. "You think it's Elder, don't you?" she said, then rolled her eyes when he started to protest. "Oh, come on. No need to keep up this charade. You want to see the Antiquarian, so you must suspect this is Elder Race sorcery."

Kerin pursed his lips, nodding.

"Whatever the Shadows are," Bas Jelaska continued, "they are sensitive to what happens in our world. The power of that artifact must be what is interesting them. They might even be mindlessly drawn to it, instinctually . . . like, as you said, how insects are drawn to a moon's brightness."

"You know something about them? More than you said before?"

Bas Jelaska shrugged. "I've read the accounts. The first sightings happened not long after the thalani arrived. There have been lots of theories put forth about what they are – maybe the ghosts of the ones that built the spires? Some indigenous creatures that have always lived here? Or perhaps they stowed away on the thalani star-beasts during the Diaspora and are as foreign to this world as we are. That possibility shouldn't be discounted." She coughed, then paused to stare in reproach at her smoldering cheroot. "They gave the name to the whole cluster, you know. The Umbral Cluster. Dust was the first world settled when the Streams shifted a century or so back."

Kerin hadn't known that. He would have assumed the Rest or one of the more hospitable planets had been the first. It must have been quite an exciting time. Streams rarely changed course, and it was rarer still when such a large and promising cluster suddenly became accessible to the rest of the stellar tributary. His gaze wandered around Bas Jelaska's home. If the Stream had opened up a few centuries earlier, maybe the vanished people who built the spires would have joined the rest of the Younger Races. But they had been cut off from the galaxy for too long, and had perished as their planet withered, leaving only the structures they'd built behind. And the Shadows. Maybe.

Kerin suddenly remembered something the Black Dawn mage had mentioned in passing. "When we were in the Old Market your name came up. They said you were a historian."

Bas Jelaska crushed her cheroot and dropped it in the urn. "That's true. I came here thirty five years ago to study the spires and their makers. I was hoping a paper on pre-starbeast primitives and why these ones disappeared might earn me a robe and cowl in one of the scholar cabals, maybe put me on the track for tenure at a collegium."

Thirty-five years. Kerin couldn't imagine spending half a lifetime trapped in a single place with nothing to show for it. "Did you ever publish your findings?"

Bas Jelaska's mouth twisted into a bitter smile. "Oh, yes. And the doors of academia slammed shut in my face."

"But it's not your fault there was nothing left behind. These people were so undeveloped they never even learned how to work metal or write."

"You misunderstand," Bas Jelaska said with a shake of her head. "I carefully studied the ruins here for months. I traveled into the wastes to walk among the fragments of the city of shards and also the warrens beneath the crystal desert. And over that time, I began to suspect that the original inhabitants of this world were far from primitive."

"What?"

Bas Jelaska gestured to where the slightly curving ceiling flowed into the walls. "It looks simple. But if you were to measure the grade and the angles you'd find that every aspect of this spire was carved with incredible precision. No people squatting in furs and with only simple stone tools could have hollowed these spires. Nebulas, I doubt the thalani or even the Mandate could shape stone so precisely today."

"But there are no artifacts. No drawings or writing on the walls."

Bas Jelaska seemed to be staring at something very far away. "Yes. And *that* was the thesis of the paper that made me a laughingstock among the cabals. I claimed that all evidence of this ancient people had been intentionally removed. Destroyed, or perhaps hidden away."

"Why?"

"Who knows?" Bas Jelaska said. She stood abruptly, brushing ash from the front of her tunic. "And in the end, as I found out, who truly cares?"

Kerin visited the privy while Bas Jelaska busied herself with making a pot of her viciously strong coffee. By the time he emerged, Nala was seated at the table with a steaming cup in front of her, the effects of the brew evident by the stiffness of her whiskers and the rapid flicking of her tail. Kyrathi were by their nature a rather high strung race, and coffee only exacerbated that trait. Nala was much easier to deal with if she woke up to a cup of weak tea, but that couldn't be helped now.

"Ho, Nal," Kerin said, sliding into a chair across from her.

"Kerin," the kyrathi said, her paw twitching. He suspected that she was fighting the urge to sharpen her claws on Bas Jelaska's table.

"Did you sleep well?"

Nala snorted. "As well as can be expected with a half-dozen lightsphere blazing around the bed."

"Because I'll be honest, you don't look like you slept well."

The kyrathi scowled at him and sipped her coffee. "It's not just the lights. Sep is terrified. Even when she does manage to fall asleep she has nightmares. She whimpers and cries out and pleads with whatever is stalking her in her dreams." She put down her mug and stared at him. "She needs to leave this planet. You saw how interested those shadow things were in her. Or interested in what's eating her arm, at least."

"They won't hurt her," he said, but he didn't even sound convincing to himself. After all, what did they truly know about the Shadows?

"Maybe, maybe not," Nala continued. "But I'm worried for her mental health. She's already a fragile thing – I'm not sure how much more it would take for her to slide over sanity's edge. And if that happens..."

Nala's eyes flicked to Bas Jelaska, who was clearly paying attention to their conversation as she waited for the water to boil. He knew the kyrathi didn't want to finish her thought out loud, as the old woman had no idea that the crystal artifact creeping up Sep's limb was so dangerous. But he knew what she meant. If the attention of these Shadows shattered Sep's mind, many people could die.

"Well, what can we do except wait for the Antiquarian to summon us?" he said, a bit too forcefully. "Do you have any other ideas?"

Nala held up her paw to show she'd heard his frustration. "No. He's our hope, may the Queen of Cats save us all. But what happens if he somehow removes the alvaren weapon and the Shadows keep bothering her?"

"Then we leave Dust."

"And she comes with us?"

Kerin sighed. "Yes." He really couldn't imagine another way forward. He'd spent his entire life scoffing at his grandfather's habit of collecting the broken and the lost and inviting them to join his crew. And yet here he was about to do the same thing.

Nala closed her eyes, and Kerin thought he saw something like relief in her feline features. A very big change from not so long ago, when she was angrily imploring him to throw Sep overboard.

"Good," she said. "Then we should start preparing, which means we need to find work, get something lined up that will replenish the coffers. A courier job, maybe, something within system. With so few starbeasts around I'm sure someone is willing to pay to bring goods to the Rest or H'shen."

Kerin nodded. That made sense. A few quick jaunts in the cluster to build up some reserves, then they could look for more interesting work that would take them back towards the busier branches of the stellar tributary.

"Any idea on where to find leads?"

Nala shrugged. "The usual places, I would think. Trading houses. Glimmer dens. Streamsurfer taverns. I thought I'd make a circuit today and see what's on offer."

Kerin accepted a scalding-hot cup from Bas Jelaska. "*Ow*. Uh, thank you." He just managed to set the coffee down without dropping it, then returned his attention to Nala. "I'll come with you."

"No," the kyrathi said flatly. "Apparently everyone knows who you are, and that you cause trouble. Let me ask around and see what interest I can get on my own."

Kerin frowned. He'd really been hoping for an excuse to leave the spire for a while. He took a tentative sip of his still-molten drink. "All right. So another day staring at the walls waiting for the Antiquarian to come calling. Wonderful."

Nala grinned, showing her fangs. "You should cherish these days, Kerin. I'm sure soon enough things will get much more interesting."

After the kyrathi had departed, Kerin sat and slowly drank his coffee as Bas Jelaska bustled around the kitchen annex whistling tunelessly to herself. Nala was right that they should try and escape Dust as soon as possible, as this planet was clearly on the verge of erupting into violence. But the thought of leaving Tessa after finally finding her again made him feel almost nauseous. Would she even care, though? Clearly, she'd carved out a life in the Mandate and risen far higher than she ever could have if she'd stayed a streamsurfer.

Kerin was studying the silty residue at the bottom of his cup when the screaming started. He leaped to his feet, snatching *Mercy* from where he'd laid the sword down the night before and rushed to the bedroom shared by Nala and Sep. He hesitated for the barest fraction of a moment, then barged inside with his hand on the hilt. Immediately he was accosted by the brightness of the spheres scattered about, and he blinked to try and clear his vision.

Sep was sitting up in bed – mercifully clothed in one of Bas Jelaska's old sleeping shifts – clutching a blanket to her chest, her pale hair a tangled mess. Her wide, frightened eyes found his own.

"What is it?" he asked, glancing around the small room.

Sep swallowed hard, the fear draining from her face. "I thought . . . I thought there was one of them standing over me. But . . . I must have been sleeping." She shivered, her knuckles white from holding the edge of the blanket so tightly.

Bas Jelaska entered the room, shoving him aside.

"Oh, child," she murmured, sinking down onto the bed and gathering Sep up into her arms.

As the girl collapsed into Bas Jelaska's embrace, Kerin made a quick circuit of the room.

Nothing was amiss, and unless the Shadow had crawled out from under the bed there wasn't even any darkness where it could have emerged. Or perhaps these things didn't even need darkness to manifest.

"Just a bad dream," Bas Jelaska whispered, rocking Sep gently.

Kerin was inclined to agree, but he still hadn't taken his hand from the hilt of his sword. Though he had to admit that he found it unlikely metal could do anything to hurt a living shadow anyway. That made him feel like an idiot, brandishing his sword and looming over Sep while she was being comforted by Bas Jelaska, so he quietly withdrew from the bedroom.

A nightmare. It must have been. Nebulas, who could blame the girl? The amount of trauma that she'd been subjected to over her short life – and in particular the last few days – would shatter a lot of minds. Sighing, he laid the sheathed *Mercy* on the table and threw himself back down into his chair, wondering if there was any more coffee in the pot Bas Jelaska had brewed earlier.

He had just decided to go and see for himself when Sep shuffled into the room, Bas Jelaska a step behind her. She found her customary seat at the table but didn't meet his eyes, instead staring blankly at his sword's gleaming metal hilt, her shoulders slumped and her face slack. Kerin felt a pang of worry, as this reminded him of what she'd been like on the swim out from Jegriddsl. For endless sandglasses she'd sat and stared at nothing while the gobber played his card games.

Bas Jelaska touched her lightly on the shoulder as she passed behind her. "You need breakfast. Meat and eggs? A cup of tea or coffee?"

Sep made no reply as the old woman began banging pots and pans in the kitchen annex. Bas Jelaska cast a worried glance at the girl before she bent to chop some sausage.

His attention was drawn to her arm. The long ladies' glove she never took off anymore disappeared into the sleeve of her sleeping shift, but he thought he could see a subtle darkening above where the ruffled hem must end. If so, that meant the crystal had nearly reached her shoulder. How much time did they have before it passed beyond her arm? And what would happen when it did?

Kerin started when he realized that she had mumbled something while he'd been lost in thought.

"What did you say?" he asked, leaning forward.

Sep did not lift her eyes from *Mercy's* tarnished hilt. "The Light. I have to return to the Light."

Kerin's grimaced. That was *not* what they needed right now. The noises in the kitchen vanished as Bas Jelaska stopped her cutting to listen.

After a long moment of silence when no one spoke, Sep licked her lips and took a deep breath, as if to steady herself. Then she looked up, her gray eyes meeting his. "I left the Light, and that is why these dark things are following me. If I go back, the Light will burn them away."

"The Shadows have been on Dust a long time, child," Bas Jelaska said slowly. Her lips were pursed as she stared meaningfully at Kerin. "Long before the church of the Searing Light arrived."

"That means the Light was needed here," Sep continued, her voice strengthening. "To illuminate the darkness and drive out wickedness." She drew herself up a little straighter. "I will go to the church today and speak with the Sister of the Thorns. She will help me."

Kerin's jaw was aching from how hard he was clenching it. He wanted to shake Sep, to shout at her that the cult she'd been raised in cared nothing for her, but he restrained himself. She was so fragile, and she must feel helpless, unable to do anything to stop the thing eating away at her. Could he really blame her that she'd grasp for help from the only thing she'd ever known?

"All right," he said finally, barely managing the words.

Behind Sep, Bas Jelaska's eyes bulged. "Kerin . . ." she began, but he shook his head curtly to quiet her.

"We'll go to the Searing Light, Sep. But you and me together, not on your own. And you're not going to join them again or offer to take anyone's pain. You have enough of your own right now, yes?"

The smile that spread across her face stabbed at his heart. "Yes," she said, and for the first time in a long while he saw hope in her eyes. "We will go together."

13

OUTSIDE THE SPIRE the air felt heavy and swollen, pregnant with a storm impatient to be birthed. This surprised Kerin, as he'd assumed it almost never rained on Dust, but from the emptiness of the streets and the abandoned stools where the old thalani men typically wiled away the days *something* certainly was approaching. The usually golden sky had darkened to bronze, and roiling, wine-colored clouds were flowing over the mountains. As he watched, blood-red lightning flickered down to lick the apex of a distant spire.

"We should go back inside, Sep," he said uneasily. "There's a storm coming."

The wind strengthened, howling through the canyon created by the spires rising up on either side of the street. Sep frowned, her long blue dress rippling and her hair dancing as she faced into the sudden gust, but Kerin saw no wavering in her resolve as she started in the direction that would lead them back to where the faiths had established their temples. Cursing under his breath, he hurried to catch up with her. Grit stung his eyes, and the ubiquitous dried fronds that the street food vendors wrapped their delicacies in swirled around his boots.

He couldn't see anyone else, which was a strong indication that they shouldn't be outside right now.

Sep squinted at the massing clouds. "The Dark is trying to keep me from the Light. We can't turn away."

Kerin grumbled a reply but he followed her as she strode down the center of the street. The path back to the religious district was simple enough, and Sep apparently remembered the way. He'd already walked this route a few times, and his hope that she would get lost faded quickly.

And yet . . . this didn't look right. He had been sure they were going the right direction, but these spires looked different, hewn from a darker stone and a bit more worn. The lightspheres that lined all the roads here were nowhere to be seen.

Sep had also realized that something was wrong, as her pace slowed, and she began to look around with a confused expression.

Kerin turned, trying to orient himself by finding Bas Jelaska's canted home, but either they had walked farther than he'd thought, or it had vanished behind another spire. The day was rapidly darkening, the indigo clouds they'd glimpsed in the distance now unfurling in the sky above. A cold droplet spattered his cheek, and when he wiped it away he found his hand was streaked with something more viscous and silvery than water.

"Where are we?" Sep asked, sounding scared. She'd stopped in the center of the street and was looking around frantically as dark blotches appeared on her dress.

"I don't know," Kerin replied over the rising wind. Another drop struck his face, and this time he tasted something bitter and metallic. One nearby spire caught his eye: it looked like it had been broken roughly in half, with jagged walls rising up around a dome of some dark material. He'd never seen anything like it, and the strangeness extended beyond this roof. The soaring, arched entrances of the other spires had always been open, but this one had had been sealed completely with what looked like gray stone or concrete.

Kerin jumped as a sword-stroke of red lightning slashed across the sky. The storm was about to unleash its full fury, and they needed to take shelter inside one of the spires.

And then he stopped. Coming towards them with small, mincing steps was another of the fox-men. It wore a similar formal waistcoat and vest as the one they'd met in the Old Market, though this vest was red with silver buttons, and Kerin was fairly sure the spectacles here had a different, more rounded shape. Was the fur a bit darker as well? Kerin wasn't certain. Then again, it very well might be the same one. The creature seemed unhurried, as if the burgeoning storm was no great bother.

"Sep," Kerin said warningly, but the girl had already noticed the approaching fox-man. She shot a worried glance at him, her ungloved hand gripping a handful of her dress fiercely.

The creature stopped a few paces away and blinked up at them through silver-spattered lenses. Thick droplets of liquid dripped from its long snout as the wind rippled its red fur. After a moment it removed its spectacles, folded them carefully, and then slipped them into its breast pocket.

"The Antiquarian will see you now," it said simply in its reedy voice.

Kerin could see Sep's jaw tighten. "No," she said firmly. "We are going to the Light."

The fox-man cocked its head slightly, its beady black eyes narrowing. "Very well. Do not seek us out again." Then it turned and with its precise, careful steps began to walk away.

Nebulas. "Wait!" Kerin cried, rushing in front of the creature and holding up his hands to stop it. The fox-man paused, watching him incuriously. Behind it, Sep had crossed her arms like she was hugging herself.

"Wait," Kerin repeated, more quietly this time. "We still want to meet your master." His gaze shifted to Sep. "This was always the plan," he told her. "It's why we came to Dust."

"Things have changed, Kerin," she said, but he barely heard her over the wind. "The Dark is here. This man cannot save me, only the Light has that power."

Kerin tried his best to keep the frustration from his face and voice. "All right. Then we just shelter with the Antiquarian until this storm passes. We'll continue on to the church and you can see what they can do to help." He pressed his hands together. "Please."

As if to punctuate what he'd just said another crackle of lightning rent the sky, bathing them all briefly in lurid red light. Sep frowned and glanced up at the churning clouds. The silvery rain was falling faster now, hissing upon the street stones.

With a sigh, Sep uncrossed her arms and gave a tight nod.

"Good," Kerin said in relief, turning again to the fox-man. It wasn't watching them anymore, its attention drawn to a tiny orange lizard that had crept out from between a crack in the ground to lick at a spot of wetness with its tiny flickering tongue.

"Excuse me . . ." Kerin began, but then he was shocked into silence as the fox-man pounced with a yipping cry, its claws closing around the lizard. In one smooth motion it scooped the squirming creature from the ground, brought it to its mouth and with a quick snap of its jaws bit off its head. The moment of wildness passed as quickly as it had come, and with perfect decorum the fox-man slipped the still-spasming corpse into its breast pocket, right beside where it had placed its spectacles. Then it returned its attention to them, its gaze placid, as if nothing had happened. Kerin found he couldn't take his eyes from the stain spreading on the creature's vest.

"Good," it said solemnly, then resumed its brisk walk. Kerin realized it was headed towards the broken spire with the blocked entrance, and he motioned for Sep to follow.

He wondered if the fox-man was going to lead them to another way inside, but it did not waver or slow at all as it strode closer.

"Where is it going?" Sep murmured just before it reached the gray stone wall.

Kerin tensed, expecting the fox-man to reel backwards with its face bloodied, but instead the substance blocking its way roiled like a dense fog bank, and the creature plunged into it without breaking stride.

Kerin and Sep shared a look, and he held out his hand for her to take. Whatever was beyond that barrier, he didn't want to risk being separated from her when they went through it. She stared at him for a moment, then hesitatingly slipped her ungloved hand into his, lacing their fingers together. He felt a sudden pang of guilt. What kind of creature was he delivering her to? Some of the stories he'd heard suggested the scholar would care little about Sep's well-being, so long as he obtained what he desired. The thought that he might be betraying Sep made his stomach twist, but he forced himself to give her a comforting smile. She returned it shyly, and then he stepped closer to the gray wall. He reached out but stopped just before touching its smooth surface.

"What do you think we—" he began, but then gasped as the grayness shivered and the fox-man's head suddenly thrust back outside. It bared its fangs and stared at them reproachfully.

"Come in! Hurry! Master waits." Then it vanished again, the ripples from its passing quickly growing still.

Kerin sighed, then tentatively edged forward. The tip of his foot disappeared with only the slightest resistance. Steeling himself, he walked forward, pulling Sep with him into the grayness.

Mist closed around him, clammy tendrils brushing his skin. For a moment he could see nothing except the swirling murk; then it cleared, and they stumbled into a great soaring space.

"Nebulas," he breathed softly, gazing about in wonder. They stood just inside the threshold of the broken spire, but where the ground floor of other spires he'd seen had been mostly empty, this one was cluttered with all the strange artifacts that he'd remembered from when he was young and his grandfather had brought him to the Antiquarian's shop. The severed stone head of a tusked creature loomed over them like a sentinel guarding the door; elsewhere, he saw sculptures and contraptions of verdigris-scarred metal, along with all manners of chests and boxes and reliquaries. Freestanding shelves were scattered about, some laden with smaller objects and others stuffed with piles of scrolls and ancient books. The light seemed to be coming from the flurry of silver motes that were slowly drifting down like snowflakes; he glanced up to what was above them and sucked in his breath. The underside of the black dome he'd seen from outside was speckled with a vast profusion of these same glimmering silver points, each linked by barely visible golden threads. It looked like an incredibly complex web had been spun across the ceiling, and after a moment of staring in slack-jawed surprise he realized that this was a map of their branch of the stellar tributary. If he concentrated long enough he suspected he'd be able to find the Umbral Cluster and even the tiny gleaming dot that represented Dust's star.

Movement out of the corner of his vision made him start, drawing his gaze from the star map above. A few small shapes were shuffling between the shelves and the larger artifacts: fox-men, all dressed in formal wear and carrying clay tablets and styluses. None of the creatures paid them any attention, instead remaining intent on their duties. Of the fox-man that had preceded them through the gray portal there was no sign.

Something else was jarring. The sound of the wind and the grumble of the skies outside had vanished, as if by stepping through the grayness they had been transported to someplace very far away.

"Don't touch anything," Kerin warned Sep as he noticed her drifting towards a huge nacreous disc held fast in a stand of blackwood. As the silver sparks falling from above neared this artifact, ripples of opalescent light passed across its surface. Sep slowly extended her hand, and a humming resonance swelled. In alarm, Kerin took a quick step towards her and pulled her arm away.

"Don't worry, it's not dangerous!"

Kerin looked around. For a moment he couldn't find who had spoken, but then the clatter of something falling over and a pained yelp drew his attention to the shelves. A man emerged from their depths, bent over and rubbing his knee where he must have bumped it. As he hobbled towards them, he raised his other hand in greeting.

"At least, I don't think so. It was found on the library world of an Elder Race. No idea what its purpose was, but it makes a nice decoration, yes?"

"Ho, Antiquarian," Kerin said.

When the man reached them he straightened, wincing as he flexed his injured leg, then smiled broadly and extended his arm. Kerin blinked in confusion at the gesture. After a moment he remembered how to respond to this ancient greeting and clasped the Antiquarian's hand in his own.

"Kerin thon Talisien," the scholar said warmly, pumping his arm vigorously "You've certainly changed!"

The same could not be said for the Antiquarian. If anything, the man had gotten younger in the twenty-something years since last Kerin had seen him. His bald pate was unnaturally white and smooth. It almost looked as if he was wearing a very cleverly designed mask.

"You look the same," Kerin replied, extricating his hand from the Antiquarian's clammy grip. "But your shop has certainly gotten more impressive."

The Elder Race scholar waved his arm dismissively. "This old place? You're too kind. I found my spot in the market was attracting the wrong kind of attention"—he gave an exaggerated wink, which Kerin found ridiculous because clearly there was no one around to overhear them—"the tattooed kind, if you get my meaning, and so I returned to my old residence, as unfashionable as it may be."

The Antiquarian turned to Sep, and his face brightened. "Greetings, my dear," he said reaching out to take the girl's hand. Kerin's heart dropped when he realized that the scholar had seized her crystallized arm, but Sep seemed too shocked by his friendliness to be upset.

The Antiquarian bowed slightly, raising Sep's arm so he could brush his lips against her glove. As he did this, his dark eyes widened.

"Well, well," he said after releasing her hand and stepping back. "How *very* interesting. Please, come with me, both of you." Then with a swirl of his overly-large robes he turned on his heel and began striding away, still limping noticeably.

Kerin glanced at Sep, and in her face he saw a healthy mix of surprise, wariness, and confusion. He suspected he looked much the same. The Antiquarian he remembered had been mercurial, overly friendly until young Kerin had touched the wrong artifact, and then his dark anger had sent him scurrying to his grandfather. This version of the Antiquarian seemed far more . . . irreverent.

"Come on, come on," the scholar said impatiently, pausing and motioning for them to follow him.

Kerin caught Sep's eye again and shrugged, then together they started to move through the gently drifting silver motes. He reached out tentatively to let one settle in his open palm, wincing in alarm as it dissipated in a brief flash. There was no pain, though, so he decided to try and ignore the flurry of falling stars.

Ahead of them was a desk that looked the twin of the one the fox-man had been sitting behind in the Old Market. A pair of stools were placed on the side closest to them, while on the other rose a much more impressive high-backed chair. Affixed to the wall behind this throne was the bony remnants of an enormous set of jaws. Only a few of the teeth still remained, cracked and yellowing, but they were each about as tall as a man. Kerin wondered if the remains belonged to a starbeast or some other giant animal.

The Antiquarian slipped behind his desk and settled into the formidable chair, clasping his hands together and smiling broadly as he waited for them to take their own seats. Gingerly Kerin sat on one of the stools, very aware that the Antiquarian's chair made him loom over them like a lord gazing down on his subjects. Sep joined him, her gaze fastened on the vast mouth seemingly poised to devour them all.

The Antiquarian noticed where she was looking and half-turned in his chair to also regard the jaws. "Impressive, yes? I had this brought out of storage when I knew you were coming. This was a gift from your grandfather."

Kerin blinked in surprise. "A gift?"

"Yes, indeed." The Antiquarian gestured with his spidery hand towards the hilt at Kerin's waist. "Surely you know the story."

It took Kerin a moment to understand what the man was referring to. "That story is *true*?"

The Antiquarian gave an exaggerated shrug. "I have no idea what embellishments Cal added to the tale, but I suspect the broad strokes are the same as what he told you."

"What is he talking about?" asked Sep, sounding confused.

Kerin swallowed, his mind whirling. He had always assumed that the story his grandfather had told him about *Mercy* had been one of his fables.

"My family's sword," he said slowly. "My grandfather claimed he'd found it on the edge of the Unknown, buried to the hilt in the skull of a dead starbeast that was just drifting through an empty system." He pointed at the vast jaws. "*That* is from the same starbeast?"

"Indeed. At that time I was very interested in extinct starbeasts, the kind that once served the vanished races of the universe, and Cal sold the location of this one to me so I could have it salvaged. I tried to convince him to part with that sword as well, but he'd already fallen in love with it." The Antiquarian's eyes brightened. "I don't suppose you might be willing to sell?"

Kerin gave a quick shake of his head, and the scholar sighed in disappointment.

"Ah, well. But you've brought me something perhaps even more interesting." He turned his attention to Sep and tapped the black wood of his desk with two fingers. "Come, my dear. Let me see what is generating those remarkable resonances."

Kerin nodded when she glanced at him uncertainly. "You can trust him," he told her, trying to convince himself of this as well.

Sep let out an unsteady breath. Despite her nervousness, she laid her arm on the desk where the Antiquarian had indicated. Then she pulled off her glove, whimpering softly as the crystalline flesh was revealed.

"Fascinating," the Antiquarian said, leaning forward to examine the glittering facets more closely. He reached out, but hesitated touching her when he saw her flinch. "May I?" he asked, and she replied with a tight nod.

The Antiquarian laid his hand in hers, his fingers curling around her narrow wrist. Kerin could sense how tense she was, but she did not pull away.

"Hmm," the Antiquarian murmured softly, sliding his grip up her arm. "Alvaren, I would say. From around the time of the Rivening."

"The Rivening?" Kerin asked, his heart beating a bit faster when he saw a shimmer of light travel up Sep's arm.

"A civil war," the Antiquarian said distractedly, his brow knitting as he examined the artifact. "Not all the alvarens wanted to pursue transcendence. It got rather messy, as I understand."

"Can you get it off?" Sep asked softly in a trembling voice.

Abruptly the Antiquarian released her arm and sat back, grinning broadly. "Of course, my dear. If you would be willing to donate this artifact to my collection, I would be very happy to remove it for you."

Sep let out a small gasp, and it took her a moment to recover from her surprise. "Will my arm be all right?"

The Antiquarian waved his hand, as if to dismiss her concern. "Just as it was before, my dear. Your flesh and blood has been transformed by alvaren sorcery, but such a process can be reversed."

Sep visibly sagged in relief. "Thank you," she whispered. Kerin felt almost light-headed, and without realizing what he was doing he grabbed her flesh-and-blood arm and gave it a squeeze. Thank the First Mover.

With an expression of avuncular affection, the Antiquarian leaned forward again and gently brushed away a tear as it trickled down her cheek. "Now, now. Don't cry." To Kerin's surprise and slight discomfort, the scholar brought his finger to his mouth and licked at the wetness. Sep didn't even seem to notice. "But I will need a few days to prepare," he continued. "Promise me you won't go looking for help elsewhere, yes? The chimericists would make an absolute mess separating that artifact from your arm, I assure you."

Sep nodded earnestly. "I promise."

So no trip to the church of the Searing Light. Kerin wasn't disappointed about that.

The Antiquarian clapped his hands together loudly. "Well! How exciting." His gaze shifted to one of the fox-men as it suddenly appeared beside Sep. "My dear, I have some other business to discuss with Kerin. Please allow my associate here to introduce you to some of the wonders I've collected."

Sep flinched as a tiny paw plucked at the sleeve of her dress, but after a moment she rose. As the creature led her away she cast a nervous glance over her shoulder at Kerin, and he returned a comforting smile.

The Antiquarian was quiet for a moment as he watched the girl and the fox-man approach one of the largest artifacts in the spire, a huge orrery of a binary system. A half-dozen gleaming planets of varying sizes moved smoothly around a pair of stars, sliding along the arcs of their elliptical orbits.

"It has changed her, you know," the Antiquarian said. "More than what can be seen."

Kerin twisted around to face the scholar again. "In a good or bad way?"

The Antiquarian shrugged. "Who knows? She is different now than before it attached itself to her, isn't she?"

Kerin nodded slowly. "When I met her, she didn't speak."

"It's healing her," the Antiquarian mused, rubbing his smooth chin. "Repairing some damage that was done. I sensed strands of the object extending all the way into her skull, changing the patterns in her brain."

Kerin shifted uneasily. "And what happens if you remove the artifact?"

"I believe the alterations are permanent and will persist afterwards. But there are few certainties in this universe."

Kerin swallowed, watching Sep as she stepped between the swooping planets, her hand now enfolding the fox-man's paw. The relief he'd felt moments ago was rapidly eroding. "And if we do nothing?"

"Then eventually she will be transformed beyond recognition. Into what, I do not know. It may be that the artifact is preparing her for a time when it takes over completely. It does not want a flawed host. When the healing is complete, the artifact will accelerate whatever it is doing."

"What are you saying?"

"It will absorb her and become whatever it was meant to be."

A coldness settled in Kerin's stomach. "And what is that?"

The Antiquarian frowned. "Almost certainly a weapon. A terrible weapon with capabilities far beyond what she may have already shown. Her consciousness will become subordinate to the artifact, and it will attempt to fulfill its original purpose."

"You said it was designed to kill other alvarens. And there are no more of those." Kerin's thoughts were racing as he tried to process what the Antiquarian was saying.

"Nevertheless, I propose we don't allow things to progress that far. I doubt you want to discover what ranked second on their most-hated list."

"Even if removing it returns her to how she was before."

The Antiquarian's expression became pained. "Even so."

Sep's amazed laughter drifted from where she stood in the center of the orrery. The planets had quickened, as if she was in the middle of a ballroom and the music had suddenly changed, the dancers swirling faster around her.

His breath caught in his throat. To see her like this, a child delighted with something wondrous, finally experiencing emotions that had been denied her for so long...

"Of course I will compensate you well for bringing me this treasure."

Kerin tore his gaze from Sep and the hypnotizing pattern made by the orrery. He found the Antiquarian staring at him, his long pale fingers steepled.

"Ten million Mandati tribunes, or the equivalent in star sapphires."

Kerin's heart began to beat faster. That was a fortune, easily enough to clear all his grandfather's debts and allow him to live the rest of his life without worry. No, not just without worry – in unimaginable luxury. He'd suspected the Antiquarian would pay well for this Elder Race relic . . . but that amount was still beyond all his expectations. He could afford a manse on the Hethian moon where all the rich guildmembers retired, dredge a lake for Drifter to wallow in when they weren't swimming in the Streams, buy the freedom of Nala's littermates, which he knew was the kyrathi's most deeply-held desire. Nebulas, he could found his own small guild, something that might grow in time to rival the Starfarers.

A tiny crease appeared on the Antiquarian's brow while he waited for Kerin's reply. "The money is not enough? Well, I have something else I'm sure will interest you."

Kerin swallowed. The money was more than enough, but he was damned curious what else this man could offer him.

"What?" he asked, a little hoarsely.

"This."

The Antiquarian extended his hand towards Kerin. Nestled in his unlined palm was a small black sphere. It looked like an obsidian ball carefully cut to display countless glittering facets.

"What is it?"

The scholar pursed his lips. "Many cultures and creatures give them different names. They were a creation of an Elder Race, and the knowledge of their fashioning has vanished with their progenitors. The most common name in the stellar tributary for such an artifact is a memory pearl."

Oh. Kerin was familiar with such objects – still incredibly rare, but relatively more common than most of the other artifacts the Elder Races had left behind. They must have been mass-produced sometime in the distant past for so many to have survived down through the eons. If what he'd been told was accurate, memory pearls captured an imprint of a person's mind, complete with all their recollections, desires, and knowledge. When great thinkers or leaders arose, powerful empires could use a pearl to fashion a reflection that could be consulted later for its wisdom. Kerin had even heard rumors that the powerful Revani merchant house was ruled by a council of memories imprisoned inside these pearls.

Such an artifact was near-priceless. It made no sense for the Antiquarian to offer him one Elder Race artifact for another. Or perhaps . . .

"Do you want to make an imprint of *me*?"

The Antiquarian's lips twitched, and Kerin had the sense that he had just barely suppressed a smile. "Oh no, my boy. I'm offering you a conversation with the man in here." He tapped the faceted sphere lightly.

Realization hit Kerin like an avalanche. "Who do you have?" he whispered, even though he was certain he knew what the scholar's answer would be.

"Calvan thon Talisien," the Antiquarian said, rolling the ball around in his hand. He kept speaking, but to Kerin the scholar's words seemed very far away, drowned out by the roaring in his ears. "A fascinating man. I collect such interesting personalities, and so I convinced him to let me preserve him . . . for posterity."

Oh, that wouldn't have taken much convincing, Kerin thought numbly, still reeling from the Antiquarian's claims. *He would have leaped at the chance.*

"So you will . . . give him to me?"

Now the Antiquarian did smile, fluttering his long fingers as if the very idea was preposterous. "No, no, no. Calvan is part of my collection now, where he is safe. No offense intended, but I'm quite certain that within a generation or two this pearl will be lost if I passed it on to you." He paused, blinking quickly, as if something surprising had just occurred to him. "And, I have to admit, I've come to enjoy his company. Your grandfather has a very unique perspective on the universe."

Had. He had a very unique perspective. Or . . . is he really in there? Kerin eyed the pearl uneasily. *Was this just a lifeless reflection . . . or would I truly be able to speak with my grandfather?*

"But if you agree to my offer I will let you visit with him. I'm sure you have many things you wish to talk about."

Wonder and surprise were quickly giving way to other emotions. Anticipation. Excitement. Not a small amount of anger for how Calvan had abandoned Kerin in such perilous straits, crushed beneath a mountain of debt owed to some very dangerous people. And . . . fear. His grandfather would be disappointed in him, he was sure. Cast out of the Starfarers Guild, their respected family name now derided throughout the tributary. Kerin was even willing to trade a broken girl for a chest of star sapphires . . . he felt a flush of hot shame. His grandfather would have at least refused payment, if only to keep his conscious clean.

He wasn't his grandfather.

"How do I know you're telling the truth?"

The Antiquarian put his hand over his chest, as if Kerin's suggestion had wounded him. "I should hope my word is enough! But I suppose I could let you visit briefly with your grandfather. As a token of good faith." The scholar held out the pearl.

Kerin eyed the sphere warily. He knew he was going to take it up in the end, but for a long moment his apprehensions kept him from reaching for it.

"Enfold it completely in your hand and close your eyes," the Antiquarian told him, seemingly oblivious to Kerin's doubts.

Gritting his teeth, he finally accepted the pearl. It was cool and hard, and his Anathema blood barely stirred at the touch. The Antiquarian watched him with a bemused grin, as if he couldn't understand why he was waiting.

Do it, you coward. Kerin shut his eyes, concentrating on the feel of the sharp-edged sphere in his hand as he squeezed it tightly. He expected a surge of sorcery, the sensation of falling or being transported somewhere else, but nothing happened. He still felt the dry coolness of the Antiquarian's spire and the hard wood of the stool beneath him. Letting out a breath he hadn't realized he'd been holding, he opened his eyes feeling a mix of relief and disappointment.

And found himself in the solarium aboard Drifter. Kerin gaped, looking around wildly. He was seated on the other side of his grandfather's desk, across from an empty chair – or, at least, he assumed it was the same desk he'd smashed into when he'd fallen through the ceiling. Most of the surface was covered by a mess of star charts, but from what he could see this desk had a deeper varnish, and the scratches and scuffs he remembered as always being there were missing. He glanced upwards. Beyond the intact panes of glass set in their copper frame the darkness of a Stream seethed and roiled. He swallowed, reaching out for Drifter's familiar emanations.

Nothing. He was sitting in the solarium with a Stream rushing past and Drifter was not here. That made sense, of course, but he still found it unsettling. Shakily, he pushed himself to his feet, steadying himself on the brass and copper optical tube of his grandfather's telescope. He felt a momentary pang of guilt seeing the ancient device whole again.

The thumping ring of heavy footsteps sounded on the metal staircase outside. He swallowed, wondering what he should do. Sit? Stand? Open the door for him?

Before he could decide, the door swung wide and his grandfather was there, glowering at him like he'd found a thief sneaking around in his house. Kerin could only stare, his thoughts suddenly scattering. The man who filled the entrance was most certainly Calvan thon Talisien, but he looked very different from Kerin's memories. His unkempt gray beard was now sharply trimmed and the color of a smith's anvil. Even more striking was the full head of equally black hair, something Kerin had never seen before. It had almost entirely vanished by the time his grandfather had first taken him from the slums of Deval, reduced to just a slight fringe around his age-mottled scalp. His grandfather couldn't have been more than a few years older than Kerin was now, as his face was barely lined and his shoulders broad and powerful. He scowled as he stomped into the room, slamming the door behind him.

"Who in the bloody stars are you?"

Kerin's jaw worked but he couldn't summon forth any words. He felt the same fear and awe he'd experienced when he was a boy and a terrifying bearded apparition had suddenly emerged from the hissing rain to fill the doorway of his small home.

Calvan stalked across the room, coming to stand behind his desk. Although they were almost the same height, his grandfather still seemed to loom over him. He folded his burly arms across his chest and studied Kerin through narrowed eyes.

"What did you do with Ixial?"

Kerin found his voice. "Ixial?"

"The scholar. The Antiquarian."

"He, uh, he's fine. He's letting me talk with you."

His grandfather studied him for a long moment, his gaze lingering on the metal hilt at Kerin's waist. "You're wearing my sword."

Kerin realized with a start that an identical copy of *Mercy* was sheathed at Calvan's side. It didn't look to have changed at all.

"My sword now."

His grandfather's jaw hardened beneath his thick black beard. "You killed me?" he asked, his hand drifting to rest on his sword's pommel.

"No! No. You died, and *Mercy* passed to me."

Calvan blinked, his fingers slipping from the hilt. "Then you are . . ."

"I'm your grandson, Kerin."

Surprisingly, his grandfather appeared to take this revelation in stride. "Hmm," he grunted, waving for Kerin to sit. Then he lowered himself into his own chair and leaned over to open a drawer. Moments later he set two glasses and a familiar dusty bottle between them on the desk. Kerin stomach twisted at the sight. His grandfather pulled out the stopper and poured a healthy amount of the amber liquid into each glass. He lifted his and leaned back, regarding Kerin from under heavy brows.

"Pye is your mother?"

Kerin reached out to take the other glass. Everything felt so real – the weight of the drink, the crystal under his fingers – it was hard to remember that he was actually experiencing his grandfather's preserved memory. He brought the glass up to his nose and sniffed. Nebulas, it even smelled just as rank as he remembered. Surely he couldn't get himself drunk here, though, right?

He sipped the vile drink and then nearly coughed it back up. The same taste. "Yes," he said, putting the glass down again. "You found us on Deval."

"Was she . . . all right?"

Kerin swallowed away a lump in his throat, surprised by the strain he heard in his grandfather's voice. He shook his head, not trusting himself to answer.

Calvan frowned and drained his glass. "Hmm. Her mother . . . was difficult. She left me. I suppose I'm difficult, too," he admitted after a moment, then chuckled humorlessly. "Even as a baby I knew Pye was her mother's daughter. And I'm sorry about that, lad."

They sat in silence for a while, both lost in their own remembrances. This version of his grandfather seemed far more maudlin than the older man Kerin had known. Calvan had never spoken of his daughter except to push away Kerin's questions, never showed emotions like this. Whatever had happened between him and his daughter, Kerin realized, was far more recent and raw, the scars not yet faded.

There were so many more answers he wanted. About his family, and about the choices his grandfather had made that had come to haunt Kerin. He'd fantasized about this moment many times in the years since his death. And now that it had somehow, impossibly come to pass, he couldn't imagine where to start.

For one thing, this man knew nothing about him. All the years they'd spent together, all the history that had flowed so wide and deep between them . . . it was as if it had never happened. There were so many questions he simply could not answer. Why had he let Tessa walk away? Why had he wasted his life sifting through the worthless remnants of dead peoples? Why had he left Kerin with such terrible burdens?

He could still ask these things, he supposed. This reflection of Calvan might even have some insights.

Kerin opened his mouth, but it was his grandfather who spoke first.

"Did I ever find the Labyrinth?" Calvan asked. He looked like he both desired and dreaded the answer.

Kerin's thoughts scattered like leaves in the wind. "The what?"

Calvan's face twisted, his gaze drifting to the star charts piled haphazardly on his desk. Then he swept out his arm, sending most of them flying. The half-empty bottle went as well, exploding into shards when it struck the floor.

"Then it was all for nothing," he said, so softly that Kerin thought he must be speaking to himself.

"What is the Labyrinth?" Kerin asked. "Why did you never speak of this before?"

A corner of his grandfather's mouth lifted. "Now, there's a tale," he murmured, with more than a trace of bitterness.

Nostalgia stabbed at Kerin to hear his grandfather say this again, and the feeling was so overwhelming that he struggled to focus as the old man – no, the young man – continued speaking.

"Perhaps I wanted to spare you my obsession," Calvan said with a sigh, his gaze wandering to the Stream rushing past overhead. "It is the beginning and the end, lad. Like a snake eating its own tail. Hints and clues scattered across a thousand worlds. Gather them up and just maybe the entrance will be revealed. That's what I was told, anyway. But first there's something you have to know—"

His grandfather's face trembled, like his skin was suddenly water and a rock had been flung down, obliterating his features in a blur of colors. Kerin surged to his feet in horror, knocking over his chair.

With a harsh spasm the vague shape sharpened again, but it was no longer his grandfather.

The Antiquarian folded his arms together on the desk and smiled cheerily at Kerin.

"What did you do?" Kerin asked hoarsely. "Bring him back."

The scholar glanced at the mess of star charts and broken glass. "What did *you* do? Calvan rarely gets so . . . emotional."

"The Labyrinth," Kerin said, righting the chair and lowering himself back down onto it.

"Ah," the Antiquarian said, nodding knowingly.

"What is it?"

"You can ask him after the alvaren artifact is safely in my possession."

"Tell me now."

The Antiquarian cocked his head to one side, studying Kerin. His eyes were pools of black deeper than the abyss beyond the Streams.

"No."

Cold shadows rushed in to fill the solarium. Blinded, Kerin cried out in alarm, leaping out of his seat again just as the light returned.

He stood on the other side of the Antiquarian's desk, panting, as silver motes drifted lazily down from the firmament spread above. The great bony jaws fixed to the wall seemed to be smiling mockingly at him. Kerin swallowed hard, running a hand through his sweat-slicked hair. He glanced over to where Sep was still examining the orrery, the fox-man beside her. The movement of the planets had slowed, but Kerin had the sense that it had only been moments since he'd first clutched the memory pearl.

The memory pearl. He stared at his empty hands, then at the floor around his feet. Had it slipped from his grasp?

"It's here," the Antiquarian said, and Kerin glanced up to find the faceted black sphere held between two of the scholar's long grub-white fingers.

"Please, just let me . . ." Kerin croaked, his hands clenched into fists.

"Well, it appears we have a bargain," the Antiquarian said. "Agreed?"

Kerin licked his lips, staring at the tiny little pearl that contained the last fragment of his grandfather in the universe. Then his gaze slid to Sep, who was coming back towards them now, still clutching the fox-man's paw. Her eyes were bright and her face flushed.

The object was reaching into her brain . . . changing the patterns . . . and removing it might return her to what she was like before. Or kill her.

He closed his eyes. "Yes. We have a deal."

～

When Bas Jelaska opened the door, Sep fairly threw herself into the old woman's arms, babbling excitedly.

"Careful, child," Bas Jelaska said sternly, staggering back a step, but Kerin could hear the warmth in her tone. She met Kerin's eyes over Sep's shoulder, her brows raised in surprise. "Good to stand in the Light again, I see."

"Not the Light!" Sep said, her words tumbling out faster than Kerin had ever heard before. "The hairless man! And his little friends! He promised me he could fix my arm, make it like it was before. Oh, his friends are so wonderful! And the things he has in his house . . ." Her words trailed away as she struggled to summon up the proper descriptions.

"Ah. You visited the Antiquarian," Bas Jelaska said more coolly, extricating herself from Sep's grasp.

"Yes! The ceiling is covered in stars, and they float down but they don't burn when they touch you! And there's a mirror that sings when you get near it, and there are planets spinning around . . ."

"Planets?" Bas Jelaska said in disbelief. "But we're standing on a planet."

"Not real ones! They're made of metal, and so are the suns . . ."

Kerin shut the red door behind him and made his way towards the divan on the far side of the living space. He badly wanted to throw himself down on the cushions and sleep for a day and a night. What had happened in the Antiquarian's lair may have filled Sep with hope, banishing the darkness that had been crowding around her ever since she'd seen a Shadow, but he felt emotionally emptied. His mind had been in a tumult ever since meeting his grandfather, and he could barely remember them leaving the broken spire and making their way back to Bas Jelaska's home.

Out of the corner of his eye he saw Nala skulking in the corridor leading to the bedrooms. He was about to call out to her, but something about the way she was standing kept him quiet. Kerin could see how tense she was, her shoulders hunched and her tail lashing about. She saw him looking at her and crooked a claw. Concerned, he followed the kyrathi into the bedroom she shared with the girl.

Nala whirled on him before he could ask her what was wrong. "We have a problem, Kerin," she hissed quietly, glancing at the open doorway behind him.

He could think of several large problems they had, but this sounded like something new. "What?"

She licked her paw and smoothed down her trembling whiskers. "I wandered around today, to the Whimsy and through the trade halls, kept my ears up for whispers of work. But no one is talking about jobs right now. The entire cluster is paralyzed with fear."

"Why?"

Nala bared her teeth. "H'shen's system has been invaded. The qan tried to put up a fight and sent out a school of their biggest, meanest fish, but apparently they were quickly turned into bait."

Kerin put his hands on the kyrathi's shoulders, trying to calm her. "Nala, what's going on?"

She shook herself free of his grip, her golden irises flaring. "The lich, Kerin. Xerivas is in the cluster. He's looking for us, and this time he's brought his legions."

14

THE REST of that day and the one that followed seemed to drag on interminably. Kerin wished he'd pinned the Antiquarian down on exactly when he'd be ready to perform the procedure on Sep, or at least how to get in contact again. Was he supposed to bring Sep outside and wander around looking for a shattered spire? The wait kept him on edge, knowing that Xerivas was out there in the cluster, searching for them. Nala told him that giant undead birds had been seen soaring through the systems of the Rest and Bel Atoch, as if looking for something. The lich and his minions had not yet left the systems controlled by the qan, but the streamsurfers Nala had spoken with had been sure they'd eventually breach Mandate space. The dead cared very little about imperial boundaries. Kerin could only offer up prayers to gods he didn't believe in or actively disdained that the Antiquarian would contact them soon, Sep would be cleansed of the alvaren artifact and they could flee the cluster laden down with sapphires.

Then maybe this tightness in his chest would finally go away.

Kerin tried to distract himself by reading one of the battered adventure novels he'd brought from his starbeast, but his thoughts kept drifting and he found it impossible to follow the threads of the story. He spent most of his time staring out the glazed window reliving what had transpired inside the memory pearl, ruminating on what his grandfather had told him. Across the living space Bas Jelaska was setting up a board game on the table where they ate their meals. Sep was seated across from her, her brow furrowed as she watched the old woman shake the pieces out onto the wood. Nala was doing what kyrathi preferred to do during the day, which was find a quiet sun-warmed corner and curl up to nap.

"Come, child, let's play a game."

Kerin's gaze slid back to the table, where Sep was now staring at Bas Jelaska like the old woman had just spoken to her in incomprehensible gibberish.

"Why?"

"Because it's fun."

Sep blinked slowly. She didn't look convinced.

"Kerin?" Bas Jelaska said, twisting around to find him on the divan. "Are you interested in helping me demonstrate to Sep the concept of casual fun?"

He pushed himself to his feet, shaking out a tingling arm he'd held in the same position for too long. "What are you playing? Is that t'skelcha?"

"It is indeed," Bas Jelaska replied. "Been a few years since I had anyone to play with. I must be terribly out of practice."

"Sounds like you're trying to get me to lower my guard," Kerin said as he approached the table. "I expect you'll tell me next you want to put a small wager on our game to make it interesting."

"So you do want to play."

Kerin pulled out a chair and sat. "In the interest of educating Sep."

Bas Jelaska's face crinkled into a smile, then she held out her closed hands. Kerin tapped the one on the left lightly, and she opened it to reveal a small red stone nestled in her lined palm.

"Fire for your first move, streamsurfer."

Kerin grunted and turned his full attention to the board. Bas Jelaska's set was an antique design, from back when the fashionable shape of a t'skelcha board was a spiral galaxy. Several wooden arms curved away from a circular central space that would be the most hotly contested battleground on the board – whoever controlled that area would almost certainly win the game, but getting bogged down in the middle and neglecting the periphery could just as easily undermine his chances.

He spent a long moment chewing his lip and considering his options, then placed his fire stone on the border between the spoke and the largest of the arms. A strong base to build out from, he hoped. If Bas Jelaska claimed the middle he could snatch more territory in the arms, and if instead she focused on the edges he would move swiftly to build an unassailable position in the center.

The old woman wasted no time in mirroring his opening by placing her first stone – a polished blue crystal, as this t'skelcha set was one of the popular elemental variants – at the edge of the arm directly across the spoke from his own piece. A conservative strategy, and not one that his grandfather had often played. Calvan had been an aggressive player, always searching for brilliance with daring gambits that occasionally succeeded but more often led to ruin, and Kerin had exceeded his grandfather as a player before he'd surpassed him with a sword.

The game proved as interesting as he'd hoped. Bas Jelaska was a canny player, and long-dulled regions of his brain gradually sharpened as he struggled to stay one move ahead of her traps and tricks. T'skelcha wasn't a complicated game, but beyond the apparent simplicity was a depth that could take a lifetime to master. Kerin made sure to describe each of his moves so that Sep could start to understand the rules and the strategies, and to his surprise she quickly seemed to become fully invested in the unfolding drama on the board, her brow scrunched down as she carefully studied everything that happened.

After all forty pieces had been placed, and the first entrapments and conversions had cleared out the weakest positions on both sides, the real action began. Kerin realized almost immediately that Bas Jelaska had made some structural mistakes in her initial placements, and slowly he began to whittle away at her defenses. She began muttering to herself, her hand hesitating between several pieces as she struggled with how best to respond.

"No."

Bas Jelaska paused, her fingers brushing the stone she'd finally settled on moving, and turned to Sep. The former pain conduit was staring at the board with an almost feverish intensity.

"Not that one."

Bas Jelaska glanced at Kerin in bemusement, then back to Sep. "Do you have a better idea, child?"

Sep extended her flesh-and-blood hand to indicate a cluster of three blue stones deep in Kerin's territory. "Those."

"They're lost," Bas Jelaska explained. "I can't save them."

Sep shook her head vehemently. "Look."

Bas Jelaska chuckled and bent forward to better examine the board. Kerin watched her follow the possible lines of attack, testing the various permutations that followed every move. A strong player could see no more than a half dozen moves ahead, as by that point the branching possibilities had usually become too many to consider at once. Finally, she frowned. "There's nothing there, child."

But maybe there was. Kerin could discern the faint outline of something, though only its hazy edges. It was impossible that after watching half a game that Sep was able to see deeper than two experienced t'skelcha players.

Still . . .

"Let her try and save your position," Kerin said, settling back with his arms crossed.

Shrugging, Bas Jelaska shifted the board closer to Sep and gestured for her to make the next move.

The girl's gaze traveled from Kerin to Bas Jelaska to the board and back to Kerin again. He couldn't decipher what she was feeling right now, but it looked to be surprise tinged with a healthy amount of nervousness.

"It's alright," Kerin said soothingly. "We're just having fun."

Swallowing hard, Sep sat forward. With careful deliberateness she lifted the blue stone she'd indicated earlier and moved it several spaces closer to Kerin's pieces. She winced at the clink of crystal on wood, glancing at Kerin guiltily.

He set his elbows on the table. "An interesting move," he said, and then slid one of the red stones he'd designated as defenders closer to where Sep was threatening.

Sep stared at the board, her gray eyes flickering about like she was imagining the outcomes of possible moves. But surely that couldn't be what she was really doing. She certainly did look deep in thought – strands of her pale hair had slipped down as she leaned over the board, and she'd started chewing absentmindedly on the ends. This was the first time, Kerin realized, he'd seen her fall into something other than herself.

She moved another piece. Kerin countered. The chewing intensified. He still wasn't sure if this was beginner's luck or if she did have a grand strategy, but with each passing turn his suspicions that she saw something on the board was growing stronger. Bas Jelaska was watching the unfolding game with her head tilted to one side, her brow creased like she was straining to see what Sep was working towards. For Kerin that picture was growing clearer, and it was very surprising . . .

They all jumped when someone knocked on the door. Kerin glanced at Bas Jelaska and Sep and found them both staring back at him. Another, harder rapping came. It sounded impatient, and far too strong for a fox-man who stood barely three span high.

"Who is it?" Bas Jelaska asked, sliding from her chair and going over to the large cabinet where she kept her antique crossbow.

"Open in the name of the Golden Emperor!" came the bellowed reply. Bas Jelaska hesitated, her hand hovering over the crossbow's stock, and then she shut the cabinet door and turned again to Kerin. In her expression he saw helplessness, and he couldn't blame her. She could not refuse the Mandate.

"Now, Historian!"

"I'm coming, I'm coming," she said, sliding back the deadbolt. Before she could pull on the door it swung open, pushed hard from the other side. Kerin rose from his chair, glancing to where he'd set down his sword. Nala had appeared from deeper in the apartment, and though he couldn't see aether in her paws, the stirring of his Anathema blood suggested she was gathering sorcery.

Bas Jelaska stumbled back as a half dozen Mandati soldiers entered. Kerin relaxed slightly when he realized their swords were sheathed, but still he cast a worried glance over at Sep. Who knew what might happen if she felt frightened?

"Kerin thon Talisien," said one of the soldiers, addressing him. He took off his gold crested helm, tucked it under his arm, and then bowed shallowly.

"That's me," Kerin said slowly, confused by the formality.

"You are requested to accompany us."

"Am I in trouble?"

The captain shook his head firmly. "I am instructed to tell you that you are not. You are needed by an agent of the Inquisitarium to assist in an investigation."

Tessa.

"And if I refuse?"

The Mandati soldier blinked, as if such a response would be unthinkable. He was quiet for a moment as he mulled his response. "Then we will regretfully rescind the request and replace it with a command."

Just what Kerin had assumed. He sighed, his gaze traveling from Nala to Sep to Bas Jelaska. All three were staring at him apprehensively, but there was only one possible answer to such a summons.

"All right, then. Lead the way."

Unblemished white stone rose around Kerin, blazing in the harsh midday sun. They'd passed through the checkpoints with only a cursory nod to the soldiers on duty, then walked the perfectly straight, gleaming road that cut through the heart of the administrative district the Mandate had built after claiming this planet in the name of the Golden Emperor. He noted the magistrate hall where he'd last seen Tessa, with clerks hurrying up the steps burdened by piles of scrolls, and other large, pillared buildings he assumed were similarly populated by bureaucrats and civil servants.

These impressive edifices gradually diminished as they moved deeper into the district, replaced by more blocky, utilitarian structures that Kerin guessed probably housed the regular Mandati citizens on Dust. There were children here, their skin as of yet unmarred by tattoos, rushing about playing games on the edge of the street as their mothers hung washing or gossiped with their neighbors. Some of them ran up alongside the soldiers accompanying Kerin, shouting questions asking whether he was a spy they'd captured or begging them to draw their swords. The soldiers ignored them, and eventually one of the mothers chased them away by swinging a reed switch that always seemed to just miss connecting with their legs.

Finally they arrived at a compound with high walls and a large golden onion dome. Kerin eyed that uneasily. If he remembered correctly, this would be the residence of the planet's exarch, someone he truly did not want to meet. Green creepers spotted with bright red flowers veined the building, as if the white stone were weeping blood. The guards milling around the black-iron gate were ashen-faced, almost dazed, as if something terrible had happened. This disquieted Kerin.

The soldiers led him through the compound's lush courtyard, where a spray of silvery water arced from the upraised hand of a stern-looking stone man in the imperial robes of state. Kerin had seen that heavy brow and bearded face before: Prime Legate Halkus, prior to his transformation into the Mandate's Golden Emperor. Several thalani and Mandati in the garb of servants were prostrate before the statue, their foreheads pressed to stone. Kerin's uneasiness about what had brought him here deepened further.

They entered the main villa, passing down high vaulted corridors and ascending a staircase decorated with gold leaf and chips of quartz. Officious looking functionaries were clustered outside a set of double doors carved of red wood, murmuring nervously, and when one older man in purple robes saw them approaching he knocked softly and then slipped inside the room. Moments later he poked his head out and beckoned frantically. The soft murmurings stopped as they moved through the crowd and entered the chamber. Given the demeanor of everyone they had passed so far, Kerin had expected to find blood splashed on the walls and body parts strewn across the floor.

But this was not the case.

It was the living quarters of someone very important. Gauzy pastel strips of silk hung from the ceiling, stirring gently in a breeze coming in through the open doors that led out onto a balcony. Expensive-looking furniture of wrought copper was scattered about: a wide bed beneath a shimmering canopy, intricately carved wardrobes and dressers, and a few low couches placed around a malachite tea table. Sprawled on one of these was a body, but the couch's gilt frame blocked most of his view. Kerin could only see a slim white hand scrawled with red tattoos hanging limply over the side, its fingers nearly brushing the floor. Kerin knew the woman was dead, as the red markings had stilled.

Standing over the body and looking down with pursed lips was Tessa. She glanced up as he entered and made a curt gesture to dismiss the soldiers that had brought him here. Kerin heard thumps of fists striking leather as they saluted, and then the ringing of boots as they hurriedly retreated from the room. Tessa watched them depart, her face bleak. Then she turned to Kerin.

"Thank you for coming."

"I ... didn't think I had a choice."

She sighed and returned her attention to the body on the couch. "You didn't."

He glimpsed something out of the corner of his eye, a flash of red. Turning, he found to his surprise that he and Tessa were not alone. Kneeling motionless with their backs to one of the walls were the three k'zar guards Kerin had seen before. Their heads were bowed, their red-crested helmets placed on the floor in front of them, along with their swords.

Kerin swallowed, his gaze coming back to Tessa. She was watching him again.

"Yes," she said, indicating the body with her chin. "It's her. I need you to come closer and tell me something."

Slowly, he approached, wishing he was at this moment anywhere but here. An exarch's daughter was dead. Things were about to get very messy on this planet

She could have been sleeping, if not for her wide, staring eyes. There were no marks of trauma that he could see, no blood on her alabaster skin or golden sleeping robe. Her insect wings were folded on her back, the veined membranes extending past her shoulders. On the green stone table was an assortment of sliced red fruit, and it looked to Kerin like she had been overcome while eating breakfast. A small puddle of wine stained the floor beside where a silver goblet had fallen.

"What happened to her?" Kerin asked, his gaze lingering on her face. She did not appear to have died in pain or fear. Her beautiful features were untroubled, as if her soul had simply abandoned its body and winged its way through the balcony's open doors and into the golden sky beyond.

"I don't know." Tessa's voice was flat, without emotion. Kerin knew her too well, though – he'd heard that tone countless times before. She was frustrated.

Kerin studied the woman's beautiful face. Her lips were parted, her cheeks still slightly flushed.

"Have you determined what killed her?"

"No," Tessa said, her head turning as a fat man in dark red robes slipped into the room. Kerin recognized him: the mage of the Crimson he'd seen rushing down the street after the spire collapsed. He looked even sweatier now than when he had been running.

"Crimson Halas," Tessa said as the man slowly approached the couch.

The mage blanched when he saw the sprawled woman clearly, mopping at his ruddy face with a cloth. "Shroud," he said, his small black eyes darting to Tessa. "This is terrible. Terrible."

"It is," Tessa agreed, folding her arms.

"What will he do? He is coming, you know. He should arrive soon, if he has not already."

"From the city of shards?"

"Yes. Exarch Veshkent was inspecting the work there."

Tessa pursed her lips. "I would prefer if we have something to tell him. Do you sense anything here, Crimson?"

The battlemage swallowed, glancing at the dead woman with a pained expression. "Nothing, Shroud. I can't—"

"Get closer. I want a thorough examination."

"Very well," he whispered, bending over the woman and letting his hands hover over her face. He paled even further, and it looked like he was on the verge of fainting. Kerin glanced at Tessa questioningly, and to his surprise her fingers flickered quickly in guild cant.

Battlemage. Squeamish. She paused, rolling her eyes, and then added: *Ridiculous.*

Crimson Halas straightened, swaying slightly. "I still cannot sense any sorcery. I would say this woman died of natural causes."

"Young healthy women rarely expire while eating breakfast," Tessa replied, the note of frustration now becoming more evident. "There's no poison in her body or anywhere in this chamber. And no poison I know of would kill her and leave her looking so . . . peaceful."

The Crimson opened and closed his mouth several times, but no words came. Finally, he pulled out his sweat rag again and wiped his brow. As he did this, he seemed to catch sight of Kerin for this first time.

"Who is this?" he asked, gesturing with the cloth.

"He is assisting me in determining the cause of death, since everyone else is being so spectacularly unhelpful."

The plump battlemage peered at Kerin more intently. "Truly? Is he an investigator?"

"He is Anathema," Tessa said sharply, and Kerin had to hide his smile as the man took a hasty step back, his jowls jiggling. This Crimson must be one of the many mages who harbored an irrational fear of those born Anathema. Kerin had heard the same stories as the Crimson no doubt had, about how the power of his blood could leach into the very air and sap mages of their sorcery, but those were only fables.

"Kerin," Tessa said, the edge still in her voice, "examine the exarch's daughter."

He nodded, moving closer to the body. The summons now made sense: he was even more sensitive to sorcery and its residue than those that wielded it. If there was any trace of it clinging to this corpse he would detect it.

Kerin crouched down beside the body, his head nearly level with hers. What had been her name? Dierdra? She looked more at peace now than the two other times he'd seen her. He remembered her lips twisted into an angry sneer as she'd stalked through the plaza. If it weren't for her glassy, staring eyes he would be certain she was still alive. There was also no smell, he realized. She hadn't voided her bowels when she'd died, nor had she begun decomposing.

Kerin waited for his Anathema blood to stir, but it remained quiet. Whatever had killed the exarch's daughter, he doubted it was sorcery. His gaze followed the sweep of her arm that was not dangling over the couch, to where her hand rested in the folds of her shimmering golden robe. The red markings under her skin had died with her, solidifying into an intricate pattern of whorls and barbs. Kerin had been told that during funeral rites in the Mandate the deceased was ceremoniously flayed, and their tattooed skin given to their next of kin. If they had attained a sufficiently impressive rank the family might decide to display the skin prominently in their home to remind visitors how powerful and respected the dead had been. Kerin couldn't imagine a father desecrating his daughter like that, but he'd encountered stranger customs ...

His thoughts trailed away as something caught his eye. It was a smudge of dirt or dust on the inside of her wrist, noticeable because the rest of her was so clean that she looked to have just stepped from a bath. He reached out towards this blemish and heard a sharp intake of breath from the Crimson.

"Shroud," the battlemage said with a note of warning, "I would not touch her until the exarch returns..."

"What is it, Kerin?" Tessa asked, ignoring the Crimson's admonition.

"Perhaps nothing," he said, lightly brushing the blackness with the tip of his finger. It tingled strangely, faintly numbing.

It reminded him of ash, or the residue from charcoal. What had she been doing that this had ended up on her?

A strangled sound from the Crimson made Kerin look up. Halas had raised his head like he was listening intently.

"Shroud," the battlemage hissed, "he comes!"

The fear in the mage's voice made Kerin glance uneasily at Tessa. She was staring at the room's closed door, her face taut.

"Kerin," she said. "Go stand with the k'zars. Quickly."

He hesitated, about to ask a question, and she stepped closer and yanked him up from his crouch. "Now!" she insisted, giving him a shove towards the three white-armored warriors, who were still silently kneeling.

He stumbled over to where she was indicating, between the last k'zar and a cabinet of red wood. None of the warriors glanced up at him as he came to stand beside them.

For a moment no one moved or said anything. Tessa and the Crimson were staring at the door apprehensively, and both jumped when a thump sounded from outside. Kerin found that he had broken out in a cold sweat.

The door swung wide and a tall figure glided into the room. The man – if it was a man – wore purple robes trimmed with silver, and his face was hidden by a featureless golden mask. Kerin's pulse quickened. He'd seen a similar garb and mask before from a great distance, on an imperial world in a faraway system. This was the ceremonial attire of a Mandati exarch, the archmages whose authority was only superseded by the Golden Emperor himself. This man was one of the few citizens who had attained the tenth and highest rank of the empire: the freedom to rule.

Tessa and the Crimson both went to one knee, and Kerin

hurriedly mirrored them. The sense of power swirling around the exarch was so great he was surprised to find that his Anathema blood was not stirring. The authority the exarch was exuding must be natural and not augmented by sorcery, but Kerin also knew for certain that this was one of the most powerful sorcerers in the entire Umbral Cluster.

The exarch drifted closer to the couch. He rested long, fine-boned fingers on the gilt back and stared down at the body of his daughter. The silence was total, and Kerin's breathing thundered in his ears.

Finally, the exarch reached down and brushed closed his daughter's eyes. For a moment he rested his spidery fingers on her face, and Kerin felt a brief surge of sorcery as questing tendrils slipped into the body.

"Shroud," the exarch intoned, his golden mask making his voice sound hollow. "Why is my daughter dead?"

Tessa's answer was quick and precise. "I do not know, Lord."

The exarch's fingers slowly traced a path down her cheek, lingering on her parted lips. Everything that Kerin knew about the Mandate and its ruthless leaders suggested that this was a rare and unexpected moment.

"Give me your best guess."

"Poison. Something the empire has never encountered before. It either dissolves seamlessly in the blood, or is still about her person and we simply do not know what to look for."

The exarch straightened, though he stayed staring down at his daughter. "I sense no sorcery, but there is something . . . odd. A flavor I do not understand. It smells of the grave."

That might be the corpse, sir, Kerin thought, then had to stifle a small, almost hysterical laugh.

"I will continue my investigations, Lord."

The exarch grunted. Finally he tore his gaze from his daughter, swiveling to face Tessa. "You were brought here, Shroud, for two purposes. To discover how the Dawn had killed my predecessor, and to protect my family from a similar fate. You have failed spectacularly in both these tasks, have you not?"

"I have, Lord," Tessa said, her voice barely more than a whisper.

The exarch pointed a bony finger towards where Kerin stood against the wall. He had a brief flash of panic that the sorcerer was indicating him, but then he realized the gesture was meant for the kneeling k'zars.

"My daughter's bodyguards know the price of failure. What is it, k'zars?"

The shouted response came in perfect unison. "Death, Exarch!"

"Are you willing to fall upon your swords, warriors?"

"We are, Exarch! Give the word, Exarch!"

Kerin edged away from the k'zars, hoping to avoid any sort of guilt by association.

The pale hand curled into a fist. Sorcery burgeoned, swelling dark and shimmering. The crackling puissance made Kerin's veins throb, and the crystals illuminating the chamber flickered in their holders.

Then the rising power dissipated, as suddenly as it had come. "No," the exarch said softly. "I shall give you a chance for redemption. What say you, k'zars? Death or vengeance?"

"Vengeance, Exarch!"

"Very well. Find who killed my daughter. Bring me their heads, and the heads of all they love. Do this, and I will absolve you of your failure."

"It shall be done, Exarch!" barked the kneeling warriors. Then as one they stood, sliding their swords into their sheaths with harsh clangs before donning their helms.

The exarch's golden mask nodded at this. He once more looked to his daughter. Kerin saw a shudder go through him, his shoulders slumping, as if the grief he was trying to hide was close to overwhelming him.

"All of you," he rasped, waving his hand sharply. "Go now." Kerin saw a droplet fall from the bottom of the mask. Then another. The splatter each made on the white floor was red. It looked to him like the exarch was weeping tears of blood.

Tessa was already moving towards the door, her gaze averted from the grieving exarch. She beckoned frantically in his direction, and Kerin hurried to follow her.

"Shroud," the exarch murmured just before they escaped.

Tessa paused in the doorway, turning back with an expression that suggested she was dreading what he might say.

"Yes, Exarch?"

"He is coming."

"Who?"

The exarch's response was distant, as if distracted. "The Golden Emperor. There is something on this planet he wants. You will have to answer to him when he arrives, so prepare yourself."

Tessa looked shaken, but she managed a tight bow before she left the room. Kerin stayed only a few steps behind her. As he passed out on to the landing where the servants and sycophants were still waiting in a nervous flutter, Kerin risked a glance back into the chamber before the door swung shut. His final glimpse was of the exarch standing with bowed head over the body of his daughter. The sorcerer had removed his mask, revealing the gaunt features of a middle aged man, his face covered in writhing red tattoos. Cutting through these markings were lines of deeper red, the tracks of bloody tears.

"What did you just involve me in?" Kerin asked as he hurried to follow Tessa. He caught up with her as she was striding through the garden that led back to the compound's main entrance. She ignored him, and he reached out to grab her arm. "Tessa!" he said angrily as she shook herself free. "Talk to me!"

The Shroud whirled on him. "What?"

Kerin matched her glare. "Eight years, Tess! We were like brother and sister for eight years. Then you vanish. And now here you are, but every time we meet you're using me. To send a message to the thalani. Then the legions. And now you bring me to the murder scene of the exarch's daughter?" His voice was rising, but he didn't care. He sensed heads nearby turning towards them, and apparently so did Tessa as she hissed something in frustration and began to drag him deeper into the gardens. When they were recessed far enough among the white-blossom wrapped statues that they were out of sight she whirled on him.

"This isn't a game, Kerin! If you want to survive you need to keep your head down. No one will care about you if you're just a random streamsurfer, an old friend of mine from a previous life. But keep talking loudly *here*, of all places, and you'll bring down attention you do not want, I promise you."

Kerin's anger was white-hot now, fierce enough that he had to fight the urge to lay hands on the Shroud.

"Did you know the Black Dawn has marked me?" he asked. "They kidnapped a girl in my crew who is not any older than you were when you left us. They know where I'm staying. They threatened my friends! How could you be so selfish as to risk our lives by bringing us into this mess?"

Tessa's golden eyes flashed. "You're only alive because of me," she spat back. "You ignorant fool."

"Oh, really?" he replied, folding his arms across his chest.

"Yes," she replied harshly, "you idiot. What were you thinking, trying to loot an exarch's tomb? The Mandate has a dozen safeguards in place to protect against robbers, especially incompetent ones like you."

Kerin blinked in surprise, his rage suddenly subsiding. "What are you talking about?"

"I'm saying I saved your life, Kerin. Do you know what happens to robbers caught in a barrow moon? They get executed, horribly. *I* intervened. I made promises to powerful people, going into their *debt* to keep your miserable head attached to your neck!"

He stared at her dumbly.

"I told you, the Inquisitarium hoards information. And I made sure they let me know every time Drifter entered a Mandate system. I *wanted* to go to you. Many times. To show you that I'd made something of myself. But I didn't. And then you went and tried to *steal* from the empire? You're so lucky I was watching you!" She glanced up at the golden sky, her chest heaving. "Others know who you are. Factions both inside the Mandate and out, like that sniveling guildrat in the tavern. When I let myself be seen with you . . . I was sending a message that you were under my protection. That if anything happened to you they'd have to deal with the Inquisitarium!"

Kerin could only swallow in response to this outburst. His mind was reeling from the revelation that *Tessa* had been the one who saved them from the Mandate. Before he could think of anything to say she continued, her tone bitter.

"Do you want to know why I left Drifter? Why I abandoned you and your grandfather? Because I saw what my future would be. *You* would bond with Drifter. *You* would inherit your grandfather's sword and his legacy. If I stayed with you I would always be in your shadow. I would have to follow where *you* led, become a character in *your* story." She looked him up and down, her lip curling. "And as much as I cared about you, I knew how that story would end. You're not your grandfather, Kerin. You make rash, impulsive decisions, and it will only be so long until your luck runs out . . . when you don't have someone watching over you to save you at the last moment. What are you doing here on Dust? Running from another mistake? I'm right, aren't I?"

She stepped away from him, the anger in her eyes replaced with something far colder. "I'm done with you, Kerin. For good this time. I suggest you leave Dust as quickly as you can."

Then she whirled and strode away, crushing the white blossoms that had squirmed onto the garden paths viciously beneath her boots.

"Tess!" he cried, but she did not turn around.

15

WITH THE CRACK of a whip and an aggrieved bleating the cage began its shuddering ascent. Kerin leaned against the rickety wood, staring blankly down at the dwindling thalani and his plodding beast. He felt empty inside, as hollow as this spire. Tessa. Nala. His grandfather. He'd failed all of them. The glory he'd dreamed about since he was a boy would never be his; truthfully, he thought bitterly, it was the striving for that glory that had brought him so low. Tessa had been right: he wasn't his grandfather. He had never deserved Drifter and everything else that had been given to him.

Nala would leave him soon, he realized that now. And without the guild's name behind him he'd eventually find it impossible to keep Drifter fed. Then what? Hire out as part of a caravan, hauling trade goods between the systems? He imagined Drifter laboring under a load of black iron or the blocks of white stone the Mandati quarried on their home world, and the thought made his heart ache. His proud starbeast reduced to being a pack animal, Drifter's shell creaking under the terrible burdens they carried through the tributary. Kerin had visited the caravansaries where the great merchant consortiums stabled their starbeasts: he'd felt contempt at the time for those broken-down creatures with their empty eyes and bowed backs. His eyes prickled when he imagined Drifter as one of them.

Kerin wiped angrily at his face as the cage bumped against the ninth tier's platform. He would never allow that to happen. He'd sever his bond with Drifter and gift him to the Starfarers Guild before it did, so they could in turn bequeath the starbeast to a promising young streamsurfer. Someone who would take care of the turtle as well as his ancestors had. Kerin leaned for a moment against the stone of the spire, collecting himself as he tried to banish these thoughts. If the Antiquarian's offer was genuine, he might never need to worry about money again. He just had to survive on this cursed planet until the scholar was finally ready to remove the artifact. Please, by all the sundered stars, let that happen before the lich decided to investigate Dust.

The red door swung open as soon as his knuckles grazed the wood, as if Bas Jelaska had been standing on the other side waiting for him to return. Kerin blinked down in confusion at the old woman as she grabbed a handful of his steelsilk shirt and practically dragged him inside.

"What's going—" he began, and then his mouth clicked shut when he saw what waited within. *Oh.*

Seated at Bas Jelaska's table was one of the Antiquarian's fox-man servants. The furry creature was intent on a dried sausage, its little paws wrapped around the piece of meat as it gnawed away enthusiastically. It was wearing an identical green, golden-buttoned waistcoat as Kerin remembered from the Old Market. The creature growled, ripping away a chunk of the sausage and chewing furiously, completely ignoring everyone else in the room. That included Sep, who was seated across from the fox-man and staring at it with wide eyes. The half-played t'skelcha board was still set up on the table, as if Sep had been waiting for him to return and finish the game.

"It showed up not long ago wanting to take the girl away," Bas Jelaska said, her lip curled in what looked like mild disgust as she watched it messily devour the sausage. "But I refused to let it until you came back."

"Thank you for that," Kerin murmured as he approached the table, resting his splayed hands on the wood as he stared down at the Antiquarian's servant. The creature did not acknowledge him as it continued to worry at the sausage, bits of meat spraying everywhere.

"Where's Nala?" he asked Bas Jelaska as the old woman moved to take a simmering pot from over her fire.

"Went out not long after you did," she said, setting the container down and reaching for a cup. "She wanted to find out what was happening around H'shen. Also said you'd know what she was talking about. I assume she was referring to the dead setting up residence in the cluster."

Kerin grunted distractedly. He was finding it very hard to look away from the mess the fox-man was making.

"Do you want some?" Bas Jelaska asked as she poured coffee into the cup in front of her.

"No," Kerin said. "We should go."

"Look!" Sep cried, clapping her hands together. "He's almost finished!"

Moments later the last bit of sausage vanished, and the fox-man began licking the grease from its paws. Kerin was strongly tempted to grab the little creature and shake it roughly for the delay.

As if finally realizing it was the center of attention, the fox-man stopped cleaning itself and settled its beady black eyes on Kerin.

"Talisien!" it suddenly barked. "Master waits for you and the girl!"

"We are ready," Kerin told it in exasperation, and in reply the little creature hopped down from its perch. It glared at him, then sneezed.

"Follow!" it cried after wiping its little snout. "Master is waiting!"

"You said that already," Kerin said, turning to Sep. She looked nervous. "Are you ready?" he asked her.

She nodded, her lips pursed as she slid from her chair.

Bas Jelaska hurried over and wrapped her in an embrace. "Oh, child!" she cried, squeezing Sep so hard the girl's eyes widened in surprise. "Don't be afraid. You'll come back here whole and safe."

Something occurred to Kerin and he stepped over to where he'd set down his travel bag. Quickly he rummaged through a tangled pile of dirty clothes and pulled out the cube of gray metal he'd taken from the treehold. Bas Jelaska's mention of the undead horde squatting in the cluster had reminded him that he should try to discover why the lich wanted this alvaren artifact so badly. And they were about to go see just the fellow to ask.

When they reached the street the fox-man drew fewer curious stares than Kerin expected. The old thalani men who spent their days smoking and grousing near the spire's entrance barely spared a glance at the creature as it scampered out of the gloom and paused blinking in the harsh sunlight, its nose raised like it was searching for a particular scent. The Antiquarian's servants must be well known to the citizens of Sanctum if their appearance did not even warrant a surprised grumble or a pipe waved in their direction.

The fox-man turned slowly with its snout still in the air, then gave a little yip and set off down the street. Kerin and Sep shared a glance, then moved to follow. The creature bounded ahead, and for a moment Kerin feared he might lose sight of it, but it paused when it arrived at the nearest crossroads and began sniffing again. Whatever smell it was looking for must have been stronger here, as it peered intently in one direction, its bushy tail quivering in excitement. It managed to restrain its enthusiasm until they were close, then it dashed away, faster than before.

"Are you scared?" Kerin asked as they quickened their pace.

Sep was quiet for a moment. "Yes," she finally said softly, not looking at him. Kerin waited for her to elaborate, but that seemed the extent of what she was willing to share.

From up ahead the fox-man gave a gleeful bark. Kerin looked in the direction it was running and was shocked to find that the Antiquarian's broken spire with its entrance of solidified gray fog had somehow materialized in a place it should not be. He shook his head, bewildered. He'd walked this street several times already, and he was certain that a different spire had been here. Kerin grimaced. How could regular folk ever make sense of the universe if sorcerers kept tinkering with reality?

The fox-man didn't slow or alter its stride as it plunged into the grayness and vanished. Kerin glanced at Sep and found that she was watching. She looked nervous, which was understandable, so he gave her a comforting smile and slipped his hand in hers.

"Ready?" he asked, and her head jerked slightly in affirmation.

"Good."

Trying to calm the slight fluttering in his own chest, Kerin pulled Sep into the doorway. Why was he so nervous? For the child's safety? Or – and now he felt a flash of guilt at the thought – because he feared something would go awry and the Antiquarian would rescind his wildly generous offer?

They emerged from the mist into the Antiquarian's shop. Or what had been his shop. The cluttered shelves and artifacts were gone, though a few hulking shadows pushed to the periphery of the great space suggested that some objects had merely been moved away from the middle of the room. The area where they had once been now resembled a sprawling workshop: Kerin saw anvils and bellows and contraptions of metal and wood, along with troughs of water and barrels overflowing with glittering substances. Scorch marks marred a large swath of the floor, as if an inferno had briefly raged and then quickly subsided. The air smelled of earth and fire, heavy with the acrid bitterness of burning coal and the more subtle sweetness of hot melted iron.

Kerin looked about in wonder, and he noticed Sep doing the same. If it weren't for the glimmering map of the stellar tributary stamped into the ceiling, or the softly falling motes of silvery light, he would have thought they'd been transported to a completely different place than where they had been before.

"Aha! You're here at last!"

The Antiquarian was coming towards them, threading his way between squat metal devices that looked like they would be equally at home in a forge or a torture chamber. His robes were covered in splotches, and a smear of black dust covered one side of his pale face.

Dark circles bruised the area under his eyes, but he was still smiling broadly and moving with an almost manic haste. Behind him trailed three of the little fox-men, indistinguishable save for the colors of their elegant waistcoats.

"Wonderful, wonderful. Everything is ready!"

"What is all this?" Kerin asked, indicating the jumble of tools and machinery.

The Antiquarian gazed around at the clutter with wide eyes, as if seeing it all for the first time. He rubbed his bald head, his hand leaving a dark stain on his scalp. "Ah, this? I've been busy since we last spoke! Figuring out how to disassociate an Elder phenomenon from its organic host is no easy task, let me tell you. But I've done it!" He leaned closer and chucked Sep under the chin, his eyes twinkling. "Yes, you'll soon be free, my dear."

He moved to one side and swept out his arm to indicate his servants. "And I've also been baking! To celebrate, let us first indulge in sweetcakes."

Sweetcakes? What?

One of the fox-men stepped forward, struggling to hold aloft a silver plate covered with what indeed looked to be small yellow cakes. Kerin could only stare at the delicacies, unable to comprehend what was happening.

"They are delicious, I assure you," the Antiquarian said, plucking one of the cakes from the pile. "If I was not the foremost scholar of Elder Race artifacts, I'm certain that I would be working in the kitchens of an emperor." He popped the entirety of the cake into his mouth and swallowed it without chewing.

Slowly Sep reached out and took a cake. The smell, Kerin had to admit, was intoxicating. The Antiquarian grabbed another and lifted it towards Kerin. "Don't insult me . . ." he said, dislodging crumbs as he waggled the cake.

Fine. Might as well go along with this madness.

Kerin chose his own cake, but before he could bring it to his mouth the Antiquarian lightly touched it with his own.

"*Avola!*" the Antiquarian exclaimed, which Kerin recognized as what certain cultures cried out before drinking or going into battle, and then tossed the cake into his mouth. Sep followed, much more tentatively, but once it touched her lips her eyes widened, and she finished the rest in two quick bites. Kerin tried his, and though from Sep's reaction he did expect to be impressed, he still wasn't prepared for just how delicious it was.

"Good, yes?" the Antiquarian said with a satisfied smile.

Sep grunted something unintelligible as she reached for a second.

The Antiquarian laughed and clapped his hands together sharply. "Ha-ha! Now that we've enjoyed the ceremonial sharing of victuals, let us get down to our business! Come with me."

He led them to the same desk they had all sat around before. Settling into his ostentatious throne the scholar beamed down at Kerin and Sep.

"Just a moment, please, while my servants make some final preparations."

Kerin glanced around. The three fox-men had vanished.

"Will it hurt?" Sep whispered.

The Antiquarian's smile became more comforting. "I promise you, child, you will feel nothing."

"Oh," Kerin said suddenly. "Perhaps this is the best time for this, scholar, while we have a moment." He fumbled in his pocket for the gray metal cube and then placed the object on the desk with a hollow clunk.

The Antiquarian stared at the artifact placidly, without any sort of recognition. "And this is ... ?"

Kerin blinked in surprise. He'd been sure the Antiquarian would recognize the cube, or at least sense whatever sorcery was inside. "Well . . . to be honest, I don't know. But someone very powerful is chasing after it. I thought you might be able to tell us why."

The Antiquarian reached across the desk and picked up the cube. He frowned, examining it from several sides. "It's not just simply metal. But there's also no great sorcery, I can tell you that, unless they've hidden it exceedingly well." He shook the cube hard, his head cocked as if hoping to hear a rattling coming from inside. But there was nothing. "It almost has the same resonance as something I'm very familiar with . . ." His nostrils flared, and Kerin could almost see the connection as it was made behind the Antiquarian's void-black eyes. "Aha! A memory pearl! It's different, yes, but the similarities are too great to be a coincidence." He shook the cube again, more gently than before. "Hello? Who's in there?" He reached down, and Kerin heard a drawer sliding open. Moments later the Antiquarian raised a large mallet, holding it poised above the artifact. "Should we smash it and see who's inside?" He looked almost gleeful.

"No!" Kerin cried, his hand flashing out to snatch away the cube. If the crystal rod attached to Sep could harness the power of a sun, who could guess what this artifact would do if broken . . . especially since it was what Xerivas had most desired in the treehold. Kerin had a vision of the entire planet destroyed by the singularity that would emerge from the shattered ruin of the cube. A memory pearl? That hardly seemed likely. Far too sentimental for a ruthless undead demigod. Perhaps the scholar was indirectly trying to remind Kerin about the reward for agreeing to let him remove the artifact from Sep.

The Antiquarian shrugged, as if Kerin's refusal to break the cube meant nothing to him and returned the mallet to its drawer. After doing this, he hefted an iron-banded box that had been at his feet and placed it on the desk with a grunt.

"What's this?" Kerin asked, returning the cube to his pocket.

With some effort the Antiquarian flipped back the heavy lid. Kerin rose slightly from his chair to see what was inside, and then sucked in his breath. Hundreds of sapphires were piled inside, some rough and others polished, all imprinted with small white blemishes like stars. And sitting on top of the priceless heap, like a tiny black dragon perched upon its hoard, was the memory pearl.

The wealth contained in this box was staggering. A single star sapphire could sustain Drifter and him for a year. A handful and he'd be richer than any of his ancestors had ever been.

And all he had to do was give the Antiquarian a little girl's arm.

Kerin looked over at Sep, and the pangs of guilt he was feeling were subsumed in a sudden panic. Her head was lowered and her eyes closed, though the gentle rise and fall of her chest suggested she was only sleeping. He reached out and grabbed her arm, but she didn't stir.

"Sep?" he said, then gave her a hard shake.

"Calm, Kerin," the Antiquarian said soothingly. "She should not be awake for what is about to happen."

He glanced at the Antiquarian. "You drugged her?" he asked angrily. "The cakes?"

The scholar nodded, his expression pained. "Yes. It is for the best, I promise you. And when next she opens her eyes this strange nightmare will be over for her." He shifted his empty black eyes to something beyond Kerin. "Ah. My servants are returning. It is nearly time to begin."

Kerin twisted around in his chair. Two of the fox-men were struggling to carry a large metal and wood contraption, while a third was dragging a wheeled stone urn, wisps of smoke escaping from within. A blackened metal handle was protruding from its opening.

"What is all this?" he asked, staring at the strange device warily as the fox-men slid it onto the desk in front of Sep. Its base was a block of pitted wood, and on either side a frame rose up to where a blade of what looked like glass was suspended.

Kerin's unease strengthened. It looked very much like a chopping block. "Is that what I think it is?"

The Antiquarian pursed his thin lips and sighed sorrowfully. "Yes, unfortunately. You see, Kerin, despite applying my formidable intellect to the task of drawing forth the artifact from the girl's arm I could not conceive of how to do it without potentially ruining the device." He expression became even more distraught. "So I think it is best if we make one clean cut and take her arm off just below the shoulder."

"That will kill her!" Kerin cried, rising from his chair in alarm.

"Please, you insult me," the Antiquarian replied with a shake of his egg-shell head. He gestured at the fox-men again, who were clustered around the smoking stone urn laying out a collection of small metal instruments. "My servants are well-trained in surgery. They shall quickly tie off the brachial artery and then . . ." He snapped his fingers and the fox-man in the red waistcoat gripped the blackened hilt protruding from the urn and lifted it. Kerin winced when he saw that its other end was broad and flat and glowed with tremendous heat. "We seal the wound," the Antiquarian said with satisfaction. "After you can bring her to the chimericists and she can have any arm she likes as a replacement. You certainly will have the funds to pay for the most talented of mixmages."

"You said you would save her arm!"

"I hoped I could!" the Antiquarian cried, fluttering his long fingers. "But my confidence was never as strong as I perhaps projected. I simply did not want to scare the poor girl!"

"Don't you think *waking up without an arm* will terrify her? And you said there were strands from the crystal extending into her brain. What will happen to her when they are suddenly severed?"

Kerin sensed that the Antiquarian's expression was meant to suggest that *he* was the one being unreasonable, and this made him all the more infuriated.

"When she wakes she will no longer have an Elder Race weapon attached to her. Surely you can recognize the danger the girl poses to this city – no, the entire planet – right now." The scholar leaned back and spread his arms wide. "But I understand your concerns. If you wish to carry the girl back to the historian's spire and lay her down in her bed and pretend when she wakes that this was all a dream, I will not stop you. Just remember" and here he flipped closed the lid of the box filled with star sapphires "what else you will be giving up."

Kerin swallowed hard, forcing himself to stare at the slumped Sep. A thin strand of drool stretched from her slightly parted lips, darkening the collar of her blue dress. The Antiquarian was right. He had seen the destruction the alvaren artifact could unleash, and it needed to be separated from her as quickly as possible. But to just slice it off? And despite the scholar's confidence that his servants could staunch the bleeding and cauterize the wound before she went into shock and died, Kerin knew how dangerous such procedures could be. Her life would spin at the end of a fraying thread, and if the surgery took only a few moments too long that thread would snap, and she would die.

But then there were the jewels. His gaze slid to the box of sapphires. A chance at a new life for Drifter and Nala and him. Another opportunity to speak with his grandfather, as well. The question of what the old man had meant by 'the labyrinth' had been gnawing at the back of his mind. Maybe the mysteries that had frustrated Kerin for decades could finally be explained.

He licked his dry lips. This would be a betrayal of her trust, he couldn't avoid that fact. Drugged, her arm cut away without her consent, her life put at risk . . . Kerin felt lightheaded. What choice did they have? What was the other, better option?

He nodded, hating himself.

"Good!" the Antiquarian cried, slapping the desk with his open palm. "Do not fear, Kerin. Hard choices should mean difficult decisions, and I can see the struggle in your eyes. But soon she will be free of this thing, I promise." He whistled sharply and the fox-men who had been waiting patiently jumped into action. One of them lifted Sep's arm from her lap while another tugged off the long glove she wore, revealing a limb almost completely given over to gleaming crystal. Kerin forced himself to watch as the creatures wrestled her arm up and placed it inside the contraption beneath the suspended glass blade, gently bringing her body forward so that she slumped across the desk, her cheek on the wood. The fox-men chittered and fussed, trying to align her arm perfectly so that when the glass fell it would only cut through flesh. Kerin stole a quick glance at the Antiquarian and found him watching all this with an expression of avid interest.

Finally they withdrew, each taking up one of the implements they'd left scattered on the floor. Sep murmured something in her sleep, and guilt like a jagged knife stabbed at Kerin. Nebulas, what was going on? How could he let this happen? A shimmer of silver light passed across the hovering blade, and in his mind's eye he saw it plunging down and blood spurting and the fox-men rushing forward to try and keep her from bleeding out . . .

"No," he said thickly. He reached for her but somehow the Antiquarian's hand was already on a small lever connected to the contraption and with the flick of a finger he snapped it down.

The blade fell.

Kerin averted his eyes, staring instead at Sep sprawled upon the desk.

A chime as the blade struck crystal. He tensed, expecting chaos as blood arced and the Antiquarian's servants leaped into action to try and save her.

Nothing. Dead silence. Steeling himself, Kerin looked again at the Antiquarian's device, unable to imagine what he might find.

Her arm. It had twisted in the eyeblink it had taken the glass to descend and somehow caught the blade in its hand. The sound he'd heard had been the gleaming edge striking her palm. Kerin's jaw dropped. Sep was still unconscious, her eyes closed, and her arm had apparently moved of its own volition.

"Fascinating," the Antiquarian breathed, and then he emitted what sounded to Kerin like a squeak of fear as light blossomed in the depths of the alvaren artifact.

"Oh, no," Kerin whispered as the world fractured into radiant shards.

16

PAIN.

Kerin opened his eyes. He was lying supine, staring up at a ceiling of dirty quartz riven by golden cracks. Hard, jabby things were pushing into his back, and with a groan he forced himself to sit up. Dust and larger stone fragments slid from him as he looked around, blinking.

Daylight was pouring into the ruin of the spire through massive gashes in the walls and ceiling. He shook his head, confused. Was this the Antiquarian's spire? In the harsh light of day the various artifacts and contraptions looked ancient and broken, as if the spire had been abandoned long ago. He glanced up again. There was no indication that an intricate star map had ever been incised into the ceiling, nor that silver motes had once drifted down from above.

What had happened? Where was the Antiquarian?

Wincing with the effort, Kerin climbed unsteadily to his feet. Beside him was the shattered remnants of the Antiquarian's desk, now nothing more than scorched chunks of wood. He noticed a few glittering slivers among the detritus, perhaps the glass blade that Sep had somehow caught.

Sep.

Kerin turned slowly, taking in the devastation. As he did so, a large piece of the ceiling came tumbling down, crushing a many-limbed device of dark metal. He shielded his eyes from the flying debris, then had to blink as more light flooded the devastated spire. He couldn't see the girl.

"Sep?" he croaked, peering through the dusty haze.

No answer. The grayness that had filled the spire's entrance was gone, and he could see out onto the street, which looked to be empty. Wait, there was something, a shiver of movement from just outside the door.

"Is that you, Sep?" he called out as a hollow booming came from above. Kerin looked up in alarm, noticing that the cracks above seemed to have widened. There might be only moments until the entire ceiling came crashing down.

Trying to ignore that thought, Kerin crouched and began to sift through the wreckage of the desk. He hissed in pain as he cut his finger on a shard of the glass blade – nebulas, that was sharp. He shuddered at the thought of it slicing through Sep's flesh, sucking at the welling blood as he continued searching with his other hand.

There. One side of the box had been vaporized, spilling out most of the star sapphires into a glittering pile. Kerin took several large handfuls, filling every pocket and pouch he could with the gems. Another loud cracking made him look up, and he swallowed nervously. He needed to get out of here. But where was the . . . ah. He grinned triumphantly as he spotted the memory pearl. The faceted black sphere nearly blended with the charred wood of the desk, and he had to reach deep into the debris – while being wary of more glass shards – to pull it free.

"Hello, grandfather," he murmured as he slipped the pearl into the pocket that also contained the alvaren cube.

Now to get out of here before everything came crashing down. Kerin stumbled towards the entrance, trying to catch again that flicker of movement he had glimpsed earlier.

He stepped out into the day's dazzling brightness. This area looked abandoned: the spires rising up around him were nearly as dilapidated as the broken one he had just exited. Large chunks were missing from most of them, with rubble and shadows choking their entrances. The Antiquarian's servant had seemed to lead them not far from Bas Jelaska's spire, but this was an entirely different area of the city. He couldn't see a single soul, although several orange lizards were splayed out sunning themselves in the empty streets.

The three fox-men were crouched off to the side, intent on something on the ground between them. Their ears perked up when they heard him approaching, and as one they turned to regard him with eyes of liquid black. A moment of disinterested attention, and then they glanced down again at what was in the dirt at their feet.

"Bloody stars," Kerin breathed softly when he saw what it was. Staring up at the fox-men, its mouth twisted into a silent scream, was the Antiquarian's face. Its edges were jagged, and it appeared to be made of something like porcelain. Had it been a mask all along?

Slowly, one of the fox-men reached down and lifted the ceramic face. The creature turned it this way and that, examining it closely. Chattering erupted among them, a debate ended when the one holding the mask yipped fiercely, raised it high, then dashed it hard against the ground. It shattered, fragments skittering. Then, to Kerin's shock, the three creatures started tearing at their clothes. Tiny claws shredded their waistcoats into fluttering strips that soon joined the pieces of the mask in the dirt. As soon as they had divested themselves of their clothes they went down on all fours. More yipping, and then they scampered into the street, bushy tails raised, leaving the torn remnants of their clothing behind. Their appearance startled the lounging lizards, sending the creatures scurrying into the shadows of the spires. Barking in excitement the foxes followed, and in moments they all had vanished from Kerin's sight.

He stared dazedly after them, unable to comprehend what he had just witnessed. It had the surrealness of a dream, but if this was a dream he should really try to wake up.

Finally he came back to himself with a shake. Sep. He had to find Sep. Guilt washed over him. She must feel scared and alone and confused.

Betrayed.

The star sapphires felt like iron ingots pulling him down, their weight an accusation. He'd sold her for a pocket full of gems.

Shielding his eyes from the sun's glare he stared at the spires rising in the distance. He thought he could see a flash of white, the unblemished Mandati stone of the administrative district, and that gave him something to orient himself by. Where would Sep flee? Back to Bas Jelaska's spire, most likely. That would be the best case scenario, he supposed. She would be distraught, but if anyone could calm her down it would be the old woman.

Where else could she go?

Oh. Oh, no.

Before the Antiquarian had summoned them, Sep had wanted to visit the temple of the Searing Light. A lifetime of litanies and scripture had taught her that salvation could be found through pain. But what would happen if she went there now? Kerin remembered the surging crowds of faithful in that plaza, and then his gaze went back to the spire she had destroyed. Large holes pocked its sides, the stone melted as if something incredibly hot had lanced out from within. Which was exactly what he suspected had happened.

How had he survived? Had Sep spared him?

He had to go the temple of the Searing Light. Maybe, he fervently prayed, she had returned to the safety of Bas Jelaska's home. He clung to that hope, hollow as it felt.

Kerin started walking in the direction of the temple district, grimacing at the twinges of pain coming from his ankle. As he passed the collapsing entrance of another spire his attention was drawn to something stirring in its recesses. Jagged limbs bent at unnatural angles unfolded as the Shadow crept closer to watch him. Kerin turned to face the thing, throwing up his arms in exasperation.

"What?" he shouted, sorely tempted to hurl a rock at it. "What do you want?"

The Shadow did not respond.

"Bloody stars," he grumbled again, turning away from the listing doorway and continuing to limp in the direction he had been going.

What a disaster.

~

By the time he reached the temples he felt like he had traveled from one extreme edge of the city to the other. Midday had come and gone, but the sun was still high in the sky, beating down mercilessly. He was filthy, sweaty, and bound together by a varied assortment of aches and pains, but over the long walk he'd concocted a plan for if Sep had returned to the Searing Light.

She'd been drugged by the Antiquarian, insensate to what was transpiring, and there was no reason to think she knew that he *hadn't* been likewise incapacitated. She'd seen him eat one of the cakes, after all. He'd claim the scholar had betrayed them both.

Of course, that was where his plan fizzled out. The artifact was still consuming her, and apparently it had a strong self-preservation instinct. If the Antiquarian couldn't remove it, who else in the stellar tributary had a chance? The mixmages were no experts in Elder Race sorcery. Maybe the pooled wisdom of a scholar cabal could come up with a solution, but it would take at least a score of solar days to arrive at the closest of the great university worlds.

And he had the strong sense that the sand had nearly finished slipping through the glass.

He paused at the edge of the temple plaza, relieved to find that it hadn't already been reduced to a smoking ruin. If anything, it looked even more crowded than when they'd passed through it a few days ago – the thalani must be a devout people. Not surprising, he supposed. They had been enslaved for centuries, and Kerin understood how oppression like that could create a strong religious streak in a people. To keep going they needed to believe that salvation was coming, in this life or the next. Or maybe they were trying to make good with their gods after learning that a lich had recently moved into the cluster.

The large crowds might also be explained by the cascade of bright flowers draping the walls of the Sower's sanctuary. It must be a festival day for the entity some believed to have seeded the stellar tributary with life. Of all the faiths, this was one that made the most sense to Kerin, as it provided a reason for why the same creatures – or very similar, at least – existed on worlds separated by unfathomably vast distances. Many Starfarers adhered to a variation of this belief, though their version was more a scientific theory than a religion. They held that it was starbeasts who had sown the universe with their spawn, and that the great creatures were the original progenitors of all life. The turtles that existed on a thousand worlds were distant cousins to Drifter and his god-like mother, just countless generations removed. When Kerin had broached this idea with Drifter the starbeast had snorted in derision at the thought that the mindless denizens of ponds and streams were in any way related to him. But Kerin still found the idea appealing, that life in the universe was a vast, connected web, its strands the Streams that bound together the tributary.

He saw no such value in the church of the Searing Light. Kerin frowned as he gazed upon the jagged temple of fused black iron hunching in one corner of the plaza. A religion devoted to inflicting pain and claiming it righteous . . . how could anyone believe that this pleased the divine?

Kerin began to shoulder his way through the milling believers, watching the crowds carefully for any sign of Sep. The buzzing activity in the square was not restricted solely to the Sower's sanctuary; there were so many Mandate citizens waiting to enter the temple of the Golden Emperor that they'd formed a line that nearly wrapped the white-stone building. Kerin wondered if they'd heard what the exarch had told Tessa, that the Golden Emperor was in fact travelling to Dust. He doubted that they had, given how this had been a surprise to the Shroud just yesterday. But then again, such news would certainly spread like wildfire once it became known. It wasn't every day that a living god came to visit.

No one was preaching outside the Searing Light temple, and as he came closer Kerin didn't see any worshippers approach the formidable door of wrought black iron. Perhaps this was a day of rest for the torturers of the Light and Sep had already been turned away. He pounded on the metal with his fist, loud enough that the hollow booming would be impossible to ignore if anyone was inside.

Hinges squealed as the door was drawn slowly open by a figure shrouded in white robes. The man or woman was a head shorter than Kerin, their face hidden by a cowl. The skin on the hands looked young, though laced with old scars.

"I'm looking for a girl . . ." Kerin began, but before he could finish the figure turned and shuffled away. Unsure what he should do, he followed, and as he stepped inside the door clanged shut behind him.

He stood in a small courtyard dominated by an altar of gray stone, above which hovered a pulsing sphere of blue-white light. No heat flowed from this radiance, and Kerin wondered if it was an illusion of some kind. Real or not, the patterns churning in its depths were hypnotic, and he found it difficult to look away.

"Embrace the Light, supplicant," came a familiar voice, and Kerin forced himself to look past the sphere to where a small set of steps led up to the arched entrance to the temple proper. The woman who he had seen preaching out in the plaza stood before him, the one who had entreated Sep to join her. She was dressed in the same black leather as before, the barbed whip he remembered coiled at her side. The black tears trickling down her cheeks glistened wetly, as if they had recently been repainted.

"I'm looking for a girl," Kerin said as the woman descended the steps. What had Sep called her? A Sister of the Thorns?

"We have girls here," the Sister said, cocking her head to one side as she regarded him. "Although we usually do not let supplicants choose their conduits. We prefer not to let the relationship grow too . . . personal."

"I'm not here to make someone suffer," he said through gritted teeth. "The girl I want to find might have come here. She has pale hair and is wearing a blue dress."

The Sister of Thorns crossed her arms. "Are you her father?"

"No."

"Lover?"

He clenched his hands into fists at the suggestion. "No."

She regarded him coolly. "Then I see no reason to answer your question."

"The girl is my . . . ward. She's confused. And dangerous."

The woman arched a sculpted eyebrow. "Dangerous?"

"Is she here?" Kerin persisted, taking a threatening step forward.

The Sister must have heard the fraying patience in his voice, because she pursed her black-painted lips. "She's here. The girl is a true believer."

"Bring her to me. Or take me to her."

The woman chuckled, shaking her head. "No. She has shared a great donation with the Light and descended into the catacombs. Even now, a blessed conduit is taking her pain."

"A great donation? She doesn't have any money."

The Sister of Thorns raised her arm. At first Kerin didn't know what he was supposed to be looking at, and then he saw the bracelet of blood-red jewels encircling her wrist. Nala's gift.

"She pleased the Light with her offering. So much so that she was granted the great boon of being allowed to personally transfer her pain to a blessed conduit."

Kerin had heard enough. Embracing his anger he strode forward, but before he could reach the steps the Sister of the Thorns moved to bar his way.

"Come no further, infidel—" she began, but whatever else she was about to say ended in a strangled squawk as he shoved her roughly to one side, sending her tumbling.

As he passed into the shadowed interior of the church he felt fingers scrabbling at his mind, then a hot rush as his Anathema blood obliterated whatever sorcery she was trying to conjure. He turned back to her and wagged his finger. The Sister's face was a mask of outrage and surprise where she lay at the bottom of the steps.

"Brother Charix!" she cried. "Stop him!"

A bulky shape in white robes glided from the shadows. Beneath the cowl of this acolyte was a countenance more suited for absorbing blows in an alley than leading morning prayers. As the thug reached for him, Kerin didn't hesitate, smashing his fist into the man's jaw. The acolyte dropped like a sack of grain, his head striking the edge of a stone plinth before he went sprawling on the floor.

"Send anyone else after me and next time I'll draw my sword," he called down to the Sister. She glared at him hatefully as he turned back to the interior of the church. Kerin knew those like her, bullies who reveled in inflicting pain on those weaker. They were also almost always cowards.

He stepped over the unmoving temple thug and entered the church proper. The nave filled most of the building's interior, glistening black beams curving together high above like the ribs of a giant beast to form a peaked roof. Alcoves lined the walls, but instead of the statues of saints or gods each contained what looked to be an abstract, barbed form writhing in agony. Rows of pews marched towards a raised dais supporting a great circle of obsidian or some other glistening black substance. A light pulsed in the depths of the darkness, similar to what he had seen outside. The entire space was empty except for a few white-robed initiates who were cowering among the pews as they stared wide-eyed at him.

Kerin stalked over and grabbed one of them roughly, hauling him to his feet.

"Where is the girl?" he hissed, shaking the boy hard enough that his cowl slipped back, revealing a terrified face covered in scars. Kerin felt a flicker of sympathy – someone had taken a blade to him many times before.

"Catacombs," the boy squeaked.

"Are you a pain conduit?" Maybe he was as much a victim as Sep had once been. Though he could speak, at least.

The boy goggled up at him. "No, thank the Light's infinite mercy."

So apparently being a pain conduit was not a coveted position here in the church of the Searing Light. Somehow he was not surprised. "Better pray for *my* mercy now," Kerin growled. "Now, show me how to get down there."

∾

The boy led him to a small vestibule hidden behind the hanging obsidian disc and a narrow set of stairs leading down into darkness. When Kerin pushed him towards the steps he collapsed to his knees, shaking as he babbled desperately about how it was forbidden and that only those that gave and received pain could enter the catacombs. The temptation to throw the acolyte face-first into the blackness was strong, but Kerin actually felt sorry for the youth as he watched him beg to be spared whatever terrible fate would befall him if he entered the catacombs. His terror was real.

Shaking his head in disgust, he left the boy blubbering behind him and started on the stairs. The darkness, he realized, was not absolute. Before he'd descended very far, he noticed a dull lightening below. There was also a smell, rising up, something that brought to mind organic matter rotting. It reminded him of a midden heap in the hot sun, or an alley where night soil pots were emptied.

His eyes had largely adjusted to the gloom by the time he reached the bottom. A corridor stretched away in front of him, lined by cells that were pockets of deeper blackness. He thought that nothing lurked in their recesses, but honestly he couldn't be sure. The faint light he'd noticed earlier emanated from a space at the end of the passage, and so he set off in that direction, his hand on the hilt of his sword. The place seemed abandoned, but the smell suggested that had not always been the case. Others had lived or been imprisoned down here, suffering in the darkness.

He saw Sep before he'd gone half the length of the long corridor. Relief swept over him, followed by a surge of self-loathing that his actions had compelled her to come to this place. She was on her knees, facing away from him, her head bowed as if in prayer. The chamber she knelt in was much larger than the cells he'd passed. An ancient lightsphere dangled from the ceiling, flickering and hissing, its radiance the sickly sepia of a dying crystal. Dry rushes crackled under his boots as he entered the room. The smell was much stronger here, nearly overpowering. There was no furniture, no suggestion that this was anything but a place for animals.

"Sep," he ventured, approaching her cautiously. He didn't want to scare her or have her lash out in anger. "Are you all right?"

She did not acknowledge his question. As he edged closer, he felt a shiver of surprise.

Sep was not alone. Huddled in front of her was another girl, her back pressed up against the mold-scarred wall. She was dressed in the same ragged, dirty white robes that Sep had been wearing when she came aboard Drifter. They were far too large for her, but even still, this could not hide how emaciated she was. Her cheeks were sunken, her arms where they emerged from frayed sleeves stick-thin and covered in weeping sores. Her hair was long and matted and encrusted with filth. She looked like a prisoner, but there were no chains on her arms or legs.

"Who is this?" Kerin said softly, crouching down. Sep did not answer, continuing to stare intensely at the girl in front of her. Tears were running down her cheeks, hissing and crackling when they struck her crystal arm.

The girl across from her would not meet Sep's eyes, and she was writhing as if in pain. For the first time Kerin saw objects scattered among the rushes: implements of black iron, some bladed and others blunt, and a coiled whip. The girl's arm was extended towards these things, her grasping fingers opening and closing. She moaned wordlessly, the sound sending a shiver up Kerin's spine.

"We need to get out of here, Sep," he said, reaching out to lightly touch her shoulder. "Let's go. There's nothing for you here."

She did not shake away his hand, but she also did not let him pull her back.

"Please, Sep, I—" His words died in his throat. The traceries of veins in her upper arm where the flesh had not yet been completely transformed had begun to glow.

"Oh, no. No, no, no," he murmured as his Anathema blood stirred. "Not here, Sep. Not this."

She ignored him, and in horror he could only watch as the shining lines spread like trickling water down the length of her arm. He had to get her away from here. In a cold panic he bent to gather

her up, but as his arms went around her a wave of force sent him sprawling backwards.

He lay still for a long moment, dazed, staring up in shock at the decaying lightsphere dancing above him. His blood was on fire; he could feel it surging in his veins as it struggled to dissipate the sorcery coursing through his body. Another surge of power from nearby tore apart the cobwebs clotting his thoughts and he forced himself to his feet. Sep was still kneeling in front of the terrified girl, but her arm was now filled with radiant light, wisps of energy swirling around her. Sorcery was flowing in a gathering wave, and he knew his Anathema blood would boil in his veins when this power finally crested.

"Sep, stop!" he cried, but she ignored him. The tears falling from her cheeks gleamed like diamonds. The pain conduit across from her had stopped writhing and gone utterly still, her wide-eyed gaze finally focused on Sep.

Kerin tried to take a step towards Sep but the air had thickened around her into a shell. Scalding winds rose, lashing him and stirring the dried straw covering the floor. Sep's hair and dress were unaffected; she was at the center of the maelstrom, an eye of calm within this building storm of sorcery.

When it finally broke, he would die.

"I'm sorry," he gasped, skirting Sep to reach the girl pressed against the wall. The power streaming from Sep was overwhelming, and it was all he could do not to collapse under the tremendous pressure. He picked this temple's pain conduit up – she weighed virtually nothing – and held her to his chest as he ran towards the stairs. She was like Sep, an innocent victim of the Searing Light's madness. Once, maybe, he would have scrambled to save only himself, but not now, not after watching Sep recover from what had been done to her. Behind him came fracturing explosions, followed by buffeting waves of heated air. The girl was limp in his arms, her eyes watching his face dully as he took the steps two at a time.

Kerin burst into the church of the Searing Light. A crowd of white-robed acolytes had gathered in the nave, along with the Sister of Thorns. The man Kerin had punched earlier was sitting on one of the pews with his head in his hands, but there were now several other Searing Light disciples just as large and imposing who must have arrived while he was in the catacombs. They stared in open-mouthed surprise as he ran towards them with the girl clutched to his chest – all except for the enraged Sister, who gestured at him with her thorned whip.

"Kill him!" she screamed.

"Get out!" Kerin shouted back, not slowing at all. "Flee, you idiots!"

The Searing Light acolytes shared uncertain glances, but still several of them moved to bar his way.

Kerin was considering trying to barrel through them when the floor exploded. A lance of roiling sorcery thrust upwards a dozen paces away from him, sending fragments of stone and chips of wood flying. It pierced the ceiling with a rending shriek and kept on going, vanishing into the sky. Somehow he managed to keep his balance, but the Sister and most of her followers were flung from their feet. When he reached the young boy who had first opened the temple door, Kerin paused and hauled him up, shoving him towards the door.

"This place is going to be destroyed!" he screamed, loud enough to be heard over the crackle of the erupting sorcery. "Run!"

Before he turned and fled he saw, to his relief, that most of the disciples were starting to stagger towards the temple doors. The Sister of the Thorns was not one of them, however. She'd regained her feet and was screeching at the others to stay, lashing the air with her whip.

They wisely were not listening. The coruscating pillar of sorcery was swelling, blasting apart more of the pews as it expanded, and the ground was now shaking so hard it felt like fissures would start opening at any moment.

He ran outside and found the black iron outer door already cracked open. Despite the girl's lightness, she was starting to slip, and he readjusted his hold on her as he hurriedly crossed the courtyard. The pulsing light that had greeted him earlier was gone, as if it had also abandoned the temple. He noticed the girl's gaze was transfixed on something over his shoulder; he spared a glance behind him, then nearly stumbled in shock. The sorcery had continued to grow, becoming a radiant pillar holding up the golden sky.

"Nebulas," he whispered, forcing himself to look away. How large would the sorcery get? Was the city itself in danger? His eyes were burning from staring into that roiling power, but it was nothing compared to the blood singing in his veins. He felt light-headed, and if his survival was not at stake he probably would have slumped to the ground in exhaustion and pain.

Kerin turned sideways to slip through the door, but still he accidentally struck the girl's head on the metal. He winced at the sound, but there was no flicker of pain in her empty face as she continued to stare up at the roiling sorcery.

Outside, the square was chaos. The crowds had fled the area around the temple of the Searing Light, but the streets leading away from the plaza were too narrow for the crush of people. Bottlenecks had formed, with bodies being dragged down and trampled by the panicked thalani. Kerin hesitated, unsure where to go. Every exit from the square was blocked and any attempt to push through would be like risking his life on a throw of blood knuckles. He glanced back at the church. It might have been wishful thinking, but it did look like the sorcery had stopped expanding. Maybe they could shelter in one of the other churches and hope that Sep would exhaust herself before the alvaren weapon obliterated the entire city.

Hitching the girl he carried up higher he started running towards the Sower's temple. Others who had found the press of people trying to flee down the narrow streets impassable had evidently arrived at the same idea, as suddenly they were surrounded by a crush of thalani fleeing for the safety of the Sower's gardens. No, he was wrong, he realized, the crowd was actually being driven back from the closest street mouth by a wedge of Mandati soldiers trying to enter the plaza. Kerin heard screams of pain now instead of terror, and he glimpsed dark-spattered blades rising and falling as the soldiers carved a path into the square.

A fat thalani man fleeing from the swords clipped Kerin's shoulder, spinning him around and almost knocking him from his feet. Someone else collided with him, nearly ripping the girl from his arms. It was an old thalani woman, and she stared up at him with terrified eyes just before she was dragged down by the surging mass of people. Buffeted from all sides, he felt the girl slipping from his grip.

And then she was gone. "No!" he cried, lunging for where she'd been swallowed by the crowd. His boot caught on someone sprawled out on the ground and he fell, barely managing to keep his face from smashing into the cobbles. Bodies swirled around him as he tried to struggle back to his feet. From his position, he searched the shifting forest of legs for any sign of the girl. Something struck the side of his head, and he dropped to his hand and knees again. His jaw was cracked hard, then another blow to his temple nearly made him black out. His fingers scrabbled for his sword hilt, as if he could somehow defend himself from the crush of terrified thalani, but even as he pulled *Mercy* free he found he was too weak to hold on, and it was torn away. Darkness pressed at the corner of his vision, and a cold tide was rising up inside him. As he sank into the black water, he thought he felt strong hands seize his arms and start to drag him across the stone.

17

WHEN KERIN finally opened his aching, sleep-gummed eyes he thought for a moment he was blind. He lifted his head from the uneven rock he was laying on and looked around wildly, then let out a deep sigh of relief when he saw that in one direction the blackness was not as complete, suggesting that there was light somewhere in the distance. He subsided again, laying back down and staring up into the dark, trying to work out what had happened and how he had come to be here.

From the rock beneath him it felt like he was in a cave or somewhere underground. The air smelled musty, and the utter silence was disconcerting after so many days of city living. Gently he began to probe his body. He ached a little, but he didn't seem to have taken any serious injuries. A minor miracle. His hand closed around empty air where *Mercy's* hilt and the memory of the sword being ripped from his grip returned to him. Damn. Something else occurred to him, and he fumbled frantically with his belt pouch. Before he reached inside he knew what he'd find, and his heart plummeted into his stomach. The star sapphires were gone. For a brief, glorious moment he'd been rich beyond his wildest imaginings. He sighed, patting the empty pouch forlornly. As he did so, his hand brushed something hard in one of his pockets. The alvaren cube. Of course. The damn thing just didn't seem to want to leave him. And there was another object, a small bulge nestled beside the artifact . . . he slipped his fingers into his pocket and touched something round and faceted. His grandfather's memory pearl. Whoever had brought him here hadn't known that these were a pair of incredibly valuable Elder Race artifacts. A bit of luck, at least.

He noticed something else, the feel of cold metal encircling his ankle. With a grunt he sat up, reaching down for confirmation of what he expected – yes, a manacle connected to thick iron links, and when he tugged on the chains they barely budged. He was indeed a prisoner. Some Mandate dungeon, he supposed. Well, maybe when the guards appeared he could use Tessa's name to get out of here. And find out what had happened to Sep. He hoped that after she had unleashed the artifact's power she'd fallen unconscious, as had happened before. The exarch and the Crimson would want to study her, to learn how she had channeled so much raw sorcery. Surely they wouldn't simply kill her, as then they'd risky losing the opportunity to harness and wield such power. He hoped.

Kerin wasn't sure how long he lay there in the dark, but eventually his wandering thoughts and bouts of self-pity were interrupted by the sound of approaching footsteps. Light swelled in the distance, illuminating a corridor rough-hewn from the rock, and after a moment a sphere of harsh white radiance drifted around a bend, followed by a man in gray robes. Kerin had been expecting a milk-white Mandate face, and he was surprised when he realized it was a thalani coming towards him. And that he had met him before.

"Ho, *kalaman*," the man said when he entered Kerin's prison. He grinned, the sorcerous light making his perfect white teeth glow phosphorescent.

"Ho, Rel," Kerin replied, holding up his hand to shield his eyes from the light.

The thalani mindmage from the Old Market dipped his head in acknowledgment. "Excellent memory, Kerin thon Talisien. My friends and I must have made an impression."

"I suspected we'd meet again."

The mage gestured, and the light dwindled to a less abrasive glow. "Probably not like this, though," he remarked, looking around the barren chamber. He kicked at the large iron ball at the end of the chain connected to Kerin's ankle, and a hollow clang echoed in the stillness.

"Where am I?" Kerin asked.

"Someplace safe," the mage replied.

"Are we still in Sanctum?"

Rel shrugged. He began to make a slow circuit of Kerin's cell, running his fingers along the stone walls.

"What happened?"

The thalani paused, turning towards him with eyebrows raised. "What happened? You ignited another wraith crystal and obliterated the church of the Searing Light."

Wraith crystal?

"No, I didn't."

His eyes narrowed. "Well, then what was it? Some Elder Race artifact? What could possibly create that kind of explosion?"

"I don't know."

"Bloody stars, you don't," Rel muttered. He sighed and leaned in closer. "Look, *kalaman*. It's better if you just tell me. I have friends in the Dawn who specialize in making stubborn folks tell their secrets. You really don't want me to call them down here."

"Why do you think I had anything to do with it?"

Rel smirked as he pulled a round tin from his pocket. He unscrewed the lid and dipped his finger inside. Kerin saw the unmistakable nacreous sheen of raw glimmer coating his fingertip before he sucked it clean.

The thalani's pale blue skin darkened, and his nostrils flared as the drug swept through him. So the mage was a glimmer fiend. No wonder he always seemed to be in such a good mood.

"Well, *kalaman*, the problem is that I just don't believe in coincidence. You were in the Bowery when the wraith crystal brought down the spire. And then there you were again, stumbling out of the Light's church just before it exploded even more spectacularly." He shook his head slowly, as if in admiration. "I have to admit, you have the face of a card maven. When we met in the Old Market I never would have believed you were responsible for the mess in the Bowery."

Kerin was having trouble keeping his thoughts in order. Everything was very confusing. "The Black Dawn destroyed the spire."

Rel's face creased in frustration. "You can drop that fiction, *kalaman*. I'm in the Dawn, and you and me both know we didn't do it."

Kerin didn't know what to say to this, so he just stared at the mage stupidly.

Rel snorted. "Wish I could get my claws into your brain, Kerin. Real curious what you know and where you came from. Damn Anathema blood. As I said, if you don't start cooperatin' we'll have to do this the old fashioned way, involvin' lots o' pointy and sharp things."

"I wish I could let you in my mind," Kerin told the mage. "Then you'd know I haven't been blowing up any buildings."

Silence descended. Rel tilted his head to one side, studying Kerin with his cheeks sucked in. Then he sighed and shook his head. "Should've guessed the Mandate would train you up good. All right then, we'll see whether Mazrem can make you talk when he gets back."

Mazrem? That name tickled Kerin's memory. Bas Jelaska had mentioned it back when they'd first arrived at her home. The mysterious leader of the Black Dawn.

His situation just kept getting better and better.

~

After Rel departed, his sorcerous light trailing behind him like an obedient dog, Kerin crawled across the floor until the chain around his leg went taut and leaned his back against the wall. Darkness had poured back into the chamber, blacker than before. The Dawn had left him his lightspheres, but he didn't want to risk exhausting the crystals. He had no idea how long he would be imprisoned, and the ability to see might be of desperate importance later. Instead, he drew forth the memory pearl. His grandfather had claimed to have escaped from worst predicaments than this, and while Kerin wasn't sure which of the old stories he believed, Cal might have some useful advice for him.

And he also just really wanted to talk to his grandfather.

Taking a deep breath, he clenched his hand around the pearl and closed his eyes. What would the old man think of all that had happened? Would he even believe Kerin? Liches and Shrouds and Elder Race artifacts. He certainly would have scoffed if his grandfather had told him the same story. Just another Talisien tall tale. Sighing, Kerin counted twelve heartbeats, then opened his eyes.

Darkness. He was still sitting on stone, pressed up against the wall.

"Grandfather?" he tried, but there was no reply except for the echo of his own voice.

Bloody stars. Kerin rolled the memory pearl around in his palm. Had the Antiquarian activated it earlier back in his spire? Perhaps it required a little trickle of sorcery to unlock the moment frozen within.

It was then that he felt it.

A crack had spread across the pearl's tiny facets, barely perceptible. But enough, perhaps, to destroy the artifact's delicate sorcery. A hollowness swelled in Kerin's chest. He'd found his grandfather again, only to lose him.

With numb fingers he slipped the pearl back into his pocket. Maybe it could be fixed. Maybe some fragment of his grandfather could be salvaged.

Sep. Tessa. His grandfather. He'd lost all of them. He slammed the back of his head against the rock wall. Pain flared, but it felt distant. Everything he did ended in disaster. Tessa had been right to leave him all those years ago. She had foreseen where he would end up, rotting away in the blackness of some gaol. Kerin had been given a name, a sword, and a starbeast, and in the end he'd amounted to nothing.

When they finally came for him, he felt something like relief to be rescued from his own thoughts. There were eight, a mix of men and women, all hard-eyed and dressed in the roughspun tunics and leggings of the Sanctum lower classes. Most had knife scars, though these looked more ritualistic than the result of back-alley brawling, similar to what Kerin had noticed on Rel's thuggish companion in the Old Market. All had long daggers prominently displayed at their waist, though two also carried cumbersome-looking crossbows that they trained on Kerin like they expected him to snap his chain and lunge for them.

"Boss wants to see ye," rumbled the thalani with the darkest age veins as he bent to unlock the manacle around Kerin's ankle. "Don't do nothing stupid."

Kerin wanted to laugh at this, but he couldn't summon the energy. Instead he stared bleakly at the man as the iron circlet popped open. The thalani seemed to sense his state of mind, because he grunted with satisfaction and then motioned for two of his compatriots to haul Kerin to his feet.

"This one's a Shroud?" one of the scarred women said dubiously.

"Didn't say he was a Shroud," replied the older thalani. "But boss thinks he's an agent of the milkies. Brought down the spire in the Bowery, he did. Apparently had something to do with the mess at the churches as well."

Mutterings swelled at this, surprised glances. Kerin ignored them. The aching emptiness inside had brought him well past caring. If these Dusters truly believed he was the terrorist who had blown up large chunks of their city, his fate was sealed. And he wasn't frightened at what they'd do to him. He just felt numb.

"Let's go, then," the leader said, then sent Kerin stumbling forward with a shove. He almost allowed himself to go sprawling on the ground, if nothing more than to annoy his captors who'd have to drag him up again, but to his surprise he felt a little flash of indignation when he heard a snort of amusement from one of the others. Kerin steadied himself and turned to stare a challenge at the thalani who had pushed him. He may be a dead man walking, but he wasn't about to give these idiots the satisfaction of seeing him grovel.

Something sparked in the older thalani's eyes, maybe a glimmer of respect. "All right, all right," he grumbled, gesturing down the corridor. "Let's get going, boss don't like waiting."

They fell in around him in a loose phalanx, the ones carrying crossbows taking up the rear. Despite their guffaws, they were still not taking any chances.

The thalani in front carried lanterns, and from the way they moved and how they peered down every side passage Kerin sensed they did not often come here. He saw no evidence of habitation. There was no furniture, no lightspheres dangling from the rocky ceiling, no garbage to suggest that anyone had ever lived in this maze of empty corridors and chambers. And it *was* a maze, as Kerin quickly lost count of the many twists and turns they took. From the sheer size of this place he assumed they must be underground, beneath the city. There were no buildings in Sanctum large enough to contain this place. And it was old. He felt the same sense of suffocating age in the rock spires. He would bet his life that this warren was carved out by the vanished primitives who had once ruled Dust. Despite himself, he felt his curiosity stirring.

A string of lightsphere affixed to the wall ahead of them suggested they were passing into an occupied section of the tunnels. There were other signs as well: discarded wooden skewers like those the street food sellers used to thread the insects they grilled, graffiti chalked on the walls, and the murmur of distant voices.

An entrance grander than any they had yet passed loomed in front of them, a craggy thalani nearly as wide as he was tall leaning against the wall outside. As Kerin was marched past him, the blue man muttered something and glared at him.

The room inside was larger and higher than what Kerin had seen before, and unlike the rest of these catacombs it was not empty. Stone urns filled the vast space, placed in neat rows like soldiers on parade. A group of thalani stood among these urns, and they turned towards Kerin as he was escorted into the chamber. He recognized several of them: the mage Rel was there, his vacant smile and glazed eyes suggesting he'd recently indulged in glimmer, and also Kapper, the bald thug from the Old Market. To his surprise the beggar was also present, slouching in the same tattered robes he'd been wearing that day, keeping himself upright by resting his plague-scarred hand on the lip of one of the urns.

"Ho, Mazrem, we got the streamsurfer here," said one of the thalani accompanying Kerin, just before another shove sent him staggering forward.

It was the beggar who drew back the cowl of his robes, his eyes narrowing as he studied Kerin. He was young, his age-veins barely visible, but his skin was mottled, and the hand gripping the stone urn visibly trembled.

This was Mazrem Tou, the leader of the Black Dawn? The man who had orchestrated the murder of an exarch and brought whispers of revolution to a Mandate world?

The disbelief in Kerin's face must have been obvious, as the thalani's scabbed lips twisted.

"Surprised, thon Talisien?"

Kerin shrugged. "I suppose so."

The beggar chuckled. "I like being underestimated. As do you, it seems."

"What do you mean?"

Mazrem raised one of his arms and made a gesture that encompassed Kerin. "Truth now, look at you. Your disguise is impressive. You appear to be nothing more than a disgraced streamsurfer so destitute and pathetic he must impose upon one of his grandfather's old lovers. His once-celebrated name – if it is ever still spoken in the tributary – now accompanied by snickers and shaken heads. And yet, suddenly, it is revealed that you're an agent of the empire." He snorted. "I have to say, that day in the market, I looked at you and saw a fool who had accidentally become entangled in all this. You're a dangerous man, Kerin thon Talisien."

"I don't know what you think you know, but you're wrong. I couldn't care less about your rebellion. And I certainly have no friends in the Mandate."

"Even your pretty Shroud?"

"She's not my Shroud. The last time I saw her she told me she never wanted to see me again."

Mazrem gave him a long, considering stare. One of his eyes was purple, Kerin realized, the other a dark green.

"We've been following you, thon Talisien. My men saw you stumble out of the Searing Light church just before it was obliterated. I want to know what you used to destroy it."

"It wasn't me."

Mazrem scratched at his pocked cheek. "I thought you might be less than forthcoming. So I prepared a little demonstration." He whistled sharply, and a pair of thalani entered the room, half-dragging and half-carrying a soldier of the Mandate. The red markings on his face writhed, blending with his dark bruises, and his head lolled like he was barely clinging to consciousness.

"This fellow tried to follow us home," Mazrem said. "Bad luck for him."

The soldier's eyes fluttered open, and he croaked something that might have been a plea for mercy. In response, the bald thalani Kapper stepped forward and struck him hard across his face, grinning when blood sprayed from the soldier's shattered nose.

While this was happening, Mazrem had pulled a thick leather glove like a blacksmith might wear over his pocked hand. He inspected it for a moment, as if searching for something. Whatever he saw satisfied him, as then he reached down into the closest stone urn. When the glove withdrew several of the fingers had darkened, smeared with a substance. Mazrem hobbled over to the slumped soldier and reached up to his slack face. He traced the path of one of the red tattoos where it writhed over the bruises, leaving a trail of dirt or ash. When he finished, he hurriedly stepped away, and at the same time the two thalani released their hold on the soldier and also scrambled back, letting him fall to his knees.

The soldier brought a trembling hand to his face, wiping at the blackness. Kerin sucked in his breath when he realized that he'd seen this substance before. In the chamber of the exarch's daughter, clinging to her cold skin . . .

"They come," Mazrem rasped, dread and excitement in his voice.

The soldier swayed, his gaze unfocused. He did not seem aware of the sudden tension, or that the thalani had retreated to the edges of the room. A hand tugged at Kerin, and he joined the others, leaving the dazed soldier on his knees among the stone urns.

Something flowed past Kerin in a rush of frozen air, a darkness with vague limbs flickering. From all directions the Shadows came, emerging from the ancient stone of the walls and rushing towards the soldier like sharks drawn by blood. Above ground, in daylight, they had seemed harmless, almost child-like . . . but here in this dark subterranean realm the sight of them filled Kerin with fear. They swarmed the soldier, caressing his flesh with their insubstantial arms. There was no terror in the Mandati's face, no pain. But something like fingers of pale mist was leaking from his mouth and nose. It unspooled in the air, and several of the Shadows converged, drawing whatever it was into themselves. As they did this, their forms seemed to harden, as if gaining substance.

Kerin heard the death rattle from across the room. The soldier toppled to one side, and when his head struck the stone with a fleshy thud the Shadows scattered, melting away. The last to vanish were the ones that had swallowed the man's essence; they lingered, then began to move away sluggishly, as if engorged. When they reached the walls they finally dissipated like smoke, trickling into cracks Kerin couldn't see.

For a long moment no one spoke.

Then Kapper stepped forward and spat in the direction of the sprawled soldier. "Good riddance."

Mazrem hobbled over to the dead man, beckoning for Kerin to approach as well. When he hesitated, another hard shove came from behind, sending him stumbling forward. He nearly lost his balance, and he felt a surge of fear that he would reach out blindly to catch himself and accidentally plunge his hand into one of the open urns.

"The death does not appear painful," Mazrem said to Kerin, indicating the soldier with a jerk of his chin. That seemed to be true. The man's face looked untroubled where it lay upon the stone, as if he had merely decided to rest for a moment. Only his staring, glassy eyes suggested that life had fled his body.

Fled, or been ripped away and devoured. Those Shadows had been swollen with the man's . . . what? His soul? His life?

"This is how the exarch's daughter died," Kerin murmured, and Mazrem glanced at him sharply.

"Yes. And the exarch who preceded her father. The Shadows are the vengeance of Dust made manifest."

"What are they truly? What is in these urns?"

Mazrem shrugged, his expression suggesting he did not care to know.

"It's organic," Rel suddenly interjected. His voice sounded distant, like he was floating far above them all. "The ash. That's why we call this room the Crematorium."

"Quiet!" Mazrem hissed, scowling.

"Don't matter if he knows," Rel said defensively. "He ain't getting topside again."

"You're not giving him much incentive to talk," Mazrem remarked acidly. He dipped his gloved hand into an urn, then studied his dark-smeared fingers. After a long moment his blood-shot eyes slid to Kerin. "My associate is wrong. I will offer you the chance to swim another Stream. Just tell me why you destroyed the church of the Searing Light. And how. Tell me about the Shroud and her plans. Tell me why you serve the Mandate." He waited for a long moment, and when Kerin said nothing Mazrem's gaze moved past him, to the others in the room. "Seize him," he said, stepping closer.

Strong hands grabbed his arms. He tried to run, but something hard slammed into the back of his legs, dropping him to his knees. Fingers tangled in his hair, holding him immobile as Mazrem extended his gloved hand towards Kerin's face.

"The destruction of the Searing Light had nothing to do with the Mandate," Kerin said, nearly babbling, unable to look away from the darkened glove as it drifted closer and closer. "It was the girl. She used to be a pain conduit. That was . . . revenge, I think, for what they'd done to her. And to others." Mazrem's outstretched fingers were less than a hand-span from his cheek. Kerin strained to pull his head farther back, away from the black-smeared glove.

"The girl?" Mazrem scoffed. "The child from the Old Market?" He glanced at Rel. "Is that possible? Is the girl some kind of sorcerer?"

The Black Dawn mage shook his head. "No. But there *was* something strange about her."

Mazrem grunted. "The Shadows, you mean. The way they swarmed her."

"Somethin' else, also," Kapper interjected in his gravelly drawl.

The diseased thalani's brow furrowed. He drew his hand back, and Kerin gasped in relief.

Kapper approached Mazrem, eyeing the ash on the glove warily, and leaned in close to whisper in his ear. A look of surprise passed across the Black Dawn boss's face, then confusion. "Interesting," he murmured, giving Kerin a thoughtful look.

"What is it?" Rel asked, then giggled like he'd just remembered something funny.

"It seems the girl has come into our possession again," Mazrem said slowly.

Kerin's head snapped up. "What?"

"We found her wandering in the rubble of the Searing Light, the only survivor after the explosion. The Mandate were about to seal off the area, so my men hurried her away to see if she had any answers about what had happened."

"Please, take me to her," Kerin said, his words coming out in a tumbling rush. "She's innocent in all this." *And alive. Sep was still alive.*

Mazrem carefully peeled off the ash-smeared glove and dropped it inside one of the urns. "You just said she was dangerous."

"Through no fault of her own. She just . . . lashed out."

Mazrem stared at him for a long moment, then pinched the mottled bridge of his nose and sighed. "Kapper, tell your men to meet us at the pit with the girl. Maybe Kerin will be more forthcoming when her life is the one at stake."

Rel let out a high-pitched giggle, quickly stifled when he slapped his hand over his mouth.

Mazrem winced, as if the sound actually pained him. "Bloody glimmer fiend," he muttered, shaking his head.

18

Kerin sensed the vastness of the undercity as the Black Dawn insurgents escorted him through a sprawling maze of twisting passages and chambers. The way they traveled showed signs of permanent habitation – lightspheres strung along the low ceiling, deteriorating furniture strewn about, refuse piled in corners – but there were many more tunnels they passed that vanished into darkness. When they encountered other thalani their sudden appearance seemed to be a surprise, but after a flurry of questions most fell in with the men and women accompanying Kerin. He sensed from their excitement that this was not a common occurrence.

Their numbers had swelled to two dozen or so by the time Mazrem slowed his already hobbling pace. In front of them loomed a much larger and grander doorway. Like everywhere else in the undercity, there were no carvings or decorations, but the sheer size of the blocky pillars flanking the soaring entrance suggested that whatever was beyond had once been of great importance. Kerin noticed that the mood of the thalani around him had shifted. Now, there was nervousness in their faces, quick glances at the yawning darkness and then to their companions, hands touching the hilts of swords or crossbow stocks.

Mazrem showed no such apprehension, though, passing between the great pillars and vanishing into the blackness.

"Rel," his voice floated back, sounding slightly annoyed. "Light."

The mage blinked, as if returning to himself from very far away. "Hmm? Oh, yes," he murmured, then a moment later radiance blossomed between his fluttering fingers. The light swelled, and after molding it into a sphere Rel released his sorcery, allowing it to float into the chamber Mazrem had entered.

The space beyond was so vast that its full dimensions were lost to the darkness. For perhaps a dozen paces the floor continued, and then fell away abruptly. Mazrem stood upon this ledge, peering down into whatever was below. Kerin approached the Black Dawn leader hesitatingly, unnerved by the mystery of what lurked in the blackness.

Mazrem did not turn as Kerin came up beside him. "Show him," he commanded, and the ghostly light began to sink. Kerin sucked in his breath at what was revealed.

The bottom of the pit seethed. For a moment, it reminded him of things he had glimpsed after staring deep into the Streams – unclear shapes writhing in darkness, with just enough coordination to suggest that somewhere behind this movement lurked an unknowable intelligence.

They were Shadows. Thousands of them, covering the floor in a shifting layer, a lattice of flickering black limbs so dense that the sorcerous light could not reach the stone beneath. And there was a sound drifting up, a faint susurrus like insects murmuring. Whispers in a language unlike any Kerin had heard before.

"What is this place?" he asked softly, horrified.

Mazrem shrugged. "We don't know. But I believe they are guarding that." He extended a blackened finger towards the far side of the room, which was just coming into focus as Rel's light continued to drift across the pit. A deeper blackness was set into the distant wall, and it looked like the entrance to a tunnel.

"Where does that go?"

Mazrem hacked a laugh that ended with him spitting up something over the edge of the pit. "The Mother only knows. You saw what happened when that ash touched living flesh, how the Shadows swarmed and killed whoever had been marked? The same happens when someone is lowered into the depths here. If we could make them scatter for a moment you could see the bodies of several brave souls who tried to make their way to that tunnel." Mazrem shook his head. "Probably just bones now. They were good men, some of the first to swear themselves to the cause."

"And that cause is killing Mandati?" Kerin asked, unable to tear his gaze from the almost hypnotic pattern made by the Shadows.

Mazrem snorted. "Freedom. And yes, that does mean killing the ones with their boots on our necks. But no one else, if it can be helped."

"So, you're saying you wouldn't have brought down that spire?"

The Black Dawn leader scowled. "Of course not. Do you still think you can convince me you had no part in that? I'm no fool, Kerin."

Heavy footsteps made them turn. A pair of grizzled thalani had stepped out onto the ledge, and between the Black Dawn thugs – hunched over, staring blankly at the floor – was Sep. Her pale hair was wild and tangled, partially obscuring her face, and the long glove that had once hidden the alvaren artifact was gone. Almost certainly incinerated by the sorcery she had unleashed at the church.

"Sep!" Kerin called to her, taking a step in her direction. She did not look up, and the thalani flanking her moved to block his way. "Are you all right?" he asked, but again she did not answer. She looked physically whole, at least, but what about her mind?

"Girl's broken," rumbled one of the thugs, speaking to Mazrem. "Found her wanderin' the plaza. Kapper recognized her, said she was in his crew." He jerked his head in Kerin's direction.

"Mmm," Mazrem murmured, studying Sep with pursed lips. "I remember the Shadows took such an interest in her. And I'd wager anything your concern for her wellbeing was not feigned." He nodded sharply and gestured with his pocked hand for her to be dragged closer.

Kerin stepped forward, but more of the Black Dawn approached to interpose themselves between him and Sep. Kapper folded his arms across his chest and giving Kerin a look that suggested he wanted him to try something.

Sep stumbled towards Mazrem when one of the thalani who had brought her here gave her a push from behind. Kerin could see her face more clearly now – it was empty, as if she was not even aware of where she was or what was happening. Dirt smudged her cheeks, and much of the blue dress Nala had bought for her had been reduced to charred tatters.

Kerin clenched his fists. She'd come so far, slowly emerging from the horrors that had shaped her life, and now it looked like she'd tumbled back into herself. Used by the Searing Light. The lich. The Antiquarian. By him. Kerin swallowed back the lump in his throat. And now Mazrem wanted to use her to make him tell secrets that didn't exist.

The unfairness of it all made him want to throw himself at the Black Dawn.

"Interesting," Mazrem murmured. He had taken Sep's limp, glittering arm and was examining the faceted crystal fingers. "Did the mixmages do this?"

Kerin watched Sep's arm, but no light glimmered in its depths. It looked dead, an empty chunk of stone carved to look like a human limb.

Oh, to the abyss with it all. What did it matter if they knew the truth? "That's what destroyed the church of the Searing Light. It's an Elder Race weapon."

Mazrem's lips twitched. "My, my. You have quite the imagination." Still, he held Sep's hand up higher. "Rel, what can you feel?"

The thalani mage drifted forward. He leaned closer, studying the crystal with glazed eyes. "Don't feel nothing. But if it's Elder, might be beyond my abilities."

"Elder," Mazrem muttered, shaking his head as he let Sep's arm fall. "Ridiculous."

"Well, they did try an' see the Antiquarian . . ." Rel began, but Mazrem cut him off with a snort.

"Kerin here has clearly been trained by the Inquisitarium to fashion layers of lies intended to confuse and mislead." He seized Sep's crystal wrist and yanked her closer to him. She stumbled, barely keeping her balance. Kerin's heart stuttered – if she'd fallen forward she would have tumbled into the pit where the Shadows roiled. "But I do believe that you do care about this one. So here is your last chance to save her. Tell me about the Shroud's plans and I will not feed her to the things down there."

"I don't know anything!" Kerin cried. As he tried to get to Mazrem and Sep hands gripped him, holding him back.

The boss of the Black Dawn shook his head in disgust. Then he pulled hard on Sep's arm, sending her toppling over the edge. She did not cry out as she vanished from sight.

"No!" Kerin screamed, ripping himself free and rushing to where he'd last seen her. His heart was flailing wildly – how much time did she have? Would his Anathema blood protect him from these things? Could he somehow save her? Below him, the Shadows writhed and chittered, the sound almost like laughter. Shouts of alarm rose up, boots pounding stone as the thalani surged forward to seize him again. Fingers curled around his shoulder; he shook himself loose, and knowing this would be his only chance he seized it blindly.

Kerin jumped.

Searing cold, and then the breath was driven from him as his shoulder slammed into stone. Pain lanced up his arm, making spots of color bloom in his vision. He lay there, gasping for air, his cheek pressed against the floor.

He needed to get up. But it felt like there was something heavy squatting on his back, crushing him into the ground. Kerin moaned, his fingers scrabbling at the fractured rock as he tried to muster the strength to push himself to his knees. The whispers were swooping around his head like birds, swelling and then fading. He thought he heard Mazrem shouting from far away.

He was among the Shadows. He could feel them slithering over his body, freezing gusts of air, plucking at his hair and running cold fingers along his exposed skin. The sound of them strengthened even as he sensed his consciousness trickling away. Cold gave way to heat, like he was slipping into a sun-warmed sea, a prickling wave carrying him out of sight of the shore . . .

Kerin returned to himself as something hard struck his face. He spluttered, suddenly remembering to breathe.

Panic clutched at his chest as he struggled to rise. The hardness that had slapped him was now holding tight to his collar. What had grabbed him? The darkness shivered and convulsed like a living thing, but still he could see nothing. With one hand he pushed himself to his feet, and with the other he reached out for what had a hold of him. He felt something cold, and faceted like a cut gem . . . gasping with relief, he clutched at Sep and let her lead him stumbling through the darkness.

The Shadows battered him, sliding across his flesh and murmuring into his ear, but the feel of Sep's hand in his own anchored him, and they could not drag him down.

Step after step, each a struggle. He was wading underwater into a dark and cold current, a terrible pressure building in his skull. He held his breath, unwilling to allow the Shadows any chance to coil around his soul.

And then he was staggering forward, crying out in relief as he emerged from the oppressive pit into a darkness that did not murmur and dance. "Bloody stars," he gasped, shivering as the last of the clammy filaments unwound from his skin. He tried to stop so that he could catch his breath, maybe let his flailing heart settle, but the hand gripping his own was insistent, dragging him along.

He wasn't sure how long they continued on like this. His sense of time frayed, and when he finally managed to fumble a lightsphere from his pouch with numb fingers he couldn't be sure how long had passed. He shook the sphere, kindling the crystal within.

Radiance slid along stone walls and a ceiling flecked with some glittering substance. The way ahead was lost to darkness, the light illuminating only a dozen paces or so ahead of them before fading. Almost certainly they had entered the tunnel Kerin had glimpsed from the lip of the pit, what Mazrem had guessed the Shadows had been guarding.

"Sep," Kerin croaked, his mouth dry. He wasn't expecting her to stop, but she did, releasing his hand. She didn't respond or turn to him. Instead, she lowered her head to stare at a spot on the ground.

"How are you?" he asked, coming around in front of her. She did not raise her gaze, though he thought he saw her flinch as he stepped closer. One side of her face was mottled by a spreading bruise; he suspected she'd gotten that from falling into the pit. The other side . . . he hissed in dismay when she saw how far the crystal had spread. It had crept from her shoulder, turning part of her neck translucent and extending a glittering tendril up her jaw to caress her cheek. In the glow of the lightsphere he could see the dark shadow of her throat and the veins etched beneath her changing skin.

He reached out instinctually to touch her face, but then realized what he was about to do and withdrew his hand. "Does it hurt?" he whispered, but still she did not respond.

A flicker of movement caught his eye. The light was dancing on the wall, but that made no sense as it wasn't a flame he held . . . ah. He turned to face the Shadow as it slid across the stone like a spreading stain. It did not acknowledge him, eventually merging with the darkness at the edge of the radiance thrown by his sphere. He watched where it had vanished, and then his attention was drawn to another of the creatures pressed against the far wall. This one was crouched like it was ready to pounce.

So they had not left all the Shadows behind them. Some had followed them . . . or perhaps these ones had always dwelled here. Their behavior was far less aggressive than the ones in the pit, at least. Kerin had thought he sensed rage as they battered him back there, but the Shadows here seemed different.

What were they? Rel had claimed that the ash summoned them.

The Crematorium, he'd called that room with the urns. Was the ash the remnants of the Shadows' physical bodies? And did that mean they were indeed revenants of some kind, haunting the world that had once been theirs?

"Is she all right?"

Kerin's attention snapped back to Sep. The girl's voice was barely a whisper. Her head was still lowered, but he caught her gray eyes watching him from behind snarled bangs.

"Who?" he replied, crouching slightly to bring his face to the same level as hers.

She licked her lips. "The girl."

The girl? Kerin's mind raced. *What was she talking about?*

"The one who walked in the Light."

Oh. Everything since the Antiquarian had tried to separate Sep from her arm had merged into a messy tangle in his mind, and he hadn't even spared a thought to the pain conduit he had carried from the temple. But Sep had remembered.

"I think so," Kerin told her gently. "I carried her outside. It was chaos, everyone was running . . . I lost her, but I think someone must have found her." Kerin forced a bit more confidence in this statement than he was actually feeling. Many people had probably been trampled as the crowds surged, and he remembered the flash of swords as the Mandate soldiers tried to cut their way into the square. But there was no reason to upset Sep.

She was silent for a long moment, as if considering this. When she finally spoke she sounded pained. "I didn't know."

Kerin glanced past her at the darkness through which they had just come. He thought he'd heard something, but it seemed unlikely that the Dawn could follow them.

"Didn't know what?" he asked, distracted as he peered into the black.

"She was inside, hiding. I looked into her eyes and I saw . . . I saw . . ."

Her voice broke. Luminescent tears were running down her cheeks, glimmering in the glow from his lightsphere. She was struggling to finish her thought, but Kerin was almost certain he knew what she would say.

She'd seen herself.

"I lost control," she finally whispered, then wiped at her face. A shudder of revulsion passed through her when she noticed that she'd done this with her crystal hand.

"Believe me," Kerin assured her with as much conviction as he could muster, staring into her eyes, "that girl was the only innocent in that church. And I brought her out. Whatever happened to the others, they deserved it."

Sep jerked her head slightly in what might have been a nod. Kerin waited to see if she had anything more to say, then he straightened and stared into the direction they had been going.

"We have to go this way, I think. Unless you can talk those Shadows into letting us out where we came in. But then we'd have to hope we could avoid the Black Dawn."

"Yes, we must go forward" Sep agreed. "There's . . . something. It's calling me." She resumed her shuffling walk down the tunnel, into the darkness.

Calling you? Kerin wanted to ask Sep what she meant by that, but instead bit back the question. He doubted Sep had any idea what she was talking about. His gaze lingered on the Shadows, for as Sep had started walking again they had stirred to life, slipping from where they crouched against the walls to follow her. Sighing, he hurried after her as well.

19

THE DARKNESS STRETCHED ETERNAL.

Kerin had no idea how long they had been travelling down this tunnel, but from the exhaustion seeping into his bones and the ache of his legs he thought the better part of a day, at least. Sep must be even more tired than him, but she kept up her plodding pace, one faltering step after another. She didn't say anything, even when Kerin asked her questions about what she thought waited for them at the end, and eventually he gave up. Instead, when he found the silence thickening the air had become too oppressive, he found himself talking.

It wasn't a conversation, as she never responded, but he sensed that she was listening. He talked about his life, from his earliest memories on Dival. Growing up crouched in corners, watching his mother's parade of lovers warily. Some had ignored him, and he'd like those ones the best. Others had raged, imprinting their frustrations on his body. The worst had been the one that showed kindness when his mother was there – at least physically, if not in spirit – but then changed when she ventured out to find her next pinch of glimmer or sip of halatz, smiling viciously as he made Kerin cry out in pain.

He still dreamed of that smile, he told Sep as they trudged along. He'd come awake clawing for breath, filled with the same helpless fear he'd felt all those years ago. No matter how big he grew, no matter how good with a sword, that smiling face was always watching from the shadows, waiting for the day when he'd be alone again.

And then his grandfather had come. He'd been terrified of the old man, certain that behind his eyes lurked the same kind of monster. Better at hiding, perhaps, but he'd learned that the most dangerous were often the ones that seemed the kindest. He'd sobbed and clutched at his mother's leg, begging for her to save him from this bearded apparition. But she'd only stared down at him with empty eyes as his grandfather pulled him away and carried him thrashing from that dark room that smelled of rot and damp. Years later he'd learned that halatz dulls the emotions in those that use it. What his mother otherwise would have felt had been carried away on a numbing tide, and maybe – he still hoped to this day – that when she awakened to herself she had cried when she had looked upon where he'd once curled up to sleep.

Not long after his grandfather's death, Kerin had against his better judgement returned to Deval. He wasn't sure what he was looking for. Closure, he supposed, maybe some tiny bit of under-standing about why his mother had been the way she was, but all he'd found in the foul slum was a collapsed hovel that hadn't been inhabited for years by anything except the rats that ruled the rotting bits of the city. An old rag-woman had emerged from her den and told him that the last woman who'd lived there had died a few years back, though she couldn't remember of what. The rag-woman had seen something in his face, and she'd gestured for him to enter her home. There, he'd found a hoard of junk and other decaying items scavenged from the wreckage, and she'd pressed into his arms a few things she'd taken from his old home. A cloth doll, its face eaten away by moths. A bracelet of colored glass that he did not recognize. And a wool blanket that he remembered sleeping under on those rare nights when the usually steamy Deval evenings turned chilly.

He realized he was speaking as much to himself as he was to Sep.

She still gave no indication that she was listening. He wanted to ask her if she remembered her early childhood, the time before she'd come to dwell in the catacombs of the Searing Light. Did she have memories of her mother? Her father? Did she have family back on Jegriddsl, or had she been left as a babe on the steps of the church?

But he did not give voice to these questions. As they continued on, Kerin wondered what she must think of him. Was she angry about his betrayal of her to the Antiquarian? Did she even realize what had happened at the scholar's spire? She had saved him from the Shadows back in the pit, after all. He watched her shuffling along, her eyes fixed on a point on the floor just a few lengths from of her. What was going on inside her head?

The Shadows were still there, keeping pace with them. Sometimes they skittered ahead, merging with the blackness of the tunnel, but they would eventually reappear nearby, etched by the light of his sphere, crouched and waiting.

"They are talking to me."

Startled, he glanced at Sep. She had turned her head to watch him while he'd been staring at the Shadows.

"Telling me things. No, not telling. Showing. They've forgotten words."

He swallowed, his mouth dry. "What are they showing you?"

She shrugged. "It's confusing. I don't understand. They might not understand, either. The Shadows were . . . broken. Into pieces."

"And what do they want?"

Silence followed Kerin's question. Sep seemed on the verge of saying something, but then she hunched her shoulders and returned her gaze to the floor. Either she couldn't put it into words, or she truly didn't understand what she was seeing.

The Shadows flowed across the walls to either side of her, like attendants fluttering around their mistress. Kerin frowned, not for the first time wondering why they were so interested in the poor girl. Surely the universe had piled enough burdens on her frail shoulders? Sighing, he hurried after her.

~

Kerin couldn't remember the last time he'd felt so terrible. The exhaustion that had been pressing against the inside of his skull had finally seeped into the rest of his body, making his limbs feel like they'd been dipped in lead. The only thing keeping him from begging Sep to stop for a while and rest was the gnawing ache in his stomach and the dryness of his mouth. If he curled up to sleep, he wasn't sure if he'd have the strength to crawl back to his feet when he woke. Also, his lightsphere had gradually been dimming as the crystal in its core eroded. Fairly soon they would be plunged into darkness, surrounded by shadowy ghosts. So long as they were moving forward he could maintain his hope that the end of this tunnel was just beyond the limit of their light.

He was so distracted by the pain in his belly and the heaviness in his head that at first he didn't realize that the tunnel had changed. It was only when Sep stopped walking and he nearly bumped into her that he glanced around and saw that something was different.

The gray stone of one of the tunnel's walls had vanished. In its place were long, faceted panes of smoked quartz or glass. Kerin stepped closer to inspect one wall, raising one hand to brush his fingers against the smooth surface. His reflection did the same, although it was so blurred that it was little more than a vague splotch of colors. All he could see of Sep was a haze of dark blue – the remnants of her dress – and the halo of pale hair around her featureless white face.

Suddenly his blood went cold. Rising behind Sep's reflection in the dusky glass was a tall, thin figure. It loomed over her, its arms bent at odd angles and its elongated head obscured by a gray mist. Kerin cried out in alarm, whirling around and ready to lunge towards the apparition . . . but there was nothing there. Sep blinked her gray eyes at him, her brow creasing in concern. Kerin approached her, looking around wildly. Movement caught his eye as the small Shadow that had been pressed against the far wall slid away, flowing across the stone like ink spilled in water. Kerin turned quickly back to the reflective wall, watching as the preternaturally thin creature stalked from the light.

"That's what they once looked like," Sep breathed, watching the Shadow's reflection until it merged with the darkness beyond the light shed by Kerin's sphere. Another of the creatures appeared from the opposite side end of the tunnel a moment later, gliding towards them.

"Are they communicating with you?"

Sep nodded slightly. "These ones remember. A little. I see flashes of light, an opening to elsewhere. Blinding pain, and then emptiness."

He watched the thin figure warily, but it did nothing threatening. Kerin swallowed, which reminded him how thirsty he was. He needed water. "We should get going."

Sep turned to stare down the tunnel. "Yes. We're not far now."

Even though Kerin had been expecting it, he was still surprised when the end of the tunnel finally loomed from the darkness. He wasn't sure what he'd thought it would look like – something grand or ornate to justify this leagues-long trek, perhaps – but this unornamented doorway was not it. The frame was simple gray stone, cracked and pitted, high, but barely wide enough for him to pass through without his shoulders brushing the sides. Beyond was a seamless black, but he sensed a great, soaring space.

Kerin hesitated before going through the doorway. "What's in there?" he asked Sep, but the girl shrugged. Her face was pale and drawn, and he thought he saw her swaying slightly. She hadn't complained once during this journey, but she was clearly also suffering. He realized this with a pang of guilt, then shivered as a Shadow flowed past her and into the darkness. If beyond this entrance was just a dead end, then they would also be dead.

"I don't know," she whispered. "They want us to go inside, though."

During their grueling march he'd only seen one or two of the Shadows at a time, flitting at the edge of his light. But many more than that had been accompanying them. A score or more of the dark shapes now hunched against the tunnel's stony side, clustered together unmoving, barely larger than children. But in the dusky glass of the opposite wall loomed their tall and blurred reflections.

Watching and waiting.

Kerin tore his gaze from the hovering ghosts and raised his sphere, then stepped through the doorway.

Shapes bulked in the darkness, vast and angular. They sliced down from above like the blades of giants, vanishing into the gloom. His sphere was fading, the puddle of light it cast barely half the size of what it had been earlier. Kerin could sense that his instinct had been correct and that this room was vast . . . and filled with enormous objects.

Which were starting to glow. A faint luminescence now infused the hanging shapes. Gradually it swelled, growing brighter . . . and then stopped as Sep came to stand beside him. He glanced over at her in surprise. She was staring up, her mouth open in silent wonder.

"Sep," Kerin whispered, "walk forward."

She gave him a quizzical look, but she did as he said, taking a few more steps into the chamber.

The light swelled further. She gave a little exclamation of surprise, then continued walking and the great space was revealed.

They stood in a cavern, the walls knobbed with rocky protrusions and riven by crevices, the uneven floor studded with stalagmites. The burgeoning light was emanating from great slabs of crystal that were thrusting down from the darkness above at seemingly random angles. Some stretched all the way to the cavern's floor and vanished, forming unbroken, softly glowing panes.

"What is this place?" Sep murmured softly.

Kerin could only shake his head mutely, stunned into silence. He felt insignificant, like an insect that had crept into the abode of giants.

He caught movement out of the corner of his eye. One of the Shadows had slipped into the chamber and was flowing across the wall. As he watched, it started to ascend, and it took Kerin a moment to realize that steps had been incised into the rock.

"It wants us to follow," Sep said.

"Maybe it's a way out," Kerin replied as he approached the first of the stone steps. It looked to have been hewn directly from the rock and polished smooth by the passage of countless others. That smoothness sent a pang of vertigo through Kerin. If one of them fell while climbing, they'd crack open like an egg when they struck the stone floor. There were no handholds that he could see cut into the rock, nothing to grip during the ascent. It would be dangerous even if they both weren't already weak from hunger and exhaustion.

The Shadow had paused twenty steps up and seemed to be waiting for them to follow. Kerin beckoned for Sep to join him.

"You go first," he told her. "Keep your hand on the wall for balance. If you feel dizzy, close your eyes and lean against the rock until it passes."

She swallowed, her face ghost-pale in the light of his sphere. "I'm scared," she whispered.

He attempted a reassuring smile. "I'll be right behind you, and if you slip I'll catch you. I promise."

Sep nodded shakily and started to climb. Kerin followed, trying not to look down through the gaps between the stairs. The higher sections of the crystal fragments had at first remained dark, but as they ascended light kindled within these facets, illuminating the way forward. At one point Sep's slipper skidded, sending pebbles tumbling over the edge, and Kerin's heart leaped into his throat. She managed to steady herself, and after taking a long moment to recover she resumed the climb, this time more slowly.

Stalactites dripped from the ceiling, clustered where the crystals pierced the rock. For a terrifying moment Kerin thought the stairs simply ended, leaving them stranded a thousand span above the cavern floor, but then he saw that with a small jump they could reach a ledge that nearly brushed the top of the cavern. And set into the stone of the ceiling there was some kind of trapdoor. Of the Shadow that had led them up the stairs there was no sign.

"Careful," he murmured as Sep hesitated on the final step, apparently gathering her courage to make the leap. Kerin made the mistake of looking down, and immediately had to grab at the wall as a wave of dizziness washed over him. As they'd gotten higher, the light had faded from the lower reaches of the slabs, so that the jutting blades now vanished below them into the murky darkness.

He was still staring at the lichen-scarred rock a hand-span from his face when he heard the scrape of Sep's slippers, and then a thump followed by a pained grunt. Kerin glanced over to see that she'd cleared the gap and was now sprawled on the ledge looking back at him, her gray eyes wide.

Ignoring the tingling numbness in his toes, Kerin climbed the last few steps and leaped before he could think about the abyss yawning below. He came dangerously close to braining himself on the ceiling before landing in a heap beside Sep, his heart hammering.

They'd made it. Now, he pleaded silently, please let it be possible to open this hatch. Please, by the mercy and grace of the First Mover and the Sower and – bloody stars – even the Searing Light. Sorry about the church, you stupid sadistic god, just please, please let this door not be stuck shut.

Sep watched him apprehensively – clearly also aware of the stakes – as he rose to his feet and pressed his palms against the smooth stone slab. Kerin breathed out slowly, holding her gaze, and then pushed upwards.

The door lifted smoothly. He was so surprised by the ease with which it opened that he could only stand their dumbly for a long moment, slab held over his head. A narrow chute stretched upwards through the rock, with metal rungs bolted to one side. It terminated far above in a circle of light.

For the first time in a long while, Kerin allowed himself to believe that they might just get out of this place alive.

Sep slowly rose, staring dubiously up the shaft.

"I can smell the fresh air," Kerin said, crouching down and lacing his fingers together to make a step for her.

The girl returned a trembling smile, then steadied herself on his shoulder as she put her foot on his waiting hands. Her crystal fingers brushed his neck, making him shiver, but he ignored the cool tingling and lifted her up. She vanished into the chute, her legs kicking. After a moment Kerin slipped his lightsphere into a pocket and followed her by leaping and grabbing hold of the lowest rung. His arms spasmed, but despite his weakness he managed to haul himself up.

About halfway to the illuminated circle above he paused and looked down. He could see nothing. The light that once had limned the crystals in the cavern below had faded, but even still it seemed unnaturally dark. Bracing himself in the narrow space he fumbled out his sphere again and shook it, trying to make the crystal within flare brighter, then lowered it slightly to see if he could push back the blackness welling up from below.

He gasped as he glimpsed what was filling the chute, the sphere slipping from his fingers. As it fell, the light it shed revealed countless writhing shapes, layers of dark flickering limbs and empty upturned faces. Then the blackness rushed in again, the sphere dwindling until it smashed against the rock ledge below and ignited in a brief eruption of silver sparks.

Kerin clung to the metal driven into the rock, staring down into the dark he now knew seethed with Shadows. He had thought only a few of those things had followed them through the tunnel. He'd been wrong. How many had he seen in that momentary glimpse? Dozens. Hundreds. What were they doing here?

"Kerin, are you all right?" Sep said, her voice floating down from above.

He took a deep breath to steady himself. "I'm fine. I dropped my lightsphere. But no matter, we'll be out soon."

A momentary pause, and then he heard her resume her climb. She was close to the top now, having very nearly reached the light.

"I see the sky!" Sep suddenly cried out excitedly, and the sound of her hands and feet scrabbling on the metal rungs grew louder as she quickened her pace.

"Be careful!" Kerin shouted back, but she was already scrambling out of the shaft and into whatever was beyond.

Cursing under his breath, he followed as fast as he could. Through the exit he glimpsed a golden sky threaded by wisps of purple clouds, and he breathed deep of the deliciously fresh air. In its last few lengths the shaft suddenly constricted, until he had to wriggle his body in places to keep from getting stuck. By the time his head cleared the hole it was just barely wide enough for his shoulders. He hoisted himself free with the last of his strength and flopped onto his back on the red earth. His vision was swallowed by the day's dazzling brightness, but as he lay there, panting hard, his sight gradually returned. Around him rose fragments of the same crystal that had penetrated into the cavern below, canted at random angles.

He lay there, stunned that they had somehow survived this whole horrible ordeal.

Sep's head appeared over him, blocking his view of the sky. In the late afternoon light the crystal climbing up her jaw gleamed, making that side of her face flash.

"Where are we?" she asked.

20

THEY HAD EMERGED into the center of a bizarre geological phenomenon. Kerin had never seen anything like it before: a forest of crystals, leaning this way and that, overlapping above them to form a glittering lattice. Some barely came up to his waist, while others soared many lengths into the sky and were so thick that a dozen men might not be able to encircle their bases with arms linked. Most were transparent like quartz, or a pale, sickly green, but there were also more exotic blossoms, blue and yellow and red. Some had been broken, stabbing at the sky with ends like shattered sword-blades, while others were whole and unmarred.

Kerin's unease grew as they wandered through the faceted maze. He thought he saw scuff marks in the loose soil, but there was no sign that anyone had been here recently. Even assuming they could figure out in which direction Sanctum lay, how would they survive an overland trek back to the city? When he'd stood on Drifter's deck while the starbeast swum across the sky he remembered seeing very little water on the surface of the planet. Just thinking about the arid sweep of Dust's badlands made the little saliva he still had thicken in his mouth. He guessed it had been over two days since he'd drunk anything. Sep must be about the same. They needed water, and soon.

Perhaps they were close enough to the city that he could contact Drifter. The distance was certainly too great for fully-formed messages, but if he concentrated very hard he might be able to alert Drifter that they were in trouble, and then give the starbeast a sense of where to find them. Maybe if he—

As Kerin turned the corner of a crystalline pillar he collided with someone coming the other way. He stumbled back a step as the much smaller man went sprawling in the dirt.

"Gah! Watch it, you oaf!" cried the fellow. He was wearing a red robe covered in golden geometric designs, the cowl thrown back to reveal a tonsured head of graying hair. Kerin thought he recognized these clothes, but never had he seen a member of a scholar-cabal wear robes that were so ill-fitting. This fellow's sleeves were so long that they dragged in the dust as he fumbled to retrieve his spectacles.

"Sorry," he mumbled as the scholar finally settled his glasses back on his face and glared up at Kerin.

"Sorry? Sorry? I could have broken my spectacles, and wouldn't *that* have been a disaster? Probably not a halfway decent grinder anywhere on this backwater world."

Kerin's patience was rapidly thinning. "Who are you?"

"Who am I? Who are *you*? Because you're certainly not supposed to be here." He blinked owlishly through the thick lenses, his face visibly paling as something occurred to him. "Wait? Are you thieves? Robbers come to the ransack the site now that the soldiers have been called back to attend the emperor?" He gulped, the apple in his scrawny neck bobbing. "I have nothing of value!" he squeaked, holding up his hands to show that they were empty. "Nothing! I am a lowly academic, probably even poorer than you, ruffian!"

"We're not thieves," Sep said softly, coming to stand beside Kerin.

The man frowned at her as he scrambled to his feet. "Not thieves? Excellent! But then why are you trespassing in the city of shards?"

The city of shards? The name was familiar, fluttering like a moth at the edge of his memories, but he couldn't remember exactly where he'd heard it before. Was it something Bas Jelaska had mentioned when she'd told him of her historical research? Or Tess, speaking about the Mandate's interests on Dust?

"We didn't mean to trespass," Kerin said wearily. "We're lost."

"Lost?" the man exclaimed incredulously. "Lost? This entire site is strictly off limits, orders of the exarch. Not to mention you'd have to cross ten leagues of inhospitable wasteland to get here from Sanctum."

"We came from underground," Kerin said. "There are tunnels . . ."

The man gaped, his bushy gray eyebrows rising. "Tunnels, you say? I knew it! I knew it! You need to show me where! Oh, won't Helviticus be humiliated to be proven wrong. The fool!" He rubbed his hands together gleefully.

Kerin swayed, and he had to steady himself on a knob of crystal. "Later. We need food and something to drink."

The old man blinked watery eyes. "Eh? You're hungry? How can you think of your stomach when we're on the threshold of a major breakthrough? Tunnels! Underground! How incredible!"

"We eat, and then I'll show you where we came from."

The old man pursed his lips, visibly trembling with excitement. But then he nodded and turned on his heel, his long robes flapping as he strode away. "Very well! Come with me. My name is Qillian Trex, and I am an under-adjunct of the Truth Seekers. Worded three times, the most recent pubbing in Incandescent Dreamings, quite a well-read periodical among scholars of primitives. Though you probably knew that already." He snuck a hopeful glance back at them, but then frowned and turned around again when he saw Kerin's blank expression.

This disappointment did not stop his babblings, which washed over Kerin, largely incomprehensible. He knew there was a complicated subculture among the scholar cabals of the tributary, with ranks and prestige based around publications in academic journals, but he'd never cared enough to learn the jargon that this Qillian Trex was tossing about.

"My name is Kerin, and this is Sep. So you are studying something out here?"

The scholar waved his hands at the crystals soaring around them. "Yes! The city of shards is a class two anomaly, unique but believed by most to be natural in formation." He shook his head sharply as he ducked beneath a crystal protrusion. "But not me! And not the emperor, either, I believe, otherwise why the exarch's interest?"

"Not . . . natural?" Kerin's head was whirling as he tried to follow along with what the scholar was saying.

"There's a pattern here!" the scholar cried triumphantly. "Incredibly complex, but undeniable. And yes, before you say it, I know that nature is composed of similar patterns, fractals and ratios and the like. But this is different! This is not simply a repeating algorithm writ large. The arrangement of crystals here is in fact a carefully calibrated focusing mechanism!" A long pause. "Or such is my very educated guess," Qillian added, sounding a bit more sheepish. "My mathematics have proven insufficient in isolating the exact pattern at work. But perhaps your subterranean approach will shed new light on the problem!"

They'd encountered a madman, Kerin realized, and he was apparently unconcerned that Sep had a crystalline arm. Maybe he thought it was some new chimericist-created fashion trend. Well, if he led them to water he could blather on as much as he liked about fractals and patterns. While Qillian continued to drone, Kerin glanced over his shoulder, looking for any evidence of the Shadows that he'd seen following them out of the cavern. No sign of the creatures, but in Sanctum they'd materialized and vanished in bright daylight, so perhaps even now they were somewhere close.

"Eat what you like," the scholar said. "I don't think the Mandati will be returning anytime soon."

That statement snapped Kerin's attention back to what was in front of them, and he let out a little moan. They'd reached the edge of the city of shards, and beyond the last of the crystal pillars spread a large camp that looked to have been hastily abandoned. There were tents, including one much larger than the others dyed a deep imperial purple, a paddock with a single hairy, horned beast – Kerin had learned somewhere over the last few days these were called ethka –

the remains of campfires, and also a number of long trestle tables. Breakfast had apparently been in progress when the inhabitants of the camp had been pulled away, as scattered upon the tables were heaps of blackening fruit, loaves of bread, and ceramic pitchers. Kerin stumbled forward, as if unable to believe his eyes, and then he rushed towards the closest table, nearly knocking over a pitcher as he fumbled for its handle.

As he gulped down the water he saw Sep out of the corner of his eye. She was hunched over another table stuffing grapes into her mouth, her cheeks swollen like she was a rodent storing nuts for winter. With a gasp he lowered the empty pitcher, letting it slip from his fingers to thunk heavily on the ground. He grabbed a chunk of dark bread, ripping pieces away with his teeth and chewing furiously; it was slightly stale, but still one of the most delicious things he'd ever tasted.

During all this the scholar continued to talk at a rapid clip. "The exarch left a few days ago. Very suddenly, very unorthodox. Messengers rode right into camp, disturbing some extremely delicate work with all the snorting and the stomping. Some problem with his daughter, from what I gather. Then, just this morning as we're sitting down to break our fast a second messenger comes, this one looking even more panicked and harried than the last. The Golden Emperor has come to Dust, he said! You should have seen the faces of the Mandati. Well, every one of them, along with all the soldiers rode out of here like they'd been personally summoned for an audience." The scholar scratched at his scalp and sighed. "And this just happens to be the day that you two also wander out of the shards claiming to have come up from underground. A half-year I've been here and *now* the site gets abandoned? The universe has a sense of humor!"

Qillian's rueful chuckling was suddenly cut short, trailing off into a strangled gasp. Frowning, Kerin turned to see what had alarmed the scholar. A Shadow lurked on the edge of the city of shards, hunched in the lee of a listing crystal. "A visitation!" squeaked Qillian, pointing with a shaking finger. "Seventy-two days since the last sighting. What a confluence of events we have! I must take notes!"

Sep lowered the goblet she'd been drinking from, her gaze also fixed on the Shadow. Then she began to walk towards where it waited.

"Sep? What are you doing?" Kerin called out, hastily dropping the fruit and bread he'd filled his hands with and moving to follow her.

"It wants to show me something," she said, her voice sounding distant. "Something important."

The scholar gasped, pulling a battered notebook and crushed quill from his robes. "The visitor is communicating with you? Remarkable! What is it saying? Be precise, please." He flipped open the book, his quill hovering over a page in anticipation.

Sep ignored Qillian. When she had come within a dozen paces of the Shadow it suddenly moved, flowing deeper into the crystal maze. It did not vanish, though, stopping again while still in sight. It appeared to be waiting for her.

"By the Pen, look at her arm!" the scholar exclaimed as Sep moved to follow the Shadow. He had just *now* noticed that one of her limbs was made of crystal? Kerin would have thought a scholar would be more observant.

He hurried after Sep. She was drifting almost like she was in a trance, her steps slow and measured. When she came closer to it, the Shadow retreated further.

Kerin came up alongside her. "Do you know what you're doing?" he asked, keeping a wary eye on the dark creature leading them deeper into the crystalline labyrinth.

"There's something here," Sep breathed, her voice distant. "Something important."

Kerin frowned, but he didn't try to stop Sep. The forest of crystals grew thicker as they wended their way between the shards, sometimes growing so close together that they had to turn sideways. Behind them, Qillian continued with his incessant chattering, mixing observations about the crystals with questions about where they were going, all of which Kerin ignored.

After passing between a pair of blood-red pillars Sep suddenly halted. They'd entered a slightly cleared space, noticeably emptier compared to the thicket of crystals they'd just traversed. Otherwise there was little to suggest that there was anything special about this particular spot. The Shadow had also paused here, beside a crystal that was slightly broader and darker than most of the rest and had a noticeable fracture down the middle. Kerin expected it to turn and scurry away, as it had before when they'd gotten close, but it did not. It seemed to be watching them expectantly.

"Do you feel something?" Kerin asked as Sep approached where the Shadow waited.

"Perhaps," she said softly, reaching out so that her flesh-and-blood fingers lightly touched the crack splitting the crystal. "This place is special. Something happened here."

A strangled gasp from the scholar made him turn. Qillian stood between the two red crystals, but he was no longer alone.

Shadows. Hundreds of them, crowding along the edges of the cleared space, extending back into the city of shards as far as Kerin could see. Silent and motionless.

"This is where it ended and began," Sep murmured, staring deep into the crystal. A reflection was there, hazy and indistinct, the gathered Shadows replaced by the same tall, etiolated shapes they'd seen in the tunnel below.

The Shadow that had led them here suddenly moved quickly towards Sep. Alarmed, Kerin lunged in her direction.

"Be care—"

Before he could finish his warning, the Shadow stepped *into* Sep. She stiffened, throwing her head back, a shimmer of light coruscating along the crystal consuming her body.

"Sep!" Kerin cried, but before he could reach her she held up her shining hand, the palm aimed at his chest. He skidded to a halt, knowing his Anathema blood was useless before the power of the artifact

Sep's gray pupils were darkening, and as he watched, this blackness spread in her eyes like ink spilled in water. And that was not the only difference. Her posture had shifted, her shoulders settling back and her head thrusting forward. He was so used to the way she usually stood, with her body hunched and her face lowered, that this change was jarring.

"Sep?" he repeated, but this time it was a question. He hesitated, unsure what he should do.

Lifting a corner of her mouth, she turned from him to face the crystal. Then she stepped forward and pressed her crystalline hand to the fracture.

A flash of light, and the world sharpened.

No, not the world around them. It was the reflection in the crystal that had suddenly become clear, the tall, hazy shapes coming into focus.

They were thin-limbed and narrow hipped, with skin the color of ash. Their oval faces had slashes for mouths and luminous golden eyes. And the color of their hair ranged from a storm-cloud gray to the luster of polished silver.

Kerin had seen one of them before, somewhere very far away.

Alvarens.

Light crawled down Sep's arm, passing into the crystal where her palm rested over the fracture. That wave spread in a blinding ripple, radiating outward as it leapt among the crystals ringing them until it vanished into the reaches of the city. Another great pulse of sorcery made Kerin light-headed. Droning sounds were rising up from the Shadows – no, they were alvarens, or at least the remnants of them – a humming that made Kerin's bones vibrate, something deep and primal. It rose and fell as more bursts of light flowed into the cracked crystal.

Something was changing inside this fracture. A darkness was pooling there, but it was not merely the absence of light: it had weight and substance. Awareness. Kerin felt like something was peering back at him through this tear. The only time he'd experienced anything like this before was when he'd stood on Drifter's deck and stared into the Streams.

A hot wind swirled through the city of crystals, stirring Sep's long hair and making the strips of her ragged dress snap and dance. A cry came from Qillian as his quill was torn from his hand and sent spinning into the sky. Kerin felt like the gusts were pushing him towards the blackness filling the fracture.

And he was not the only one. The Shadows streamed around him as they surged forward, leaving a tingling numbness when they brushed his skin. The dark children barely came up to his waist, but in the crystal's reflection he had disappeared in a sea of much taller alvarens.

The first of the Shadows reached the crystal, its body contorting as it wriggled inside the fracture and vanished. Sep grimaced and let out a cry of pain. Kerin shook his head, trying to clear it. What was he doing? He should be pulling Sep away from whatever was happening. But when he tried to move he found that his feet were stuck fast. Kerin strained, crying out in frustration. He could only look on helplessly as the tide of Shadows reached Sep and the crystal.

And then began to dwindle. Like that first Shadow, as each of the others reached the crack they slipped within and did not emerge again. In the reflection, the alvarens stepped gracefully forward and then vanished. One after another, a continuous stream. And while this was transpiring, great surges of sorcery emanated from where Sep touched the crystal, flowing out. Kerin felt like some tiny sea creature trapped in a tide pool as the ocean surged in and out. Relentless and inexorable, vast beyond comprehension. He was lucky this sorcery was not affecting him directly, for if his Anathema blood had tried to protect him he was certain that he'd be reduced to ashes. As it was, the sorcery was simply washing over him as he tried to keep himself perfectly still and unnoticed by whatever intelligence had summoned this power.

And then it was finished.

All the Shadows were gone, swallowed by the fracture. With some effort, and a gasp of pain, Sep pulled her hand from the crystal. She stood there for a moment, swaying, and then collapsed in a heap. The unnatural darkness that had filled the crack evaporated, revealing dusky crystal once more.

Suddenly Kerin could move again. He rushed to Sep's side and knelt, gently turning her over. Her breathing was shallow but steady, her eyes closed.

"Sep?" he said softly, unsure whether he should try and shake her awake.

Her eyes fluttered open. To his relief, as she tried to focus on him he saw that the black in her eyes was gone. Yet he hadn't seen the Shadow that had entered her leave her body.

"Kerin," she whispered weakly. "What happened?"

He shook his head. "I don't know. Do you remember anything?"

Her gaze moved past him, her brow furrowing, as if she was straining to recall some hazy memory. "Maybe . . ."

"Remarkable! Incredible!"

Her attention shifted to the scholar. Qillian's fringe of hair was standing up in tufts, and his eyes were wild.

"Do you know what this means?" he babbled excitedly. "This proves my theory correct! These crystals are no natural phenomenon, but a vast artifact arranged for a very specific purpose! A purpose, young lady, you have just revealed!"

"And that is . . ?" Kerin asked.

The scholar shrugged. "I have no idea! But we witnessed it! Oh, I must write down your perspective of what happened. Yes, that would be invaluable! And of course, I'll have to study you, my girl, to find out what you just did and how you did it!"

Kerin saw the fear growing in Sep's eyes. "We're leaving," he said firmly, gathering her into his arms.

"Oh, you must stay!"

We must not, thought Kerin. Every sorcerer on the planet surely had a nosebleed and a splitting headache right now, from the lowliest back-alley auger to the exarch himself. Some of them would be rushing here to discover what could have possibly resulted in such an eruption of power . . . and if it could be harnessed for their own ambitions.

Kerin started to retrace their path back to the Mandati camp. Sep was limp in his arms, utterly drained, but the look in her eyes as she watched his face was calm. The Shadow that had possessed her had either joined its brethren in their exodus or retreated deep inside her.

Qillian's crunching footsteps and pleading entreaties followed them all the way to the camp, but Kerin wasn't listening. His mind was racing as he tried to figure out a way forward in which none of them ended up dead or imprisoned or being vivisected by a mixmage. They'd have to flee. Return to Sanctum, find Nala, get back on Drifter and try to reach the Stream mouth before the Mandate realized that they were the ones who caused this sorcerous surge. First things first, though, they had to cross the badlands. That meant they'd need...

His gaze alighted on the hairy animal in its makeshift paddock. Kerin didn't see any tack or a saddle, but he remembered Jenks clinging bareback to his ethka as he galloped across the stable grounds.

It would have to do.

"Wait, what are you doing?" said the scholar as Kerin kicked open the paddock door.

"We're taking this thing," he replied. The animal watched him with huge wet eyes as he approached, chewing placidly. It didn't look dangerous, but those horns were perfectly capable of goring him.

"I must insist you do not!" Qillian cried, grabbing hold of his arm. Kerin ignored the scholar, dragging him forward a few steps before the scholar let go with a squawk of outrage.

"We have to study the girl and her remarkable arm. Find out if what she did can be replicated! We are on the verge of a major discovery here!"

Kerin ignored the increasingly desperate-sounding scholar. He looked down at Sep's wan face and found that she was still watching him, her expression serious.

"I'm going to put you down," he said, and when she nodded slightly he helped her find her feet. She swayed, and he had to put his hand on her shoulder to steady her.

After making sure she wasn't about to collapse, he walked over and unlooped the rope that secured the ethka to its hitching post. A nearby barrel bristled with what might be riding crops, and Kerin chose one before turning back to the creature. Watching all this, Qillian was fairly dancing up and down as he waved his arms in agitation and spluttered nonsense. Kerin ignored him, something he was getting good at doing.

The animal brayed as Kerin lifted Sep up onto its broad back. In moments, she was slouched forward between its shoulder blades, resting her head on the thick hair covering the ethka's neck. He wasn't sure how she was suffering the smell rising from the beast, but otherwise the spot she'd found looked very comfortable.

"If anyone asks," Kerin said to the scholar as he grabbed fistfuls of the animal's hair and pulled himself up behind Sep, "tell them we're with the Black Dawn."

Their mount seemed to know the way, quickly finding a faint trail of trampled earth after they'd left the paddock. It had turned its head around to stare at him in annoyance when he'd flicked the crop across its flank, refusing to go any faster than a brisk canter. Even still, the beast's rolling gait made it necessary to hold tightly to its long hair, so Kerin decided to let it continue at that pace across the badlands.

Despite the bumpy ride, Sep had fully succumbed to the rigors of the last few days and passed out in the nest of hair. Kerin couldn't help but envy her, though he doubted he could fall asleep right now even if he was curled up in bed in his quarters on Drifter. His mind was whirling as he tried to sort through what exactly had happened in the city of shards.

The Shadows had once been alvarens, unless that was some sort of strange illusion pulled from his recent memories. But assuming it was true, what did that mean? Had they been left behind when the others had transcended? Were they ghosts? Something else? Kerin struggled to recall what little he knew about the alvarens. The Stream to the Umbral Cluster had opened up about a century ago, he believed, and that would align with when that Elder Race had abandoned the universe. It seemed like there was a connection. Had Dust once been an alvaren planet? Perhaps even their home world? He realized to his surprise that he'd never heard anything about where the alvarens had originated, or even what branch of the stellar tributary they had once inhabited. That by itself was odd.

So what had just happened back there? And was Sep free of the Shadow that had entered her? He eyed the sprawled girl warily. She had alvaren blood – he knew that to be true, as it was why the treehold had opened for her. The artifact devouring her arm was alvaren. The Shadows that had shown such interest in her and then used her to do . . . something . . . had apparently been the remnants of alvarens. For a long-vanished Elder Race, they certainly seemed to be clinging to the reality they had supposedly moved beyond.

A flash of gold on the horizon brought Kerin back to the present. He felt a stirring of unease. He wished he'd looked around for a sword at the Mandati camp, just so that he'd have something to deter would-be bandits. Sep had demonstrated the ability to obliterate just about any possible threat, but Kerin was starting to fear that the tremendous amounts of energy she'd summoned forth again and again since the Antiquarian's ill-fated attempt to claim the artifact might damage. Surely there must be a cost.

Another glint in the far distance, larger than before. He tightened his grip on their mount's fur as he realized that it was not on the land, but in the sky. And that meant it almost certainly could only be one thing. He wished he had his spyglass with him so he could at least relieve himself of this gnawing suspicion.

It continued to swell as they thundered across the wastes. Other objects emerged from the wash of the bronze sky, darker and smaller, a swarm accompanying the great golden shape.

It was moving alarmingly fast. Before he could even think about trying to find cover among the rocks and scree of the badlands it passed overhead.

And it was what he had expected and dreaded. The brilliant golden gleam was the armor that sheathed the body and mantle of a massive war kraken. Its trailing arms moved in unison, helping to propel the starbeast as it slid across the sky. Given how high it was, Kerin couldn't tell for certain its size, but the black shapes accompanying it were now also recognizable: a retinue of war krakens, more than a dozen of them. They looked small enough that the gold-armored starbeast could have grabbed each of them easily with one of its two longest arms – and given that all the other war krakens he'd had the misfortune of meeting were about the size of Drifter, this suggested that the one they accompanied was gargantuan. If Kerin had not encountered Xerivas's undead dragon, then this starbeast would easily be the largest he'd ever seen.

The Golden Emperor had indeed arrived on Dust. Master of a hundred systems, a sorcerer who could challenge any other power in the stellar tributary. And he was swimming overhead, intent on reaching the city of shards, no doubt drawn by what had just happened there. A tingling numbness spread through Kerin as he stared at Sep where she was sprawled unconscious. There was a tightness in his chest, the feeling that impossibly high walls were closing in around them. They had attracted the attention of beings that were only a breath away from godhood. Yet despite knowing that their situation was hopeless something was growing inside him. They might fail at freeing her from the crystal before the lich or the emperor found them – they *would* fail, almost certainly – but he would not abandon Sep. Her life had been a litany of betrayals, one after another, and that would end now.

Kerin glared at the golden kraken as it began to dwindle behind them, then leaned over the side of the ethka and spat in the dust churned up by its pounding hooves.

Let them come.

21

KERIN LET OUT a sigh of relief when the rock spires of Sanctum finally appeared in the distance like the spearpoints of a marching army. He'd been unable to fully quash the niggling doubt that they were riding in the wrong direction – which, of course, would have been disastrous. Their continued survival was very much dependent on getting to Drifter and fleeing Dust before the Golden Emperor or his minions even knew they should be hunting them.

There were no walls girdling Sanctum, of course, as there wasn't a rival population center on the planet large enough to threaten the thalani who had settled here, but before they passed into the city proper they had to wend their way through the outskirts. It reminded him of the slums of Deval, with skinny children squatting outside crudely-built structures – on his home world, those houses had been lashed together from rotting silverwood scavenged from the great forests fringing the city, while here they were piles of rust-colored rocks covered with tarps of woven scrub. The poverty was the same, as listless thalani in ragged clothes watched him pass down the makeshift streets with empty eyes.

Kerin wondered what the people here thought of their new imperial overlords. Clearly this area had been poor for a long time, well before the Mandate krakens had arrived in the golden sky. He worried that some of the thalani watching them might be sympathetic to the Black Dawn and had heard of what had transpired in their hidden refuge, but there was little he could do about that now. Likely they were apathetic – he had witnessed the gestation of revolutions on other planets, and they had never been driven or fully supported by the truly oppressed. It was the tier raised slightly above the very bottom – those who had experienced a taste of what the upper classes enjoyed, and wanted more – who fought to upend the social order. And if it was successful, those revolutionaries would ascend to the top, but the people in the slums would stay exactly where they had always been.

Their ethka was not challenged in the fringes of the city or when they rode down cobbled streets in the shadow of the spires. The Mandate was more visible in these districts, as he saw several squads of marching soldiers, though none with red-robed battlemages. The few thalani braving the streets seemed on edge, giving the imperials a wide berth as they hurried about their business.

Sep did not stir until they arrived outside Bas Jelaska's home, and then she raised her head groggily, squinting up at the canted spire picked out against the gleaming sky.

"Home," she murmured, and what he heard in her voice made him clutch the ethka's fur more tightly. This would be their last time coming here, and Kerin doubted Sep had ever felt as safe anywhere as she had in this spire. They had no choice, though. And they could only stay long enough to say goodbye and grab their things – and hopefully Nala as well – before fleeing to the stables and Drifter. Hunters would be on their trail soon enough, if they weren't already.

Kerin slid from the back of the ethka and helped Sep dismount. She was wobbly on her feet, barely able to stand, and Kerin had to half carry her into the gloom of the spire's interior. He left their mount snorting and snuffling in the street, as he didn't see any hitching posts, but the animal seemed content to rest after their long ride across the badlands.

He had no coin to pay the operator of the lift, but the old man took one look at Sep's tattered dress and their drawn faces and shuffled over to lift the whip from the hook where it hung. Kerin helped Sep inside, then sagged in exhaustion as the platform began to rise. He closed his eyes, dispatching a prayer to the nameless gods of the abyss that Nala was waiting for them above. Kerin didn't know what he would do if the kyrathi was somewhere else in the city –maybe leave a note explaining what had happened and that they'd fled to the stables, with a coded message letting her know where in the tributary they could rendezvous later.

All these plans were swept away as they approached the slightly-ajar red door to Bas Jelaska's home.

Something had happened.

For a brief moment he considered turning around and fleeing the spire, leaping back on their mount and riding towards the stables. Then he remembered all the kindness Bas Jelaska had shown them, and he thought of her held hostage by Mandate soldiers as they waited for Kerin to return.

Wishing again that he had any sort of weapon, Kerin propped Sep up against the wall so she at least wouldn't topple over if he let go of her. She squinted at him in confusion as he lowered his face to hers.

"Wait here and don't make a sound."

She frowned, but eventually nodded. "Where are you going?"

"To find Bas Jelaska. I'll be right back."

He slipped inside. The main room and kitchen annex looked undisturbed, motes of dust glimmering in the light pouring through the circular window. His eyes traveled slowly over the furniture, looking for a sign of who had invaded the apartment . . . and if they were still here.

A cold shock went through him as his gaze alighted on the table around which they'd spent many a meal. Lying on the wood was a length of glistening black metal threaded with golden cracks.

Mercy. His sword had somehow found its way back.

Kerin crept closer to the table. When *Mercy* had been torn from his hand during the riot in the temple district he thought he'd never see his grandfather's sword again. Very slowly he reached out, his fingers curling around the hilt of cold, smooth metal.

"You took your time getting here."

Kerin whirled in alarm, raising *Mercy* in the direction of the voice.

Then sagged in relief. Tessa leaned against the entrance to the passage leading to the bedrooms, her arms folded across her chest. She was dressed in the cloak and dark leather tunic he'd seen her wearing at the magistrate's office, the cowl drawn up to shadow her face.

"Tess," he breathed, taking a step towards her and then halting. Was she still angry with him? What was she doing here? "We just arrived in the city."

She pushed her hood back, her golden eyes narrowing. "Arrived from where?"

Kerin briefly considered lying to her, then discarded the idea. There was no way in his current state that he could spin a tale that would hold up under her scrutiny.

"The city of shards."

Her brow crinkled. "What? Why would you go there?"

Kerin slid *Mercy* into the empty sheath at his side. "Long story and we don't have time. What are you doing here? Where are Nala and Bas Jelaska?"

She stared at him for a moment, then pursed her lips. "You should see something," she said, beckoning him deeper into the apartment. Suddenly she froze, her gaze focused on something beyond him.

He turned. Sep stood in the doorway . . . no, she *filled* the doorway, her shoulders thrown back and her head held high. Gone was the meek girl barely clinging to consciousness. Her eyes swept the chamber imperiously, her lip curled almost scornfully.

Her eyes. Blackness had again welled up to swallow everything, but Kerin knew *something* was looking out from within the girl. She took an awkward step into the room and nearly fell, as if unused to walking. Her crystal arm flashed out, the fingers splintering the wood of a side table as she caught herself.

A shudder passed through Sep, her head falling forward. When she looked up a moment later the blackness had vanished. Her eyes darted about in confusion, as if she didn't know how she'd gotten here.

Kerin rushed forward and caught her before she could collapse. "What..." she murmured, clutching at him while he carried her over to the divan and laid her down gently.

When her head touched the pillow she fainted dead away. He watched her for a few moments as her breathing deepened, then turned as Tessa came up beside him. The Shroud stared down at the unconscious girl with pursed lips.

"What was that, Kerin? And what happened to the girl's arm?"

Kerin rubbed at his face. How much did he dare tell Tessa? She may have been his friend once, but she was also an agent of the Mandate. Where did her loyalties truly lie? He remembered her striding away angrily in the exarch's garden ... but in the days before that she'd shown him some affection. That couldn't have been faked, could it? And she'd saved them after the debacle on the Mandati barrow moon. He let out a slow breath. The simple truth was that they were not getting off this planet alive without her help. Kerin closed his eyes and could almost hear the rattle of the blood knuckles being cast. He had to take a chance that under those tattoos she was still the girl he'd grown up with.

"The crystal is an artifact that can summon forth a tremendous amount of sorcery. We found it in an ancient ruin, and it attached itself to her. At first it wasn't even up to her elbow, but it's been slowly devouring her. This is why we came to Dust. I was hoping the Antiquarian could help remove it, but when he tried the artifact defended itself, and I think maybe killed him. Sep ... the girl, I mean, that's her name . . . she was confused after that. She ended up going to the temple district and . . . well, destroying the church of the Searing Light. She was a former pain conduit, you see."

"*This girl did that?*" Tessa hissed, her eyes wide.

Kerin nodded. No going back now. "The Black Dawn captured us in the chaos afterwards. They thought we were working for the

Inquisitarium. We escaped and fled to the city of shards. While there Sep was . . . possessed by a Shadow. It did something, used the power of the artifact to cause some reaction. While we were returning to Sanctum I saw the Golden Emperor swimming overhead towards the city of shards. I think he sensed whatever she'd done."

Tessa was silent for a long while, her lips pursed as she studied the sleeping girl. She looked overwhelmed. "I'm going to believe you, Kerin," she said slowly, "because I know she wasn't the only one affected by what happened in the city of shards."

He glanced at her in surprise. "What do you mean?"

"Come with me," she said, and turned away.

Kerin followed her as she led him to the bedroom where Nala and Sep had slept, then pushed open the door. Glass covered the floor of the chamber – it looked like all of the lightspheres that Sep had insisted be placed here to protect her from the Shadows had shattered. In the dimness, Nala was curled up on the bed, her head tucked into her body. Panic clawed at him for a moment until he saw that her flank was rising and falling in a sleep-grooved rhythm.

"I found her collapsed in the other room," Tessa said softly. "When I was helping her lie down in here she kept mumbling about the light burning in her head. I know she's a mage, and I thought she must be having a reaction to something that erupted elsewhere. What happened in the temple district made it very clear that powerful sorcery was loose in the city." She shook her head in disbelief. "I never thought your young friend would be the cause, though."

Kerin gestured back towards where Sep had fainted. "To be fair, it's her and not me. I'm just trying to keep her safe."

"Kerin, is that you?" Nala murmured, her voice weak.

He quickly stepped into the bedroom and crouched beside her. "Yes. How are you feeling?"

She blinked her large amber eyes, trying to focus on him. "Better. There was a surge like I've never felt before. It was like . . . like reality itself was being torn to pieces, and me along with it." She grimaced, showing her canines. "I finally managed to pull myself back together. What happened?"

"Sep happened."

Nala snorted, then gave a little mew of discomfort. "Of course."

"Whatever she did, I think it attracted the attention of the Golden Emperor. We need to get off Dust as quickly as possible."

Nala gave a jerky nod. Then she hesitated, as if seeing Tessa for the first time.

"Who's this?"

"Tessa."

"And she's a Shroud?"

"Yes."

Nala growled, unsheathing her claws. "And you just told her what Sep can do. You're an idiot, Kerin."

"He is," Tessa said quickly. "A complete fool. However . . ." she rolled her eyes up to the ceiling and shook her head slowly ". . . as usual, he's not going to suffer too greatly for his stupidity. I'm going to help you get off this planet, kyrathi. His grandfather showed me kindness long ago. He saved me, and what I'm doing is for his memory. And the turtle."

Nala eyed her suspiciously, but her hackles had subsided. "What *are* you doing here, Shroud?" she asked.

Tessa gestured at the sword hanging from Kerin's side. "*Mercy* was found in the plaza after the Searing Light's temple was destroyed. I recognized the sword, of course, and brought it here to return to Kerin."

"And where is Bas Jelaska?" Nala asked. A dangerous note had crept into the kyrathi's voice with this question.

Tessa held up her hands, as if asking for calm. "She's fine. Truly. The historian was summoned to the imperial district because she once wrote some paper on the city of shards. Apparently the Golden Emperor is fascinated by that place and has even read Bas Jelaska's writings about the site."

"So someone did care," Kerin murmured softly, remembering the bitterness in the historian's tone when she'd told him of the scorn that had greeted her life's work.

"What did you say?" Tessa asked.

Kerin shook his head. "Nothing. Look, we need to go quickly. Nal, can you move? If we're not on Drifter within a sandglass or so I think we'll be spending the rest of our short, pain-filled lives in a Mandate dungeon. We met a scholar at the city of shards and I'm certain he has already informed the Golden Emperor about the handsome streamsurfer and the girl with a crystal arm. They'll be looking for us soon."

Nala nodded, grimacing, and held out her paw for Kerin to help her up.

Tessa stepped forward first, offering her hand. The kyrathi hesitated for a moment, then allowed the Shroud to pull her to her feet.

"Doesn't mean I trust you," she grumbled.

"That means you're smarter than him," Tessa replied, jerking her head in Kerin's direction.

"Not a very impressive height to reach."

"All right, all right," Kerin said, turning back to the main room where Sep was still passed out on the divan. "You ladies can keep talking about me on the way to the stables."

The streets of Sanctum had almost emptied once again, just like when the spire had fallen in the Bowery. There were no bells clanging in the distance this time, so Kerin assumed that what had sent the thalani scurrying for shelter was related to the shards of glass littering the ground. Every lightsphere and lantern in the city had been shattered by the looks of it, wrought-copper holders clutching at nothing, empty chains dangling from posts forlornly. Kerin thought back to the broken lightspheres surrounding Nal and Sep's bed. His best guess was that the sorcery that had rippled out from the city of shards had caused all the light crystals in the city to explode, meaning that it would be a dark few nights on Dust before an emergency shipment could be brought in from elsewhere in the cluster.

Nala and Sep slumped on the back of the plodding ethka as Kerin walked alongside it, occasionally flicking its flank with the crop when it paused to investigate the piles of dung its brethren had deposited in the streets. Tessa kept pace on the other side of its great shaggy head, her long sleeves rolled up so that her writhing red tattoos were visible. The Mandati must have been able to decipher something from those flickering patterns, as the lone patrol of soldiers they encountered on the way to the stables gave them a wide berth after coming close enough to see Tessa's markings clearly.

"Are you worried they'll report having seen you with us?" Kerin asked after the soldiers had marched away twice as fast as when they'd first approached.

Tessa was quiet for a moment. "I don't think I can pretend I don't know you. I'm sure our meetings in the Whimsy, the magistrate's offices, and the exarch's villa were all noted. I expect to have to answer all sorts of questions."

"Are you in danger?"

She shrugged on the other side of the moist bulge that was the ethka's nose. "I'm usually the one asking the questions. The Inquisitarium is the most feared organization in the Mandate, and I have a powerful patron. The presence of the Golden Emperor here on Dust makes things a bit more complicated, though. Even the exarch would be loath to move against me on his own given whose shadow I stand in, but the emperor's authority is supreme, and he fears no one." She raised her head to squint into the golden sky. "The ice is certainly thin, but I've danced my way off other lakes before. Comes with being a Shroud."

"Well . . . thank you. I'm sorry about what I said earlier, in the exarch's garden."

Tessa let out a long sigh. "To be truthful, I should not have called you there. It's just . . ." She lapsed into silence, and Kerin could tell she was struggling with what she wanted to say. Finally she shook her head. "Oh, bloody stars. I wanted to see you again, Kerin, before you left. Talking to you in the Whimsy and in the magistrates offices it felt like a part of me I'd thought long dead was stirring back to life." She shook her head. "I had no idea the exarch would learn so quickly about his daughter's death, or that he'd be able to return to Sanctum before her body was even cold. It was selfish of me, endangering you like that."

"You wanted to see me?"

Tessa scowled at him across the ethka's monstrous face. "Nostalgia. Nothing more."

"I see."

"Wipe that stupid grin off your face or I'll do it for you."

Annoyance radiated from Tessa as they continued on in silence. He knew Nala was correct and that he shouldn't trust the Shroud, but he found it impossible to even consider the possibility that Tessa would betray them. Underneath those red tattoos she was still the same girl that he had sat beside while learning astrogation from his grandfather, taking turns making faces behind the old man's back. Whatever terrible things she had done in the service to the emperor, whatever wounds had been inflicted and scarred over in the years since that day on Heth, she was still undeniably Tess.

A growl and a shifting from atop the beast made Kerin glance up. Nala was perched on the edge of its broad back, her legs dangling over the side. She still looked faintly nauseous, but her eyes were clearer than they had been back at the spire.

"Feeling better?"

Nala nodded, then pushed herself off the ethka to land lightly beside him. "Yes."

"Good," he said, "because we're almost there." Kerin pointed up ahead, where the white-fabric of the stables was just visible between two of the tiered adobe dwellings.

"And what's the plan?"

"We make straight for Drifter. If we're challenged by anyone from the Mandate, Tessa gets us past. Once we're on the old boy we take off. Since the Golden Emperor is here, the skies must be swarming with imperial starbeasts, but hopefully they haven't been told to be on the lookout for us yet. We swim for the mouth and try to lose them in the Streams."

Nala's ears flicked in the direction of Tessa. "And is she coming with us?"

He shook his head. "No." When Drifter's flippers lifted from Dust, he supposed she could once and for all close the door on her time as a streamsurfer, the debt she owed to the ghost of his grandfather cleared in full.

"Have you told Drifter we're coming?"

"He's sleeping," Kerin said, questing out briefly to make sure the starbeast hadn't woken since the last time he'd tried to contact him. Still slumbering. Starbeasts hoarded energy like desert animals did water. They could stay awake for weeks at a time while swimming through the Streams, but when in port they spent most of their time asleep.

Wouldn't Drifter be surprised when he rapped on his shell? Kerin grinned, imagining the turtle blinking blearily as his great head emerged, and then the rush of thoughts and emotions that would result from Kerin telling the starbeast that they needed to flee Dust *now*, maybe while out-swimming a fleet of Mandati war krakens.

They passed beneath the expanse of white fabric. The stables seemed even emptier than when they had first arrived: he could see a dark mound in the great distance that he suspected was Drifter, but otherwise the vast plain was bereft of other starbeasts. Perhaps they'd fled when the Mandate emperor and his fleets appeared in the skies, or maybe it was the appearance of the lich in the cluster that had spurred them to leave. It was fortuitous, in any case, as there would be fewer witnesses to their departure. He glanced around, half expecting to see a cloud of dust on the horizon as Jenks galloped towards them, but there was no sign of the stablemaster. Kerin owed him for a few days of berth, and usually he wouldn't dream of departing without settling his debt, but this was now a matter of life and death.

"Kerin . . ." Nala said warningly, and a moment later he saw what the kyrathi's excellent eyes had already spotted.

Figures waited for them up ahead, blocking their path to Drifter. The light filtering through the fabric above made the armor three of them wore gleam like bleached bone, while the last, a more rotund fellow, was attired in robes of deepest red.

Kerin's heart fell. Even though he was too far away to see their faces clearly, he knew who waited for them.

"Tessa, do you see this?"

She grunted affirmation. "K'zars, and I believe that's the Crimson, Halas."

"What do they want?"

"Perhaps they want to wish you well on your journey."

Kerin snorted. "Can you get us past them?"

"I believe so. The Crimson and I have roughly the same rank, but I know he's a coward and easily intimidated."

Still, Kerin's fingers rested on *Mercy's* pommel as they approached the Mandati. He hoped it wouldn't come to a fight. K'zars were known throughout the stellar tributary as exemplary swordsmen – despite coming from a primitive culture that had lacked starbeasts, they had managed to hold off the invading Mandate legions for years before finally succumbing to the empire's overwhelming strength. Following their world's subjugation, the Golden Emperor had allowed their unique warrior culture to persist, so that k'zars could be employed as incorruptible and deadly guards for the Mandate elite.

Kerin stepped in front of the beast to make it halt across from where the k'zars and the battlemage waited. He tried to guess their reason for being here by studying their expressions: the Crimson looked nervous, a sheet of sweat on his plump face, but the stone-faced k'zars betrayed nothing. Just like him, their hands were resting on the hilts of their swords, and circular bucklers were strapped to their forearms. They looked ready to fight.

"Ho, Crimson Halas," Tessa said, stepping forward. The tattoos on her bared arms darkened, as if to remind him what she was.

"Shroud," the battlemage replied. He licked his lips but seemed at a loss for anything else to say. His gaze flickered to the silent, waiting k'zars, as if imploring them for assistance. None came.

"I'm escorting an old friend to his starbeast," Tessa finally said.

The Crimson wrung his hands together. "I'm afraid you can't. Do that, I mean."

Tessa folded her black-etched arms across her chest. "I won't let you arrest them, Halas. I can assure you with utmost confidence that they are not working for the Dawn."

The battlemage blinked in confusion, then wiped at his glistening brow with his sleeve. "Them? Who are they? We are here to bring *you* to justice, Shroud."

Cold surprise flooded Kerin, and he saw Tessa stiffen. "What are you talking about? By whose authority?"

"Exarch Veshkent."

Her head rocked back as if she'd been struck. "Why?"

The Crimson sighed heavily. "Oh, I'm certain you know. For the murder of his daughter."

"I didn't kill Dierdra," Tessa said forcefully, but Kerin saw that she'd widened her stance and shifted her weight to the balls of her feet.

"Get ready," he murmured to Nala, barely moving his lips. "If this gets ugly you need to deal with the battlemage."

"The evidence is damning, Shroud," the Crimson said, shaking his head.

"What evidence?"

"The evidence uncovered by my esteemed companions here," he told her, sweeping out his arm to encompass the motionless k'zar. "It turns out they are surprisingly skilled investigators."

"Apparently not, as I had nothing to do with the death of the exarch's daughter."

"Then you deny setting the wraith crystal that brought down the spire in the Bowery?"

"I . . ." Tessa glanced over at Kerin, and a hollowness opened in his chest at what he saw in her face.

"That is Inquisitarium business, Crimson," she said through gritted teeth, then paused, and when she spoke next her voice was tight. "Dierdra was not supposed to be there."

"She almost died in that attack, then days later was successfully

assassinated. And you knew she was speaking ill of you to her father."
The battlemage looked pained. "Forgive me, Shroud, but I also
believe you need to answer questions about this . . . coincidence."

"I refuse."

"It is the exarch's orders. You are under arrest, as well as these . . .
companions of yours, to see what they know as well. But you should
feel grateful that the exarch is merciful, as the k'zars advocated for
your immediate execution."

Tessa threw back her cloak, revealing her twin golden-hilted
swords. "Let them try."

The battlemage swallowed, his piggish little eyes flicking from
Tessa to the k'zars. The warriors were all staring at her intently, the
grips on the hilts of their blades white-knuckled. "Then you will not
come with us peacefully?" he asked, sounding nervous.

"No. And I claim Inquisitor Serevus's protection. You cannot
punish me until he can adjudicate on this matter."

The Crimson sighed heavily. "Since you were placed here by
request of Exarch Veshkent he believes he has ultimate authority
over you."

"And what do you believe?"

"I believe the exarch is very near, while Inquisitor Serevus is very
far away."

"Coward."

The battlemage shrugged. "I prefer pragmatist." He turned to the
k'zars, mopping at his face again with the hem of his robe. "Seize her.
But please, make sure she lives."

Metal chimed as the three Mandate warriors drew their swords. A
flicker of movement almost too fast to see, and Tessa's twin short-
bladed swords were also in her hands.

Bloody stars. Kerin ripped *Mercy* from its sheath and hurried to
stand beside Tessa, but a bolt of red energy erupted from the Crimson's outstretched hand to strike him in the chest. It was like being
shoved hard: his breath fled in a ragged gasp as he tumbled backwards, nearly losing his grip on his sword. If it wasn't for his
Anathema blood his flesh would have blistered and sloughed away

from his bones; instead, the aether only harmed his poor shirt, the steelsilk threads blackening and curling. He groaned, pushing himself back to his feet as a large chunk of his ruined shirt fell away. Nebulas, he was running out of clothes.

The Crimson was staring at him in shock, his mouth agape. Apparently he had forgotten that Tessa had told him Kerin was Anathema, or he hadn't recognized him from when they'd met in the exarch's manse. Kerin hesitated, unsure whether he should charge the battlemage and finish him off or help Tessa. She was being hard-pressed by the three k'zars: she moved with uncanny grace as she danced between them, swords flashing, but the Mandate warriors were equally as well trained. His decision was made as a torrent of green aether arced from somewhere behind him and impacted upon a red-crystal shield the Crimson had conjured. At the same instant, Tessa gave a grunt of pain as the tip of one of the k'zar's swords sliced her thigh shallowly, sending her hopping backwards out of the reach of their curving blades.

He bellowed as he rushed the closest of the k'zars, trying to distract them before they could press their advantage. All three turned to him, and Tessa suddenly stopped her retreat and lunged forward, her swords arcing. Two of the k'zars caught her blades with their own, shivering the air with a metallic chiming, while the last moved to meet Kerin's charge. He swung hard, hoping to overwhelm the k'zar quickly with the ferocity of his attack, but the warrior turned his sword aside. Unbalanced, he couldn't avoid the k'zar's buckler and it smashed into his face. Bone crunched as something popped in his nose, and he desperately threw himself backwards to avoid the follow-up slash that would have disemboweled him.

Somehow, he managed to recover, warding away the k'zar's flickering sword with a desperate defense. The man fought with an unnatural calmness, no emotion at all in his face, as if this was a training session and not a life or death duel. Kerin realized, with a sinking feeling, that he was overmatched by the k'zar and that it was only a matter of time before one of the warrior's precise strikes broke through. He was on his heels, unable to even attempt a counterattack.

Nebulas, he'd really thought he was a damn good swordsman. Of all the painful truths he'd been forced to confront over the last few days, somehow this one stung the most.

Green and red light flared on the periphery of his vision, each flash followed by a boom that made his Anathema blood throb. He wanted to sneak a glance to see how Nala was faring against the Mandate battlemage, but it was taking all his focus just to keep himself from being skewered. The k'zar was relentless, and *Mercy* was growing heavier and heavier, each parry he made a hair slower than the last.

Sharp pain stabbed his wrist, and his sword's hilt slipped from his numb fingers. For the first time emotion appeared in the k'zar's face, a flicker of satisfaction as he drew back his blade to plunge it into Kerin's chest.

White light struck the Mandate warrior, crawling over his ceramic armor. The k'zar collapsed, and before Kerin could process what had happened the blazing energy gathered itself and leapt from his twitching body, crackling towards where Tessa was still fending off the other two warriors. It struck one of the k'zars in the back, then passed through him to blast the other, sending both sprawling. For a moment, Tessa could only stare at their steaming corpses, and then she raised her head to stare in wide-eyed surprise towards where the sorcery had come from. He turned as well, knowing what he'd find.

Sep stood upon the back of the beast, her legs sunk to the knees in the mounded hair. The right side of her body was shining like a star, almost too bright to look upon – Kerin was surprised that the beast beneath her hadn't panicked, but then he saw that its legs were trembling and its eyes rolling around in their sockets, as if something was holding it still. Her eyes were pockets of blackness, her hair writhing in the air like a nest of snakes.

Nala and the Crimson had stopped their aether duel and were also staring in shock at Sep and the crackling penumbra of sorcery wreathing her. The Mandate battlemage was the first to recover, shrieking in terror as he hurled a sphere of roiling power at the girl. It carved a glittering path through the air, but just before it struck Sep

she raised her shining arm and caught the sorcery. It hissed and sputtered in her grip, dripping aether like gobbets of flame from a torch.
Then she released the crackling sorcery and it sped like an arrow
back towards the Crimson. He just had enough time to emit a squeak
of fear before the aether plunged into him, tearing a gaping hole
through his chest.

"Tooth and claw," Nala murmured as the Mandate battlemage
collapsed. She looked at Kerin, her face showing awe and fear.

Kerin gathered himself and took a step towards the creature that
had once been Sep. The entity that had entered her in the city of
shards had clearly risen again. He could only hope that since it
helped them this meant it was friendly, or at least not an enemy.

"Who are you—"

Crackling sorcery lanced down from above, tearing a hole in the
stable's fabric roof. Kerin reeled back, his Anathema blood throbbing
as his sight was consumed by coruscating light. The last image
imprinted in his mind's eye was Sep perched atop the ethka
vanishing within that pillar, utterly consumed by the radiance. Hot
droplets spattered Kerin's face in the moment after the vast aether
surge, along with wet chunks of something soft. The liquid tasted
warm and salty on his lips. Blood.

"Sep!" he cried as his vision slowly cleared.

The great hairy beast was gone. It had been reduced to its compo-
nent parts, a mound of bubbling flesh and burning hair, with a few
mostly intact limbs scattered about. In the middle of the obliterated
ethka huddled a small, unmoving form.

"Sep!" he cried again, rushing towards the girl, dread closing
around his heart. Nothing could have survived that.

He skidded to a halt as a shape floated down through the charred
rent in the white fabric. Purple and gold robes rippled in an unfelt
wind as the exarch alighted beside the ruin of the beast. His golden
mask regarded his handiwork for a long moment, and then with
slow and measured strides he approached the corpse of the
Crimson.

Tears stung Kerin's eyes as the exarch knelt beside the Mandate battlemage and began tracing the hole carved in Halas's chest with his finger. Sep could not have survived that attack.

"Exarch!"

The sorcerer rose, turning towards where Tessa stood, swaying, beside the crumpled bodies of the k'zars. She was favoring one leg and blood sheathed her left arm, obscuring her Mandate tattoos.

"I claim the protection of the Inquisitarium and the right to a trial by tribunal!"

From beneath that featureless gold mask came a harsh laugh. "You stand among the corpses of a revered battlemage and k'zars sworn to the empire and you demand justice, Shroud?"

"They attacked us!" Tessa shouted back, drawing herself up straighter.

"By my orders," the exarch snarled. Purple radiance swelled around his hands, and the day seemed to darken. "I care nothing for the proprieties of the empire anymore, only that you suffer for what you have done."

A wave of shimmering green aether washed over the exarch. Nala moaned as she wrung every last drop of sorcery from the reserves inside her, the emerald flames around her paws sputtering.

When it faded the exarch stood unharmed.

"This shall not be quick," the Mandati archmage promised, raising his arms. Violet lightning crackled forth to first strike Tessa and Nala and then leapt to Kerin. His Anathema blood surged to meet the sorcery, but the strength of the exarch still drove him to his knees. He screamed as a hundred knives were plunged into his flesh. Darkness pressed down as he shivered, wracked by great pulses of pain. Somewhere far away Nala was yowling, the agony in her voice cutting through the haze that had wrapped him in a suffocating embrace.

Nala.

His blood hammering in his veins, Kerin pushed back against the storm of knives and struggled to his feet. He took a stumbling step in the direction where the exarch stood wreathed by purple lightning. The pain was overwhelming, but he focused on Nala's screaming.

He had to save her.

His shuffling feet bumped against his sword, and with a tremendous effort he reached down, his fingers closing around *Mercy's* hilt. The feel of the cold metal in his hand seemed to deflect some of the flashing blades of sorcery flowing from the exarch, and his next step was stronger. He gritted his teeth as his Anathema nature warred against the overwhelming power of the Mandate archmage. It was like fighting through a raging hurricane, if the winds of such a storm carried slivers of razor sharp metal.

The exarch at the eye of this maelstrom turned to face him. "You are impressive, Anathema, but I am no simple mage."

Kerin cried out as the buffeting gusts of sorcery strengthened. His Anathema blood flared red-hot, but he felt its power flaking away, simply overwhelmed. He collapsed, *Mercy* tumbling from his numb fingers. Kerin screamed into the ground as the exarch's power scoured him, stripping away the final layers of his protection.

The ground shook as a great crash sounded, and a moment later the raging sorcery vanished.

He lay there, panting, breathing in the loamy smell of the red earth with dirt on his lips. Why had the exarch stopped his assault? Did the sorcerer think he was dead? *Was* he dead? Unlikely, given the Anathema blood pulsing in his veins as it strove to purge the sorcery from his body. Kerin wanted to raise his head and see what was going on, but he was afraid that the exarch would then realize he hadn't quite managed to kill him.

Well, that's disgusting.

Kerin gasped, then coughed as he sucked in a lungful of dirt. He looked up.

Where the exarch had been standing there was now a massive green and brown mottled flipper. Drifter's head loomed over Kerin, casting him into shadow, and he saw himself reflected in the turtle's great black eye.

Drifter!

The turtle's head turned slightly to regard his flipper. *I really don't want to lift this and see what's underneath. It feels... gooey.*

Kerin staggered to his feet, dazed and still reeling from the exarch's sorcery. He saw to his relief that Nala and Tessa were both moving weakly, trying to get up. Above the starbeast a massive hole had been torn in the fabric of the stable's roof. Drifter must have awoken, launched himself into the air when he'd realized what was happening, then descended with the force of an avalanche.

Crushing an exarch of the Mandate into goo.

"Do you know who that was?" he rasped.

A mage of some sort.

Kerin coughed again, unable to say more, but he waved his hand frantically to demonstrate how wrong the starbeast was. "Exarch," he finally managed. "You just squished the exarch of this system."

Drifter blinked slowly, which Kerin knew indicated great surprise. *The exarch. Huh.*

He was going to kill us, so thank you. Kerin thought, switching to their mental bond as another wave of coughing struck.

You're welcome. I suppose we need to get out of here quickly, then. Are the others all right?

The others. Kerin stumbled away from Drifter towards where Nala squatted in the dirt. She licked a blackened paw and rubbed at her face, her eyes widening in horror when she realized the whiskers on one side had been burned short. A little ways beyond her, Tessa had pushed herself up onto her hands and knees, her head hanging down. The Shroud cleared her throat loudly and spat out a wad of blood.

"Anyone dying?" Kerin asked, and they both turned to stare at him bleakly.

"Maybe," Tessa muttered, wincing as she slowly stood. She grimaced, glancing at the dark blotch spreading on her leggings. She'd clearly lost a fair bit of blood from the cut on her thigh, but if she was able to stand, then likely the k'zar's blade had missed her artery. They'd have to get her on Drifter quickly and wrap her leg with a tourniquet, though, before she fainted from the blood loss.

"Sep?"

Kerin shook his head at Nala's question. The ruin of the beast she'd been atop was still steaming, a barely recognizable pile of melted flesh and bone. The moment the sorcery had arced down from above to consume her was still frozen in his mind's eye. That had been a killing blow. The exarch had wanted to torture them, to make them suffer, but he'd taken no chances with the girl who had so effortlessly slain his Crimson and k'zars.

Bloody stars, she had deserved better.

Nala hung her head, her arms going limp in her lap. A sound rose from her as she stared at her paws, low and mournful. It made the hairs on the back of his neck stand up. Kerin had heard this only once before, when he'd brought her to see his grandfather sitting in the solarium, watching the Stream flow past with empty eyes.

Tell Tessa it's good to see her.

Kerin swung his attention back to the Shroud. "Drifter says it's good to see you."

She looked up at the vast head looming over them, a rueful half-smile on her bloodstained face.

"It's good to see you, too, you big dumb reptile," she said. Her gaze traveled from Drifter's giant black eye to the flipper where the exarch had been standing not so long ago. "Are you sure he's dead?"

The starbeast snorted explosively, which was as close to laughter as he could manage.

Oh, yes. Very much so.

"He's dead," Kerin assured her, finally starting to move in the direction of the ruptured beast that had carried them all the way from the city of shards. He truly did not want to see what had become of Sep, but he owed her something, at least. A burial in the Streams where what remained of her could exist forever, a few words to let her spirit know she would not be forgotten, maybe they could even salvage some small token to remind them of her . . .

"She's alive."

Sep was curled into a ball in the middle of the ethka's corpse, her eyes clenched shut. She murmured nonsense and slightly shook her head, as if denying something in her dreams, her body uncoiling from its fetal position. Kerin swallowed when he saw what had happened to her. The remaining shreds of the blue dress had been utterly immolated by the exarch's sorcery, but Sep's flesh was pink and unburnt. There was less skin than just moments ago – her arm was entirely given over to the artifact now, and the crystal had crept down the right side of her body, all the way to her abdomen. One of her small breasts was now faceted and partially translucent, threaded by dark strands, and tendrils of crystal were reaching up from her cheek to claw at her eye. It looked like whatever she had done to survive the exarch's sorcery had accelerated the crystal's spread. This new growth was more opaque than her arm, as if it was still in the process of transforming the flesh.

When the ethka had died so spectacularly its blood and viscera had exploded outwards – Kerin remembered the feeling of warm, soft chunks hitting him with a mental shudder – but somehow Sep at the very epicenter of the strike had remained largely untouched. There was probably more gore on him than the girl.

"Nebulas," Tessa breathed as she hobbled over to stand beside him, looking down at Sep. "How is she not dead?"

"The artifact must have protected her," Kerin said numbly, still having trouble coming to grips with all that had just happened. "It's Elder Race, as I said. Alvaren."

Tessa's head snapped around to stare at him in surprise. "Alvaren? Are you sure?"

Kerin nodded. On the ground, Sep moaned, moving her arms and legs feebly.

"Stop gawking and help her," Nala said, shouldering past Kerin. Sep stirred but did not open her eyes as the kyrathi bent down and gathered the girl in her arms. Then Nala flicked her ears in the direction of Drifter. "Let's get her aboard."

Kerin shook his head as he followed Nala towards the rope ladder that led up to the structures clinging to the starbeast's shell. The kyrathi had been frantic to remove the girl and the unpredictable weapon swallowing her from Drifter not so long ago, and now just a few days later here she was carrying her back on board willingly.

Kerin had already decided of course that Sep should come with them, but their opinions wasn't the only ones that mattered.

How do you feel about this? he asked Drifter as the turtle's great black eye tracked Nala's approach.

The sensation he received in return was something like a mental shrug. *If I was afraid of taking risks I would have severed my bond with your family long ago. By the whorled shell, I would have found a quiet little water world to retire on. To be a streamsurfer is to court danger. Bring her up – I like the girl.*

Kerin couldn't keep a smile from creeping across his face. *I'm glad to hear that.*

Nala had begun to clamber up the rope ladder while also somehow holding Sep pressed to her chest. The girl must be at least partly conscious, as her arms were wrapped around the kyrathi's neck. Kerin chewed on his lip as he watched the crystal limb glitter. How long until it swallowed her completely? And could they arrest its spread?

He started as Tessa appeared in front of him, looking serious.

"Tess."

"Kerin."

"That was a disaster."

Her eyes slid from Kerin, looking around at the evidence of what had just transpired. Her gaze lingered in turn on the smoking corpses of the k'zars, the Crimson with the hole carved through his chest, and the flipper that Drifter seemed reluctant to lift until he absolutely had to.

"It appears my time as a valued citizen of the empire has drawn to an end."

"You'd leave the Inquisitarium?"

Tessa snorted. "I don't think I have a choice. There's no way I'd avoid punishment for what just happened here. An exarch died, Kerin. Killed by my old friend's giant turtle while I was helping him escape the city."

"What will you do?"

Her gaze returned to him, and he saw in her face the immense frustration of someone having to deal with a simpleton.

"Well, I need to get off this planet pretty quickly. Know anyone who is leaving soon?"

Kerin coughed to cover his embarrassment, and then motioned for her to climb the ladder.

"After you."

"Mmm," she murmured, and then turned away to start her ascent.

Above her, Nala's face appeared over the balustrade. "Hurry up! We've got company."

Kerin spared a glance over his shoulder. A cloud of dust was rising in the distance as a herd of ethkas stampeded across the stables. He couldn't tell whether these were Mandati soldiers astride the beasts, Black Dawn revolutionaries, elegantly-dressed fox-men, or some other faction they'd unknowingly managed to enrage, but there was little chance they were friendly. With a sigh, Kerin shouldered his charred rucksack and began to climb the ladder. Almost as soon as his boots found the first rung Drifter pushed off from the ground, his flippers raising billowing clouds of dust.

Don't tell me what it looks like Drifter begged, but of course Kerin couldn't resist glancing down at the now-revealed remnants of the exarch, just visible through the haze.

Huh, Kerin mused, staring at the receding smear on the reddish earth. *It's not so bad. Ever squeeze a grape until it pops?*

Luckily, no.

Then I guess I can't really describe it. Or maybe it reminds me of—

Kerin grinned as he felt Drifter's consciousness pull away, and then focused on getting up the now swinging ladder without losing his grip. He would prefer not to end up as another stain on the fast-receding ground.

Brightness washed over him as the starbeast surged through the torn roof. Kerin tried not to think of the widening distance below him. The wind was stronger up here, howling in his ears and plucking at the tattered remnants of his shirt.

He was in a cold sweat by the time he finally swung himself over the balustrade and staggered onto the deck.

"Nebulas," he gasped, tossing his rucksack down on the wooden planks and leaning over with his hands on his knees. This wasn't the first time he'd had to scramble up a ladder while Drifter beat a hasty retreat, but it was still terrifying.

When he finally controlled his racing heart, he straightened and found Tessa standing nearby, gazing up at the Nest with an almost wistful expression. She'd found a strip of cloth somewhere and had tied it around her leg as a makeshift tourniquet.

"Welcome home," he told her.

One corner of her mouth lifted, and she shook her head slightly, as if in disbelief.

"I never thought I'd be here again."

"I hoped you would," he said, then inwardly cursed for sounding like an idiot.

Tessa looked a bit less enthusiastic. "I'm not rejoining the crew, Kerin. We're both fleeing for our lives in the same direction, nothing more. Convergent interests. Get me to a world outside the Mandate and we'll go our separate ways."

An indigo murk settled over the deck as Drifter ascended into the sky. Kerin wiped the condensation from his face as they burst free of a cloud bank, the seamless bronze sky suddenly unfurling above them. Twilight was not far off, and the ghostly outlines of the moons could be seen, as well as a spattering of stars.

"I understand," Kerin said. "But before we think about that, let's concentrate on getting out of here alive."

22

NALA REAPPEARED on deck while Drifter was passing the larger of Dust's two moons. The kyrathi looked bedraggled, with her filthy fur and burned whiskers, but there was resolve in her amber eyes as she came to stand beside Kerin and Tessa.

"She's sleeping," Nala said before either of them could ask. "Whatever reserves she had have been utterly exhausted. I bumped her head against a door and she didn't even stir."

"You checked for a pulse?"

Nala gave Tessa the kyrathi version of a withering look. "I know when I'm carrying around a corpse, Shroud. She's alive, just pushed well beyond her limits."

"That's probably true for all of us," Kerin muttered, rubbing at his aching temple. He wanted to lie down and sleep for a month, but he wouldn't dare rest until they had left the cluster.

What was most important now was how quickly the Mandate started the pursuit. There was no fleet of war krakens boiling up from the surface, so it seemed that no one had realized yet that the squabble in the stables had resulted in the death of an exarch and the flight of the girl responsible for the sorcery in the city of shards. But they would. Once they peeled apart the remains of the exarch Drifter had left mashed into the dirt they'd find his imperial robe and fragments of his golden mask. And then the hunt would begin.

When Kerin finally dragged his gaze from Dust, he found Nala staring at him with arms crossed.

"What happened to Sep?" she asked, an edge to her voice.

"What do you mean?" he replied, though he knew very well what she was talking about.

The kyrathi's low growl made the back of his neck prickle. "Don't play dumb, Kerin. You've been gone for days. Bas Jelaska said you'd been summoned by the Antiquarian, and since I didn't think I could find his spire I decided to wait for you to return. Then the bells started clanging again. Bas Jelaska went out to get word of what had happened and returned with tales of the disaster in the temple district, how the church of the Searing Light had been utterly consumed by an explosion of raw sorcery. Seemed like far too much of a coincidence, and that the only possible explanation was that the Antiquarian had failed spectacularly at removing the artifact. Now Sep reappears with black eyes and far more control over her powers. She caught an aether blast like it was a ball, Kerin! What in the bloody stars is going on?"

While Nala had been talking, Tessa had adopted a posture similar to the kyrathi, with her arms also crossed and her gaze fixed intently on Kerin.

He sighed. As the moons shimmered off Drifter's starboard side, he told them everything that had happened since he'd returned to Bas Jelaska's home and found one of the fox-men gnawing on a sausage. Nel's growling strengthened when he admitted the Antiquarian had decided the best way to remove the artifact was to slice off Sep's arm. He tried to impress how conflicted he'd been, but he still felt a hot flush of shame about what had happened. Tessa's attention sharpened when he told her about the underground city where the Black Dawn had taken him after rescuing them from the chaos of the temple district, and she sucked in her breath when he explained how Mazrem Tou had used the Shadows to assassinate his enemies, including the old exarch.

"One of the Dawn let slip that they'd determined the ash they used to summon the Shadows had once been organic . . . they thought it might actually be the cremated remains of the beings that had become the Shadows."

Tessa was staring at him intently now. "And did they claim to know anything else about these beings?"

Kerin shook his head. "No, but given what happened in the city of shards I believe they must have been alvaren."

"Alvaren!" Nala hissed, her tail dancing.

Tessa looked far less surprised. She knew something.

"We escaped the Dawn by fleeing through a tunnel that led to the city of shards," he continued. "Shadows followed us, and at the time I thought it was only a few, but when we emerged above ground it turned out to be a much larger number."

"How many?" Tessa asked quietly.

Kerin shrugged. "Maybe . . . all of them? I don't know. And it was in the city of shards that their true nature was revealed. In the reflections of the crystal they appeared as what they had been before: alvarens. There were males and females, young and old . . ." He turned to Nala. "The massive surge of sorcery that gave you a headache was from when one of the Shadows, uh, entered Sep and used her to do something in the city."

"And what was that?" Tessa prompted him after he'd been silent for a moment.

Kerin sighed, rubbing at his brow in frustration. "I'm not sure. There was . . . a crack in one of the crystals. Like it had been broken. The Shadow inside Sep forced her to pour a tremendous amount of sorcery into the fracture . . . but not to heal it, I don't think. Maybe wrench it fully open, because the gathered Shadows threw themselves into the crack and vanished."

"All of them?" Nala asked.

"Well, clearly not all of them," Tessa replied, and now it was her turn to give the kyrathi a condescending look.

"Apparently not," Kerin answered Nala. "When the Shadow first possessed Sep in the city of shards her eyes turned black."

"Oh," Nala said softly, casting a glance at the doorway that led to where Sep was sleeping. "And so that's where her new abilities came from."

"Yes," Kerin agreed with a slight nod. "It wasn't really her."

"So you're saying an alvaren ghost is sleeping in our passenger berth?" Nala asked.

He shrugged. "Sep's there, too. The Shadow has only . . . used her a few times, and you can tell when it does by the way her eyes change. What I want to know is why it didn't follow the other Shadows through the door it opened in the city of shards."

"Perhaps it has something left to do," Tessa mused. From her expression it seemed like she was trying to align what Kerin had just said with something she already knew.

And he wanted to know what that was.

"You glanced at me strangely the first time I mentioned that the artifact was alvaren. What do you know, Tess?"

The look in her unnatural golden eyes was measuring. Then she sighed, her shoulders slumping. "Nebulas, what does it matter anymore? I've already signed my death warrant – a few imperial secrets won't make my execution any more painful."

"Secrets?"

"The knowledge is closely guarded in the Mandate, by orders of the Golden Emperor himself. Dust was in fact the alvaren home world, the planet from which they emerged epochs ago. I was told they called it Ganamere. The Younger Races remember alvarens as diminished and fading, but apparently they were quite the fierce warrior people and had once dominated a large swath of this branch of the stellar tributary."

"But there's no evidence that they lived in the spires," Kerin said. "No artifacts, no writing, not even tombs with alvaren skeletons."

Tessa shrugged. "They must have scoured all evidence of their habitation before they transcended."

"Did they transcend?" Nala asked, her amber eyes narrowing.

"From what Kerin has said, perhaps not," Tessa replied. "Or maybe a group of them were left behind. All I know is that the

Golden Emperor was very interested in Dust and the alvarens, which is why the Mandate first pushed into the Umbral Cluster."

"And it must be why the Antiquarian took up residence on the planet," Kerin said slowly, pieces slotting into place. "I came to Dust because he was an Elder Race scholar, but the reason he was there in the first place was because the planet had once been the home world of the alvarens. We accidentally returned the artifact to where it had come from."

They were passing close to the second of Dust's moons, and Kerin's attention was drawn to the surface. What looked like an artificial lake had been scooped from the rock and floating in the silvery water he could see black specks that he suspected were war krakens. Many of them.

"But why is the emperor in this system now?" Kerin asked, eyeing the vast fleet nervously. "To protect Dust from the qan . . . or the lich's horde?"

Tessa shook her head. "Neither. Though the last message I got from my superiors in the Inquisitarium they were absolutely frantic with worry about what the undead were doing here." She swooned slightly, then gritted her teeth and steadied herself. "But no, the Golden Emperor isn't here because of the lich. It takes weeks in the Streams to arrive at the Umbral Cluster from the imperial core, so they must have left long before the undead appeared. When I asked the same question I was told that several of the most puissant alvaren artifacts the emperor has collected – and because of his fascination with the Elder Race, he has quite a few – had suddenly stirred to life about a fortnight ago. After that happened, the Golden Emperor immediately departed for Dust, gathering the exarchs of other worlds and their fleets as he passed through the empire."

A fortnight ago. Kerin shared a quick glance with Nala and saw in her face that she was thinking the same thing as him. That would have been just about the same time they'd entered the Crucible and the alvaren treehold had awoken. It couldn't be a coincidence.

"Well," Kerin said finally, turning away from Nala before Tessa could notice what was passing between them. "Hopefully the emperor is too focused on what happened in the city of shards and we can slip away."

"Slip away to where?" Tessa asked.

"I'm thinking Reaver's Rest," Kerin replied. "That's the seat of qan power in the cluster. I don't think the emperor would risk war with the reptiles by chasing us there . . . but if he does, maybe we can slip away in the chaos."

"And what about Sep?" asked Nala, and Kerin heard the strain in her voice. "How can we help her?"

He ran a hand through his hair. "We seek out a mixmage. I'm sure there's a renegade or two on the Rest. There are always a few on those outlaw worlds." Kerin remembered the way the artifact had protected itself when the Antiquarian had tried to cut it away. They would be courting a similar response by asking a chimericist to remove it, but what other options did they have? Hopefully the alvaren ghost that had taken up residence in her would depart if the artifact was separated from her body.

He turned to Tessa. "And you can find other streamsurfers on the Rest, ones headed somewhere in the tributary that's far beyond the reach of the Mandate."

She nodded slightly, her expression inscrutable. For the first time, Kerin wondered how she was truly handling all that had just happened. Years of ascending the intricate hierarchy of the Mandate, achieving a rank where she could speak almost as equals with an exarch, and now suddenly reduced to being a fugitive. She looked as stoic as could be expected, given the circumstances.

There was something else he had to know.

"Is it true, Tess? What the exarch said?"

She blinked. "About what?"

"About the spire. That you brought it down."

She glanced away, staring out at the stars. He noticed her hands were clenched into fists. "The explosion wasn't supposed to be that large. Just a small piece knocked loose, hopefully with minimal casualties. There was . . . a miscalculation."

"But why?" he asked.

"The Dawn was growing more and more popular among the thalani. According to the social algorithms of the Inquisitarium, the planet is on course for a full-scale rebellion. That means thousands of deaths, maybe tens of thousands. The explosion in the Bowery was an attempt to turn the common people against the Dawn." She swallowed, hanging her head. "I don't know what Dierdra was doing there. Or why the wraith crystal was magnitudes more powerful than I had been told. The whole operation was a disaster, but I promise you I was trying to save lives."

"By killing a few innocents," Nala muttered.

"Better than thousands of others when the planet erupted in a full-scale rebellion."

Kerin bit back on what he wanted to say.

His starbeast's thoughts intruded on his own, flavored strangely. *Kerin.*

Drifter, you were listening? Kerin didn't chide him for eavesdropping, as the turtle deserved to be a party to this discussion.

I was. You want me to swim towards the Rest.

Yes.

And then you'll turn the girl over to the chimericists. A pause, and Kerin could feel the displeasure radiating from the starbeast. *Whoever you find on the Rest will be as much butcher as mage.*

It isn't what I want, either. But we need to remove the artifact before it consumes her utterly. If you have a better idea, please share.

Another silence, longer than before. *We make for the Rest.*

Kerin allowed himself a grim smile. Drifter's agreement, however grudging, meant his judgement in this was probably sound. If the starbeast had insisted on an alternative plan – or simply refused to deliver Sep to a chimericist cutting table – Kerin didn't know what would happen. When a handler and his starbeast engaged in a contest of wills it was usually the first sign that their bond was fraying.

There's something else.

And that is? Kerin asked, unnerved by the swirl of emotions coming off Drifter.

The krakens are stirring. I can feel their agitation, and they've started chattering.

Fear slithered through Kerin. *What are they saying?*

I don't know. The imperial starbeasts have their own unique patois. It sounds just like a whispering babble to me . . . but it's swelling. Something has them excited.

"Kerin!"

Nala's annoyed voice intruded on his conversation with Drifter, and then her tail thumped him in the side. Blinking, he returned to himself. Nala and Tessa were staring at him with worried expressions. They must have seen something in his face.

"What did Drifter tell you?" asked the kyrathi.

Kerin swallowed, trying his best to compose himself. No reason to frighten them until he was certain the krakens were in pursuit. "Nothing. He's just worried about Sep." He forced a smile. "You two should go get some rest. You both look like you need it. If anything changes here, I'll ring the bell."

Tessa's gaze was flat, her lips pursed. She always seemed to know when he was skirting the truth. Then a shudder of pain crossed her face, and with a grimace she clutched at her leg.

Kerin stepped forward to help her, but Nala was closer and she hooked an arm under the Shroud's shoulder.

"We need to stitch that up," the kyrathi said, nodding at the dark blotch on Tessa's leggings. "Come with me. I've put Kerin back together enough times to know where all the pieces go."

After a brief foray to his quarters to retrieve his spyglass and change into a fresh steelsilk tunic and trousers, Kerin made his way to the afterdeck and searched their wake for any sign of pursuit. With his naked eye he couldn't see anything except the night-cloaked Dust and its moons, but when he peered through his spyglass he noticed motes of a deeper blackness picked out against the starscape.

They're coming.

Kerin had been expecting Drifter's confirmation of his suspicions, but still his heart fell.

How far behind us?

Less than a turning of a sandglass.

Can you stay ahead of them until we reach the Stream's mouth?

Most certainly. But I can't promise we'll reach the Rest before they catch us. Krakens are devilishly fast.

So it sounds as if we'll have to fight. How many are chasing us?

I can't be sure. Too many.

Give me a guess.

I would say . . . around one hundred.

Kerin fumbled with his spyglass, nearly dropping it.

*A hundred? A **hundred** war krakens?*

My estimate is on the lower end. I was trying not to depress you.

That . . . is an armada. We're being pursued by the largest Mandate fleet in the tributary.

Yes. Congratulations. None of your ancestors ever managed to aggravate an entire interstellar empire before. It's really quite impressive.

Shaken, Kerin slipped his spyglass into his belt. *Then we need to hurry.*

Drifter did not answer, but from the emotions flowing across their bond Kerin sensed how hopeless the starbeast considered their situation. Still, there was also a hard core of determination. The starbeast wasn't demoralized or despairing. He would swim as far and as fast as he could, and when the first kraken's arm brushed his shell he would turn and fight.

Let me show you what happened on Dust, Kerin thought.

He felt Drifter's curiosity stirring. *This should be interesting.*

Kerin summoned his memories of his time on the planet, hurrying past the days spent waiting impatiently in Bas Jelaska's home to concentrate on everything that had transpired since the Mandate soldiers had brought him to the exarch's manse. He felt the starbeast's disapproval at his acquiescence to the Antiquarian's desires, and then his shock at the destruction Sep had caused in the scholar's spire and the church of the Searing Light. There was also quite a bit of satisfaction leavening Drifter's feelings here as well, and Kerin sensed little sympathy for those that had been subjected to the sorcery she'd unleashed. The starbeast watched his unspooling memories after their capture by the Dawn with rising apprehension, letting out little exclamations of surprise as Kerin detailed their escape and entrance into the city of shards. When he arrived at his first clear glimpse of the Shadow's true forms Kerin paused, holding the image in his head.

Those are alvarens, aren't they?

Drifter was quiet for a moment as he examined the reflections of the tall, thin creatures. *They are indeed.*

What do you know about them?

The starbeast offered the telepathic equivalent of a shrug. *Not much. They had nearly vanished from this universe when I was still young, barely more than a century old.*

A century is still a long time.

Not to me. And not to creatures like them. Their species was already ancient when I poked my head from my egg. Every one of them I encountered seemed to carry this great weight on their shoulders, as if wearied by the endless eons of their race's existence.

Were they violent? War-like?

Not with other species, thankfully. Their sorcery was very advanced, even for an Elder Race. They were secretive, I remember, protecting the location of their home world and core systems—

The Umbral Cluster and Dust, Kerin interjected.

Yes, it would appear so. But although they did not conquer or enslave weaker races, I do remember rumors of a great civil war. It did not spill over into the rest of the tributary, but they could not entirely hide what was happening. The entire tributary trembled at times with the sorcery being unleashed.

The Antiquarian mentioned something about this. He called it the Rivening.

Yes, that was it. My own memories are hazy, but I recall a stream-surfer who had crewed with a renegade alvaren telling your great-great grandfather about how the strife was between two brothers of unsur-

passed power, each of whom believed in very different destinies for their people.

And who won?

I suppose the one who wished for the alvarens to transcend, as it was after this Rivening that they disappeared from the universe forever.

Kerin frowned. Or had they? The Shadows had apparently been some remnant of the alvarens. Had they failed in their bid for transcendence?

Kerin mulled this over as Drifter carried them ever closer to the Stream's mouth. The starbeast was swimming as fast as Kerin had ever experienced before, save for when a favorable current would sometimes carry them through the Streams like a leaf in a flood-swollen river. Drifter would tire quickly at this pace, but if there was ever a time he should exert himself beyond the limits of his endurance, it was now. With one final glance through his spyglass at what was behind them, Kerin began to make his way back to the foredeck.

He had consciously avoided sharing his memory of meeting the echo of his grandfather with the starbeast. Kerin wasn't sure how Drifter would react to the knowledge that some shred of his grandfather had persisted. The relationship between them had been deep and strong, forged over decades of being bonded. His grandfather had been far closer to Drifter than he had been with Kerin, and he suspected that the starbeast felt the same.

Kerin arrived outside the Nest and stepped up to the railing, resting his elbows on the pitted wood. He watched Drifter's head bobbing up and down as the starbeast strained forward. If, by some miracle, they somehow survived this mess, Kerin supposed he would have to tell Drifter about the memory pearl. His grandfather's enigmatic words still haunted him, and if anyone knew about this 'labyrinth' it would be the starbeast that had shared Calvan's mind for nearly fifty years.

Relief flooded him as the Stream's mouth appeared in the distance. Really there was no reason to feel anything about leaving the system, but still it felt like they'd made it at least part way to freedom. Now they just needed to stay ahead of the Mandate fleet for a solar day or so in the Streams, until they reached Reaver's Rest. And then they'd find out if the Golden Emperor was willing to risk a war with a power as great as the Mandate to capture them. Kerin's gaze drifted to his laboring starbeast. He could only hope the krakens tired as easily as Drifter when they were swimming so fast. Most of them dragged around all sorts of armaments—

KERIN.

Drifter's surprised cry exploded in his mind as the great turtle attempted to arrest his momentum, sending Kerin lurching forward into the balustrade.

Nebulas, Drifter! What's going on?

The starbeast's flippers were churning frantically as he tried to turn them from the path they'd been on. *The mouth!*

Kerin's glanced at the rippling curtain of multi-colored light. Around the hazy edge of the hovering entrance to the Streams a long, dark shape was emerging from where it had been hidden. Tentacles flared wide as the war kraken surged towards Drifter – it looked to Kerin like the same starbeast that had been on sentry duty when they'd come through the mouth weeks ago. And it had most definitely been informed that they should not be allowed to leave.

Kerin's jaw tightened as the kraken slid across the distance between them, its nest of tentacles squirming. He gripped the balustrade, preparing for the collision that was coming. Drifter bellowed a battle cry as the kraken swam closer, and the Mandate starbeast answered with a shriek from its clacking beak that set Kerin's teeth on edge.

The first of the two longest tentacles slapped against Drifter's shell, tearing loose a walkway between the decks and sending bits of wood and rope tumbling into the abyss. The impact rocked Drifter, but Kerin kept his feet. The other great tentacle latched on to one of Drifter's flippers, and through their bond Kerin felt a stab of pain as the great hooks on the underside of the arms sunk into the turtle's flesh. He grimaced, reeling away from the railing as Drifter shuddered. The starbeast tried to wrench his limb away, but the kraken's grip was firm and he only managed to deepen the agony flowing from his flipper.

The war kraken had drifted close enough by now that its smaller, thicker tentacles could also grab onto Drifter. One of the smaller structures that thankfully had not been occupied since his grandfather's day was ripped away from the shell. Drifter was straining so hard against the grasping arms that he was now slowly dragging the kraken away from the mouth, but Kerin could tell that the starbeast wasn't about to rip fully loose. The arms were far too strong – much larger and stronger starbeasts than Drifter had failed to free themselves from a war kraken's embrace.

Kerin cursed, rushing down the stairs leading to the lower deck. The kraken had aligned its body parallel with Drifter, its arms now bent at an awkward angle. Kerin stared across the diminishing gap between the starbeasts at the Mandati marines crowding the platform built along the kraken's mantle. An officer with a gold-crested helmet was shouting commands at a contingent of soldiers as they wrestled boarding planks closer to the edge of the deck. On a slightly higher forecastle built where the mantle flared widest stood the captain, who must be the one bonded with the kraken, as well as a man in bright red robes. They also saw him, as the robed man gestured and crackling flame lanced from his hand. Heaving a sigh for his rapidly diminishing wardrobe, Kerin did not even try and avoid the sorcery as it flashed closer. Better it struck him directly than the wood he stood upon. His Anathema blood pulsed, his vision was consumed by light, and when he could see a moment later he saw that his tunic had been charred but he was otherwise unhurt.

A pair of the great planks now stood on end, towering high above the kraken, then they were tipped forward so that they came crashing onto another of Drifter's lower decks. Kerin drew *Mercy* and hurried along a walkway to where the boarding was about to begin. Footsteps pounded the deck behind him, and then Tessa appeared. She glanced at him, her golden-hilted blades ringing as they slid from their sheaths.

"You hold the left!" she cried, and then hurried to where one of the planks had obliterated the deck's balustrade. She was favoring one leg, but being hobbled wouldn't give the Mandati any advantage if they had to fight her while also trying to cross a narrow beam. Kerin followed her lead, setting himself across from where the first of the marines were just starting to edge out over the void, spurred on by the exhortations of their captain.

"Crossbows!" Tessa screamed, pointing one of her swords at where a group of soldiers had rushed up to the railing on one of the kraken's slightly higher decks. Kerin swallowed. Such weapons were notoriously inaccurate, but did he really want to take the chance that they would all miss? He was just considering throwing himself to the deck and taking cover behind what little of the balustrade remained when a wave of swirling green sorcery consumed the soldiers. Their ragged screams drifted across the chasm between the starbeasts as they rolled on the deck trying to extinguish the emerald flames devouring their flesh.

Nala.

Kerin had no time to look around for the kyrathi, as the first of the marines had nearly crossed the plank. His armor was different than the soldiers Kerin had seen on Dust, a less-bulky scale mail instead of the banded plate of the planetside legions, but the broad, short-bladed sword was the same style as Kerin had wielded when training with Tessa. Good, the extra reach *Mercy's* long blade gave him would be an advantage.

The marine realized this as well and lunged forward to try and get within his guard before he was set. Kerin anticipated this and met him before he could close, forcing him to fend off a quick flurry of slashes. One of the parries came a heartbeat slow, and *Mercy* scored the marine's side, sending him stumbling back a step. Kerin grinned and moved forward to press the Mandate soldier further. It was refreshing to cross blades with a warrior who was not a Shroud or a k'zar. Maybe he wasn't as hopeless a swordsman as he'd been made to feel recently. Then again, the marine's footwork was basically nonexistent, as one wrong step would send him toppling to his doom.

They were at an impasse: Kerin wasn't about to leave the safety of

Drifter's deck, and the soldier seemed reluctant to attack again. He stared at Kerin with frightened eyes, his pale face knotted with pain. The officer back on the kraken was screaming at him to charge Kerin, but it wasn't until one of the marines crowding the plank behind him gave him a shove in the back that he came staggering forward again, swinging his sword awkwardly. Kerin batted aside the blow easily, knocking him off balance. With a despairing cry the poor fellow went tumbling off the plank, the sound of his voice quickly fading.

The next marine advanced more warily, shuffling forward with his sword raised behind the buckler strapped to his other arm. Kerin set himself again, lifting *Mercy* to a guard position. In the periphery of his vision he noticed eruptions of green and red light. Nala and the battlemage trading sorceries. He desperately hoped she dispatched the Mandati sorcerer quickly, as eventually the marines would realize that if they all rushed at once they'd overwhelm him by sheer weight of numbers.

Kerin Drifter's mental voice sounded strained, but also surprisingly calm.

Yes? Kerin thought in return, jabbing out with his sword to keep the marine in front of him at bay.

Get away from the edge and hold on to something.

What?

Now.

Kerin felt the deck shift beneath his feet. Drifter had stopped pulling against the kraken and was slowly turning his great body. The marines of the boarding party cried out in alarm and crouched down, trying to become more stable as the plank moved beneath them.

"Tessa!" he yelled, glancing over to where the Shroud was also struggling to keep her feet. The blades of her swords were streaked with blood, and the marines had drawn back farther from her than on the plank Kerin was guarding. She looked at him, her face creased in confusion.

"What is Drifter doing?" she shouted as a flower of green flame blossomed on the foredeck of the war kraken, ripping apart the great ballista mounted on the starbeast's mantle.

Kerin didn't trust himself to explain what was happening quickly enough. Lunging towards Tessa, he grabbed her by the arm and started to drag her away from the shattered balustrade.

"They'll seize the deck!" Tessa cried in alarm, but she didn't try to shake herself free as he led her to where thick ropes hung against Drifter's shell. Kerin wrapped the ropes around his arm – this was exactly why they were there, to help secure passengers in the event Drifter had to maneuver sharply – and Tessa did the same after hurriedly sheathing her swords.

Despite Tessa's warning, the marines had apparently decided that they should return to the kraken right now.

They never made it.

Drifter had twisted his massive body so that his head was now facing the bulk of the war kraken. Its sinuous arms were still sunk into his shell and flesh, but rather than trying to rip himself loose, the great turtle instead lunged forward. The sudden, sharp motion would have sent Kerin flying across the deck if he hadn't tangled himself in the safety ropes, and he hoped that wherever Nala was she'd anticipated what the turtle was about to do.

Drifter roared, opening his mouth wide as he hurled himself towards the war kraken's armored flank. Kerin tensed, expecting to hear a great clang as the turtle's head struck metal, but with a deft twist of his head Drifter hooked the curved end of his beak between two of the overlapping plates. Then he pulled back hard, and with a rending shriek a huge gap appeared in the kraken's armor as a sheet of the dull gray metal came loose and tumbled away. Kerin could almost see the panic rippling through the war kraken, the bioluminescent lights visible where its flesh was unarmored shifting from blue to white, and all its tentacles released their hold on Drifter at the same time.

The fight seemed to have fled the kraken. Kerin was sure it now wanted nothing more than to flee, but Drifter was not yet finished with the Mandati starbeast. The great turtle thrust his head forward again, just as powerfully as before, but this time he plunged his wickedly serrated beak into the kraken's unprotected flank. A shudder went through the great creature as Drifter ripped loose a huge gobbet of flesh. Blue blood poured from the wound and the turtle let the chunk it had torn away fall from its beak, and then jabbed again into the same spot, this time going even deeper. The kraken spasmed, screeching in agony, its smaller tendrils slapping uselessly at Drifter's head and shell. His turtle burrowed his head into the kraken's side, and when Drifter wrenched his head back violently this time he had a glistening white organ the size of a wagon clutched in his mouth. With a shake of his head, Drifter tossed the chunk of rubbery meat away. Another pained shriek came from the kraken, and then a cloud of roiling blackness issued forth from where its tentacles joined with its body. The darkness swelled to obscure the starbeast, but Kerin could sense juddering movement, and when the cloud dissipated he saw that the war kraken had managed to swim a few lengths away from Drifter.

Kerin thought his starbeast was going to pursue, but then he saw what Drifter had already realized: the kraken was dying. Blue blood was gushing from the gash torn in its side, and Kerin could actually see far enough into the creature to glimpse more nested white organs. Its tentacles were flailing slowly now, like a drowning man desperately straining for the surface as he slipped below the waves. The kraken was sinking, unable to keep itself aloft, and Kerin knew that when this happened a starbeast was truly doomed.

Drifter stared after the dying starbeast, his black eyes hard and glittering, his beak stained blue by the kraken's blood.

"Nebulas," Tessa murmured from where she was beside him, tangled in the ropes.

Kerin nodded numbly. He'd only seen Drifter locked in close combat with another starbeast once before, and it had been nowhere near as vicious or bloody as this. Usually conflicts between stream-surfers were conducted at a distance, with sorcery and projectiles flung across the void. He'd certainly never witnessed the turtle gouging out chunks of flesh with his beak, nor had his grandfather ever described such a thing.

Kerin extricated himself from the ropes, rubbing at where they'd chafed his arms and shoulders. Tessa did the same, watching with her mouth pressed in a thin line as the war kraken sunk out of sight, her face pale. Kerin glanced at her leg, wondering how much it was bothering her, and if the stitches Nala just put in had burst during the battle.

Nala.

Leaving Tessa behind, Kerin pounded up the stairs back to the main deck. He looked around wildly for any sign of the kyrathi. Many streamsurfers had tumbled to their deaths when their starbeasts had moved quickly and unexpectedly, but in relief he saw her leaning exhaustedly against the balustrade. She turned to him, raising a paw in tired greeting.

"Well, that was exciting," the kyrathi said as he came up beside her.

"Looks like we can kill starbeasts without Sep's help," Kerin said, putting his hands on the railing and looking over the edge to where the Mandati kraken was now but a dwindling speck. He wondered what the surviving marines must be feeling as they plummeted through the abyss. The thought was terrible enough that he almost felt sympathy for the Mandati soldiers.

Nala glanced in the direction of the passenger cabin. "In the back of my mind I was waiting for her to show up and smite the bastards. She must be absolutely exhausted to sleep through that."

I was also hoping Sep would help. Then I decided I should just take matters into my own flippers.

Kerin sent a wave of gratitude flowing across the bond he shared with Drifter. *I didn't know you could be so savage.*

I already hated squids, and then this one had to go and wreck my beautiful shell.

You were too pretty before. And I bet female turtles love scars.

Kerin imagined he saw the edges of Drifter's huge mouth twitch. *You're right about that, luckily. Easier to see I'm a true warrior now.*

Nala's tail thumped his leg. "What is Drifter saying?"

"He's telling me that these new battle scars might help him find a mate."

She snorted. "Males."

"Oh, good. You're alive, kyrathi."

Kerin and Nala turned to see Tessa ascending the stairs. The Shroud winced, then gathered herself and hobbled across the deck to join them.

Nala eyed her stained trousers. "I should take another look at your leg."

Tessa nodded gratefully. "Yes, thank you."

"Someone should also go make sure Sep is all right," Kerin said.

The kyrathi stepped closer to Tessa and offered the Shroud her arm. "That sounds like a captain's duty."

Nala was right, he knew. Kerin sighed, wishing he could come up with some excuse that kept him on deck. He wasn't even sure why he was so reticent. There was certainly some lingering guilt about what had happened with the Antiquarian, but he also felt like she'd forgiven him, if she had ever truly blamed him. No, he supposed that he was intimidated by whatever ghost had taken up residence in her. When her eyes had gone black he'd sensed something. Disdain, perhaps? Contempt? The spirit of the alvaren – if it was an alvaren – did not care one whit for any of them, and given the power it could evidently command that made him nervous.

After Nala had led Tessa back inside the saloon to patch her up again, Kerin left the main deck by way of a wooden walkway that curved along the outside of the starbeast's shell. As he made the swaying journey across the planks to the passenger berths, he felt Drifter begin to move again towards the Stream mouth. Before he reached the platform with the door that opened into the corridor where Sep's quarters were located he felt them pass into the Stream. Reality seemed to tremble, and the cool, fresh air of Dust's system suddenly became warmer and stale, like a windowless room in summer. Kerin glanced back just before he pushed through the door. Churning darkness had replaced the star-pricked sweep of his universe, and even though he had swum a thousand different Streams he still couldn't suppress a shiver.

Kerin entered the structure that contained the passenger berths.

The corridor was darkened, the starlight that had been trickling through the windows having vanished after they passed through the mouth. Kerin reached up and fumbled for the lightsphere hanging from the ceiling, giving the glass a tap to kindle the crystal within. After a few flickering attempts the crystal finally ignited, flooding the hallway with a ghostly radiance. Apparently what had happened in the city of shards hadn't shattered these crystals, for which he was very grateful. Squaring his shoulders, Kerin approached Sep's quarters.

Gently he pushed open her door and was surprised to find that Nala must have left the lightsphere burning beside Sep's bed. Wasteful, but perhaps she was worried that Sep still feared the dark after what had happened back on Dust. That would be understandable. He slipped inside, trying not to make any noise. Sep lay in her bunk, her eyes closed and her face slack, and for a moment he couldn't understand how Drifter's maneuvering hadn't tossed her from her bed. Then he saw the safety straps fastened across her chest, holding her tight to the bunk. Nala must have suspected that their swim wouldn't be smooth and prepared accordingly. Wise.

Kerin approached the girl, relieved to see the gentle rise and fall of her chest. He remembered being in nearly the exact same spot after they had fled the alvaren treehold, Nala hovering at his side as they watched Sep sleep. It felt like years had passed, though in truth it had only been a few weeks. So much had changed. She'd been a stranger to him then, just a nameless girl whose life he'd saved almost on a whim. He felt a prickle of shame remembering how he'd looked down at her arm and his first thought had been trying to figure out where he could possibly sell this priceless Elder Race artifact. He'd had no intention of bringing her into his crew, making her part of his family. Now . . . he would fight to the death for her.

And that's almost certainly what would happen.

"Kerin."

Her voice was barely a whisper, and he hadn't even seen her lips move.

"Sep," he said, crouching down beside her. "How do you feel?"

She grimaced and tried to sit, only to find that she was strapped to the bed. "Not good. Why can't I get up?"

Kerin leaned over and undid the buckles. "Just a precaution. Nala thought there might be some rough swimming and she didn't want you getting tossed from the bed."

Freed from the restraints, Sep pushed herself into a sitting position. She gazed around the room as if seeing it for the first time.

"We made it," she said in surprise, then her face creased in confusion. "But how? The last thing I remember was sitting on the ethka and those men had appeared in front of us. They were angry. You started fighting them. Nala and the man in red were throwing fire at each other . . ." Her gaze became distant, as if she was trying to remember something that was stubbornly refusing to come to her. "And then nothing. Did I fall?"

Kerin licked his lips, unsure what exactly he should tell her. Was she ready for the knowledge that something had taken over her body and killed the Mandati?

In the end he never had to make that decision. Her eyes widened slightly as realization swept over her. "It happened again," she murmured, raising her flesh and blood hand to lightly touch the crystal crawling up her cheek.

"Yes," Kerin said simply, hoping she didn't want to know any details.

"I think I can feel him," she said softly. "He's inside."

Kerin frowned, eyeing Sep's faceted arm warily. "Inside the artifact?"

She was quiet for a moment, as if considering this. "Yes. Maybe. I don't know." Her fingers drifted to her forehead. "He could be . . . in here."

"It's definitely a 'he'?"

This time there was no hesitation. "Yes. I'm sure."

Kerin let out a slow breath. What were they going to do? He'd told Nala and Tess that they'd find a renegade mixmage on the Rest, but the artifact had claimed most of the left side of her face. How could they remove it without killing her? And would cleansing the alvaren crystal even remove the Shadow inside her?

Sep shifted her gaze to the flowing blackness that was visible through the room's small window. "There was noise earlier, loud sounds. And everything was shaking. I thought I was dreaming . . ."

"Yes. The Mandate tried to keep us from leaving the system."

Sep's hands tightened around the blanket covering her. "They're chasing us, aren't they?"

Kerin answered before he could even consider lying. "Yes."

Sep turned to face him again. "They want me. For what happened in the place with the crystals."

"Not just that. Other reasons as well." *Drifter squished an exarch.*

Sep shook her head. "No. I've felt him out there, searching. He wants me."

Kerin blinked in confusion. "Who?"

"The Golden Emperor," Sep murmured, staring at something far away that only she could see. She was quiet for a long moment, and then her gaze sharpened on him.

"You could have left me behind. Left me for *him* while you ran. You could have escaped." She swallowed, and he saw tears trembling in her eyes. "You would have been safe."

He attempted a smile. "You're one of us now. Not that that's any great thing, mind you."

Sep wiped at a tear as it trickled down her cheek. "It is," she whispered, then reached out to touch his wrist lightly with her fingers.

23

KERIN WAS on the main deck staring out into the churning dark, his thoughts drifting in the emptiness, when Nala found him later. She sighed deeply as a greeting, then leaned against the balustrade, a steaming bowl of tea clutched in her paws.

"How is Tess?" he asked, returning to himself.

She lapped at her drink. "Resting. She lost a lot of blood. I don't know how she was still standing."

"She was always tough," Kerin murmured, tracing an imperfection in the wooden railing with his finger.

"And now she's a Shroud," Nala replied, shaking her head.

"You two seem to be getting along."

Nala plucked a chunk of meat from her tea and popped it into her mouth. "I don't think I've truly come to grips with what she is," the kyrathi admitted as she chewed. "Calvan talked about her so much I feel like I've known her for a long time. I used to be a little jealous about the light that would come into his eyes when he mentioned her, silly as that sounds. But I always suspected I would like her if we ever met, given the stories . . . and I do."

"What do you think about what the Crimson said?"

"Eh?"

"About Tessa igniting the wraith crystal in the plaza and bringing down that spire. Killing all those people."

Nala's tail lashed the air behind her as she looked away. "I don't know."

"I don't either," Kerin admitted, rubbing tiredly at his aching eyes.

"How long has it been since you've slept?" Nala asked, concern in her voice.

"A few days," he replied.

Nala flicked her ears in the direction of the Nest. "You should go rest. A sandglass or two would do wonders, I think. I just took a nap and I feel ready to take on the entire Mandate."

"You just might get a chance to do that," Kerin muttered.

Her tail thumped his leg. "They're still following us, then?"

He nodded. "For a while Drifter couldn't feel them, since we'd left Dust's system, but then they also passed into the Stream. They're getting closer."

Nala's gaze shifted to Drifter's massive head. It was bobbing up and down with the effort the starbeast was expending. "I wanted to ask you . . . are we swimming a little slowly?" Her voice was a whisper, as if she didn't want the starbeast to hear.

Kerin gave a curt nod. "Yes. Look at his port flipper."

She glanced over the railing, and a moment later gave an uneasy growl. "That looks . . . not good."

"The worst of the bleeding stopped, at least. It's incredible he's managed to keep up this pace with the wounds he's taken."

"All so we can throw ourselves at the feet of the qan," she muttered, shaking her head. "Can we actually make it to the Rest?" Her tone suggested how ridiculous she thought it was that they were fleeing to the reptiles for solace.

Kerin shrugged. "He insists he can. But when I reach across his bond . . . he's in great pain. It's like he's trying to run a race with a ruined ankle."

Nala did not respond to this, and silence descended between them for a while. There was nothing either of them could do to help Drifter. They could only hope the starbeast somehow found the strength to keep ahead of the Mandate fleet until they reached the mouth that emptied into the Rest's system.

"And how's Sep?" Nala asked suddenly.

"She's . . . all right. The crystal has spread a bit more, but I think she has a few days left, at least. The bit that has reached her face doesn't look like it's fully set. The crystal is opaque rather than translucent."

"Do you think she can use the weapon against the krakens chasing us?"

Kerin pursed his lips. Nala had just given voice to what he'd been considering while watching the Stream flowing past.

"I think so. She seems to be able to summon that power when in danger. But Nala . . . Drifter said there were at least a hundred krakens behind us. *A hundred.* Even an Elder Race weapon can't destroy that many starbeasts. And every kraken will have a Crimson battlemage. Tess even said that several exarchs are here as well, summoned along with the fleets from their systems. And each is an archmage." A hollowness had opened in his stomach just thinking about the armada pursuing them. Their predicament was beyond hopeless.

He leaned forward, setting his elbows on the wood and burying his face in his hands. "I'm sorry, Nal," he said, his voice ragged. "I did this to us. It's my fault."

The kyrathi snorted. "Don't be ridiculous."

"No, it's true. If my grandfather was still alive we wouldn't be in this situation. He never would have let it come to this. I've failed all of you."

Nala's tail thumped him hard. "Enough, Kerin. I won't listen to this."

When his head remained in his hands she laid her paw on his shoulder.

"Ow!" he cried indignantly, pulling away from her as she flexed her claws through his steelsilk shirt.

"Now that I have your attention," Nala said, inspecting the tips of her claws as if to see whether she'd drawn blood. "Keep your mouth closed and listen."

Her amber eyes found his. "With Calvan at the helm, we'd be in the same sort of trouble. Nebulas, maybe even worse. Why are we here? Because you showed mercy to Sep. You could have left her in the treehold, as I was telling you to do." She held up her paws quickly. "And no, I'm glad you didn't. The girl deserved a chance, and you couldn't have known what would happen. But once she was on Drifter it was inevitable some terrible power of the tributary would try and take her from us. Happened to be the Mandate, but it could just has easily been the qan matriarch if we'd gone to the Rest, or one of the Triumvirate if we'd fled to the Embers, as I almost suggested. Or maybe even something worse." Nala saw him opening his mouth and waved at him to stay quiet. "Don't talk, listen. That instinct, Kerin, the one that led you to give me Sep before you saved yourself, even as the treehold was collapsing on top of you . . . it's the same instinct your grandfather had. He saved Tessa and me, brought us on Drifter and gave us new lives. I would be dead, and I'm not sure what the life expectancy of a gutter rat like Tessa was, but I don't think many of them reach adulthood, let alone leave their home planet. And you, too. I know what your life was like on Devali. All of us – you, me, Tessa – in our own ways we were just as broken as Sep is now. The only difference is that we didn't come with an Elder Race weapon . . . but you couldn't have known that Sep did." She was quiet for a moment. "Though, even if you had, I think you still would have tried to save her. And by tooth and claw, Calvan would have done the same."

Kerin didn't trust himself to answer the kyrathi without showing the emotion her words had stirred up, so he only nodded jerkily. She watched his face for a moment, as if searching for something, and then she nodded as well when she seemed to find it. Nala placed her paw on his shoulder again, but she kept her claws sheathed this time as she squeezed lightly.

"I'm going to go nap some more. Ring the bell if anything changes here."

Then she was gone, silently padding away. He stared where she had been for a long time, until he felt Drifter intrude upon his thoughts.

She's right, you know.

Kerin winced as the pain the turtle was feeling seeped across their bond. *You were eavesdropping.*

Well, you were whispering while standing right behind my head. Isn't that even ruder?

Kerin couldn't keep the corner of his mouth from lifting. *I suppose it is.*

That's one thing I've always liked about you, Kerin. You take responsibility. You admit your faults and shoulder blame. Not all of your ancestors were the same.

I doubt they made as many spectacular mistakes as I have.

A booming snort reverberated in Kerin's mind. *Oh, you're not the first Talisien to make questionable decisions. I'd put you far from the worst, actually. As Nala claimed, you're more similar to your grandfather than you realize.* Drifter paused for a moment, as if gathering his thoughts. *You must know it's rare for a starbeast to stay with a single family for so long.*

I've noticed.

That's because it's demanding to be a streamsurfer, and not everyone is suitable. The universe is a dangerous place, even for starbeasts. If I had thought you would not make a good captain I would not have bonded with you after Calvan's death. But I had watched you for years, and I saw the same qualities that had first drawn me to your family. Cleverness. Curiosity. Compassion. We all have a finite time in this universe, Kerin. Those are the characteristics I want to define my time here, and that is why we are well-matched.

Kerin hung his head.

But speaking of finite time . . .

Yes?

The Mandati have closed the distance. Grudging respect flavored Drifter's thoughts. *The squids are fast. I'm not sure if I could stay ahead of them even if I wasn't hobbled.*

*Don't feel so bad. You **are** a turtle, after all.*

If there was one thing I could change about your family, it would most certainly be the terrible sense of humor.

Kerin chuckled. He supposed it was a testament to their bond that even when standing at the gallows with the rope around their necks they could still find humor in the moment.

You can't make the Rest?

He felt the starbeast's attitude become far more sober. *I'm sorry, Kerin.*

That tiny flame of hope he'd been nurturing began to gutter. *How long do we have?*

A sandglass, maybe a little longer.

Kerin let out a slow breath, his mind racing. He thought back to those dusty charts in his grandfather's solarium, the tangle of Streams that knotted the Umbral Cluster. He chewed the inside of his cheek as something occurred to him.

Well, if it was their only chance...

The lights from the Mandati fleet had appeared in the blackness by the time the Stream's mouth could be glimpsed in front of them. His hand had been on the bell's rope for so long that his arm had started to tingle – he'd wanted to wake Nala and Tessa so they could join him on deck, but he also felt guilty at the thought of doing this. Likely this was the last bit of rest they'd ever enjoy. Kerin had no illusions about what would almost certainly happen in the next short while.

He pulled the rope hard, and the bell clanged. Sighing, he lifted his spyglass and tried to focus on the vague shapes behind them picked out against the Stream's roiling darkness. Most were still just splotches of pale light, but one was markedly different than the rest – many times larger, and gleaming gold.

Kerin lowered the spyglass slowly as a prickling numbness spread through him. The Golden Emperor himself was leading the Mandate armada. It seemed unbelievable. The emperor was a living god to the inhabitants of a hundred systems, and right now he was churning the Stream as he strained to catch *them*.

Kerin actually felt a twinge of pride.

Footsteps drew his attention, and he turned just as Tessa emerged from the saloon. Her red hair was tangled and wild, as if she'd just woken up, but her face looked noticeably fresher than before as she stumped across the deck to him favoring her uninjured leg. Nala appeared a moment later, swinging up from a lower walkway and landing silently. Kerin took a step towards Tessa, his hand held out to help her, but the Shroud waved him away.

"We've arrived at the Rest already?" she asked, peering past him at the curtain of light shimmering in the distance.

Kerin winced inwardly when he heard the hope in her voice. "Not . . . exactly."

Nala narrowed her eyes at him. "What does that mean?"

"Well, not at all, in truth."

The kyrathi smoothed down her whiskers, scowling when her paw reached the shortened ends on the left side of her face. "Then where does that mouth lead?"

Drifter's consciousness entered his own, interrupting him before he could answer. *Kerin.*

What is it?

We'll pass through the mouth in less than a hundred heartbeats. Are you sure about this?

Kerin swallowed, turning to stare at the points of light glimmering behind them. *Yes. But it's too soon. I need you to wait until the Mandate is almost upon us.*

He felt the starbeast's uncertainty, but Drifter didn't try and argue. The turtle had exhausted every possible argument in his previous unsuccessful attempts to convince Kerin that this was a very bad idea.

"Kerin!" Nala cried, yanking him away from Drifter. Her paws were on his arm, claws pricking his skin. "What system is on the other side of that mouth?"

He looked at her, and from the fear in her eyes he suspected she already knew the answer.

"H'shen."

~

Now, Kerin thought, and Drifter surged towards the rippling light.

As his starbeast lurched into motion again, he kept his spyglass trained on the vast armada rapidly swelling behind them. Mandati marines were visible on the platforms built across the mantles of the closest war krakens, scurrying about as they readied weapons and boarding planks. Dwarfing this vanguard, but still a ways behind them, was the starbeast of the Golden Emperor himself, sheathed in shining armor. Kerin could see only a small, pavilion-like structure attached to the vast bulk, and he wondered where the imperial entourage and attendants were located on the great starbeast. The emperor looked to be the only inhabitant on the leviathan.

"I hope you know what you're doing," Nala murmured as he lowered his spyglass and turned to face the Stream's mouth.

"I most definitely do not," he replied just before they passed into the hovering radiance. Cold, stark light washed over the deck as everything around them trembled, as if wood and flesh had suddenly become less solid, and then a moment later the universe sharpened once more as they emerged into the star-spattered darkness.

H'shen. Kerin had never been here before, and he quickly surveyed the system, trying to get his bearings. The Stream's mouth was closer to the star than in most other systems, and a large blue and black mottled planet loomed off Drifter's starboard side, taking up most of the view. This must be H'shen itself, as Kerin remembered it was famous for its thick, dark oceans and vast azure deserts. To port the system's yellow sun blazed, but between them and the star were countless points of hanging darkness – an asteroid belt, probably the remnants of a planet that had met some cataclysmic fate long ago. Kerin's heart began to beat a little harder. That was exactly what he'd hoped to see. So far luck was with them.

Drifter's flippers churned the system's cold air as they soared away from the mouth, taking a path between the planet and the belt.

Beside him, Nala was standing rigidly as she peered into the emptiness, her hackles raised and her claws gripping the railing so hard the wood had splintered.

Can you sense them?

Drifter's response was immediate. *Oh, yes. And they know we're here. Their thoughts are so cold, so . . . empty.*

Are they doing anything?

They're swimming straight for us. Most of them, anyway.

How many

A pause, as if the starbeast was trying to make a count. *I don't know. Hundreds.*

"What's wrong?" Tessa asked. She was staring at him uneasily, and Kerin realized his reaction to what Drifter had just said must be showing in his face.

"Do you truly need to ask?" Nala growled, stepping in to answer before he could gather his scattered thoughts. "We're swimming towards a lich's undead horde. Of all the things in the universe one should never, ever do, this is right at the top of the list."

And now we have company behind us as well.

Kerin turned, craning his head to see around the curve of Drifter's shell. Long, dark shapes were spilling from the Stream's mouth, mantles rippling and tentacles writhing. The war krakens took a moment to orient themselves as they adjusted to this dimension, and then their tentacles flexed as they slid away. Kerin had to commend their bravery – the Mandati starbeasts certainly sensed the vast horde of undead lurking in the system, but they showed only the slightest of hesitation before continuing their pursuit of Drifter.

Or perhaps they were more frightened of their master. Kerin sucked in his breath as the war kraken of the Golden Emperor materialized from the mouth. The sheer size of the behemoth was staggering, many times longer than its brethren swarming around it. It truly was the starbeast of a demigod.

Above us! Drifter's warning came a heartbeat before a massive shape emerged from the blackness ahead of them. It was the corpse of a bird large enough to pick Drifter up in its talons, a few desiccated feathers still clinging to its great wings. Kerin instinctually ducked, but the undead starbeast soared over them without glancing down. Its silence was eerie, only the swirl of disturbed air to mark its passage. Then it was past them, swooping towards the leading war kraken.

Kerin looked at Tessa and Nala and saw awe and shock. He realized his own jaw was hanging open when he tried to speak.

"Was that a Thryssian roc or a—" he began, but Nala hissed for him to be quiet and gestured frantically with unsheathed claws in the direction Drifter was swimming.

He turned and saw that emerging from the emptiness was a legion of starbeasts. Kerin recognized many of them, while others he had never encountered in his travels. There was the flensed hulk of a ghenabakan dreadnought, the warren of tunnels threading its stony flesh exposed to the abyss through which it was swimming. A swarm of reapers soared on insectile wings, their scythe-like front limbs crossed over cracked and punctured thoraxes. An ancient serpent-starbeast that had been picked clean of all organic matter slithered past, so old its decaying bones had turned yellow. Other members of the horde looked more recently deceased: a school of qan razor fish were still covered in barbed scales and flesh, and if it were not for the gaping wounds or the shattered remnants of the structures once attached to their backs they could have passed as still among the living.

None of the undead starbeasts spared a glance at Drifter, intent on the Mandati fleet still boiling from the Stream's mouth.

"Tooth and claw," Nala breathed, and Kerin could only nod mutely in agreement.

Kerin ... I can sense Xerivas's dragon ahead of us.

The lich clearly had other priorities right now, but still Kerin didn't want to present himself before the undead sorcerer quite yet. His hand went to his pocket and the hard outline of the grey-metal cube. Thank the stars he hadn't tossed the artifact into the void, as trading the cube for their lives was really their only hope of surviving at this point.

The asteroid belt Kerin thought, his gaze drawn to the vast field of floating rocks. *We'll hide there until the fighting is over.*

He felt Drifter's affirmation, and then the starbeast turned away from the parade of dead starbeasts.

"They're letting us go?" Nala murmured incredulously when none of the lich's servants made an attempt to stop them.

"Xerivas knows we're trapped," Kerin replied as they approached the fringe of the asteroid belt. "There's only one mouth in this system, and very shortly there's going to be several hundred starbeasts tearing themselves to pieces between us and it."

Drifter slowed as he passed between the first of the great floating rocks. *Do we try to hide deeper in the field?*

Kerin gave a mental shrug. *It doesn't really matter, does it? And to be honest, I'd like a good view of what's about to happen.*

Me too.

Drifter descended towards an asteroid on the edge of the field, one with a relatively smooth and flat surface. As soon as his flippers touched rock, Kerin felt a flood of relief from the starbeast as the pulsing waves of pain diminished. He realized that the starbeast had been trying to hide the extent of his injury by keeping the worst of his agony from leeching across their bond. Sympathy swelled in him, but Drifter pointedly ignored his concern. The message the starbeast was trying to impart was clear: they had more important things to worry about.

Such as being dangerously close to a battle between two of the tributary's great powers.

Flashes of red light were erupting as the first wave of undead starbeasts collided with the vanguard of the Mandati host. Kerin brought the spyglass to his eye, but he could only catch snatches of what was happening between the intense bursts of sorcery. He saw a war kraken convulsing as it died, impaled by the long spiraling horn of an undead monstrosity that looked to have be soldered together from several different starbeasts. Elsewhere one of the insectile reapers blazed like a torch, crimson aether consuming its desiccated wings. A bolt the length of a wagon leapt from the ballista perched on the mantle of a kraken and struck the skull of a wolfish, winged starbeast. The undead creature's head exploded in a cloud of bone dust, but the rest of its body kept surging forward. Its long curving claws fastened onto the kraken's armored flank and began trying to rip away the metal plates protecting its soft flesh. Not all the lich's servants were unmanned: Kerin saw tiny shapes leap from the back of one lumbering starbeast, their bat-like wings outspread as they glided towards where a group of krakens had formed a tight phalanx against the crashing wave of the dead legion.

"Nebulas," he whispered, lowering his spyglass. Tessa and Nala were also watching the unfolding battle intently – he knew the kyrathi's sight was excellent, but if Tessa could see clearly without a spyglass then her strange golden eyes must be an improvement over what she had been born with.

The Shroud gasped, the color draining from her face, and Kerin hurriedly turned and fumbled with the spyglass to see what had startled her.

The massive war kraken of the Golden Emperor had finally reached the battle's front lines. A tentacle far longer than one of Dust's spires whipped through the air, striking the disemboweled husk of the ghenabakan dreadnought Kerin had seen earlier, and the undead starbeast shattered like it was made of clay, stony fragments tumbling into the void. As if of one mind, the undead host turned towards the hulking Mandate starbeast. The great kraken seemed to realize that it had the lich's attention and it spread its tentacles wide.

Kerin nearly dropped his spyglass at what was revealed, and a surprised yowl came from Nala.

At the center of the kraken's nest of tentacles was not a beak. Instead, a huge, malformed human head, golden and hairless, roared and gnashed its teeth.

"What in the bloody stars is that?" he murmured, shocked.

"The Golden Emperor," Tessa replied softly. She did not sound surprised, though Kerin heard something in her voice: awe, and perhaps disgust.

"Impossible," Kerin whispered.

"It is not," Tessa intoned dully. "He was the first and the greatest of the mixmages. When he ascended to the throne of the empire three centuries ago he became obsessed with turning himself into . . . that." She raised her arm, indicating the massive golden kraken. As if he'd heard, the golden visage of the emperor twisted, his maw opening wide. A faint bellowing came to them that sounded more beast than man, and Kerin shivered.

"Bit by bit, molding and shaping his flesh over the decades," Tessa said.

"He turned himself into a starbeast," Nala whispered.

"No, a monster," Tessa corrected her, shaking her head. "If the citizens of the empire knew, there would be panic. Even most Shrouds are unaware that our immortal, reclusive god-emperor has become a mad abomination. Out there in the fleet, likely only the exarchs know the truth. The rest have been told this is a mindless starbeast twisted by sorcery into a weapon of the divine, and that the Golden Emperor inhabits the structure on its back, too holy to be seen by those who have not demonstrated their purity by attaining the freedom to rule."

He comes.

The dread in Drifter's thoughts pulled Kerin's attention away from the great kraken. A shape was emerging from the blackness that had birthed the lich's legions. At first it was just a swelling shadow, and then Xerivas's enormous bone dragon soared into view on outstretched wings.

"Mother of the Dark," Tessa whispered hoarsely. "What in the abyss is *that*?"

"The lich's starbeast," Nala told her. "We've met before. It ate us."

"So the dead archmage is on that thing?" she asked, her gaze swinging from the dragon to the kraken and back again. "This is about to get interesting."

The swarm of dead starbeasts that had been harrying the Golden Emperor pulled back as the dragon neared, and the kraken spread wide its tentacles as if welcoming the dragon into its embrace.

The two great starbeasts collided, and Kerin was almost surprised that the universe itself did not tremble with the force of the impact.

Claws and teeth scraped the kraken's gleaming armor as tentacles wrapped vast skeletal limbs. Blue blood misted the air as dust and fragments of bone fell away. Kerin glimpsed among the writhing tentacles the emperor's monstrous visage, its mouth twisted in a roar, its eyes wild and rolling. He looked for the speck inside the undead dragon that would be Xerivas's black throne but could see little through the monster's ribs.

The fighting swirling around these two leviathans intensified, sorcery rippling the darkness.

Kerin knew he was watching history being written here, for if the lich or the Golden Emperor perished it would change the balance of power in this branch of the stellar tributary. He couldn't look away.

A deep, rising growl from Nala slowly penetrated Kerin's awed stupor.

"What is it?" he whispered out of the corner of his mouth just before the kyrathi's tail thumped him hard in the back.

Blinking, as if surfacing from a dream, he tore his eyes from the distant battle. Nala was turned away from the balustrade, facing the Nest, her claws unsheathed and the fur on her back bristling.

Something was there.

An asteroid hanging above them had plunged much of Drifter's shell and its structures into shadow. But the darkness did not hide the two looming shapes that had appeared on the deck. Kerin's hand went to the hilt of his sword, his pulse quickening.

"Tessa," he hissed, and at his tone the Shroud whirled from the railing and drew her golden swords.

The shapes did not move.

Kerin glanced around to see if anything else strange had appeared. *Drifter*, he thought as he edged towards the motionless intruders. *What are these things on the deck?*

*What are **what** things on the deck?*

Drifter couldn't sense them. That was troubling. Maybe they were an illusion, although his Anathema blood hadn't stirred.

There's something here.

Ah. I see them. A scene of Tessa, Nala and Kerin on the deck slowly approaching the two dark shapes materialized in his mind's eye. Drifter had turned his head to see what was happening.

Kerin withdrew a lightsphere and kindled the crystal within, then tossed it towards the objects. It struck the wood and rolled to a stop a few span from the shapes, illuminating . . . feet. Silvery feet, beautifully carved. Also muscled calves, flowing up into graceful thighs, which merged with androgynous, narrow-waisted midsections. They appeared to be statues shaped from gleaming silver metal. The first difference between the two forms were the chests – one was most definitely male and the other female, though both were broad and powerful. The faces also had distinctly gendered casts, with the feminine statue's features being slightly softer and more rounded. Both were of equal height, maybe a half again as tall as Kerin. Their arms hung at their side, and what looked like silver wings were folded across their back.

"Hello?" Kerin called out, unsure whether he should draw *Mercy*. He didn't want these things to assume he was a threat . . . if they were aware of anything at all. Neither had moved in the slightest since he'd been watching them. Where had they come from?

"Are they golems?" asked Nala, and Kerin shrugged. They looked manufactured, someone's ideal of a perfect humanoid. He had to admit they were beautiful.

But what were they doing on Drifter? And how did they *get* here?

"Streamsurfers."

The voice was the crackle of ancient parchment. Familiar, and something Kerin had hoped to never, ever hear again.

Twin points of cold light flared in the shadows. The whisper of footsteps followed, bone on wood, accompanied by the heavy clump of a staff.

Nala gave a little meow of fear as Xerivas shuffled from the darkness. The lich's avatar was shorter this time, but it was still dressed in frayed black robes, and in its bony grip was the same staff that Kerin remembered. The tusked silver skull leered at him, the black-threaded red jewel sunk in its brow glittering in the starlight.

"Xerivas," Kerin said, letting his hand slip from the hilt of his sword. "Fancy meeting you here." He was surprised how steady he kept his voice.

The lich rasped a chuckle, shaking his head slightly as he approached. Kerin tensed, but Xerivas glided right past them. He shared a glance with Tessa and Nala as the undead sorcerer halted at the balustrade, resting his skeletal hand on the wood as he looked out past Drifter's half-turned head at the distant battle. Without using his spyglass, most of the starbeasts were nothing but floating specks of darkness to Kerin until illuminated by an eruption of sorcery, but the two great starbeasts around which the rest swirled were clearly visible. All of the Golden Emperor's tentacles were now grasping the dragon; some were wrapped around its arms and legs, keeping the claws away from the kraken's flesh, while others were trying to push inside the undead starbeast's hollow ribcage, as if the dragon could be broken apart from within.

The lich watched the grappling titans for a long moment, then turned back to Kerin and his companions. *"What would compel a man to turn himself into such an abomination?"*

Kerin swallowed back what he wanted to say, hoping that Nala and Tessa would show the same restraint. Glancing at them, he realized he shouldn't have worried. They were both clearly cowed by the waves of power and dread flowing from the ancient archmage.

"Clever, bringing the Mandate and their emperor here," the lich said. *"Though I have to admit to some curiosity about what you thought would happen after. Surely the victor would not simply let you swim away."* The undead sorcerer waved his bony hand vaguely at the battle raging behind him. *"Especially after such a monumental waste."*

"It looks like your pet is in trouble," Kerin said, nodding towards the undead dragon. "Why don't I give you what you want, and then you can go help? We'll swim back to the Stream and be on our way."

"You are in no position to bargain, mortal."

"Truly? You clearly desire the cube from the treehold." Kerin forced his most triumphant smile, as if he had just cast a winning throw at blood knuckles. "Which I have hidden exceptionally well. In a thousand years you will never find it, this I promise."

"It is in your pocket."

Kerin swallowed. He glanced at Nala and Tessa and found them staring at him with wide eyes.

"That can't be true," the kyrathi said, her whiskers trembling. "Right, Kerin?"

"Well, you see . . ."

"Tooth and claw," Nala whispered, covering her face with her paws.

"Enough of this foolishness," the lich intoned, lifting his arm.

Kerin's Anathema blood pulsed as sorcery swelled nearby, and he braced himself, fully expecting to be consumed by a torrent of aether. But instead he felt a warmth spreading from his pocket, and then a charred hole opened in his steelsilk tunic as the cube floated over to Xerivas's outstretched hand. Skeletal fingers clutched the artifact, and it looked to Kerin like the lich was pleased, the points of light sunk in his eye sockets flaring brighter as his fleshless mouth twitched upwards.

"No!" Xerivas cried suddenly, his skull snapping around as he thrust his staff at something behind Kerin.

Sorcery burgeoned, a vast maelstrom, and Kerin whirled around. Sep stood in the doorway to the Nest, disheveled and wild eyed, the crystal arm she had raised at the lich blazing with power. The light strengthened as the sorcery reached a crescendo, and Kerin felt a surge of anticipation at what he knew was imminent.

Nothing happened.

Kerin sensed in his Anathema blood the sudden dissolution of the cresting power. It felt like someone had ripped a hole in the universe, the absence was so jarring. Before his stunned eyes the light in Sep's arm faded, subsiding back to a faint glimmer.

Kerin was not the only one surprised. Sep's face was twisted in shock as she stared at her crystal arm. Then she gave a pained cry, stumbling forward a step before falling to her knees. It seemed like something invisible had seized her by the alvaren artifact and yanked hard, as her outstretched arm was straining towards the lich.

Sep was leaning backwards, but her arm looked like it was attempting to tear itself from her body. He tried to go to the whimpering girl, but he found his feet rooted to the deck. Despair filled him as he realized that Xerivas's sorcery had overwhelmed his Anathema nature.

"What are you doing to her?" Kerin cried.

"Correcting an old mistake," said the lich. He drew back his staff, and the surface of Sep's arm rippled.

Then fractured.

Sep screamed. The pain in her voice was a knife to Kerin's heart. But there was nothing he could do, as the lich's sorcery held him so tightly that he was struggling to draw breath.

Fragments pulled free, glittering shards that swirled around her, strengthening as more and more of her fully crystalline body flaked away. Sep's wide and terrified eyes found Kerin. The cries coming out of her were muted now, as if the gathering storm of crystal was devouring the sound.

"Stop!" he managed to grate from a mouth that could barely shape words.

Sep was nearly lost in a blizzard of light. The last glimpse he had of her as the radiance closed was her face being winnowed away, the artifact ripping itself from her flesh. Her gray eyes were pleading . . .

Sep fell forward out of the shimmering crystal swarm. The fleshy thud of her face striking wood made him gasp. A wrenching cry came from Nala.

"Bastard," Kerin hissed through a throat that felt as if it were being strangled, watching as the glittering, swirling cloud drifted towards the lich. When it neared Xerivas it began to coalesce again, solidifying into the same crystal rod that Kerin had first seen displayed on a plinth in the treehold.

Drifter, I can't move, he thought desperately, but it was as if whatever had seized him had also severed his link with the starbeast. Out of the corner of his eye he could see the turtle's great head, and it also looked to be frozen.

The lich released his grip on its staff, though it stayed standing upright beside him. Slowly he reached out, his skeletal fingers curling around the shimmering length of crystal. Xerivas turned it this way and that, as if examining the artifact for flaws.

"It was always our way," he said, but it did not sound to Kerin like he was speaking to them. *"To create things of terrible beauty that brought beautiful terror. It drove us mad, in the end."* Xerivas turned his skull, cold light gleaming in his eye sockets. A prickling numbness crawled across Kerin's skin, the lich's scrutiny a physical thing. *"Oblivion became a purpose, the salvation from what we'd done over a thousand, thousand years. The natural and inevitable end point of our flawed existence."*

The lich casually tossed the crystal rod over his shoulder. It flashed briefly as it caught some stray beam of starlight, and then it vanished over the balustrade and was gone.

"But I rejected this, and so they rejected me."

"Ver Xerivas."

The lich's skull jerked around to stare at where Sep had fallen. Kerin let out a choked hiss of surprise. Sep still lay there, but she had propped herself up with her one remaining arm. Darkness had welled up to fill her eyes.

"Always a romantic," Sep said in a voice that was not her own. She was smiling, but there was no warmth in it.

She wasn't dead, thank the First Mover. And the side of her face where the crystal had covered moments before had been pared down, but the flesh was smooth and unbroken. Her shoulder seemed lopsided, as if a chunk of it had been lost, yet blood did not darken her dress. The crystal had seemingly sealed her skin as it had been pulled away. Only her arm had disappeared, the one part of her than had been fully transmuted.

The lich tilted his skull to one side, considering the girl. *"And who are you?"*

"You do not recognize me?"

Xerivas was motionless, staring at Sep like he could flense away her remaining flesh.

"Impossible," he whispered, but then something else seized his attention, as he suddenly turned from Sep to face the distant battle.

And Kerin saw why.

The Golden Emperor had forced several of his shorter, thicker arms past the ribs of the dragon and into its chest cavity. The undead starbeast was thrashing like a speared fish, tossing its head back and forth as it roared. Kerin watched in mute astonishment as the great kraken pushed the arms it had inside the dragon outward . . . and bones splintered, wrenched from their sockets as the dead starbeast began to break apart. The necromancy animating the monster was visibly leeching away, its limbs slackening as it began to sink, and the Golden Emperor had to withdraw his tentacles from the shattered carcass before he was dragged downwards into oblivion.

Everyone on the deck, including the lich and whatever spirit was possessing Sep, seemed stunned by what had just happened.

Finally Xerivas spoke, his voice a desiccated whisper. *"Unfortunate. More time is needed."*

The lich reached to the tusked silver skull topping his staff, his bony fingers prying at the red jewel in its forehead. After a moment it came loose, falling into his hand. Xerivas held it up, as if searching its black-threaded depths for something, then reared back and threw it towards the still-raging battle. It should have followed an arc and sunk out of sight not far past the railing, but instead it shot like a ballista bolt into the distance, vanishing in a heartbeat.

Kerin watched where it had gone, his apprehension rising. The lich remained staring at where the Golden Emperor had spread his writhing arms wide as he bellowed in triumph.

And then something happened.

A cloud of roiling, churning darkness swelled to an impossibly vast size beside the great kraken. Dozens of sinuous tendrils twisted blindly, each far longer than the longest arms of the Golden Emperor and set into this monstrosity were countless gnashing mouths. There were eyes as well, which Kerin hadn't noticed when he'd first glimpsed this same horror on the threshold of the alvaren treehold, seemingly stolen from a host of different creatures. The eyes of reptiles and fish and humans and creatures he didn't know, all set haphazardly in the rapidly solidifying flesh of the creature.

It dwarfed the Mandate emperor, several times the kraken's great bulk. Kerin gaped, unable to believe what he was seeing.

The lich turned from the monstrosity he had unleashed. *"Do you remember I told you we were lucky the eldritch horror had dwindled from starvation?"* he said, and Kerin knew he was speaking to him. *"As you can see, I have been feeding it."*

Glistening black tendrils wrapped the Golden Emperor, dragging the great kraken towards the horror's maws. The ruler of the Mandate was not helpless, though, nor was he about to succumb meekly – his own more solid tentacles plunged into the hazy form of the monster, tearing loose clumps of pulsing darkness. The many mouths of the abomination stretched wide, a terrible shrieking traveling all the way to where Drifter perched on the asteroid.

Xerivas turned back to the girl, who was still lying on the deck braced by her one remaining arm. *"Now,"* the lich said, *"let us continue."*

Sep sneered at the dead sorcerer. "You don't recognize me."

The lich cocked his skull to one side. *"I have my suspicions."*

Sep's black eyes narrowed. "Perhaps this question will bring clarity. Did you ever return to the spires of Ganamere?"

The lich lifted its skull slightly, as if staring at something only he could see. *"Ah. So it is you,"* Xerivas whispered, and there was a note to the sorcerer's voice, something almost melancholy. *"And yes, I did return to the site of your great folly."*

"Then you know we were not extinguished."

"Not extinguished," Xerivas continued, *"but only the faintest ember remained. Slivers of fragments, wandering lost in the ruin of our world. All of our great works obliterated, the libraries burned, the statues torn down. Effaced from the universe, as if we had never been."*

"You know why."

The lich regarded Sep coldly. *"Because you are mad, brother. You were all mad."*

Brother? Kerin blinked in surprise. The spirit inhabiting Sep was Xerivas's brother? Surely not.

But the girl's smile had only widened after the lich's last statement. "Yes. You do know me. It is fitting that we meet again, here and now, the very last in this universe."

"In any universe."

"Not true!" Sep crowed triumphantly, her dark eyes flashing. "I did it, brother. In the end, the flaw was simple enough to heal, once I knew it was there. I sent our people through! Into what lies beyond."

The lich was silent for a moment, as if mulling what the spirit possessing Sep had said. Another violent shriek rent the air, and Kerin glanced past the undead sorcerer to find that the Golden Emperor had been half-swallowed by the horror, pulled into its seething, billowing form. But the kraken was still struggling viciously, lashing the creature with its tentacles as waves of aether from the Crimson and exarchs of the Mandati fleet carved away chunks of its unnatural flesh.

"How did you return to yourself?" the lich finally asked.

Something like uncertainty shivered Sep's face. "For a long time I was lost, wandering in mist. I did not know who I was. Then, suddenly, I returned. I found myself standing over a dead man in a golden mask, his life and sorcery flowing through me. And I remembered."

A sharp intake of breath from Tessa, probably all she could manage with the lich's sorcery holding her tight. Kerin knew what she was thinking. The Shadow inside Sep had fed on the soul of the old exarch, the one whose death she had been summoned to Dust to investigate. And that had somehow restored the spirit's knowledge of what it had once been.

And what was that? An alvaren, apparently. A sorcerer, almost certainly. The brother of the lich? If so, then Xerivas was a member of that vanished race as well.

"I returned to Ganamere after your failure," the lich said. *"I found*

those skulking, shadowy fragments, like silhouettes seared into a wall after a great explosion. Then within the crystal prism you built I also discovered the ashes of our kind, heaped before the rift you failed to open. I gathered those remains and placed them in a tomb beneath the first spires. I thought at least I owed that to the memory of our people."

He was speaking of the urns, Kerin realized. It was Xerivas who had placed the ashes of the dead alvarens in the underground city, where they'd eventually been discovered by the Black Dawn.

"You owe us much more than that, brother!" spat Sep. "If you had joined our great endeavor I would not have failed the first time!"

The lich shook his skull slowly. *"You poor fool. I was there, at the rift. I saw the hopelessness of what you were trying to do. The flaws were so deep it never would have worked. We were not ready, brother. I knew this. We had not overcome our own imperfections."*

"And yet I completed the ceremony!" the ghost inhabiting Sep cried triumphantly. "I ushered our people into what lies beyond!"

"You did not," the lich said, almost sadly.

A flicker of doubt passed across Sep's face. "What do you mean?"

"No sorcery could have elevated the sad remnants of our people to transcendence. I suspect you merely obliterated what remained, finishing what had been started long ago."

"No," Sep whispered. "You lie."

"You could always tell when I was lying. Am I now?"

Sep's mouth twisted into a snarl. "If that is true, then we are truly the last!"

"There is another, as you well know."

"You will never find her!"

"I already have." The lich raised his arm, showing Sep the cube he still held.

The color drained from the girl's face. "Impossible," she whispered. "The hold was bloodsealed and there is no more alvaren blood in the universe!"

"We are not as pure a people as you always insisted," Xerivas said, his skeletal fingers closing around the cube. For a moment it retained its

shape, then it crumbled. Glittering dust sifted down, drifting to the wooden deck.

Slowly these motes began to coalesce, swirling back upwards to form a spectral humanoid shape that Kerin recognized as the spirit from the treehold. Shimmering silver hair reached to her slim waist. Large, unblinking eyes. The alvaren wraith turned her head, looking around as if waking from a dream. Her thin mouth opened, and a stream of musical utterances tumbled forth. As before, for a moment they meant nothing to Kerin, but then something shifted in his mind.

"What is this?" murmured the spirit, her gaze lingering on each of them as she slowly turned. "Where am I?"

"Alaissa," Xerivas murmured, his voice a ragged whisper.

She focused on the lich. "Yes. That was my name long ago."

The undead sorcerer did not say more, seemingly at a loss for words.

"You should not have taken my soulveld from the Crucible," she said sadly. "It was my duty to protect what we had left behind, for I was the chief artificer. The objects within could murder billions if they were claimed by one of the Younger Races." She wrung her long-fingered hands, suddenly agitated. "Oh, I fear what has been done."

"The artifacts have all been destroyed," whispered the lich. *"I made sure of it."*

Relief trembled the wraith's insubstantial face. "Thank you. You did what we could not."

"Tell me," continued Xerivas, *"who convinced you to sacrifice yourself and pledge eternity to the Crucible?"*

Her brow creased in confusion at the question. "The leader of my people."

"Was it Malichen?"

Her huge eyes widened even further in surprise. "Yes! But . . . how do you know of him? Surely he long since completed his great project, and my people have abandoned this universe."

The lich swiveled to Sep. *"I knew it was you, brother."*

"You refused to help us!" the spirit inhabiting the girl shrieked.

The alvaren wraith's fingers fluttered to her mouth. "Malichen? Is it possible?"

Sep's lip curled. "Alaissa. Our greatest artificer, lover to our greatest sorcerer. You also betrayed us by refusing to join the project."

"Your brother was dead!" the female wraith cried. "I had nothing left to live for! I did not want to experience eternity without him!"

A clattering drew the attention of everyone on the deck. The lich's skeleton had collapsed into a heap on the deck. Standing over it was another alvaren ghost, shimmering and translucent like the one called Alaissa, but very clearly male.

"And you do not have to."

"Xerivas!" cried Alaissa.

Nala and Tessa were goggling at the two wraiths, and he was sure he looked just as bewildered. Xerivas stepped closer to the spirit that had been imprisoned inside the cube and held out his shining arm. When she took his hand, he pulled her across the deck, towards the two silvery statues hulking in the shadows.

"You cannot leave me!" screeched Sep. She had climbed to her feet and now stood swaying unsteadily, her face contorted in rage. "You cannot turn your back on our people!"

Xerivas paused. "Our people – and you, brother – turned away from me long ago. All I ever wanted to do was explore this universe with her at my side."

"You would abandon me?" Sep cried, trembling.

"I could destroy you," Xerivas said, almost tiredly. "But I think existing in this broken body is a worse punishment than oblivion for you. Just a lost spark of sorcery clinging to the notion that it was once alive." Xerivas had turned as he said this last statement, his gaze lingering on Kerin. It almost seemed like the lich was speaking to him.

"Xerivas . . ." the spirit of Alaissa began, watching Sep with a confused expression. "Is that truly Malichen?"

"He will not keep us apart anymore," Xerivas said, gently drawing her closer to the silver shapes. "Come with me." His glowing body disintegrated as he stepped into the statue of the male alvaren.

Alaissa hesitated for the briefest of moments, and then she followed him by flowing into the female statue. Light flared in the eyes of both, and the silver wings folded on their backs spread wide. Feathers glinted in the starlight as the wings beat the air, and then the two alvaren souls lifted from the deck.

In moments they were lost among the floating asteroids, and as they vanished from sight Kerin felt the sorcery holding him release its grip. He fell forward onto his knees, taking great gulping breaths as he tried to sort through what had just happened. Tessa and Nala were doing the same, staring up at where the lich had gone.

An unnatural shriek made them all turn and stare. The eldritch horror the lich had unleashed upon the Mandate fleet was being torn asunder, great oily chunks of its flesh falling away under the onslaught of the Golden Emperor and his sorcerers. It was fading, becoming insubstantial as it dwindled, and as Kerin watched it finally dissipated into shreds of darkness. The necromancy animating the other starbeasts must have also departed along with the lich, as Kerin couldn't see any sign of the undead legion now. They must now be just bones and scraps of dried flesh falling through the void, their cursed existence finally over.

But they would not be the only remains tumbling into the abyss. Kerin watched in shock as the vast form of the Golden Emperor began to sink, his body riddled with gaping wounds. Most of his tentacles had been reduced to stumps, but the few that remained grasped weakly at the air as the great kraken struggled to stay aloft.

It was hopeless. For a brief moment Kerin glimpsed the emperor's mouth twisted into a scream, his golden head lashed with blue ichor, and then the great starbeast plummeted out of sight.

Kerin.

Drifter, are you all right?

The turtle's head was twisted half around so he could see those that remained upon the deck.

I'm fine. I'm sorry I couldn't help you . . . that lich's sorcery was immense. To hold a starbeast in thrall! A hatchling of the Great Turtle, no less! He could have established a second necrocracy in the tributary if he'd so desired.

And all he wanted from the beginning was to find his lost love.

There was more to that story. Drifter's great head dipped slightly. *Well, I suppose you could ask her. Him.*

Kerin turned to Sep. The girl had staggered over to the Nest and was leaning against a wall, staring up at where the pair of silver avatars had vanished. Kerin shared a quick glance with Tessa and Nala.

The scuff of their footsteps approaching made Sep look up. She muttered something unintelligible, her black eyes flashing.

"Stay back," she hissed a moment later in Trade. "I still have power. Remember what happened to the fools on Ganamere when touched by the shades of my people."

"Leave her, ghost," Nala growled, green sparks swirling around her paws.

"Or you will do what? Burn me out?" The spirit inhabiting Sep drew her body up a little straighter, staring defiantly at them.

Kerin swallowed. What could they do? Restrain her and hope they could find a necromancer capable of exorcising the alvaren ghost? He glanced over his shoulder to where the massive battle had until recently been raging. To his surprise, there were still flashes of aether illuminating the darkness. Who were the Mandate fighting now?

"We have a chance to escape, streamsurfer," Sep said to Kerin. "The ones who chased us here are distracted. If we flee now we can slip back through the mouth before they know we are gone."

"What *are* they doing?" Nala murmured, also staring out at the battle as it intensified again.

"They are doing exactly what I would expect," Tessa replied, and Kerin thought she sounded almost tired. "The Golden Emperor has fallen. Several exarchs, all holders of the tenth rank – the freedom to rule – must have survived. They are ... establishing a hierarchy."

"What does that mean?" Kerin asked, then flinched as a great crimson rose of aether bloomed in the darkness. The exarchs out there were mighty sorcerers, each the ruler of a Mandate system. Would the entire empire dissolve into chaos like this, or could one of these archmages manage to take up the mantle of the Golden Emperor?

"It means they will be busy for a while," Tessa said. "I doubt they would bother trying to stop us even if we swam right past them on the way to the Stream."

"Then we should go now," Sep urged.

"You don't give orders, ghost," Nala snapped, the embers around her paws flaring brighter.

"My people were exploring the Streams when your ancestors were still slinking through the grass," Sep said to Nala sneeringly, then turned her attention once more to Kerin. "You know the opportunity I present, streamsurfer. I have the knowledge of an Elder Race. My value to you is incalculable."

Kerin stared at the creature that had been Sep. The bastard was right. If he returned with the last remnant of an Elder Race he would become a legend of the tributary.

He suddenly remembered what Xerivas had said. "Just a lost spark of sorcery," Kerin whispered to himself, quoting the lich's final words, "clinging to the notion that it was once alive." *Sorcery.*

Kerin strode forward and grasped Sep's remaining arm. She glanced at him, startled, as something crackled between them. His Anathema blood thrummed in his veins, and Kerin tumbled into blackness.

24

HE STOOD UPON A DARKLING PLAIN.

Numb surprise washed through Kerin as he stared into the impenetrable blackness. He hadn't been expecting this at all. He thought his Anathema blood might have some effect on the spirit inhabiting Sep . . . but it seemed like he'd been transported somewhere else. Where was he?

He shivered, rubbing at his arms. It was deathly cold here, and if it weren't for this darkness Kerin was sure he could see his breath. The ground felt smooth, but not slippery, like polished stone rather than ice. Still, a coldness was seeping up through the soles of his boots, making his feet tingle. He knelt down and brushed his fingertips against the ground, but then jerked his hand back from the searing pain. Kerin stood again, reaching into his pocket for a light sphere. He withdrew one and gave it a good shake, but the crystal inside did not ignite. He tried another, with the same result.

His heart began to beat a little faster, the whispers of panic in the back of his mind growing louder.

Trying to calm himself, Kerin closed his eyes and slowed his breathing, ignoring his thudding pulse as he listened hard for any clue that might tell him where he was. The silence enveloped him, seamless and suffocating.

Nothing.

But when he opened his eyes, something had changed.

The darkness was no longer absolute. In the distance was a hazy smear of light, so faint he worried at first it was his imagination.

He started walking. His legs felt stiff, half-frozen, and he wondered how long he could survive out here.

The light swelled quickly, and Kerin nearly staggered in relief when he got close enough to the glowing shape to see that it was Sep, curled up into a fetal position, her back to him.

"Sep!" he cried, rushing to her and crouching down. Her skin had a pearly luster, her hair a metallic sheen. He could see the rise and fall of her chest, but her eyes stared past him, empty and unblinking. Kerin gently gave her shoulder a shake. "Are you all right?"

To his relief, he saw her eyes slowly focus on him. But no recognition passed across her slack face. She did not stir, nor did her breathing quicken. She seemed entirely uninterested in him.

"It's me, Kerin. Do you remember Dust? Nala? Bas Jelaska?"

He realized with a start that she had both her arms, and her face and neck were unscarred, as if she had never been bonded with the alvaren artifact.

He'd seen her like this before. On Drifter, during the swim out from Jegriddsl, when she'd sat in the Nest and stared blankly at nothing.

"Man."

Kerin glanced up, startled by the rasping voice. Looming over Sep was an alvaren. Not an insubstantial wraith like he'd seen before, but one of flesh, though it still looked recently exhumed. Its skin was cracked like old leather and stretched taut over sharp bones, and its large golden eyes were recessed deep in their sockets. Brittle hair that appeared more steel than silver tumbled past its shoulders, reaching all the way to its sunken chest.

Kerin shivered as he stared into those unblinking eyes. "What's wrong with her?" he asked, his hand drifting to *Mercy's* hilt as he rose from his crouch.

The alvaren did not seem intimidated by this threat. "The fledgling is broken. Our sorcery healed her for a time, but now that has been withdrawn. She has returned to what she once was."

"I don't believe you."

The alvaren watched him impassively, thin lips pursed. "I speak true."

"Then what do you want?"

"Her mind is shattered, but she is still a suitable vessel."

"No."

"Hear me out, man. Before you place yourself in opposition to me, listen to my tale. Understand what is at stake."

Kerin was surprised by the note of pleading he heard in the alvaren's voice. The ghost sounded desperate.

"What you witnessed between Xerivas and I was the final act in a drama that has unfolded over centuries. We are brothers, bound by blood and sorcery, both gifted with great talent and greater ambition. But we were born in the wrong age, as the flame of our people – which had once blazed across the tributary – was now but a dying flicker. Our brethren's souls were afflicted by a rot, weighed down by an unknowable sadness. Only my brother and I still burned with the passion that had once defined our people. I knew our time in this universe was over, our species in an irrevocable decline, and that our only hope was to use the great sorcery we had refined over the eons to move outside this universe, to whatever existed beyond. We would transcend, as other Elder Races had done before us. The idea ignited what smoldering resolve remained in the remnants of my people. But we had already faded so much, and the project was so taxing. We needed my brother, the greatest sorcerer born in a thousand years. Yet he was not empty inside. Like me, he still burned. And others rallied to him, the dwindling few who thought the time of the alvarens had not yet passed in this universe."

"The Rivening," Kerin murmured.

"Yes," the alvaren shade said, bowing his head. "They resisted with a fervor that had been missing in our people for many ages, but they were too few. The war, however, weakened those that survived even further. When we attempted to complete our great project, we failed."

"And now your people are all gone," Kerin said.

The alvaren raised his thin arms, staring in what seemed like wonder at his clawed hands. "Are we truly? I find myself reborn in the shell of this fledgling."

"But the rest of the Shadows on Dust disappeared. I saw it."

"Not all," the alvaren corrected him. "Just the ones that followed me to the city of shards. There are others still on Dust, thousands of them. Perhaps, like me, they can be saved."

"What are you saying?" Kerin whispered.

"I am saying that the fate of the alvarens is in your hands. Help me resurrect my people."

Kerin felt a shiver of surprise at the earnestness of this request, his hand finally drifting from his sword.

"We still have much we can bring to the tributary!" the alvaren continued, its voice rising. "And ancient knowledge to share. The Crucible was but one treehold we hid before we attempted to transcend. Pledge yourself to my cause, and I will share with you sorcery and power beyond your wildest imaginings!"

The ghost pressed his long-fingered hands together. "Please, man." The arrogance and disdain were gone now from the alvaren's voice. He was beseeching Kerin, begging for him to give his people one final chance.

But why would he beg unless Kerin had a choice?

He glanced down at Sep. Her lips were slightly parted, her hands limp in her lap. She looked lost, empty, just as the alvaren spirit claimed. If this was all that was left of her, how could he value what remained more than the future of an entire race?

Kerin sank down beside Sep. He felt the alvaren's icy gaze watching him closely. Taking a deep breath, he leaned forward and gathered the girl into his arms. "Your people had their chance, wraith. Now she deserves hers."

The wraith hissed something guttural as Kerin rose holding Sep to his chest. The air seemed to grow even colder, and every breath prickled his lungs.

"Man, think! She is lost! At least let some good come of what has happened to her! Leave the fledgling, and I will lead you from her broken mind."

Kerin adjusted his grip on Sep, hitching her up higher. "I think if I do that I'll be abandoning her to you." He smiled grimly, staring at the alvaren's seamed and wrinkled face. "No."

"Then you will die!" snarled the wraith. "And after your death I will take her anyway!"

"Yeah, well, go ahead and try."

Kerin strode forward, into the black. Before he'd gotten more than a few steps the darkness trembled in front of him, solidifying into the alvaren. The ghost drew itself up to block his way, but Kerin walked straight through it. Its look of shocked surprise as it dissolved was immensely satisfying.

Moments later it reappeared beside him, its clawed hands clutching at his arm. He tried to ignore it, but where it touched him an icy numbness spread. With a pained grunt he pulled away, a wave of dizziness almost making him stumble. Shaking his head to try and clear it, Kerin quickened his strides as he squinted into the blackness. Beside him, he heard the clicking of the alvaren's talons keeping pace. Where in the bloody stars was he going?

Time had no meaning in this place.

The blackness through which he staggered never lightened; he felt no hunger or thirst, though his limbs were aching, and his breathing was becoming more ragged. Sep was limp in his arms, her eyes fixed on his face. He tried to talk to her several times, but she just watched him placidly, her thin lips pressed together. The alvaren stalking them continued to entreat him to abandon the girl, but he ignored the ghost, refusing to even look at it.

"This place is an endless waste, Kerin. We are in the girl's mind, and as you can sense there is nothing here. She is shattered."

Kerin's clutched Sep tighter to his chest and continued on.

"There are other things I can offer you. I know you carry a pearl; I can feel its resonance. Did you think it broken beyond repair?"

Something must have shown in his face, as when the alvaren spoke again it sounded excited.

"The pearl is not dead. Only the outer surface is cracked, and this has severed the link to the memory contained within. But it can be repaired. I was a master of such sorcery. It was I who placed Alaissa into the cube so she could guard the artifacts stored in the Crucible. She was naught but a remembrance frozen in time, in truth. As Xerivas freed her, so could the inhabitant of the pearl you carry be freed."

Kerin stumbled, nearly dropping Sep. He was so tired. So cold.

"Just leave her here," the alvaren whispered, sounding like he was right next to him. "We can do great things together, Kerin. I am not evil – I only wanted to save my people!"

"No," Kerin grated, his legs trembling as he forced himself to take another step.

A hiss of rage came from the alvaren, and another sharp spear-thrust of cold pierced his side. Kerin grunted, his grip on Sep slipping. With some effort he managed to hold on to her.

To the abyss with this bastard.

Another step.

Another.

His insides felt sharp and hard, pressing against his skin like they were trying to erupt from his body. A haze was clouding his eyes, making the luminescence radiating from Sep blur, as if she was starting to dissolve. She still felt solid in his arms, though. Heavy. So heavy. Kerin gritted his teeth, trying to not think about his aching arms.

He couldn't go on. He sank to his knees, still refusing to let go of Sep. If this was the end, so be it, but he wouldn't let her go.

Kerin.

Was that his imagination? It sounded like Drifter, but the voice was so distant.

Kerin, where are you?

He swallowed, mustering the strength to respond. *Here.*

That's not very helpful.

It's dark. I can't see anything.

That was louder. I think . . . I think I'm getting closer.

Hurry. Kerin swayed, nearly toppling forward. He knew if that happened he'd never rise again.

A wind arose, playing against his face. It felt out of place in this emptiness, like it was intruding from elsewhere.

Reach for me!

Kerin frowned. Reach for what? But he slipped one of his arms from around Sep and extended into the black.

The wind strengthened. It felt like something huge was passing nearby. His hand brushed a hardness as a great shape rushed past him, stirring the air with its passage. Concentrating hard, he forced his numb fingers into an imperfection in the surface of this thing, and then he was suddenly thrown forward, dragged along. His legs lifted from the ground, but somehow he was able to continue clinging to whatever had carried him aloft. Suddenly he realized what it was he was touching, as he'd felt it many times before. He smiled, laying his face exhaustedly against the great turtle's ancient shell.

A howl of desperate rage rose up from below as they ascended into the dark.

Kerin returned to himself sprawled on the deck, propped up against the wall of the Nest, Sep clutched tightly to his chest. He blinked blearily, unclenching his stiff fingers. Beyond the dark hump of Drifter's head a Stream's mouth shimmered, obscuring the rest of the system.

"Nebulas," Kerin rasped as feeling flooded his frozen limbs. He felt like he'd died quite some time ago, and then had his spirit shoved roughly back into his corpse.

A gasp made Kerin turn his aching head. Nala was squatting down not far from him, her tail dancing as she watched him stir.

"You're alive!" she cried, and then a moment later his face was buried in warm fur.

"This isn't helping me breathe," he mumbled through a mouthful of hair.

She drew back, wetness in her eyes. He couldn't remember ever seeing her cry before. "Tooth and claw, I thought you were gone," she said. "Your pulse was so weak. I didn't know what to do . . ."

"Drifter came for me," he said. At this, the starbeast partly turned his head so that a slice of his huge black eye was visible, then slowly blinked in an approximation of a wink.

"Welcome back," Tessa said, coming to stand beside Nala. "We didn't know what happened. You grabbed the girl and pulled her close, then collapsed. We decided we shouldn't try to move you and see if you could wake up on your own. So instead we spent the last sandglass skirting the edge of the Mandate civil war and have just arrived back at the system's mouth."

"I went inside her," Kerin said, his gaze drifting down to Sep. "I tried to help her, but all I think I did was keep that alvaren ghost from fully inhabiting her body. I don't—"

His words trailed away as she shifted slightly in his arms. Her eyes fluttered open and found his. Gray, not black.

"Kerin," she murmured softly, and her hand reached up to gently stroke his face.

25

THE STREAM ROILED and churned beyond the jagged remnants of the solarium's roof. Seated in his grandfather's chair, Kerin leaned back and concentrated on the shapes flickering in the depths of the darkness. Half-formed glimpses of another universe, maybe another reality, seemingly close enough to touch but in truth far more distant than the farthest branch of the tributary.

The tenor of your thoughts right now reminds me of your grandfather.

Kerin's lips twitched in wry amusement. Not long ago such a claim by Drifter would have annoyed him, but something had changed. The anger he'd been carrying around in a tight knot for so long had been unraveled. His grandfather had been flawed, but no one was without flaws. All that mattered was how you dealt with these imperfections.

Still no pursuit?

Kerin felt the satisfaction flowing from Drifter. *None that I can sense, and I deeply doubt any will come. Whichever exarch wins out back there will have far more important priorities than resuming the chase for us. They will swim towards the imperial capitol in all haste to try and seize the seat of Mandate power.*

Good. And your flipper?

Getting better. A few days of floating in a warm sea would do wonders, I think.

I'll keep that in mind, Kerin replied, not bothering to hide his amusement at this suggestion. Drifter had been lobbying for a tropical holiday ever since they'd escaped H'shen's system.

A sharp knocking pulled him back to the solarium.

"Come in," he said loudly, already knowing who it was.

The door swung open, and Tessa stepped inside. She glanced around at the mess he still hadn't fully cleaned up, her gaze lingering on the glittering shards and bits of metal he'd pushed to the edges of the room, and then she stared up with a frown at the mangled copper frame above them.

"If Calvan is haunting Drifter, he'd be absolutely disgusted with the state of things," she said, picking her way carefully across the solarium to where he sat behind his grandfather's desk.

"If he's haunting Drifter then he just witnessed us escape from a lich, a Mandate fleet, and the deranged remnant of an Elder Race. I can claim with some confidence he's impressed."

Tessa murmured something that sounded like grudging agreement as she righted a stool that had been lying on the floor and sat.

Kerin sniffed, noticing the faint smell of vel sticks. "You've just come from Sep's cabin?"

Tessa folded one long leg over the other and nodded. "Yes."

"And how is she?"

"In good spirits, I think. Talkative. Nala is there as well, and it seems like she's living with the girl now. Who would have thought a former ghenabakan battlemage would have such a strong mothering instinct?"

"Not I," Kerin replied truthfully with a shake of his head.

"When I left, the kyrathi was trying to convince Sep to have a tail stuck on when the chimericist replaces her arm. The girl seemed agreeable to the idea, surprisingly."

Kerin chuckled, trying to imagine Sep with a tail.

After a long pause, Tessa's face suddenly grew more serious. "Kerin, there's something we need to talk about."

His good humor subsided. He'd been dreading this conversation. "Oh? Is it what you're going to do next?"

"Yes. But first I want you to understand something." Tessa's brow creased, as if she was struggling to give shape to what she wanted to say. "Bloody stars," she finally muttered, followed by an exasperated sigh, "why is this so hard? All right, let me start at the beginning."

"The beginning of what?"

"Of my life after I left you and Calvan."

"Oh," Kerin murmured. Through the bond he shared with Drifter he felt the starbeast's curiosity stirring.

"It was harder than I thought," Tessa said, her gaze unfocusing as if she was reliving a long-ago memory. "Carving out my own life. I was barely a woman, on a planet I'd never lived on for any length of time. The skills Calvan taught me might have gotten me a berth on another starbeast, but I'd had enough of streamsurfing. I wanted some stability." She paused, twisting one of her red curls around her finger. "I started doing small jobs, errands for someone I thought was only a merchant. Turned out he was dealing with more illicit goods. By the time I realized he was a criminal I was enmeshed in his organization. Not that I would have left anyway, as I had been desperate when I'd begun working for him." Tessa pulled back her frilled cuff, staring at the red tattoos writhing along her forearm. "Then the Shroud came. It is rare that the Inquisitarium reached beyond the boundaries of the Mandate, but the merchant had been involved in something that angered powers within the imperium. So they dispatched a Shroud, and it was like an avenging demon had descended." She swallowed. "The merchant had a warded safehouse guarded by a dozen men. The Shroud murdered them all like they were children. I was left on death's threshold, my eyes ruined."

Tessa's twisting red markings darkened. "I don't know why Serevus took me with him when he'd finished. He nursed me back to health and had a chimericist replace the parts of me that were beyond saving. He made me his apprentice. And as he ascended through the ranks of the Inquisitarium, I was his right hand." She pursed her lips. "He's not a bad man," Tessa continued finally, "but he believes with utmost certainty in the principles undergirding the Inquisitarium. The greater good must be achieved, so long as the costs do not exceed the return, that there is a moral calculus that can be applied to any situation." She gazed at Kerin with eyes that were almost pleading, as if desperate for him to understand. "What I did, igniting a wraith crystal in the plaza to try and turn the opinion of the thalani against the Dawn . . . that is exactly what the Inquisitarium would encourage. A few deaths, for a large chance to avert rebellion and the massacres that would inevitably follow."

She lapsed into silence. This was not easy for her, he realized. She was making a confession.

"Let me ask you something," Tessa suddenly said, plucking nervously at the hem of her sleeve. "What if the god of the Searing Light was real? What if Sep's suffering had, in truth, opened the way to salvation for everyone she helped cleanse? A thousand people saved through the pain of one innocent. Do you think it should continue, even if she has no say over what is happening to her?"

"No," Kerin answered immediately. "If such a god was real, I would reject it on principle."

"Principle," Tessa said with a sad smile. "Serevus would have said that the universe is chaos, and we bring order to it through the same principles that govern the Mandate. He saw the empire itself as something like the Searing Light, in truth, holding back the tide of disorder by making the difficult decisions that needed to be made. And that usually involved sacrificing a few for the benefit of the many."

Kerin shrugged. "I find that philosophy monstrous."

"Severus would say you're an idealistic fool."

"I don't care. I want no part in the society he helps shape."

Tessa regarded him for a long moment, as if searching his face for something. Finally, she swallowed and leaned back, lacing her fingers across her knee.

"Do you have a place for me in your crew?" she whispered, and to Kerin's great surprise it looked to him like she was blinking back tears.

His thoughts scattered, and he could only stare blankly at her.

She hurriedly continued, as if worried about what his silence meant. "The Mandate will eventually come for Sep, or you . . . or me, but I can help you stay ahead of them. And I have resources hidden on a dozen different worlds. We can use this coin to pay for a chimericist to heal Sep and also repair what damage has been done to Drifter." There was a wariness in her face, as if she'd given voice to something she secretly, desperately desired, and now feared what the answer might be.

Kerin leaned forward, putting his elbows on his grandfather's desk and steepling his hands. Of course he would welcome her back. But there was a mystery that had been gnawing at him, and he suspected she had answers. Kerin gazed at her intently from over his fingertips.

"First I want to know something, since you told me once that the Inquisitarium hoards information." He paused dramatically, letting the moment unfold. "What do you know about the Labyrinth?"

Tessa's eyebrows quirked in surprise, and she tilted her head back to watch the Stream rushing overhead, just as his grandfather used to do. "Now," she said softly, "there's a tale."

Thank you so much for reading *The Shadows of Dust*. If you've enjoyed the adventure and would like to see more stories set in the stellar tributary, I would be thrilled to receive a review and your feedback on Amazon or Goodreads. Reviews are of tremendous importance to authors, and we are truly appreciative when we get them. Take care, and happy reading.

IN MEMORIAM

This book is dedicated to the memory of Gerald Warfield. Gerald and I met in the summer before I published *The Crimson Queen*. I'd brought my first draft to a fantasy writers' retreat, and Gerald and I were paired together – I read and commented on the book he'd written, and he did the same for me. I was very, very lucky. Gerald was a wonderful man and a talented writer. The guidance he gave me helped shape *Queen* into the book I eventually published, for which I am forever grateful. And his book was brilliant: the main character was a sea turtle, similar to the rabbits in *Watership Down* and the cats in *Tailchaser's Song*, and it has the same depth as the best of those stories. Gerald had volunteered in the Caribbean to help with sea turtle conservation, and the book was informed by his own experiences. I hope to see it published one day.

Beyond his brilliance as a writer, Gerald was just fundamentally a good person, and some of the light went out of the world this year when he passed away. I miss the emails he'd send to me every month or so inquiring about my life and writing. Drifter was in fact inspired by the character Treader that was introduced to me by Gerald.

Here is something Gerald wrote on his own website to commemorate his friends and family that had died:

"One of the compensations for death is that life goes on. From our earliest extant literature, the Epic of Gilgamesh, we find, at the end, that the hero is at last reconciled to death. He takes a friend outside Uruk and instructs him to look at the walls of the great city. Every brick has his name on it. But the point is not that Gilgamesh built a monument to himself. The unspoken assumption is that there will be people to see it. Life will go on."

Gerald's stories can be found here. They are one of the monuments he has left behind.

I miss you, Gerald. I know that you're out there somewhere, swimming with your turtles in the stars.

ACKNOWLEDGMENTS

I have many people to thank for helping this book come about.

Thank you to Chris Fox for providing the initial spark for the story.

Thank you to Phil Tucker and Mihir Wanchoo for providing very helpful feedback on the first draft.

Thank you to Inger Tucker, Michael Thies, and Christine Putoni for their eagle eyes that somehow spotted a host of typos that had slipped through the cracks.

Thank you to Septira Taruna, for being a terrific friend and for allowing me to use your name in this book.

And as always, thanks to Nancy and Dan, my wonderful parents.

ABOUT THE AUTHOR

Alec Hutson grew up in a geodesic dome and a bookstore and currently lives in Shanghai, China. If you would like the keep current on his writing, please sign up for his newsletter at authoralechutson.com.

ALSO BY ALEC HUTSON

The Raveling

The Crimson Queen

The Silver Sorceress

The Shadow King

Swords and Saints

The Cleansing Flame

The Twilight Empire

The Hollow God

The Manticore's Soiree

Made in United States
North Haven, CT
22 May 2022

19418811R00222